THE CREATURE

Lupo fought hard to remain in control. He tried to exert some kind of pressure on whatever shape his brain was now taking and, for a second, he felt himself slipping back, or maybe both ways. For a brief moment he thought he'd won, feeling nearly in control of the Creature, but then he was over and no longer Nick Lupo.

In only seconds, the transformation was complete.

He lunged at the door and howled as his nose smacked soundly into the reinforced steel. Forepaws scrabbled uselessly against the smooth surface, claws tearing—the pain lanced through his heavily muscled body like a javelin. The blood scent turned strong and inviting, for a second, until whatever vestige of his own brain that remained intact reminded him in a single nearly incoherent thought, that it was his own blood and therefore unacceptable.

He was there again, in the Creature—aware, though standing well back, like a separate consciousness.

The huge gray-black form sat on its haunches and let out a strangled howl.

W. D. GAGLIANI

WOLF'S TRAP

LEISURE BOOKS NEW YORK CITY

For my parents and Janis,
as ever my pillars of love and support....

...And in memory of my dad.

A LEISURE BOOK®

May 2006

Published by

Dorchester Publishing Co., Inc.
200 Madison Avenue
New York, NY 10016

ISBN 0-8439-5702-6

The name "Leisure Books" and the stylized "L" with design are trademarks of Dorchester Publishing Co., Inc.

Printed in the United States of America.

Visit us on the web at www.dorchesterpub.com.

ACKNOWLEDGMENTS

I'd like to thank some of my "writer friends" for their advice on this book and/or publishing, and for their most valuable gift—friendship: Don Adams, Elaine Bergstrom, Judy Bridges, Alice Henderson, Brian A. Hopkins, Tina Jens, Gary Jonas, Don Kinney, Jill Lindberg, Dennis Michel (I miss you, man!), Garrett Peck, Joel Ross, Beecher Smith, Tamara Thorne, Deena Warner, John Zemler. I've met many new friends in the past two years, and I thank them, too.

Also, for inspiration: James Blaylock, Robert Bloch, Gary A. Braunbeck, Ed Bryant, Doug Clegg, Matt Costello, Larry David, Charles de Lint, Bradley Denton, Philip K. Dick, Harlan Ellison, Ray Garton, Charles Grant, Jack Higgins, Brian Hodge, Jack Ketchum, Stephen King, Joe R. Lansdale, Richard Laymon, David Lynch, Robert R. McCammon, David Morrell, Billie Sue Mosiman, Tim Powers, David J. Schow, Michael Slade, Peter Straub, Karl Edward Wagner, F. Paul Wilson, and so many more who made an indelible mark.

And the music of: Emerson Lake & Palmer, Yes, Genesis, Marillion and Fish, The Alan Parsons Project, Kansas, Pink Floyd, Tangerine Dream, Spock's Beard, as well as all their individual musicians. Prog lives!

AUTHOR'S NOTE

Some license was taken with regard to Milwaukee and Eagle River geography. A list of important references can be found at www.williamdgagliani.com.

PROLOGUE

Cincinnati
March 2

He headed for the park again.

He went just about every day, when the weather was nice, but only once every few weeks did he feel the tingle that told him something special would happen.

Today he felt the tingle, and he smiled.

It was warm, but he wore his parka anyway. The mushy ground seemed to spring under his step, still wet from the last snow, but the benches were dry.

He pulled himself into character, easily enough.

He was so happy. He was going to see a girl.

He'd been seeing her every day for a couple of weeks now, and had managed to say hello in his own shy way. And Susan had just as shyly told him her name when he'd pressed her for it a few days before, after she told him she liked to watch him feed squirrels. Maybe it was the way the small, furry rodents climbed all over him, looking for peanuts and corn kernels, that first attracted her to him. Or because he was a nice, quiet person. He dressed well, spoke well, and made her feel safe with his subdued manner.

And maybe his priest's collar made her feel even safer.

When Susan had come up to him that first day, he'd had to admit that she was cute. Just plain, really, with a heavy dose of cute. Brown hair, gray eyes, normal nose (maybe a little bony), and no makeup except lipstick. That had made him perk right up. When she smiled, she was no longer plain.

He was a smile man, pure and simple.

And she did smile, seeing all those squirrels waiting their turn to jump up and search through the folds and pockets of the young priest's parka.

"I didn't realize they were so tame," she had said.

He pretended to see her for the first time. "Oh, yes," he said, "they're pretty used to me."

When he looked at her, he often looked at just her lips. He did that, he explained, because he was a little deaf, though not enough to require a hearing aid. He told her it helped just to see her lips forming words. It didn't hurt when the lips he "read" were so stunningly perfect.

He smiled at her, his priestly smile.

"They're so cute," she said, smiling back.

He nodded, silent because one chubby squirrel was checking out the top of his head, tiny paws grabbing on to his shoulder. When it was done, it scurried down the back of the parka, and a different fellow climbed up. He put another peanut in his hair.

"You must be a regular," she said, and he was happy to see that she wanted to keep talking. So they chatted about squirrels and rabbits and their feeding habits, and he told her that he'd been feeding them every day. He noted that when she smiled her eyes sparkled.

"Well, I have to get back to work," she said after a while, real regret apparent in her voice.

"Where do you work?" he asked. An innocent question.

She told him a lie and he smiled. "Very nice! Maybe I'll see you again."

"Yes," she said, "maybe."

So he continued going back to the park, his starched collar in place. The next day she didn't stay long—she had a lunch date—but she said hello and watched him feed a pudgy squirrel. She laughed and called him Piglet. He looked at her as she laughed. She really did feel safe, and that made him happy.

She didn't come the next three days, and he wished he had taken her picture. He had a camera in his bag, but it might have been difficult to explain why a priest would want to photograph a pretty girl. So he spent hours sitting in the chilly early-spring sunlight, throwing nuts to the gathered squirrels with little angry gestures.

She was back the following Monday, calling out a cheery hello that startled him. He looked at her eyes for a second, then her mouth. She smiled; then he smiled, too. The squirrels were insistent, though, and he had to concentrate on the feeding. She took a brown bag out of her spacious purse and sat on the next bench. That was when she first told him her name.

He told her his name, and she said, "Martin, that's a nice name."

"*Father* Martin," he corrected her, "though I'm between parish assignments right now."

He fed hungry squirrels, and she ate a sparse lunch, throwing out crumbs that the furry creatures scooped into their tiny mouths. Then, while he watched, she refreshed her bright lipstick before smiling and waving good-bye.

His hands itched, and he scratched them until they almost bled, the camera lying screaming and unused in his duffel bag. If only he could have planted an excuse, a reason, to photograph her.

But, no, a priest couldn't get away with it, not this day and age.

Martin felt a sharp pain behind his eyes. Susan's face blended into Caroline's, and he knew that her memory was weighing on him again, causing his vision to blur and his hands to itch. Her loss was the catalyst, the reason for his visits to the park this month, and for his visits to the airport last month. No, it was the moon's position, he thought, pushing the pinprick pain aside once again.

He knew it was almost showtime. His great crusade, his life's work. Everything he'd done up to now was just a warm-up an opener, a prelude. He was ready now—almost ready—to make the blood flow.

"It won't be long, Caroline," he thought. "Not long at all."

Now, as he spread peanuts on the bench and called the squirrels, he spied Susan approaching on the path from the parking lot. She was right on time—had her lunch hour planned to the minute—and she waved as he looked up. In one hand she carried one of those colorful reusable lunch sacks, and in the other a clear bag of goodies for the squirrels.

He smiled and waved, too, and wrestled his bag closer, making sure the flap was closed. He didn't want her to see his surprise too soon. It was time to move on, and the expectation surged through him like high voltage. He always enjoyed the culmination of his plans. He always enjoyed the moving-on part, and this time he had something even bigger to look forward to.

He patted the bag. One thing at a time. Finish one series of actions before beginning another.

He had planned this well. He planned everything well.

He smiled at the thought of it.

When he looked up at Susan, he knew that for the first time she could see into and beyond his bland eyes. Past his smile. Into his darkness. She hesitated, her steps first slowing and then coming to a halt.

It was too late. Understanding crossed her features just as his hand came out of the bag.

PART ONE
PRELUDE

CHAPTER ONE

Milwaukee
March 17
MARTIN

After two weeks of watching, carefully noting every coming and every going, Martin Stewart decided it was almost time to begin this new phase of his life. He had let his need build up to an almost intolerable level, to the point where the pain was almost as good as the release he could expect. Indeed, withdrawal was in this case as satisfying as fulfillment. But only to a point. Eventually, the waiting would begin to erode the corners of his facade, and he would have to plan another release.

He had enjoyed his role as quiet, trustworthy Father Martin last time. It had somehow seemed to heighten the pleasure of the release to know that someone so outwardly trustworthy could turn out to be so different, so *dangerous*. There was a certain—he searched for the right word—*justness* to it all, especially afterward, when he had seen the tiny bloodstains on the white collar. The irony was delicious, almost as delicious as the act itself.

Martin was pragmatic about his *releases*. He saw them clearly for what they were. His flesh was inherently weak, and each completed project simply an indication of how weak. That each release was also to be savored merely complicated the mixture, and Martin was nothing if not complicated. He could stand back and observe his actions and behaviors in a completely objective manner, and he was justly proud of this capability. The doctors had noted that it lent Martin a certain tragic flair. Here was a man trapped in the clutches of behavioral urges no one should have to suffer, though he both suffered and enjoyed them, analyzed them, claimed he saw where they careened hopelessly off the normal path, and finally rationalized them as the only possible outlet for his needs.

Martin kept a journal, much as his sister had always done, even through her psychiatric practice, though his was nowhere as detailed. Still, he reveled in his feelings and emotions, and he tried to outguess the doctors as to the reasons behind his actions. This practice did not stop him from committing actions that he was well aware crossed the line into abnormal, or even—as the doctors pointed out—into the realm of the dangerous. He merely considered each action an experiment, and he wrote down how he felt when he performed the action, even if he was aware of the action's negative connotations.

Martin differed from the Stevensen Institute's other psychopaths in that he was completely aware of his psychopathic tendencies, and in that he enjoyed acting on them to a degree greater than any other patient they had ever entertained. And was there any doubt, the doctors wondered, considering his earlier family life? The files they kept on Martin were full to overflowing, an even dozen folders and packets stretched to the breaking limit and held together with fraying rubber bands. Several accounts of what had transpired in the Stewart home were included, but none were as complete as Martin's own additions, written in a tiny, precise hand that resembled squiggles until more closely examined, and then became almost overly ornate. Some of Martin's journal pages were included in the folders. But most pages Martin kept to himself. Martin was very resourceful, and no one on the clinic's staff would have believed that he had been able to squirrel away several hundred pages of journal entries, besides having shared hundreds more with his various therapists.

But he had. And now Martin was filling up a whole new notebook with his perfect penmanship, noting in neat entries every time Corinne Devereaux left her building and when she returned.

At first, he had neglected Detective Lupo's schedule, but within two days, he had decided to begin a separate log with the policeman's comings and goings as well. Soon, he enjoyed the exercise of matching their schedules and wondering if and when they were together. The coffee shop from which he kept vigil was as close as he could hope to come, and they were quite accommodating, especially once they heard about the novel he was writing, little by little, in their very own humble diner. Maybe he would name them somewhere in the book, he told them. I'll have the hero meet the girl of his dreams here, he said to the blushing waitress. *Before they go to his place and screw their brains out in seven positions*, he thought but diplomatically did not add.

The waitress, Linda, had a bit of an acne problem, but she was smart enough to play up her good features. Her lips were full and sensuous, and well-highlighted with violet gloss. Her auburn hair was a supple cascade around her shoulders. Unfortunately, she must have thought her pretty, upturned nose required some adornment, because the right nostril was pierced and sported a thin gold wire hoop. Oh, well, Martin thought every time he saw Linda, we can't all be perfect. It somehow threw him off liking the girl. Still, she was flattered at his attention, and more than happy to keep his soda glass or coffee cup filled as long as the promise of some small measure of immortality hung between them.

Today, Martin watched Corinne Devereaux pick her way carefully down the rain-slickened sidewalk leading to her building, balancing on her high heels like the professional she was. He would have liked Corinne as his own conquest, he had decided. He had already walked past her once on the street, had made brief eye contact with her, and smiled.

Even in these days of mistrust, she had smiled back.

Martin was taken with her. Stunning would have described her well. A cliché—so be it. Blond, true blond, without the aid of a bottle; he'd been through her garbage on a regular basis, so he knew. Medium height, slim but shapely build, long legs flattered by the leotards and stir-rup pants she favored and, recently, those high-priced bell-bottoms that had beaten the odds and made a come-back. Facial features as fine as any supermodel's, with light blue eyes looking out over a graceful, patrician nose that hinted of intelligence and charisma. Sublime lips, outlined in her favorite bright red, put the finishing touches to a face that should have graced magazine cov-ers and cosmetics advertising. Instead, for some reason he could barely fathom—not that he really cared—she chose to make her living by escorting ugly old men to high-priced restaurants and then perhaps to their over-priced hotel rooms, where she would put those features to work in creating the illusion that she enjoyed what she did and with whom she did it.

Fools. Martin snorted. He drank a long swallow of tepid coffee and noticed that Linda was on her way—sweet, lovely, little nose-pierced Linda—with a fresh pot to re-fresh him. *Fools.* He returned to his thought after she had topped his cup and smiled at him. He smiled back dis-armingly. *All fools.*

In the meantime, Corinne Devereaux finally reached her building's lobby door and went inside. Martin could still see her through the glass, struggling with her purse. *Looking for her keys?* He made a note in his log. Time. Which direction she had come from. How long it took her in the lobby. He would like using her as his first *message*. He would like it a lot. It might double the fun, seeing how long it would take the freak cop to finally understand what this was about, whom he was dealing with. Or was that, *with whom he was dealing?* As a writer, he should know. What if Linda asked?

Martin smiled. The coffee was hot and strong—just as he liked it—and it felt good going down on such a wet, miserable day.

He turned the page and started a new column. Soon the cop would be home, and then he would enjoy imagining what those two did together. Was it a *professional* relationship? Did she trade favors for a friend—a protector—on the force?

Martin's forays into Lupo's trash hadn't helped much. Hardly any processed foods, but plenty of meat containers. Little vegetable waste, though the apartments were likely to have sink disposal units. Mail was mostly junk or bill-oriented, with little to set it apart from anyone else's. The meat made sense, and Martin smiled at the thought of any one person eating this much meat during this age of diet awareness. Oh, yes, it all made sense. Caroline's journals were—to say the least—fantastic in nature. But Martin had always trusted his sister's seriousness, even though his own relationship with her was complicated by his feelings, feelings that he had acted upon at an early age. Oh, yes, he had acted. And she would still be his, if Nick Lupo had never come along.

He picked up the coffee cup but changed his mind and slammed it back down on the table, liquid sloshing over the side and forming a puddle. Linda looked up, startled, and watched him from across the room, perhaps wondering if he needed something.

...un knew he needed *something,* but he could never
...e it again, not ever, because of Nick Lupo, and now it
was almost time for Lupo to pay.

He waved his cup at Linda, wordlessly asking her for
the pot and a rag. She jumped to his request. That was
more like it. Maybe he would keep Linda in mind, too. He
wondered if Lupo frequented the diner. It was so close to
his building, Martin guessed yes. He wondered if he could
sense where Lupo might have sat on one of his speculated visits.

Martin's hands itched, and he scratched them. Linda
approached with a smile that brought tingles to his spine.
He kept both throbbing hands under the table while she
dealt with the spill and his cup.

Linda.

He did like that name, he decided. He looked up into
the waitress's pale eyes and smiled his best smile. Her
glossy lips parted in return. "Would you like to be in my
book?" he asked.

Milwaukee
March 19
LUPO

The first detail that struck Dominic Lupo was the tang of
freshly spilled blood.

The second was the inexorable greenness of everything. The walls were green tile, the sinks a deep green
marble. And the fluorescents above made his skin green,
according to the blurred reflection he caught in the long
mirror. It made him shudder.

"In here, Detective Lupo," said the uniform, a veteran
cop by the name of Robbins.

Lupo already knew. His nose would have led him there
in moments. The prickling sensation had already begun.

In the stall, the green was overshadowed by splashes of

crimson. Maroon, where the blood had begun to dry on the metal partition, and where shoes had marred the splatter patterns on the cold tile floor.

Lupo gazed over the head of a photographer and waited with eyes closed until the electronic flash had gone off. Then he tapped the photographer on the shoulder and motioned him aside.

There was something.

But he wasn't sure what.

He leaned in for a closer look. Details, detached from all context, popped out at him like flashes of light.

Blond hair, tied in a ponytail.

Tied with a red and white bandanna.

A shapely neck, with folds of skin and pale flesh parted like sliced lard along both sides of a long, wicked cut that stretched from just below the right ear to just below the left. Head tilted to the side, nearly severed from the torso, hidden in the shadows.

Something. Lupo wished he could grasp exactly what was vaguely familiar about this messy scene, which was after all only one of many he had experienced. Not that it got any easier, but it was easier to think of the victim as a side of beef and get on with it, because overt sentimentality ruined an objective approach. Still, if he could only . . .

The red bandanna.

That was it. But why was it important? He struggled for a second, wanting to make the connection. It was familiar, but he couldn't quite place how. He squinted and started to crouch.

Then a hand was fastening around his elbow and manhandling him away from the open stall, toward the side wall, where a diaper station gaped open grotesquely as if offering a sacrifice to an unheeding plastic god. A smudged streak of blood solidified the image for Lupo. The sense of it all getting worse struck him like a physical blow. He let his partner, Ben Sabatini, lead him to the corner. As he passed the station, he was dismayed to see more bloodstains on its surface. No, not stains. Deliberate smudges. The perp had dipped his hands in blood and purposely fouled the plastic shelf. Truly a futuristic urban altar, now devoid of all innocence. Lupo shook his head.

There was something lying flat on the surface of the convenience table, sealed in a clear evidence bag. Lupo reached for it, but Sabatini stopped his motion with a trembling hand.

"Sorry, Ben," Lupo said. "I thought the boys were done with this."

Ben Sabatini, a twenty-year cop who had seen more street crime than anyone Lupo had ever known, hesitated and held Lupo's eyes with his own. He ran one meaty hand after the other through thinning silver hair—a stalling gesture, effective only for a few seconds. "They're done, Nick. But I need to talk to you before you see this."

Lupo's hair stood on end, and he felt a tiny growl work its way up his throat. Was it the sense of being thwarted, or that more was going on here than his first assessment had revealed? He almost wished he could take notes, so he could compare his response to that in other situations.

"The girl's name is Corinne," Ben said. "Corinne Devereaux."

Later Lupo would remember the way his stomach seemed to drop within his body, pressing on his intestines with nearly unbearable pressure. He would remember the squeezing of his testicles, as if they lay cradled within a tightening vise. Lupo caught his breath and realized he had momentarily halted his intake of air. A strong itch crawled from his fingers, up and over the backs of his hands, where coarse hair grew in large tufts. He jammed his hands into his pockets and drew a long breath.

"*Corinne?*" A hoarse whisper came out. Lupo tried clearing his throat, but he choked instead.

"It isn't—that's not *your* friend's last name, is it?" Ben's discomfort was obvious.

Lupo gave his partner a withering glance. "Are you sure about the name? The last name?"

Ben nodded, looking at the floor. " 'Fraid so. No ID, but her girlfriend's the one who found her. She's outside. She fainted when she was talking to Robbins. Went in to look for her friend because she hadn't come out."

Ben was a cold one, but Lupo's shocked reaction affected him, making him revert to the persona he had used all too often to break such news to an unsuspecting wife or husband. He fidgeted, embarrassed, letting the news sink in. Lupo shook his head once, as if trying to clear it of knowledge. Of the truth. It didn't work. His eyes refocused on Ben's, which now fixed him squarely.

"What happened? What the hell happened?"

"It's rough on the street, Nick."

"Fuck the street!" Lupo's voice rose despite his caution, and his hands itched even more. He dug further into his pocket. "This isn't the street, Ben. This is Westridge Mall. Not some alley under the freeway down by the docks, for Chrissakes. Now, what happened? What the fuck happened?"

Ben nodded. "In her line of work, you know how it is. It ain't unheard of, Nick. Even here."

Lupo felt the growl building inside him again and forced himself to swallow it. The consistency of his tongue was too rough, almost sandpaper, and he felt desperately in need of water. Or anything wet.

Anything.

His gaze traveled downward as he tried to escape the green-on-green decor of the mall washroom, and suddenly he was looking at the bag that lay on the diaper station and the flat object inside. It was a strip of four color photographs from a mall photo booth. Each tiny photograph depicted the same scene, with only slight variation.

It was Corinne, all right, his friend and neighbor, engaged in an activity relatively normal for hookers, but simply not usually managed in such cramped quarters, potentially in view of so many people only feet away.

She did not appear to mind, since she seemed to be smiling. It was hard to tell, because she was performing fellatio on a well-endowed male, who stood next to the tiny stool. The pictures were cut off a little above waist-high. The plastic curtain must have been tightly drawn, Lupo reasoned. Ben hadn't spoken of any reported commotion that might have been caused by public sight of the sex act, even though the booth was located near the food court, assuring constant traffic.

"Any security report on this?" asked Lupo as he gently pried the bag containing the bloodstained strip from the table and held it aloft between them.

Ben avoided his eyes. "No. They managed to keep it private. This little booth escapade is a damned new one on me, but . . ."

"Yeah, I know. In her line of business." Lupo frowned. "Question is . . . is this the guy?"

"I told the lab guys to treat this as a direct shot at the perp, but this guy's anatomy doesn't look very helpful. We don't put those in the computer." He smiled sardonically. "Some of 'em, maybe we should."

Lupo dropped the bag. "Yeah." There was no humor in his voice.

Then he was standing over the body, which had stiffened into a parody of human form. This Corinne was a marionette, cut from her strings and cast aside with last year's toys. He bent at the waist and realized that there was more, much more, that he had missed in his shock. He stretched latex gloves over his hands and began. Her eyelids seemed to have been partially sliced off, perhaps with a razor blade or utility knife. They hung uselessly next to her eyes, now widened as if in terror. Her lips were garishly painted and smeared with crusted lipstick. Lupo touched her skin and smelled his fingertips; there was blood mixed in with the Revlon. The sick fuck had re-

painted her lips with blood and had then smudged
them . . . smudged them how? He looked back at Ben,
who shrugged.

"Looks like he continued after she was dead, Nick."

Lupo wanted to let the growl out, but he contented
himself with scratching the backs of his hands and saying
a quiet good-bye to Corinne. Corinne, who'd made a point
of saving his newspaper from hallway thieves when he forgot to retrieve it. Corinne, who brought over DVDs and
chips and homemade salsa to enliven the occasional
weeknight when neither was working.

Working. That was a laugh.

*At least those nights I wasn't up in the woods, locked in
the cabin, covered with stale sweat, trembling as clouds
traversed the sky and obscured the moon.*

Her breasts were bared, the low-cut dress ripped apart.
Her nipples had also been partially sliced off, and he could
see blood and lipstick streaks there as well. Her hands
seemed intact and had been bagged for examination.

A loud racket from the doorway announced the arrival
of the coroner's field staff, and Lupo was forced to step
aside and watch as his friend's body was unceremoniously transferred to the unfolded gurney and zipped into
the waiting body bag. The last thing he saw was Corinne's
head—the wide-open, glazed eyes—and the gaping
wound below her chin. Then the guy from the meat
wagon stuffed her bloodstained hair inside after her and
roughly closed the bag, his own face a mask of disinterest.

Lupo's fist shot out and caught the side of the partition,
bending it like foil. He felt nothing.

The coroner's assistant eyed him warily as he pushed
the gurney past, no doubt wondering what the hell was
wrong with the hairy cop.

After all, it was just another hooker. Not the first to die at
the hands of a rough customer, and not the last. The guy
hummed a little ditty as he and his partner maneuvered the
gurney through the tight washroom and toward the door.

Lupo closed his eyes, and everyone and everything disappeared. In his mind's eye, which now resembled a reddish cavern, he thought he saw the murderer clearly. But only for a second, and then the image blurred and faded and he was following Ben into the mall corridor and wading through the crowd of excited rubberneckers.

He could smell their enthusiasm for the scene and all its gory highlights.

"Guess what I saw at the mall tonight? Somebody whacked a chick in the john. Can you believe it? Two more minutes and I would have been the one to find the dead body. Man, I would have freaked. Heard somebody say she was a hooker—"

There was a knot of police blues nearby, and Ben gently guided him in that direction. Corinne's friend was sitting with her head in her hands, talking to a uniform who made tight, little precise notes on his pad.

Lupo walked past the excited onlookers and tried to blur their bloated faces. *Let them all into the john to revel in the stink of blood and death. Let them all get their* Inside Edition *scoop right from the front lines.*

In his pockets, his fists curled and trembled.

He felt wretched, and barely in control.

Corinne's girlfriend was of little help. Between sobs, the story that unfolded was barely comprehensible. On a shopping—not working—expedition, the two were approached by a man who offered money for turning a trick right there in the mall.

"I think he knew Corinne, but I'm not sure. She remembered him. Something about last year, at the Hyatt. She told him we were off duty." Stacey Collins sobbed. Her makeup was smeared now, mascara running and bright lipstick askew on her full lips. Lupo wondered why he noticed such details and frowned.

Behind her, a cop chuckled at her choice of words.

"I mean, we weren't here to—" She broke off with another sob.

"Go on," Ben said, using his gentle fatherly voice. "What did he look like, and what did he ask for?"

"He was so ordinary looking. Maybe sandy blond hair, real average. Like, Docker pants and a shirt. Not much of a john, you know? He said he was going away tonight—to Silliman Valley or whatever, then to Europe."

"Did he sound European? Have an accent?"

"No—real Midwestern, just like us."

"Go on." Ben's patience with statements was legendary. "Any other details about him or the way he was dressed?"

"I think he had a shopping bag."

Ben looked at Lupo. "What did he want?"

"He said he was leaving and she could give him a bon voyage gift—right here in the mall. He wanted—I mean, he made it pretty clear he wanted a blow—I mean, you know, oral sex, right in the booth while the camera was going."

She looked at each of them in turn as if it were a secret she had just revealed. She wasn't aware of the photograph strip they had bagged.

"This was the booth upstairs?"

"Uh-huh."

"How did Ms. Devereaux react to the request?"

"Well, Corinne, she kinda dug it, I think." Stacey smiled, a little wickedly. "I mean, it's kinda sexy and it's so naughty to be in the middle of the mall and—" She caught herself and let her voice fade.

Lupo spaced in and out of the session, watching as the curious crowded around as closely as the uniforms would let them, which was fortunately too far to hear the details. The constant traffic and the sheer gall of this perpetrator, taking a victim so easily and within sight of so many potential witnesses, boggled the mind. Though it was not standard procedure, they had decided to interview the girl before taking her downtown, in case the perp was still in the mall, which was Milwaukee's largest and most sprawling. This was a procedural no-no, but Nick and Ben had conferred with Lieutenant Don Bowen and gotten an okay under the circumstances. A second forensic team was working at the cosmetics counter where the suspect had approached the women, but apparently he hadn't touched anything. And a third team had cordoned off the photo booth on the food court level upstairs.

The unsteady drone of Stacey's voice lulled Lupo into a trance. He stepped away from the knot of cops and tried to breathe regularly, though the stench of deep-fried grease and popcorn blended nauseatingly with the vivid memory of the mall slaughterhouse just a few feet away and enveloped his nostrils.

Lupo ducked under the yellow tape perimeter and headed back into the corridor that led to both restrooms and to the janitor's closet. The service closet was locked when he rattled the knob. He bowed and sipped from the metal water fountain between the restroom doors, then stood before the doors. Three doors. Why was he even here? What could three doors tell him that Stacey's account couldn't? Why was he so unconcerned with what she was saying?

Ben will get it. He'll get it all.

There would be plenty of time to go over Stacey's story. Within minutes someone would drive her downtown, and she would be asked to repeat it all again. And maybe again, depending on how it played. Lupo knew all this and wanted nothing more than to avoid it. Maybe Corinne would be magically restored if he ignored the details of her death. Maybe it would all turn out to be a mistake, a huge misunderstanding—the chorus of the Genesis song flitted through his mind like an old 33 at 45 rpm. He shook his head.

Can't seem to let go of the music.

He was standing right in front of it, and it didn't register for the longest time. Opposite the wall in which the rest-room doors were set, and behind anyone who stood before those doors, was yet another door. A different janitor's closet? Storage? It seemed narrower than the other doors. Perhaps access to the Chick-Fil-A franchise next door?

Jesus, Chick-Fil-A? Is that the guy's sick-fuck sense of humor?

On a whim, Lupo grabbed the knob and turned. Uniforms had already checked this particular egress from the scene, he was certain. Yet the knob turned freely. *Not locked, and no lights*. He pushed the door and saw bare cinder-block walls a few feet from the door. The walls formed a sort of tunnel that led away from the front of the food court.

He cast about for a light switch, blindly feeling the textured wall, and nearly sprained his hand on a fusebox with a master switch. He threw the switch even as the prickling sensation worked its way up his back. Naked overhead lights sputtered on, and Lupo stepped back, turning again toward the door and wanting to wade into the small crowd to drag Ben here and show him the access tunnel that apparently no one had even noticed, let alone considered important. But there was something here. Some vibe, or at the very least, a feeling, as well as an obvious escape route.

The lights threw the red-brown smears into a near three-dimensional relief.

The angular letters formed a crooked message: HERE'S ONE FOR YOU, NICK!

Down below the eight-inch scrawl, on the dusty floor, sat a jar half-filled with dark liquid, smeared up the sides and on the lip.

Blood. Corinne's blood. Lupo caught its scent in his nostrils.

The son of a bitch had dipped his hands into her still-warm life's blood and left a cheery message for him.

His hands itched more than ever now, and he jammed them back into his pockets.

In the harsh glare of the naked bulbs, Lupo saw that the floor dust had been disturbed. Keeping clear of them, he crouched for a few moments and examined the scuff marks in the dust, right where the bastard would have had to stand as he fiddled with his palette and canvas. A single row of faint footprints snaked its way out of the confused area immediately in front of the bloody message. Lupo squinted slightly and saw that the footprints had some sort of trite pattern on them, as if from a gym shoe, and that they seemed to lead lightly down the hallway.

The tunnel. He headed down this damned service tunnel. Fucking tunnel. How did he get the keys?

Some feet away, the hall narrowed and darkened, becoming somewhat like a single cyclopean eye that implacably returned Lupo's gaze.

He felt himself tremble slightly, and every tip of every hair on his body seemed to tingle.

Even as instinct screamed for him to exit into the well-lit corridor and alert Ben and a half-dozen uniforms that here was a viable trail to follow, that here the perp had lingered to leave a polite personal message for one of their party, and that now was a good time to assure some sort of backup, Lupo began following the footsteps.

Almost immediately, he entered the area in which the lighting had deteriorated (or the perp had purposely damaged the light strips), and even as his senses protested, Lupo still followed the scrapings a pair of gym shoes had made in the dust.

In the near-darkness, he was rewarded with a brown handprint smeared waist-high on the yellow cinder blocks. Tiny splatter marks made a pattern around its edges.

Lupo grasped his Glock 9mm, pulled it out of its holster, and hurried down the passageway, unmindful of the deepening shadows.

It wasn't an altogether new feeling.

CHAPTER TWO

1976
LUPO

The air had been electric all day.

It was as if something, some event, had announced itself only to those whose eyes were sensitive enough.

Dominic Lupo was sensitive enough, and the day felt somehow *intense.*

He had watched the harsh morning sunlight turn nearly blue in the afternoon. Grass and tree leaves wore blue-green coats, and he found he had to squint whenever he stood in the sun. He imagined ultraviolet rays skewering him like yellow beams in an all-color comic book, and he could already feel heat building up in his forearms and the back of his neck.

He manhandled the lawn mower over the pits and valleys of the backyard even though it was a self-propelled machine, believing the effort would help develop his arm muscles. Certainly, wrestling fifty pounds of machinery over rough terrain on a hot day should tighten his muscles, and it also gave him some reason to accept the fact that his lot in life seemed to be yard work.

Last week it had rained, and he'd been forced to mow the soggy lawn, which had been a nightmare. Comparatively speaking, this was better, because at least he could try to tan his arms. Jeans and his surplus army shirt covered the rest of his body, protecting him from the intense jungle-like heat. It was intense, and he liked that because the Lake Michigan humidity, the haze, and the blue sunlight helped cement his fantasy. He was some Jungle Expert in the middle of nowhere, performing a vital duty for his country.

He snickered. Well, a vital duty in the lawn-care war his father seemed dead set on winning. Why, Nick didn't know. The neighborhood was going to pot. Railroad tracks not far away, the biggest American Motors plant a few blocks farther than that, and very few home owners—and increasing numbers of renters—were having some effect. Only the Lupos' home showed the efforts of continued care and tinkering, while every other house on the block seemed to crumble slowly into disrepair. It wasn't that Nick wanted his own house to end up like that, a worthless lump of Sheetrock and siding, but he resented his father's insistence that every little thing be done just so: every task a mission, every crooked nail to be straightened, and every crack repaired or at least well-hidden. Nick just didn't understand his father's urgency, the old man's determined effort to keep some tool in his hands. Only two short weeks of summer left, and Nick had spent most of his vacation single-handedly repairing some joke Nature must have been playing on his father. Every other kid in the neighborhood cruised by on a bicycle or high-pitched mini-bike, or played softball down at the corner, where no house had ever been built, or roved in one of several mostly harmless gangs that hung out near the curb on summer evenings.

Nick wasn't free to hang out, and he knew that his

image—that of a snot-nose who didn't hang out or talk to anybody, or even go to the same school as everyone else—was at least partly earned. His real friends he never had over, inside the house as guests, because he knew his parents would disapprove of that one's hair, or that one's foul mouth. Maybe if his friends came to visit in suits and short, plastered hair. But, no, Nick was accustomed to a loner's existence. In fact, he had come to crave solitude.

Nick maneuvered the mower around the yard in ever-decreasing circles, making sure he missed no patch. No bigger perfectionist existed than Frank Lupo, and he would not hesitate to make his kid mow the lawn a second time to get it right.

Suddenly, the blade clanked against an obstruction—either a branch or a piece of gravel—and the mower threatened to quit. He pulled back desperately on the handle, raising the base of the mower off the ground until the blade cleared and sputtered back to life.

He glanced quickly at the house. Whatever his father was doing, it seemed Nick was safe for the time being. There was no angry shout or glaring face at the window. He hoped—no, prayed—that the blade hadn't snapped, then continued mowing when he was reasonably sure it hadn't. He was nervous about the effort the mower seemed to make. But now he was behind the old garage, next to the neighbors' fence and under the willow (*those goddamned tiny leaves!*), and he knew a casual look from the back of the house would not catch him resting. God forbid.

He let the mower roar for a moment, wiping a sheen of sweat from his brow, and then nearly shouted in startled surprise when he looked up and saw a face peeking at him from atop the fence.

Andy!

That fucking fool. I almost crapped my pants.

Nick gave Andy the finger, then glanced around guiltily. His father could wield the finger whenever he wanted to, or call some idiot in another car a "cocksucker," but he wouldn't stand for Nick's use of his middle digit or such language.

He looked at the fence again. Andy was just staring at him, his face an expressionless mask.

"What's up, Andy?" He had to shout over the mower's racket.

Wisps of smoke hung around his head, their edges blue from the sunlight. He hoped he had got the right proportions in pouring the oil and gas mixture. He'd never hear the end of it if he damaged the mower. He wasn't the most mechanically inclined of people, so a stalled mower was a dead mower. Nothing his father would want to deal with on his day off, no sir.

Andy still hadn't moved, though from twenty feet away Nick could see his friend blinking. Andy's blinks were slow and purposeful and not at all like his usual rapid-fire pattern of facial gymnastics.

"Are you okay, Andy?"

Something about the light that day, the blue sunlight he always associated with mid-August, yet somehow different, suddenly made him feel creepy. *Really creepy.* And Andy, just staring at him over the fence.

Nick's mouth was dry, and his voice was hoarse as he called out again.

But that was easy to explain. There was smoke all around him from the clattering mower, and the sun was weird, and he was afraid he'd broken the blade, and he was just being . . .

Why was Andy acting so strange? Why wouldn't he talk, or wave, or come to the low fence and shoot the shit like he always did?

"What the fuck's the matter?" he shouted, hoping the mower's clatter would cover his words enough to avoid earning him a punitive visit.

But Andy just stared right through him, almost as if he didn't recognize his own best friend.

What the hell was Nick supposed to do, stop mowing to figure out what Andy's problem was? *Fat chance.* In the Lupo household, if you were assigned a chore, you didn't stop until it was done, unless the supervisor stopped you to stack another chore on top.

Nick shrugged. "Hey, hope you feel better." He put his head down and pushed the mower again, hoping he wouldn't catch any hidden dog shit. Whenever that happened, a cloud of toxic fumes would envelop him and he couldn't help but think of the tiny chunks of waste that would line the rounded bottom of the mower, which he would then have to clear (after disconnecting the spark plug cable first, of course) by hand. Yuk! The thought turned his stomach and brought up a sour reminder of his breakfast. *Double yuk!*

He went on about his job, pushing the mower back and forth in front of the fence, occasionally glancing up to see if Andy was still there. Every time Nick looked, the other boy was indeed there, frozen in stone.

Andy Corrazza was the next-door neighbor's kid and Nick's current best friend by default. Andy's three sisters had no interest in Nick. A happily mutual feeling—until recently, anyway. For years, he had ignored Jackie, Ginny, and Brenda as the alien life-forms they were, and they had ignored him as the snot-nose brat next door, the one who mowed the lawn incessantly, grooving to some macho jungle fantasy world only he could visit, or the one who sat on his front porch reading—*reading*, for crying out loud—even in ninety-five-degree weather. Nick would have concurred on all fronts; only now was he noticing that their blouses were filled with mysteriously enticing things, actually quite a bit, he had gathered from Stan, a Polack-Italian mix from down the street who had the hots for all three Corrazza sisters. Nick wasn't even sure what "having the hots" meant, but he knew that whatever it took to lead boys to that condition, the three girls had it—they *all* had it. He'd seen them in bikinis out in their yard, and he had begun to understand plenty.

Andy was a normal kid, for someone who grew up with three sisters, and he could always be counted upon to sign on to any irrational scheme Nick devised—like the theft of four thirty-five-gallon drums from a warehouse near the tracks, drums that would float their super-raft (if they ever built it). Never mind that the two of them could barely lift a single drum. They had already removed four of the colorful containers and hidden them in the underbrush, then camouflaged the area with freshly cut foliage. Andy was not quite so much the dreamer as Nick, but he recognized in Nick the grandiose plans that would land both of them in the spotlight for some great feat. Nick read of great adventures, and Andy was the only other kid who listened enough to paint himself into them.

Why was Andy acting so strangely?

Nick looked up again, and Andy was gone, a slight breeze gently rustling the willow branch under which he had just been standing. Nick stood behind his stuttering mower and carefully examined the Corrazzas' weather-beaten fence. You could see through most of its length, and the rest stood barely upright because of neglect, and Nick figured he would see Andy crouching behind it, maybe hoping to play some sort of half-assed prank. How would a Jungle Expert handle a possible ambush? Would he walk into it open-eyed, only to wipe out the enemy using his superior intellect and battle-honed instincts?

But, no, Andy wasn't anywhere behind the fence.

Nick gave the Lawn Boy a reluctant half-push. What the hell, if the idiot wanted to play games . . .

The prickle he felt on the back of his neck was like a leaf or an insect landing on his sweaty skin, and at first he tried to wipe it off. When that didn't work, he stopped mowing and used both hands to feel his upper back and neck methodically. There was nothing there, yet the feeling continued.

Nick whirled and stared at the fence where Andy had been. The willow branch still swayed gently, occasionally dropping a squad of narrow yellow leaves. Nick's gaze slowly traveled up and down the rickety redwood fence, then into the shadows created by the sides of his garage and the Corrazzas', which were parallel and about three feet from the fence. The shadows were deep next to the fence, somehow enhanced by the brightness of the day. A dark window set into the back wall of his garage stared at Nick with vague malevolence. Or was the uncomfortable gaze coming from the tight little alley between the garage and the fence, the place where no sunlight whatsoever seemed to penetrate?

"Okay, Andy, you asked for it," Nick called out over the mower's erratic rattle. "I'm comin' after ya!"

He took a single tentative step toward the corner of the garage, all the while staring into the Cyclops eye of the black window.

Even in the blue heat of late summer, Nick felt a chill ripple on his skin. He swallowed hard; then he marched toward the shadows.

CHAPTER THREE

Earlier
MARTIN

Martin would remember it forever, the first salvo in his campaign against the freak cop. He reveled in the memory . . .

When he followed them through the chilly parking lot to the mall, Martin wore what he thought of as his "writer's clothes" under a light jacket. Even though it had been a mild winter, now it was almost too cold; the early-spring temperatures in this Midwestern city were rarely consistent from day to day or even hour to hour. But the comfortable deck shoes, khaki Dockers pants that were wrinkled just enough, and blue cotton golf shirt embroidered with a tiny loon he had purchased at a Midwest specialty store right in this very mall earlier in the week were altogether perfectly bland and academic. He carried a small notebook in his back pocket so he could stop to make entries in his logbook and take notes for his "book" at the same time. He carried a bulging shopping bag in one hand. He blended right in with the suburban fathers and lower-level executives he saw everywhere, hanging out at the Starbucks and the Gloria Jean's, drinking majestic and overpriced paper cups of take-out coffee between trips to the washroom to void their bladders of the stinking swill coffee turned into.

Perhaps if he had a stroller and a baby, he'd just disappear into the faceless masses of suburban escapees.

But just as the thought crossed his mind, he felt the handle of the Gerber boot knife jab his back where it was clipped to his belt inside his waistband.

Maybe he wasn't destined to ever fit in that well. He'd settle for just long enough to complete his mission.

What was his mission? Well, he reminded himself, he had intended to follow Corinne Devereaux and her friend—Wanda? Wilma?—on their off day and plan his final encounter. After several weeks of entries, he was fairly certain the two would traipse from mall to mall, groping and pawing the racks, trying on incredibly skimpy outfits balanced by the most bland of casual wear, befitting people whose shopping needs included both their public and secret lives. He had merely intended to follow and observe, but he had also begun to spin his plans into a semblance of order. There was little question in his mind as to how to gain his revenge, what to do to her that would enrage *him* to the necessary degree. But he had left open for debate the when and the where, until just now, when he remembered following Corinne and her friend here only a week before. Now the disparate elements of his plan were solidifying into a whole that he found more acceptable and more titillating every second he allowed it to play unchecked in his mind.

Maybe the when was today, and the where was right here . . .

He watched Corinne and her friend enter yet another department store and followed slowly, unobtrusively, hoping this time their destination would be the cosmetics counter.

Martin had always prided himself on his ability to map out and execute a flawless plan. He remembered well how easily he'd out-thought doctors, nurses, and orderlies for years, having his way with them even as they believed they had cracked his hidden shell and extracted the succulent meat inside, feasting on his tender thoughts and feelings. All the while he had enjoyed feeding them those bits of him he *wanted* them to have, doubling his guard on all the others. He had almost developed a two-track mind, as he saw it, one that he could allow access to, and one that he could wall away and protect from every prying technique they were likely to try. And try they had, but he had beaten them every time. The psychological games, the long sessions with various therapists, the drugs—even the drugs were ineffective in cracking him, though he wondered at times if the drugs hadn't complicated his life by becoming too enjoyable. He'd ridden that tiger all too willingly.

Corinne and her friend—Winnie? Wally?—spun watches in their display cases, priced jewelry of various kinds and eventually bought a gold chain each, then headed for the rear of the store.

And stopped. They made a right turn and approached a white-coated cosmetics clerk who wore too much makeup for her poor, craggy skin, giving her the look of a mannequin under the bright lights.

Martin brought his forward motion to a hasty halt, looked around quickly, and made for the watch display, where he became intent on a collection of sports models for divers—or people who want to pretend they *look* like divers—standing where he could see the two women as they spoke with the clerk.

From afar, they seemed like any other pair of women shoppers, but he had been close enough to see that Corinne's great beauty was almost matched by her friend, who most certainly worked for the same high-priced escort agency.

Stacey, that was it.

Martin chuckled. He had no idea why he'd thought her name began with a W.

Stacey was dark blond, her hair curly where Corinne's was straight, and much shorter than Martin liked. Her face was nearly exquisite, though, a turned-up nose over full lips—what escort girl doesn't have full lips?—and a perfectly proportioned chin. High cheekbones and clear green eyes rounded out the picture, her skin as flawless as alabaster. Nordic and Celtic, perhaps, a nice blend. Her body spoke of interminable sessions at the gym, but displayed a hint of baby fat she would never get rid of and which would always enhance her beauty. Men liked a bit of meat on the bones, and whether women realized it or not, rarely appreciated when their women were in better shape than they. Martin shook his head. There was so much women didn't realize about men.

He saw a clerk hovering and quickly spun the display, affecting a thoughtful look that said, "I'm still thinking." The clerk, an elderly woman whose perfume could knock out a horse at twenty paces, disappeared behind the cash register island to bother someone else.

As Martin watched, Corinne and Stacey worked their way down the counter pointing to this lipstick sample and that, each selecting several to try on. Martin couldn't believe his luck.

He felt himself harden at the thought, the expectation of what he was about to watch. *Bear witness to,* he corrected. Perhaps it was an omen, a sign from whoever or whatever pulled the strings that today was indeed the day.

Huddled around the mirrors, Corinne and Stacey began their show. Martin fervently wished he could capture it all on film, but why be greedy? He spun the display and then moved to another, nearer the edge of the counter, hoping the old crone would leave him be.

Twenty feet away, Stacey selected a canister, uncapped it, and spun it open, the colored tip gently rising to meet her lips.

Martin squirmed. He imagined it was his penis, which bulged in his pants to the point where he had to make sure he was facing the counter. Mesmerized, he watched as Corinne nodded her approval while Stacey colored her lips with a darker shade and then pouted into the mirror. Martin couldn't quite see, but his imagination was capable of supplying the picture. His squirming was painful, and his hands itched as if they were on fire. He ignored the pain as much as he could, but felt sweat break out on his forehead.

Now it was Corinne's turn. She opened one of her canisters, gave the miniature penis its erection, and proceeded to paint her lips with dainty, economic motions that made Martin quiver with need. Her shade was a deep, classic red, and Martin silently approved. Stacey nodded, too, taking the canister herself and trying it on after wiping her lips with a tissue. Both wearing harlot red, they then turned their attention to a bright violet. Corinne wiped her lips, then applied the violet in slow, sensuous strokes—upper lip middle to side and middle to other side, and then lower lip, same again, and then more, applying a thick coat that Martin wanted desperately to—

"Have you decided? Would you like to see one of those?"

Damn it!

He'd been so intent on the erotic display across the aisle that he hadn't heard—or smelled—the crone approaching.

"No!" he said brusquely. He gave the display another spin. "I'll call you if I need you."

She sniffed and stalked away, a grimace on her pinched lips.

Martin mentally kicked himself. He didn't want to make an impression on anyone, not if today was the day. Now it was too late, and the old broad might remember him all too well when the time came. Though with his bland disguise and style-less haircut, didn't he resemble a million other guys? He smeared his prints on the display wheel and stepped aside to ostensibly check out more watches, this time leaving his hands off the counter. But his eyes wandered.

Across the aisle, each woman was on her fourth shade. Damn, he had missed one. They were now wearing two shades of pink, from what he could see, though the color was too light to stand out from so far away. The violet and red had been bolder, much more erotic, though he supposed the pink would be just fine from up close.

They switched from lipstick to mascara and eyeliner then, and Martin lost interest—while it was still erotic to see beautiful women apply cosmetics, it was lipstick he craved. He noted that they each purchased a couple canisters and couldn't help wondering which shades ended up in their bags.

They headed away from him, and he disappeared among the counters and groups of browsing shoppers. He noted that the crone had moved to a different counter to help an elderly gentleman who was monopolizing her time with silk ties. Good, she'd be less likely to remember Martin now.

He shadowed them from store to store, both the large chain department stores at each end of the mall and a score of boutique-style stores located in between. Most of them were too small for him to enter, so he took up a post nearby at some center-court stand or cart, gazing at mindless artwork and leather products until he spotted them leaving one place for another. At the second large chain store, an uppity and expensive layout of designer clothes and other high-priced status items, the women once again made a stop at the cosmetics counter.

Martin chose men's fragrances to entrance him this time, a counter that allowed him a clear view across to theirs. And this time there was no clerk present to interrupt him. Corinne laughed at something her friend said, and the fragile crystalline quality of her voice carried over to Martin and thrilled him with anticipation. It had to be today, he realized all at once, in a rush of awareness that made his extremities tingle. He was ready, and she was ready, and the plan was making itself known to him as his plans always did, almost as if they were created whole-cloth by someone else and dumped into his brain all at once—*downloaded,* as today's computervolk would say if given the chance. Downloaded into his brain. He liked that. It was so *direct.*

Corinne and Stacey wiped each other's lips with tissues and then picked new lipsticks to try on, this time teasing him by applying the color to each other's lips, drawing carefully so that the tiny penises wouldn't stray. Martin found sudden difficulty breathing, watching the two begin what was perhaps their two-girl private show. He imagined them performing this lip ballet for some old geezer in a hotel room, or for a frat-boy bachelor party. He watched as male passersby reacted to the raw sexuality by doing double takes and as their wives shot them dirty looks and even dirtier words, tearing them away even as they wanted nothing more than to stop and gawk at the lesbian act in full flower.

Martin heard both Corinne and Stacey laugh as they admired their handiwork in twin mirrors, knowing they knew he was there, watching and appreciating. Rather than hiding, Martin felt emboldened and stepped away from the fragrance counter, stepping toward them and readying himself for the question he would ask.

Abruptly, the two women broke from their counter and made for the escalator in the center of the store, and Martin's bold approach fizzled to nothingness.

He swore.

The bag was heavy in his hand, and so was the realization that his plan would have to wait, even if he was half ready to carry it out.

He followed them up the escalator, but three obese women on the metal steps stood in a cluster and would not let him through, so by the time he reached the second level Corinne and her friend were no longer in sight.

Martin looked around almost in a panic, attempting to avoid appearing desperate and perhaps not succeeding nearly as well as he hoped. He was standing in a main aisle, but his quarry had disappeared into a forest of clothes racks. He stepped aside when the escalator deposited a blue-suited shopper onto the platform behind him.

"Excuse me!"

The man looked at him as if he were an obstacle made entirely of excrement and stepped around him with a pointedly sarcastic whole-body gesture. Martin smiled wickedly. In the Institute, the man would have paid for his impoliteness, oh yes, he would have paid dearly. But now was no time to dwell on the healing qualities of revenge— ha! That was an ironic thought, Martin realized, as the entire escapade revolved around the healing qualities of revenge. No, it was just a matter of picking his fights carefully, and sticking to the plan that had formed so wholly and completely in his mind.

Then, almost as if to caress him with the silken hand of Fate, something made him turn and—illogically—look back down the escalator he had just climbed. There they were, having somehow doubled back and down the stairs, or perhaps one of those cleverly hidden elevators. In any case, Corinne and Stacey now perused a counter full of discounted accessories not far from the bottom of the down escalator, which Martin immediately negotiated, staring at them openly as the jagged moving steps brought him closer to where they stood.

He surveyed the sales floor and saw that the timing was perfect, all visible salesclerks otherwise occupied and very few shoppers hovering nearby. The moving stairs would deposit him mere feet from where the two women stood, and he boldly allowed the momentum to carry him to a spot just beside them.

"Well, hello!" he called out cheerfully as he allowed his face to light up with recognition. He knew it did because he had practiced the trick for years. He had been told it shaved age right off him, and made him seem friendly and uncomplicated. It was an essential maneuver in his current business.

Before the two women could even turn and acknowledge his presence, he was continuing on. "Imagine running into you here! What fun!"

The two lovely faces now peered curiously at him. It was clear he was speaking to them, yet neither recognized him.

"You don't remember me, do you?" he said with a wide smile. "The Hyatt, about a year ago?" He glanced around and lowered his voice conspiratorially. "We met after a certain phone call, and—" He stopped suddenly as Corinne nodded uncertainly.

Martin smiled wider, especially to himself. She had responded to over a dozen calls from the Hyatt since he had begun to log her activities, so he was safe—an out-call out of many relegated to the shadowy depths of her memory. And he *did* look familiar, after all. Her friend saw that Corinne seemed to struggle briefly with remembrance, then nodded as the connection was apparently made.

"Hello," said Corinne quietly. It was clear she wasn't thrilled to have her separate worlds collide in such a way, but business was business and you couldn't afford to alienate what might be a repeat customer. "It's nice to see you again," she said, holding out a slender hand. She might have lied, but she was convincing—an actress to the end.

He shook it with honest eagerness. "I've also visited the Roxanne Web site, of course, but you know how it is—it's easier for me to remember *you* than for you . . . In any case, I'm really happy to see you. It's such a coincidence, because I was thinking of you just a few days ago."

"Really?" Corinne said, sliding into her customer-service mode as easily as if she had slipped on a shawl.

Her smile widened, and for a moment Martin was so lost in her lips and the dark violet shade that colored them that he almost stuttered.

"I'm flattered you have such fond memories," she said, as if reciting a speech practiced often and with great success.

Her lips turned up and he finally released her hand, which he just realized he had grasped longer than was necessary. Yet the blunder worked to his advantage, because she seemed to accept now that he had met her in a hotel room and that she had satisfied his needs once, and now she hoped to do so again. Four hundred dollars an hour plus gratuity meant that she would always accept a broadening of her client list, even if it was awkward to chat about her business in this sterile environment.

Martin sorely wished he had indeed met her in a Hyatt suite, her lips employed for his pleasure and then—but no, he must not lose track of his goal, and here he had been handed a superb opportunity to bring his Phase One to fruition much earlier than expected.

"My dear, you were much more than a fond memory, and I am not just flattering. I have thought about you for a long time, and I had hoped the next time I was in town . . . that is, I had intended to call Roxanne and, well, ask you for a date."

There, that was relatively naive and yet knowing. His hesitation was a supreme bit of acting brilliance.

"Do you have the number? Maybe I can give you a card and you can—" Her voice trailed off as she dug in her tiny purse, disentangling a business card from some sort of pouch and handing it to him with slim fingers tipped with long, wine-colored nails that made his mouth water.

He made as if to take it, but hesitantly. "I've only had a couple days here, and this was my first without a meeting. I have a flight out in a few hours," he said with real regret in his voice. It was his conviction that always worked for him. He was convinced the words he spoke were true.

"Where are you heading?"

Making polite conversation. Unhappy to see a guaranteed transaction fade away.

He finally took the card and tucked it into his shirt. "Salt Lake City to put out a fire, as they say, and then Silicon Valley to light one under a certain project team!" He laughed.

Corinne laughed politely but with true humor at his little joke. Stacey smiled, her own lips delectable in their slightly different mauve shade and only a few feet away so he could smell the cosmetic smell that made his penis swell under the baggy pants.

"Well, maybe another time." Her face showed some disappointment, though not enough to lead her to where Martin wanted to go.

He maneuvered his features so that his crestfallen look took control of all emotions. Gazing into his face was to see almost as much disappointment as a child whose Christmas had yielded not a single gift.

"I'm afraid it's not likely," he whispered. "After the Valley I'm being reassigned to the East European branch, with all those Soviet countries suddenly in need of computer equipment. Well, it could be years before I return."

"That's too bad," Corinne said, and it was to her credit that Martin truly believed she *was* sorry. "I wish there was something . . ." She turned to her friend, who had become bored and whose attention had wandered to a counter display. Stacey shrugged slightly—she was not an interested party, and Corinne could take care of herself.

Martin let his eyes light up again. *Hit by sudden inspirational thought!* He deserved a freaking Oscar. "You know," he began softly, drawing her into the conspiracy of his gaze, "you may remember that my, uh, interests are not too uncommon, and I think they can be, uh, accommodated even in unusual places. Like this mall, for instance."

Martin knew he was walking a tightrope. There was a good chance she would not consider even for a minute what he was suggesting, in which case he would have to settle for some yet-unfocused Plan B, which, in the few minutes since he had begun his charade, he fervently hoped would not be the case. Right here in this mall, this was the message he wanted to send. This was the kind of splashy communication he had sought, he had planned, and now that he was so close he was loath to give it up.

Corinne Devereaux hesitated a moment, bringing her lips together in a straight line and refreshing her lustrous lipstick as she clearly thought about what he was saying.

"I'm not—" she began.

"On duty," he finished for her. "Yes, I know. I just thought that maybe, since we seemed to hit if off last time, you might consider a bon voyage gift. With full pay, of course, and an incentive just like last time."

Martin knew that she could not remember him, but that very fact worked in his favor, because it was likely her lack of memory embarrassed her in the face of such a polite repeat customer. He could see that she was thinking it over.

Suddenly she smiled. "You have intrigued me, Mr.—"

"Just call me Martin," he said, smiling back.

"You know, I don't make a habit of this, especially on my off days."

"Of course, of course. I don't blame you. I'm glad you're willing to make an exception. Very glad." He was a nodding fool, he realized, so he stopped.

"Stacey, how about meeting in a half hour . . . where?" She turned to Martin.

Inside, Martin jumped for joy. Talk about Fate. Nothing could have improved his luck in this venture, nothing at all.

"Near the food court," he offered, as if after a moment's thought. "There's a photo booth there that'll be perfect for my going-away gift. Then we'll need the washroom, and there's one right there."

Corinne nodded, the smile on her face faltering for just

a second. Martin knew exactly why, why she suddenly caught herself, and he timed his next comment to catch her before the rest of the doubt formed fully in her mind. "That is," he said, "you'll probably want the washroom to fix your makeup. I'll be on the way to my plane."

"Okay, Stacey? A half hour?"

Stacey suddenly looked nervous. "Are you sure you should be doing this?"

"Don't be silly. It's an old friend who's leaving town. Why not?" Her lips twisted into a wicked smile. "Plus, it's kinda naughty."

Martin knew from his research that he had tapped into the woman's carefully hidden wild streak. He knew that the illogical aspect of this encounter was exactly what had intrigued her, and he knew that he had won. Just like that, Jack, he had won and his plan had fallen together even better than he had hoped. He looked at her lips, a vision of mauve lushness, and he felt himself grow rock hard.

In a moment, they had left Stacey at the counter and he was steering her to the mall entrance, after which they headed for the food court. Martin applauded himself for the careful planning and research that had gone into this scenario.

"I don't remember you all that well, Martin," Corinne Devereaux began as they took the escalator. Martin luxuriated in the glow of her beauty, and he noticed other men glance and then stare at her, for even in casual clothes, Corinne was stunning. Her lips drew many a look as did her figure, but she seemed not to notice.

So comfortable with her own beauty. So comfortable with the situation, alien as it was.

"I was afraid of that," he said. "I'm pretty average looking. And we both had a bit to drink. But I could never forget you, or your lips, or what you did with them."

This seemed to satisfy her. After all, if someone knew her specialty, then it was likely that she had encountered him during one of her many appointments.

"I'm happy to know I was memorable," she said with just enough humility.

Martin sensed that she had closed herself off to doubt, even though she had great reason to doubt everything about him. But her hunger for an interesting situation and some quick cash seemed to eclipse everything else, including the letters. Martin cluck-clucked her in his mind. *She really should have been more careful.*

They reached the food court, and Martin steered her toward the automated photo booth, off to the side. She looked at him, still doubtful. "Here, huh?"

"Oh, yes," Martin whispered, his voice full of lust. "It's a perfect place for your specialty."

And damn it if he didn't see the light go on in her eyes, as she realized that what he suggested was, indeed, very erotic.

"Martin, you dog," she whispered back, suppressing a giggle.

He held open the curtain as she stepped into the tiny booth. "One thing," he said as she sat on the stool. He set his bag down and caught a glimpse of gray cloth.

"Yes?" Her voice was deep and sexy and her eyes grew in the low light.

"Would you put on more of that lovely shade of lipstick?" Her smile made his groin twitch.

He stepped in and pulled the curtain closed behind him.

It was nearly time for Stacey to meet Corinne, and Martin stepped out of the men's washroom and quickly crossed over to the women's, where, in a flash of gray cloth, he stepped through the door, key in hand, and turned the cylinder quickly, before anyone else could try to enter.

She was in a stall. Even better. He stepped closer, quietly, until he stood only a few feet away from the stall door, far enough so she wouldn't be likely to see his shadow. It had been a wonderful twenty minutes, a memory that would last him forever and that he would cherish.

Martin breathed quietly, as he had taught himself to do as a child in the Institute, whenever he needed to pretend sleep or drug-induced relaxation.

When Corinne opened the stall door after flushing, Martin leaped into the opening and shoved her forcefully backward until she fell onto the toilet.

Before she could scream, or fight back, he was on top of her with one hand over her mouth—the smell of the fresh lipstick staining him was almost overwhelming!—blade held high in front of her eyes, which had opened even more widely than when he had spilled his copious seed deep into her mouth and down her willing throat only minutes before.

"Quiet!"

His voice was a hiss she couldn't ignore, not with the sharp blade etching patterns in the air just in front of her delicate features. He could see her thoughts churning— what could she do to placate him? Somehow negotiate her survival?

"Nothing," he said in response to his own interpretation of the question there, visible behind her eyes.

Such beautiful eyes.

When he began his work, he enjoyed watching the life drain visibly from those eyes, and he wished he could be here to gaze in the eyes of him for whom this message had been so carefully composed.

Only a minute or two later he was finished. He recovered the keys from his pocket and, looking around for a likely surface, spotted the diaper-changing station. Martin smiled. He took the strip from his chest pocket and dropped it onto the hard plastic.

Moments later, he melted into the back of the service tunnel, a flash of dark-stained gray. In his hand he clutched two small jars and his shopping bag.

Martin knew he had just created Art.

Now he would sign it.

CHAPTER FOUR

1976
LUPO

Nick headed for the shadowy area between the fence and the garage, ready to give his friend Andy a pounding. Hey, Andy was his best friend and all, but he was acting so weird today that he was asking for a good old knuckle sandwich! They didn't fight that often, but occasionally a good tussle renewed their friendship in ways no one but them could ever figure out. Maybe it came down to respect, and how much could be earned by beating the other in the field of battle. Nick hoped he could figure out what was wrong with Andy and get back to the last hour or so of lawn work before his father decided to check on his progress.

He stalked toward the back of the garage. The window was as dark as ever, half covered by odd-sized sheets of paneling and plywood and Sheetrock his father stored upright in front of the car. Only a corner of the window was actually uncovered, otherwise the garage was an airless, dank cave. For a second, it seemed to Nick that Andy was looking at him from inside the garage, standing just beyond the light and staring through that little opening in the corner.

But, no, the garage was locked. Nick had locked it himself earlier that same day. His father hadn't gone anywhere. The garage was old and homemade and no one had ever bothered to put in a side door. There was no way Andy could be watching him from the inside.

Outside, below the window's slightly rippled glass, stood a pile of leftover lumber and sheet metal, stuff that Nick's dad had used for various remodeling and upgrading projects. It was killing the grass, here in the shade of the garage, and Nick was painfully aware that when the stuff eventually got used or tossed, he would probably either have to reseed the grass or lay some new sod. His father would never leave a patch of dead grass in his yard like that, and Nick was a built-in work crew. Now, as he approached the stack, he remembered that he'd seen a rat slip behind it and disappear not too long ago. He'd at first thought the gray-brown critter a squirrel, but the whiplike tail certainly bore little relation to a squirrel's fluffy appendage.

And squirrels don't usually squeeze between stacks of lumber, he reminded himself. At least, not when there's a fence and a bunch of trees nearby.

No, this had been a rat, and now it made him wonder if sticking his nose back there was such a good idea. Rats were uncommon in this area of town, but what if this one pioneer had a family?

For a second, Nick hesitated. The sound of the mower behind him brought him back. He had to do this quickly, before his father decided to see why the mower seemed to be standing still. Nick knew that if he choked the mower's engine, his father would notice the silence and come to make sure Nick was moving on to the next phase, the raking and bagging of mown grass and willow leaves.

Then he was standing next to the pile of odds and ends, and he heard it shift—could have sworn he did—as something underneath changed position, and then he was approaching the dark tunnel between the garage and the fence, acutely aware that the rat and his cronies, if they were hiding under the lumber, could now attack him from the rear. But he had to find out what was up with Andy, and he had to do it now—without delay, without chickening out.

The strip of ground between the garage and the fence was dead. Nothing could grow there in the darkness except some weeds and all sorts of elaborate spiderwebs. Nick brushed a web from his face and stepped forward. There wasn't much space, but Nick's father had resolved to use it wisely, stacking yet more scrap wood and several empty crates along the length of the strip. The shadows came not only from the Lupos' garage, but also from the fence four feet away and from the Corrazzas' garage. The crates and stacks of leaning wood gave the area dark angles that, together with the long shadows of the garages, seemed impenetrable even on a bright day. It was like a forty-foot-long cavern, and Nick shivered a little at the thought of entering—Jungle Expert or not.

Another web brushed his lips and chin, and he spit convulsively to get it off. *Fuckin' spiders!* His foot squelched in a pool of black slime, water left over from the last rainstorm mixed with who knew what else, and Nick wasn't about to check. He pulled his sneaker out of the mess by pure force and tried to step over the puddle with the other.

Andy, I'll kill you for this!

The mower was still cranking away back in the yard where he had left it, but the sound was somehow muffled and seemed to fade with every step he took.

It's like another world. An image out of Arthur Conan

Doyle's *Lost World* popped into his head, along with scenes from both movie versions. *Maybe the rats grow to the size of horses here*. He swallowed hard. That Andy really was a fucker.

"Andy, get yer ass out here!"

Nick heard a shuffling coming from ahead, maybe ten feet into the *cavern*. He had given up thinking of it as anything but a cavern, even though if he craned his neck upward, he could still see a slice of sky between the overhanging eaves of both garages.

"Look, Corrazza, this isn't very funny. I'm gonna get in trouble pretty soon, so get out here.

"Okay?" Nick added.

There was no answer, but he thought he heard the same shuffling, as if Andy were crouching behind one of the crates and had suddenly decided to scurry to hide behind another, farther back toward the front of the garage. Maybe *slither* was a better word. Then he looked down, suddenly wondering if he should worry about snakes. Were there poisonous snakes in the Midwest? He wasn't sure, and this was no time to find out—not with bare ankles.

Okay, two more steps, and if that little turd doesn't give up I'm gonna go back to mowing the lawn. And fuck 'im!

The air was stale back here, almost suffocating. Nick realized that he was breathing hard and tried to slow his panting, but he didn't seem to be getting enough air.

I been reading too much weird stuff. He shook his head, wondering how much time he had before his father found him back here, acting like a weirdo and too afraid to walk next to his own garage. He took one step, then a second, then was about to call out to Andy—*idiotic jerk!*—that he had better things to do with his time than play this stupid game, and then he felt something furry . . .

(slick like wet fur and it tickled and made his hair stand up as it caressed his right calf)

. . . clamp onto his ankle.

Nick jumped straight up and out of the thing's grasp and heaved himself straight back in one backward leap that took him past the corner of the garage.

Well, not really *past,* since he clipped his right shoulder on the sharp corner and fell straight down, landing on his butt back where there was some sunlight, one foot still mired in the black pool of gunk, his jeans streaked with cobwebs and his shoulder flaming up into a dull, steady throbbing pain.

He eyed the darkness intently, as if waiting for something—the snake, the mutant rat, the whatever it was back there—to spring at him while he lay helpless.

But nothing sprang.

"Fuck!"

Behind him the lawn mower sputtered and died.

Probably out of gas.

Then he heard the same shuffling sound coming from just on the other side of the first crate in the hellish little cavern, and he furiously backpedaled his arms and legs, ignoring the pain in his shoulder and scraping his back on the grass, until he was another five or six feet farther away from the shadows. He jumped to his feet and staggered back to the dead Lawn Boy as if it were some sort of protection against whatever stalked him. Nothing else moved, and there was no sound from the side of the garage.

Still ignoring the pain in his shoulder, Nick turned to check the mower. He caught the movement from the corner of his eye. It was just a flash, but he swiveled his eyes and focused on the fence, and there was Andy, about thirty feet away. Near the back end of their property, still on his own side of the fence.

"Hey, you little fucker!" Nick shouted, not even remotely thinking about his father's reaction if he were within earshot. "What the hell you doin'?"

Andy just stared at him. Again. Just like before, barely blinking and with no expression on his face at all.

Nick made to take a step in that direction. *Teach that little asshole a lesson* . . .

But something stopped him. He reached up with his left hand and grasped his right shoulder, which still throbbed from smacking the corner of the garage. What stopped him was the knowledge, full and unconditional, that Andy had been nowhere near the dark space between the garages, that he couldn't have caused the sounds Nick had heard, or grabbed his ankle, or any of it. It just was not possible, unless he had an accomplice— and Nick was Andy's only accomplice. Ever. So Andy hadn't been responsible.

"Uh, look, Andy," Nick began. But the other boy was gone again.

Nick heard the back door of his house clattering open, so he bent over the mower to check the gas level. His father, coming to see if he was done.

A brief lecture about wasting time, then a thankfully retreating back. A turn to the left just inside the door— good, going to the basement; out of the way for a while. Nick relaxed, but only for a moment.

After mixing more fuel, Nick started on the lawn again. He hoped his father wouldn't notice the small area left undone near the corner of the garage. No way would he do that area today. Maybe next week, when things weren't so strange.

He resolved to catch Andy later and, if necessary, beat the truth out of him.

Now he had to finish the lawn so he could trim the front hedges before dusk. The rest of the afternoon, Nick studiously avoided even looking at the darkness next to the garage. But the whole time he felt someone's eyes on him and was always aware of where he was in relation to the garage.

Nick hoped the evening would bring answers, but it was as if the whole day had been leading up to something. Nick wasn't sure he wanted to know exactly what.

There was a crash as a crate or a stack of lumber tipped over next to the garage, and when Nick ran around to the driveway, he saw what he thought was a huge German shepherd slink into the thick bushes that lined the front of his house. Maybe the stray dog was responsible for the strange noises, not Andy. Maybe Andy was just trying to tell him about the dog. Nick looked down to where the cracked blacktop curled into the strip of grass parallel to the driveway.

A big, blotchy bloodstain seeped into the crack, turning black and disappearing even as he watched.

That dog's hurt. Better stay away from it.

CHAPTER FIVE

LUPO

The image of that man-made cave of long ago bright in his mind, now Lupo stalked another man-made cave—the mall service tunnel—his sharpened senses tasting the bitter darkness and its secrets. Old secrets and new intertwined like coiled serpents.

There was little light here, but Lupo's pupils dilated to correct for the lack. Nostrils flaring, he navigated by olfactory traces that he soon realized were evenly—or almost evenly—spaced partial handprints slopped onto the cinder blocks. The ink was blood, apparently from a second jar carried away by the perp.

Corinne's blood.

Lupo snarled. The taunting was infuriating. He could sense that the guy was gone now. There were no eddies of active smells in the corners, or in the cracks between the low-hanging pipes and conduits above. He could just barely catch the tantalizing scents of the man who had bathed in her blood and used it to cloak his own scent.

There wasn't much there, except the clear understanding of maleness and evil, and Lupo felt himself losing control.

Fight the anger, he reminded himself. Ride out the anger. Relax, and visualize a peaceful scene. Often the quiet acoustic guitars of early Genesis could lull him to an English pastoral scene, and he used the way the notes and imagery blended together to calm down. The swirling synthesizer line and Mellotron choir that followed the last vocal part of "Entangled" reduced him to tears in the right circumstances, relaxing his muscles almost as if he had no control over them. The peaceful scene was there, in his head, brought to light green and golden reality by the music in his head. He tried to push himself physically into the scene.

But it was too late.

The first sign of the Change was an infusion of smells so great that it made his head spin. It was as if his nostrils had been securely blocked but now were thrown open like shutters. Suddenly, he could smell every blood cell in each handprint, and the varieties of dust layers, and each liquid or gas carried in every hanging pipe, and the copper in the wiring, and the rubber in the gaskets. The smell of recent fresh paint in the access tunnel was nearly intoxicating, and he felt himself gasping for breath.

In his head, the lush, gentle music grew dissonant and painful.

There was little time, and Lupo knew well enough by now that he had not yet developed the self-control needed to bring himself back from the brink. He frantically removed his clothes, hoping to shed this layer of useless skin before he damaged it beyond repair. First the shirt, a straitjacket that bound his arms too tightly as his muscles hardened and grew and changed. He ripped the fabric off his torso, already feeling the constrictions around his thighs. For a moment, he couldn't help imagining himself as the Hulk—green and wearing clothes that always managed to be fashionably torn in all the right places. But there was no humor in his mind. He kicked off his shoes, quickly shucked his pants, and had just enough time to lay the pistol down on top of the pile before he was irreversibly *over* and suddenly his hands had become monstrous paws and he was galloping down the passageway, the scent of the guy strong in his nostrils

—a familiar scent intertwined with the guy's own strong one, curled around it and so achingly familiar—

and the sharpness of the blood on his tongue, bitter blood that he craved and that he knew, deep in the recesses of his altered brain, he would soon taste.

His paws scrabbled on the cold concrete, nails scratching out a lullaby pattern magnified in his sensitive ears, and suddenly images were entering unbidden into his head—images both clear and blurred, and which he realized he should not be able to understand.

There was an image of an average-looking man, perhaps somewhat good-looking but still average enough to instill a sense of safety in others, in the ones he hunted, stalked. And killed.

As Lupo ran on into the dim light, a part of him relished the fact that he was feeling more than mere instinctive responses to stimuli, that he was still somehow present in the creature as it ran, so that, in essence, he was two: this creature of the night, magical and free, and a human presence within the creature's mind, or soul, which had retreated to a corner and could observe without affecting the creature's instincts or actions. At least, could not affect instincts or actions yet, though he'd been trying for years.

He heard the chase music, faintly, at the back of his brain. He was amazed to realize that he could indeed hear an instrumental passage, with its syncopated interplay between the synthesizer and the drums. This was the first time something as important to him as music—his favorite music—had crossed the divide between his two selves.

Lupo felt as though in a dream he was running down a passageway, dreaming of another who was running down a passageway, as if he were watching a film of a four-footed creature running down the same tunnel, and then the three intersected and became one, and he knew that his own consciousness was manifesting itself from within the brain of the beast. And he felt the elation of knowing that finally, after so many years of hopelessness and failure, here was another chance to gain control over the actions of the beast.

The Creature slowed, and Lupo brought his own senses to bear. The Mellotron sounds swelled and faded, and the music was gone. There was a fork in the tunnel, but the Creature knew which passage to take, and when Lupo ordered the Creature to follow his instincts, both were soon bounding down the new path.

The bloody handprints had become less frequent, and the creature seemed to have trouble holding the scent in its nostrils between each signpost, as if his Change were fading in and out, but Lupo worked at exerting control over the Creature's actions, spurring it on whenever it hesitated because the scent softened. Then the scent would swell and grow strong and the Creature growled, its muscles bunching as its hair stood on end and its lips curled tightly, displaying sharp rows of fangs.

Lupo felt himself trying to soothe the beast from his perch in its mind, felt his control begin to manifest itself in the Creature's quieting. The growl changed to a whimper as its nose worked at a loose pile of clothing on the cold concrete floor of the passage.

Within the complicated scent was that of the perp—this Lupo *knew,* without understanding exactly how—and the now-familiar bitterness was again combined with the scent that the creature had smelled on each bloody handprint.

Lupo willed the creature to sit.

With another whimper, the creature settled back on its haunches and lowered its head.

Lupo felt a rush of confidence, like an influx of chemicals, which made him visualize the creature as under his control. And then he felt that the creature *was* under his control. Something had happened in the tunnel, something that he had been trying to achieve for years. Always slight progress would be overshadowed by regression, a regression that Caroline had attributed to the creature's magical origins. For who knew how a creature that by all rights should not—*could not*—exist would react to an everyday tied-to-the-physical-laws kind of limitation?

Caroline had been right! Lupo felt the Creature—no, felt *himself*, for he *was* the Creature—sitting at the proverbial end of the line.

The scents mingled strangely here, in the clothes. Lupo concentrated, and he could make out three separate threads. No, four. There was the perp's scent. Strong, male, somewhat distinct from a separate male smell—the second thread—that also permeated the clothes. Then there was Corinne's scent, made bitter by her fear and the pain. Here the creature—Lupo—whimpered. *The incredible mind-numbing pain.*

And there was a fourth thread there, something faint and unidentifiable but unmistakably curled around the guy's thread as if they were one, even though they weren't. Lupo was puzzled, but his control over the creature was too primitive, *too basic,* to allow further analysis.

Lupo flexed his new understanding of how it all worked, threw all his concentration into forcing a Change. It had never worked before, the Change always leaving him when it desired, allowing him no say in the matter. But now things were different; he had effected some kind of breakthrough, though he didn't know how.

He could feel it working, could feel his senses alter and his perceptions somehow spiraling back into those that Nick Lupo could recognize as completely his own. He felt the tingling again and the itching of his extremities, and then the coldness of the concrete was kissing his bare skin—his *human* skin—and he was just a man, sitting naked in a dark and dusty tunnel.

On the floor, a pile of men's clothes. Gray-green shirt. Bloodstains barely dried. Black pants. Scuffed shoes. A battered pager. The uniform of a maintenance worker. Lupo looked around. The tunnel was not a dead end. There was an emergency exit set into a corner, probably leading to the parking lots. He had slipped past them, probably not long before. Had changed his clothes here, then made his way to his vehicle while sirens stopped at the main doors. Had taken the time to taunt Lupo by name.

Who the fuck is this guy?

Lupo stood, leaving the abandoned clothes for the forensics team. There was no way the other officers could have missed the unlocked access door, Lupo now realized. The guy had still been there, had done his thing with the blood. *Then he had gone back and unlocked the door,* as if he knew Lupo would be the one to find it.

His elation tempered by the death of his friend, Lupo quickly made his way back to where he had shed his own clothes. He dressed and reholstered the Glock, then walked through the door and back into the mall's washroom area.

Ben stood a few yards away, talking to a young uniformed officer.

"I got something here," Lupo said.

"Hey, Nick, where were you?" Ben patted the uniform on the back and sent him away. "I been looking for you the last ten minutes."

"Busy." *If only you knew how much.*

The fourth thread. What was the fourth thread? Was his newfound control so tenuous, so imperfect, that he was mistaken?

Minutes later, the access tunnel was swarming with cops.

Ben stared at the wall, Lupo at his side. Lupo's lungs screamed as if he'd run a marathon. One of the Forensics guys stood with them.

The bloody words seemed to glow in the darkness. *"Here's one for you, Nick!"*

"Fuckin' Satanists!" The Forensics tech whispered, staring in awe.

Lupo turned toward him but said nothing. The guy was serious.

"Nick's another name for Satan—you know, Nick Scratch. Saw something just like this last year, in a graveyard in Green Bay."

"Yeah?" Lupo said.

CHAPTER SIX

LUPO

The strangeness of the day had translated itself into an evening ripe with weird shadows and sounds, lending the late-summer twilight a sense of foreboding.

Nick's father had grunted his acceptance of Nick's efforts on the lawn, then sat in the dark brooding over something or other—Nick didn't know what might have happened while he had wrestled the lawn mower out back—until Nick's mother called them to dinner.

The three ate quietly, watching a television documentary. Nick's mind wandered. A song he heard often on AM radio thumped through his head. It was "Money," by a band with the weird name of Pink Floyd. He didn't even much like the song, but he caught himself humming it all the time. He guessed that made it a good song, after all.

Meals were always quiet in the Lupo household. Soon long shadows crossed the kitchen walls and floor, and then he was finished and on his way to bed, where he would read as long as he could get away with it, probably until his mother softly knocked on the door and warned him to turn off his light before his father decided it was too late to be awake.

Nick's single window overlooked the driveway, and the yellowish cone from the streetlight on Brady tinged his walls amber. He started to pull down the shade. His mother always opened it to let in light during the day, but Nick himself hated to see the oblong of light from the window at night, though he resisted the urge to confess that it was a fear of seeing monstrous shadows cross the window that drove him to close and lock the sash every night and pull the drape tightly down to the floor.

He stopped, his hand on the shade.

Shouts. From the street, out front.

Another fight?

No, these were men, shouting in unison.

He jumped as a howl cut through the late-August night. And another.

Pain, and fear.

But then the men shouted again, their voices rising as they came closer, and suddenly Nick realized that they seemed to be coming up the driveway.

He saw them then, a dozen shadows carrying oversize flashlights and baseball bats, or could those long shapes be guns?—muttering loudly among themselves. Then they were past, heading straight back toward the garage, and he was tearing out of his room and into the kitchen.

Frank Lupo stood in the back door frame, rigid of back and also gripping something. In the shadows, Nick thought it was another baseball bat. Except the Lupos didn't own a baseball bat. No, it was Frank Lupo's prized Beretta shotgun, with its inlaid ivory filigrees, and Nick realized with surprise that his father was pushing shells into the breech. He never kept the shotgun loaded at home, and he always preached respectful handling.

"Go back to your room," Frank Lupo ordered.

Nick thought he heard his mother crying in the master bedroom, which, in the way of older homes, was located right off the kitchen.

"Your room, I said!"

Nick retreated, and his father was on the back staircase, the Beretta at the ready in his hands. Nick could hear him opening the door and talking in low tones with someone, maybe one or two of the men Nick had seen in the driveway. But what was going on? Had someone committed a crime? Should he call the police?

"Ma?" he half whispered from the darkness.

"Oh, my God! Go back to bed, Nicky! Go now, before your father sees you. Please!"

He almost obeyed then. He actually felt his feet beginning to turn. A slight forty-five-degree-angle turn would send him back in the direction of his bedroom and the closed drape, and nothing was going on that he needed to be a part of. Nothing at all. Just a gathering of old drinking buddies. But Frank Lupo had no drinking buddies.

No, Nick could have obeyed then, but he didn't want to. The oddness of the day's events had made him curious, and he wouldn't be cheated out of an answer now.

As he negotiated the back steps, he heard a series of howls and growls from just outside the door, maybe one of the neighbors' dogs out with the men, on a leash, tracking some criminal. Nick stepped into the darkness of his backyard, the sky a purple bruise above him.

Another howl split the night, and the men raised their voices in shouts that Nick couldn't make out, and he couldn't tell where they were. It seemed they had gone around the house in the other direction, perhaps up against the south neighbors' garage. Nick stumbled on something, maybe a garden tool, he couldn't tell, and suddenly he was on his knees and facing the largest German shepherd he had ever seen.

He flashed for a second on the shape of a shepherd slinking into the bushes earlier that day, traces of blood on the blacktop. Twin green eyes peered at him like emeralds in the gloom, he felt himself reaching out a hand to the dog as if it were a pup, and he realized the stupidity of what he was doing, but he couldn't stop himself in time. The dog's eyes fixed on his, and then the huge jaws opened and snapped shut near his hand, which he was by then rapidly pulling back.

The dog growled, low and deep in its throat.

Nick stared at the animal, wondering as he did so why he wasn't leaping for the safety of his own back door.

The light was bad, late dusk finally giving way to real nightfall and the shadows deepening all around.

Nick felt strangely fascinated by the animal, which in turn stared at him intently. He thought he saw slickness below the dog's haunches, as if the beast were sitting in blood. Instinctively, he offered his hand again.

This time the dog did leap, his jaws clamping on Nick's outstretched hand even as shouts erupted from the corner of the house and voices raised in anger interrupted the animal's concentration and it tried to come out of its leap sideways, Nick's hand still clamped in its jaws like Lassie trying to lead him to the site of Timmy's peril.

Nick felt the skin of his hand tear roughly as it raked along the dog's jawline. He yanked his hand back, feeling the sting then of ripped flesh and air settling on the open wound like water mixed with alcohol.

The dog landed awkwardly on its four paws, then immediately leaped for the darkness of the garage's shadow.

Holding his hurt hand, Nick watched him go. Even through the pain caused by the dog's iron jaws and sharp teeth, he felt almost no anger or animosity. He couldn't explain it, but there was no urgency and no desire to scream for help. He realized then that he *wanted* the dog to escape its pursuers, even if he shouldn't have.

Hide between the garage and the Corrazzas' property, Nick thought, somehow instantly aware that the commotion closely followed the dog—the men had spotted it and were approaching quickly. Meanwhile, the dog seemed indeed to be heading for the same strip of darkness Nick had faced earlier. Maybe the shadows would be even deeper there.

The knot of men followed, voices raised, brandishing weapons—all of them long guns.

The air had been sucked out of Nick's world, and he couldn't breathe at all.

The men disappeared into the blackness of the shadowy backyard, their shouts drowned out by a long howl and a savage growl that raised the hair on Nick's back.

A ragged volley of shotgun blasts nearly knocked him to the ground, and then another ripped into the echo of the first. Nick could swear he heard a whimper, then a child's voice, and then one of the men was crying loudly and the others murmured as they reloaded their weapons and stood in a circle Nick could now barely make out.

He felt wetness on his skin and looked down. Blood had welled up from several deep gouges in the back of his hand and had begun dripping to the blacktop. The wounds throbbed in a steady rhythm of pain.

Absentmindedly, he wiped the aching hand on his jeans and stuck it in his pocket.

The men were returning now, walking slowly out of the shadows, shotguns held low and heads bowed.

Frank Lupo glared at his son, who had disobeyed. Nick knew the look and prepared for the worst. Instead, the elder Lupo put his arm around his son's shoulder, a strange enough gesture, and whispered words Nick almost didn't catch.

"Time for bed. Let the man grieve how he wants." He muttered something else, a sentence or two Nick lost amid the new sounds from the backyard: a man, bawling and screaming, his Italian distorted by the night and by the low voices of the others who crossed themselves and dispersed without looking at him.

Is Mr. Corrazza crying? Nick wanted to ask. But the moment for questions was past.

Nick went to bed, wondering what the German shepherd had done, why the men had hunted it so viciously, ending its life with gunfire.

His hand had stopped bleeding by then, so he never bothered to bandage it.

The next day, news of Andy Corrazza's death in a fatal hit-and-run accident wiped the bizarre dog hunt from his mind.

CHAPTER SEVEN

LUPO

Lupo's apartment was the same cluttered two-bedroom he had occupied since the Academy. There was little furniture besides overflowing bookcases and the occasional end table, buried in a layer of books and periodicals. Research, he called it when pressed. But then, he'd never be pressed again, would he, since Corinne had done much of that pressing in the last two years?

He sat now and could almost see her standing in his doorway, a tiny smile playing over her face as she chided his housekeeping. He heard himself replying with a playful insult about her family values and saw her smile flicker at that, and then he was apologizing. She'd been serious for the next few minutes of her visit. A nonprofessional one, she would say around a wicked smile, and that had been two, no, three days ago. The last time he'd seen her. Until today.

Now she was gone, her apartment across the hall

sealed up and her body on a tilted metal slab downtown. And though she was just one less whore on the street for most people, his daily life could never be quite the same. He knew without a doubt that what he faced now would be that much harder to face because Corinne wouldn't pop in with the timely insult or friendly ear.

It was almost funny. He had resigned himself someday to hear her tell him that she had contracted AIDS, intelligent as she was and careful as she claimed to be. Still it was an occupational hazard. Though she was a hooker, Ben was incorrect in his assumption that this involved streetwalking. While she wasn't quite an executive-level call girl yet, she'd been headed in that direction, working selectively for a relatively safe escort service known in the city for its "clean" approach to a dirty business. So her "encounters" tended to be in "safe" hotel rooms and the expansive, well-decorated bedrooms of sprawling north suburban mansions, rather than in cars, alleys, and ratty flophouses. Corinne had plans to invest her trick money into a degree. She'd mentioned her interest in law as a possibility, and Lupo had never felt the urge to point out the horrible *Inside Edition* cliché of an ex–call girl lawyer.

Now she would never have her chance. The finality of it caught in his throat. Had he been asked a week before, he never would have imagined how her loss would affect him.

His gaze slid over the huge rack of compact discs that nearly covered one wall. Over two thousand CDs, some classical, with a healthy scattering of movie soundtracks, experimental and electronic, plus so-called Classic rock—but mostly Progressive rock. It was his one vice, collecting obscure prog-rock concept albums recorded by long-gone bands such as Quill and Cathedral, nearly unknown bands such as Marillion, Pallas, and IQ, as well as more popular bands such as Yes, Emerson Lake & Palmer, and the very band whose music had forged his friendship with Corinne—Genesis. She had heard him playing their latter-day output—his least favorite—and they'd started talking about their musical likes and dislikes. Corinne liked the more recent pop-heavy, pseudo-Motown hits influenced by vocalist-drummer Phil Collins, while Lupo savored the much older mythological and literary epics written by the youthful keyboardist Tony Banks and the outrageous early vocalist Peter Gabriel. But they had found common ground in the band's middle period, when Collins had stepped from behind the drums to sing on the mid-seventies albums. The song "Entangled" had become a touchstone of sorts for them, with its six- and twelve-string guitars, synthesizer, and Mellotron blended to form a visual ballad of delicate beauty and subtle English humor. Lupo had played "Entangled" for her after a lengthy discussion about the merits of Gabriel versus Collins, and it caused them to reach a middle ground. They'd become friends then, even if she did think many of his CDs impenetrably dense and too musically challenging for the average listener. Which was why he liked them, he would argue. Then they'd order pizza and have a good laugh.

Now he could barely stand to look at his prized collection. He gazed down at his cluttered desk, the abortive home office he had never quite managed to gather together. Stacks of loose papers teetered on the edge, propped by crooked piles of books and yellowing magazines.

With a sudden motion, Lupo swept everything off the side of the desk and onto the already-cluttered floor. Then he swept the few remaining books and pens off the desk, clearing its surface. He cradled his head in his arms, but he could not maintain the position long. He could feel it coming again, and he pushed the chair away from the desk and let it wash over him.

The smells! His nostrils cleared and the smells rushed into his head and made him giddy, swirling around his brain and then slowly settling into recognizable patterns of familiarity. Like the day's earlier Change in the access tunnel, Lupo found himself more aware of these occurrences than ever before, more able to process the information as a human, rather than merely react to it as the Creature. He wondered briefly. What had changed in such a short time? But then his rage was building, and—for lack of a focus, perhaps, or because the rage *was* his focus—somehow the approaching Change seemed different.

Why was he experiencing the Change in so many new ways? Why now, after all these years?

The tingling drove his senses crazy. It began under the soles of his feet and in his palms, slowly spreading first outward to his fingers and toes and then inward, back toward his torso. And the smells, heightened to lancelike points that drove into his nostrils and exploded inside his brain in the shape of olfactory fireworks, the smells made him weep with their intensity and familiarity and—something else, something he could not, in the infancy of his awareness within the maze of the Creature's mind, completely grasp. *Something.* As if the Creature itself were attempting to communicate with him, before—before the anger and rage and hurt gathered up into a single tangible emotion that began low in his stomach, and he knew he was about to go over, *just like that, it's a fact-Jack,* and even though he tried to recall or deny or alter the feelings that had suddenly spilled over into rage, he also knew full well that he could not and that his precarious new balance between Man-that-was and Creature had been tipped and was already spinning him into the Change, spinning him inexorably and without remorse, spinning him like a children's cartoon into the gray-black form only once glimpsed in the videotape he had made in the woods just before the beast toppled the camera and howled off.

He barely managed to shed the layer of clothing and

scatter it about him, heedless now of his need to collect it later.

How strange. I can sense Corinne. She's still here. No, her smell is still here. Her scent. And here's HIM—his smell is here, and the fourth thread, too. Stronger now than before.

The words passed through the narrowing focus of his mind and were gone.

Lupo fought hard to remain in control. He tried to exert some kind of pressure on whatever shape his brain was now taking and, for a second, he felt himself slipping back, or maybe both ways. For a brief moment he thought he'd won, feeling nearly in control of the Creature, but then he was over and no longer Nick Lupo.

In only seconds, the transformation was complete.

He lunged at the door and howled as his nose smacked soundly into the reinforced steel. Forepaws scrabbled uselessly against the smooth surface, claws tearing—the pain lanced through his heavily muscled body like a javelin. The blood scent turned strong and inviting, for a second, until whatever vestige of his own brain that remained intact reminded him in a single, nearly incoherent thought, that it was his own blood and therefore unacceptable.

He was there again, in the Creature—aware, though standing well back, like a separate consciousness.

The huge gray-black form sat on its haunches and let out a strangled howl.

His nerve endings tingled mercilessly now, as if insects had somehow crawled into his flesh and were digging tunnels around bone, along cartilage and sinew and between the cells themselves. Millions of tiny legs traversed organic highways and set him to scratching, though he looked at his forepaws for a moment and tried to decide—*actually felt himself trying to decide*—whether they could do the job on their own or whether he would have to enlist his rear paws, on which he now stood. Somehow, standing on the rear paws was something he had come to prefer over the years, even if he could in a second crouch on all fours and feel completely at home.

All this Lupo knew as if it were contained in a distant memory, a visual one that seemed to grow brighter and closer with every breath, more comfortable with each passing moment but still somewhat jumbled and confused. Before, he'd known that he was working his way through a roundabout thought process, a process that only Caroline had ever been able to coax from him on a regular basis. Somehow, she had spoken to him through the haze of the Change and its side effects, and she had managed to instill in him the confidence to attempt the direct brain-to-limb communication that he himself had rarely completed successfully. But now, as of today, he felt success finally within his grasp.

Even though the rage and other complex emotions within him had once again forced a Change, Lupo could feel himself gathering control over the Creature. Could feel himself consciously abandoning the reliance on instinct he had developed over the years, beginning instead to learn how to trust the instincts while still maintaining a presence, *a Nick Lupo presence,* that could impose its will on the actions of the Creature.

His awareness flickered like a loosely connected television set, and he felt himself lose some of the control he thought he had gained. Lupo heard a soft whimper, *his* whimper, and knew that the beast still imposed some semblance of control.

Now was a time for anger and fury, the beast seemed to say, and no soft voice could have coaxed anything but a vicious response from its jaws.

The Creature lunged for the door before Lupo could bring to bear his own will, backstepping and lunging again and again, feeling the pain and frustration slide into one incurable ache. At the windows, then, but the glass was safely out of reach. Though his wiry paws could reach through the reinforced steel bars sideways, the bars were

too narrowly set in their frame for him to reach the textured Plexiglas. A strategically positioned hedge along the
side of the building hid the beast's shadowy struggles
from casual view, and indeed camouflaged Lupo's "im-
provements" to the security of his apartment. But now the
Creature wanted out, and Lupo's feeble and flickering
sliver of awareness could impose no physical control.

Bloodlust struck the Creature like a sharp dagger—
Lupo felt it, too—and it howled at the futility of searching
for anything to quench its insatiable wantonness.

After abandoning the windows, Lupo attacked the rest
of the furniture, upending chairs and tilting end tables
even as the rage crested and eventually dissipated, the
scents playing in his nostrils and taunting the beast with
their inaccessibility. The sliver of Lupo seemed to glow
from the beast's brain, gaining strength again as the beast
tired and finally laid its head down onto its gigantic paws.
Soon it slept, unsated, taking Lupo with it until the next
time, his hope of learning more suddenly dashed.

When Lupo awoke, painfully parched as always, he was
lying on the floor, his bloody hands under his head. The
steel door had held firm, with its seven custom-made
locks, and the windows seemed intact as well, though
bloody streaks marked the steel bars where it—no,
dammit, where *he*—had tested *his* strength. This time, he
had not managed to loosen any of the soundproof panels, so no neighbors would come knocking to ask him to
control his dog.

Nick cried for Corinne and for himself and his
grotesque fate. Weakened by the episode, he remained in
the secure chamber, knowing that his fragile state of mind
could trigger another unwanted incident.

He smacked a hand weakly on the linoleum.

No matter how much progress Nick thought he was
making, the Change knew no master except the Moon
and his own soul's unrest.

Before he could will himself physically away from the

place he approached, his memory dredged up familiar piano chords. "Mad Man Moon," another Tony Banks composition. "Well," she had said, "that would have to be your song, wouldn't it?" She'd ducked his swat and stuck out her tongue. They had settled on "Ripples" as her song then, and the sad prophetic truth of the song—lamenting the fact that ripples never come back—came crashing down on him now. He couldn't stop the onrushing memories. He didn't want to.

Nick cried, then sank into an exhausted sleep, dreams darkening his rest with their promise and tickling his intuition with the featherlike knowledge that he was missing something, something that the beast had found and tried to communicate to him.

Lupo awoke, still thirsty.

What was it about the Change that dried his throat and palate? he wondered, as he staggered to the refrigerator and took out a bottle of water. He rinsed and spat into the sink, then swallowed several large gulps. He allowed some water to dribble down his chin, enjoying the tickling coolness on his skin, which always seemed hot and feverish after an episode. He stared at his hands, at his forearms, then glanced at the bloody marks he had left on the walls and on the door. There were no wounds or scratches, since minor wounds healed somehow on their own whenever he was in his other form. This was a phenomenon that Caroline had first observed and studied years ago, carefully documenting her conclusions in one of her hard-covered notebooks. They had speculated on the nature of the healing process, on what could possibly be happening at the cellular level, how it worked and to what extent.

Lupo snorted. It had been probably a week now since he had thought of Caroline. Maybe even two weeks. *Cheers. Let's hear it for small victories.* He toasted his haggard self as reflected in the smudged coffeepot on his counter. It was Corinne, of course. Her friendship had not quite replaced Caroline's, for no one's could, but it had allowed him some freedom to let Caroline inhabit a more remote area of his memory. She was there but not so prominent, not so accusing. Like his father, who had likewise receded in his mind until he had become a passing acquaintance, someone he had known in his youth but not so much *his father*. Some kinds of guilt were like that, Lupo knew, overlapping so they could sap your strength and darken your life at any particular moment, leading further into darkness that you ignored when working, when interacting with other people, but which you could rarely avoid when left defenselessly alone. Some kinds of guilt chewed at your soul until you started considering ways out, especially when you knew just how monstrous you really were.

There was no song for Caroline. If there had been, its sound would have surely killed him.

His friendship with Corinne had somehow made up for the loss of Caroline and his father, his two great failures. He'd started to consider himself human part of the time. He met his own distorted eyes in the curved reflection of the coffeepot, blinking and wondering who was looking at whom.

He drank another long mouthful, then put the bottle away, now with the hunger gnawing at his stomach. He could feel the full moon coming—"Mad Man Moon"— just a couple days away, and his hunger always intensified during the cycle. He would eat then, but he knew the pit of his stomach would always feel empty, even after a meal. He had always considered it part of the curse, that horrible sense of emptiness. Sometimes stress or danger caused an unintentional change even outside the lunar cycle, and the hunger would be upon him, yet impossible to fulfill. Now that he seemed to be gaining some control over his temporary changes, would there be any difference? What if the bloodlust subsided at his command, much as regular everyday hunger could be held at bay with the thought of future satiation? He wondered how Caroline might have fit the eternal hunger into her theories. He also wondered if what he was learning now, damn near at middle age, might have saved Caroline way back then, when he was young and full of himself and his strange powers.

Fuck this. He squeezed his eyes closed until they hurt.

He pulled on sweat pants and a t-shirt that hung limp near the couch. He started to straighten the mess he had made of his desk, layering papers and books more or less the way they had been, in what he called his geologic system, where the oldest items were clearly on the bottom, with progressively newer files and folders spread out and upward in strata so that the upper layer was only a day or two old. As he did so, a sealed envelope caught his eye. It was a letter, but it was addressed to Corinne.

"Shit!" He picked it up by one end and snapped it onto the edge of the desk. "Shit, shit, shit."

Corinne had given it to him just three days ago. Could it have been that long? She had brought it over, wearing a crooked smile on her face.

"Mr. Detective, find out who this guy is. He's sending me a letter a week, okay? It's getting kind of creepy."

She had mentioned the letters—three of them—once before, but had shrugged them off as hazards of her profession.

"Some kook, probably a rich one I met at a party, who got my name from Eileen."

"She's not supposed to give out names, is she?" he'd asked. *"Nick, this is a people business! Twisted people, but still people. Occasionally, a name gets mentioned. Favors are done. Payments are made. You know what I mean. Maybe he, ah, requested my expertise."*

"Yeah, and maybe he's just some pervert," Lupo had growled.

"Honey, they're all perverts."

But something about this fourth letter had spooked her, something that she had never been able to tell him about, because after giving him the envelope and asking him to check, she had been paged, and that had been the last time he'd seen her alive.

"Duty calls," she had said with a mock salute and a smirk.

He looked at the envelope now. How could the letter have spooked her? She hadn't opened it. If the other three hadn't concerned her, why this one? Just because the sender was so persistent? Had he done more than send letters? Had he called?

Why the hell didn't I get on this earlier?

He had already handled the outside of the envelope, so now it was likely too late to lift decent prints from its surface. But maybe the letter itself . . . It felt like a single sheet, folded in thirds. Very innocuous. The typing on the outside of the envelope was normal, with no unique characteristics. None of those detective story clues—no upraised or faded letters, or other distinguishing marks. The font was a boring Courier, neither output on laser nor inkjet. Probably an old, low-cost electronic typewriter, one of millions sold in the Eighties before the computer explosion. There would be no chance for a grandstand scene, in which he could dramatically match the incriminating letter with the quirky machine that had produced it. The postmark was from the central Milwaukee Post Office. No particular clue in that fact, either, as it was the busiest post office in the county. If the guy had mailed from inside, there would be videotapes from the security cameras. But it was most likely he'd used one of the half-dozen outdoor boxes.

Lupo laid the envelope on the desk and went to fetch the latex gloves he needed to continue handling the envelope and check the inside sheet. Then he zipped the envelope-open and read the vile words: *Hello, Cunt. I'm not playing anymore. You're about to die!*

Suddenly, his hands began to itch, then his feet.

What the hell was this? He hadn't done more than two changes in one day in years, and he was damned well too tired to let it happen. He stared at the envelope and held his hands just over it, hovering above it as if about to grab it off the surface of the desk. His fingertips tingled.

Blink. Vision. The envelope has someone's hands on it. They aren't his hands or Corinne's. Breathing faster, increasing. Panting. Nostrils itching, oozing. Wipes his nose, feels coarse hair on the back of his hand. Eyes begin to change, light changes, sound changes Smells intensify. Smells intoxicate.

Lupo shakes his head. Lets the spell dissipate, and it does, retreating as if following his command. He looks at the envelope, and it's as if he can see a trail leading from the desk to the door.

Lupo shook his head again, harder. The door, where the blood streaks indicated a Creature eager to chase, to follow a scent. Maybe the Creature was trying to tell him something, something useful. But could he trust himself to open the door? Could he control the Creature?

Lupo let his instincts take over this time, unsure as to what else to do. He stuffed the envelope into his pocket, grabbed his keys from the hall table, and undid the locks. Then, before he could think too much, he was out in the hall. There was a single strip of yellow tape across her doorway: CRIME SCENE MPD, repeated in block letters. They hadn't bothered to padlock the place since it was not actually where the murder had taken place, and everyone knew a cop lived just across the hall. Ben had probably figured Lupo would need access—for whatever reason—and had instructed them to leave it. Lupo turned the key, then ducked under the tape and closed the door behind him.

Corinne's scent was everywhere, and it might have overwhelmed him, if only there hadn't been something else, something that made the hair on the back of his neck stand up as it had in the service tunnel at the mall.

He had been there, in Corinne's apartment. Or, maybe, not quite. But there was definitely a trace of the same scent Lupo remembered from the tunnel.

It hit him for a second that he was remembering the scent awfully well. That he'd never recalled anything from a change state quite so easily. But he went with it, oh yeah, 'cause if he were picking this opportunity to learn more about himself and how to control his animal side, well, there was no better time. He made directly for Corinne's kitchen, noting that now he could sense another scent—what he had thought of as the *fourth thread* back in the concrete tunnel. There had been Corinne's blood scent, and the custodian whose clothes the guy had worn, and the guy's own thread. And then that fourth thread. The one he couldn't quite identify. And here it was again, in Corinne's damned apartment. What the hell?

I could have prevented her death if I'd moved quickly on the letters, and if I'd opened this one.

He shoved the thought aside and tried to listen in as part of his brain monitored the creature's.

He picked up the trash basket, a tall beige cylinder with a hinged top and a black plastic liner neatly folded over the rim, and stuck his face in it. Yes, there it was. Weak, but definitely still strong enough to sense.

He spread an old newspaper on the floor, and started pawing through the garbage. Not a pleasant experience, by any means, but he found nothing except the usual three- or four-day accumulation. Still, the scent tickled his nostrils. Ben and the lab boys would have gone over the apartment too quickly, since it wasn't the actual crime scene, and they would have found nothing because they didn't know what to look for. No letters, or any other incriminating evidence.

"I had a laugh and ripped them up, Nick," she had said

when he had asked to see the other letters. *"I mean, it's not the sort of thing one keeps to enjoy again and again, if you know what I mean."* He had complained that she might have saved them so he could have them tested, but she had shrugged. *"I didn't think of it. I figured they would stop. At least you have that one, right?"*

I sure let her down. Lupo scooped the loose trash back into the bin and looked around. *I sure fucked up.*

Out the kitchen door, onto the back landing, and down the stairs. To the Dumpster, where all their refuse ended up before being taken by a private contractor to whatever recycling plant or dump they were currently using—*Have to look into that!*—but in the meantime, it was only the middle of the week, so her trash would still be there.

He opened the four plastic panels that covered the double-size Dumpster, and the scents washed over him— not just the fragrance of decaying food and paper products, but also the guy's scent and the mysterious fourth thread, stronger here than anywhere. He dug through with his hands, ignoring the wet slime that oozed out of some colorful container, reaching a neatly twist-tied black plastic trash can liner that looked like the one in Corinne's basket. He pulled it carefully from the jumble of loose trash, but it was sagging and nearly empty.

There was a long, jagged slit in the plastic.

Someone had been through Corinne's trash.

Lupo looked up and saw a corner of his own trash bag from two days before; the stack of empty meat cartons at the top gave it away. On a whim—*instinct, maybe,* he thought—he worked it out of the tight mass of paper and plastic bags until it was lying before him, where he could clearly see the same long, jagged slit that had let out most of his garbage.

The sonofabitch had been *here,* and he had rummaged through both their trash, not a dozen yards from the back wall of their building. How many other people had touched the Dumpster, erasing prints?

Lupo closed the Dumpster flaps with a loud snort of disgust. He looked around. How close was this guy right now? Was he even now watching Lupo through binoculars? A telescope? A camera?

A rifle's telescopic sight?

Lupo felt eyes on his back all the way to the building.

CHAPTER EIGHT

1976
LUPO

Two weeks after Andy's death, Nick Lupo's destiny came crashing down on him.

At dawn, Nick awoke shivering from a nightmare, bathed in cold sweat. He was curled in a tight ball, trying to keep skin on skin so he could stay warmer. Had his mother opened the window again? Sometimes she enraged his teenage sense of privacy by opening the door to his room and entering without his permission to perform some sort of task, put a blanket away in his double-size closet, take his used laundry for an unscheduled wash load, or alternately open and close a window, a shade, or his curtains. These transgressions didn't bother her in the least, and no amount of explanation on his part ever convinced her that a mother shouldn't be able to walk in on her son whenever she wanted or needed to. Nick wondered how often he'd nearly been caught with a smuggled *Penthouse* or *Playboy* and a guilty hand.

Now he became aware of three things with startling clarity. The cold wetness on his skin, and the tiny, hard points prickling his side could *not* be his cotton sheets. And his throat screamed for water, as if he had swallowed a bucketful of sand.

He opened his eyes finally, sure that he wouldn't like what he saw, and then he leaped up, shivering even more violently, shocked to see his backyard—there was the grapevine trellis, the old-fashioned garage, and over him the drooping branches of the neighbor's weeping willow. Long, narrow leaves dotted his arms and chest. His *naked* arms and chest! Where was his t-shirt? Nick always wore a t-shirt to bed, despite the season, leaving several pairs of brand-new pajamas still in shrink-wrap. But the dark blue t-shirt he had worn to bed was gone, and so were his Jockey shorts.

He hugged himself, trembling uncontrollably. Dew numbed his toes. His penis was shrunk to thimble size, he noted with near panic, and small twigs were knotted in his pubic hair.

What the hell was going on?

He tore his hand from under his left armpit, where he felt a semblance of warmth, and cupped his genitals instead. He brought his left hand close to his face until he could see it clearly, though it seemed blue in the faint light from the driveway spot his father had installed at the back of the house the previous year. The hand itched as if ants swarmed under his skin. He shook it, but the feeling didn't stop.

It was barely dawn, the sky dappled with patches of light. A cool wind swept across the grass. His feet squished in the wet grass and he started for the back door, hoping it was open and that he could sneak inside without awakening his parents. They would interrogate him like cops, and what could he say? He didn't know what had happened to him. He stooped to swipe off some leaves and twigs and recoiled to see that his feet weren't only wet with dew—there were splashes of what appeared to be blood.

Nick's breath caught in his throat. His blood? He checked calves and ankles quickly, but no, he had no wounds he could see. Then whose blood was it?

He sidled toward the door, acutely aware that the approaching sunrise might well cause him to be seen. With a deep breath he abandoned his modesty and sprinted through the dew right to the door, which opened to his touch. He prayed a silent thanks, a habit born of parochial school, and slipped inside. His father's snoring was audible through the wall, and he climbed the stairs carefully, keeping to those stairs he knew from long experience wouldn't creak. Then he was opening the kitchen door and tiptoeing down the hall past his parents' bedroom, its door slightly ajar. He stepped carefully past the darkened bedroom, timing his steps to coincide with the snores, figuring that a break in the pattern would be more likely to awaken his father. His mother made no sound, and Nick could not guess whether she could hear him or not. He didn't worry about it. Worry would only slow him down. Within moments, he was stepping into his own room and closing the door silently. He would have to wait to wash, but in the meantime he could wipe his skin and put on some clothes. Try to figure out what the hell had happened to him.

Nick was still shivering, now with fear as well as cold.

The blood, the naked romp outside, and the lack of memory.

There was no accounting for this, none at all.

Unless.

Nick looked at his left hand again, the hand that itched unbearably as if he had a rash or had gotten poison ivy. The wound where the dog—*Andy, it was Andy and you know it!* his brain screamed—had torn the skin was both throbbing and itching. He tried to scratch it with his other hand but it wasn't enough, so he dragged his teeth across the scab and felt some relief immediately.

Nick stopped. What the hell was he doing, nipping at his hand like a dog?

What the fuck was he doing?

He shook his head, listened for the comforting rasp of his father's snoring, and found a pair of old underwear that he used to wipe the blood and bits of twigs and grass from his legs. He looked into his full-length mirror, remnant of a previous home owner, and recoiled at the sight of bloody smears all around his lips and cheeks. He felt the urge to vomit suddenly and forced himself to swallow and breathe deeply. The taste of raw meat and bone and rancid blood seemed awash inside his mouth.

He gurgled and just barely managed to spew once into the old briefs he still held.

It looked like chunks of his lungs, Nick thought at first, as he wiped his mouth. The bloody taste was still on his tongue, but for a second it didn't seem so foreign and he was able to avoid another spasm.

What is wrong with me? Nick thought, a strangled sob escaping from his lips.

The face in his mirror didn't seem his own anymore. For a second he swore Andy Corrazza's eyes looked back at him, and then it was someone else's, and yet again another stranger's, until it seemed as though dozens of pairs of eyes looked at him from his mirror.

He turned away dizzy, afraid he would be sick again. He was thankful it was a Saturday, so he could hide from the world and try to sort things out. He climbed into a pair of cutoff jeans and a t-shirt, then curled up on the floor next to his stereo cart. He made sure his headphones were plugged in and dropped a record onto the spindle.

He listened to "Dark Side of the Moon" for the hundredth time and thought he now truly understood madness. The shivers didn't leave him for hours, and the madness was just beginning.

CHAPTER NINE

LUPO

The phone's shrill bleating woke him from muddled, dreamless sleep.

It was someone from the Coroner's Office, asking if he had any next of kin to add to the report, needed so they could file her paperwork and begin the process of removing Corinne's remains from their premises.

Lupo took so long thinking that the tinny voice squawked at him. "Are you still there, Detective?"

No point taking it out on the bureaucrat.

"No next of kin," Lupo said. There was, he knew. Parents in Cincinnati or Cleveland, but they'd disowned Corinne years before. Had, in fact, requested she never return. She had been saddened, but iron-hard about her intention to fulfill their request. She had made no contact for years, and neither had they.

"What should we do with the body? I need someone to

claim it and arrange services, or the City will go the other route and take over. I can mark that option, if there's no one." The attendant's voice faded out and died, and Lupo heard in the fade the hope for some sort of solution.

He sighed and lay back down on the bed. "I'll claim her and arrange a funeral. Just put my name down and I'll take care of it when I come in later today."

"Yes, Detective." Relief.

Lupo let a nasty retort die on his lips and quietly hung up. What was the point?

He wondered, just for a moment, if he had maybe loved her more than just as a friend. Had he? Should he have? And why had it taken her death for him to question his feelings?

He fell asleep again with images of Corinne fading in and out of his vision, which seemed black around the edges.

PART TWO
DIVERTIMENTO

Chapter Ten

MARTIN

Rag's Gunshop was a cramped storefront squashed between a Laundromat and a ma-and-pa hardware, perhaps the last of its kind in the city. It was long and narrow, filled with a dusty display case down one side and haphazard shelving on the other. Behind the counter, racks of rifles and shotguns stood like tree trunks in a grove. Nothing looked new. Rag's was about as far as one could get from the freshly painted, brightly lit, suburban all-sports complexes that now sold most of the legal firearms. The floor tile was cracked and blackened with age. And the clientele, though loyal, was rarely to be seen until perhaps the month or so immediately before deer season.

Which was why Martin Stewart had chosen to frequent it, having wandered in several times to ogle the Vietnam souvenirs and the Chinese-made AK-47s that rested proudly behind Rag's counter. With some prodding, Rag had even showed Martin a trunkload of what he called "goodies," which he kept under lock and key behind the counter. These were various illegal devices, any of which would have gained Rag a federal rap and some hefty fines, had ATF been alerted to their presence.

Martin smiled. That would have been too easy. And not very smart.

Rag was proud of his stock, much of which seemed to have come by way of China, Vietnam, and Afghanistan. Martin had browsed often enough and at length to have heard many of Rag's Vietnam stories, which Rag colored with descriptive hand motions and nudges. The man's straggly gray hair and beard reminded Martin of Jerry Garcia, the late Grateful Dead guitarist, but the man's red-eyed stare called to mind more the crazed look of a terrorist. Rag had militia ties, and Rag himself had often made cryptic remarks about the McVeigh verdict and execution.

"Howdy, Rag," Martin called. A long loop of shrunken, petrified human ears rattled as the door slammed closed. Martin smiled. He couldn't help smiling every time he saw the illegal ears.

"Hey, dude. How ya been?" Rag took his right hand off the holster he wore on his widening hip. In this neighborhood, Martin was well aware, armed robbery was not out of the question, even in broad daylight. Indeed, Rag had himself foiled two attempts in three years.

"Purdy good, man," Martin drawled, sliding into the good-old-boy patois as if born to it. "How's the wife?"

"She ain't no Cindy Crawford, if ya know what I mean?" Rag grinned. "But she's okay enough."

"That's a good one, Rag." Martin grinned until he thought his cheek muscles would spasm.

He stood at the counter now, looking down through the display glass at the rows of tagged handguns. He realized that he could identify most of them. The new ones, at least. His research was paying off. Some of the old military models were lost on him, but those he didn't care about anyway. Martin felt a tingle. This was almost as good as watching high school girls trying on lipsticks at the mall. He suppressed a smile.

Rag sat on his stool and faced him, the frame of a field-stripped Colt .45 in his puffy hand. "Just got this one in—a real beaut, once I scrape off some of the crud. These people didn't care for it, that's for sure."

Martin waited patiently. Rag had a way of thoroughly depleting one track he was on before starting another, and you couldn't just try to make him switch, either; it had to be on his own terms, when he was ready. But Martin could be patient, and this was a minor inconvenience. Besides, he genuinely enjoyed Rag's machine-gun scatter of talk ranging far and wide.

"Is it really old?" he asked.

"Naw, prob'ly issued post-Nam, but it sat in this guy's basement for years. Gave 'im fifty bucks for it, put it out on the shelf tomorrow and get three–four hundred. Life is sweet, man."

Rag went back to buffing the blue-black frame.

Martin felt a twitch working its way up his left hand. Rag would take his time and get to Martin when he was ready.

"Bet you want an update on your special order, huh?" Rag grinned. He liked a captive audience.

"When you have time, bud," Martin said, struggling to unclench his jaws. "No hurry."

"Okay." Rag nodded, but he set the Colt aside on the workbench that served as his back counter. A half-dozen firearms in various stages of assembly rested in vises or under gooseneck lamps. He turned back and gestured at the case between them. "Take a look at that top one, all the way to the left."

Martin followed Rag's pointing finger. It was a bulky, stumpy, squat semiautomatic. Black. Mean-looking and all business. Martin didn't recognize it, though he knew he should have been able to. He looked up, tilted his head inquiringly, and waited for Rag to fill him in.

"It's a Glock 17 9mm. Standard cop issue. Light as a feather—about half ABS plastic. Takes a seventeen-round magazine, plus one up the spout. Hell of a gun. Six hundred, you interested?"

He waited for Martin's reaction. Martin eyed the pistol slowly, muzzle to grip. *Standard cop issue.* This was very likely Lupo's side arm, then. It looked every bit as dangerous as Martin knew Lupo to be, and he felt an obligation to get to know it.

"Can I see it?"

Rag grinned. "It's a nice one, all right." He unlocked the cabinet and slid the Glock out. In one fluid motion he snapped the slide all the way back and presented it to Martin with the breech open. As Martin carefully took it from him, Rag's finger pointed to the slide stop lever. "Push that with your thumb."

Martin did, and the slide slammed forward smoothly. Martin knew that if a magazine had been inserted into the handgrip, the slide would have chambered a round with the forward motion, and the pistol would have been ready to fire.

Fingers tingling, Martin held the Glock out, aiming it at the side of the store.

Lupo held a pistol like this when he was hunting me.

Martin handed Rag the Glock. "Not today," he said with real regret. "But it's nice," he added quickly.

Rag nodded and recased the weapon. There was a squawk and the scanner hidden somewhere on the workbench broke into a series of calls. For a moment, both Rag and Martin listened to the police broadcasts. After the radio quieted down again, Rag stood and squeezed through a doorway to the back of the store, returning in a few seconds with a wrapped bundle and two yellow and green boxes.

"Took me a little longer than I thought," Rag was saying, "but I think they turned out great. And the piece was no problem. It's clean, a Smith .44 with a four-inch barrel.

Still has a serial number, but I'm told it has no history. Not that you care, huh?"

"No," Martin agreed. "I just don't want the purchase on the books—all this gun-ban stuff going around, why should they have my name on a silver platter?"

"Right," Rag nodded. "No sweat. I get a couple a month just for guys like you—law-abiding individuals who don't want the government to come and take their guns away. So that's a hundred more, but it's worth it."

He unwrapped the holstered Smith & Wesson. Martin gulped. It wasn't quite as big as the Clint Eastwood Dirty Harry gun, but it was *big*. Martin took it. It was heavy, too. Very solid. He understood why people felt comforted by handguns—such compact power, all in the palm of one's hand.

"I like it," Martin said, flexing his fingers around the checkered grips. "It feels great."

Rag smiled. "I knew it, man. Three hundred even for the Smith. These'll run you another hundred fifty each." He laid the two boxes on the counter and slid one open. Fifty cartridges stood at attention on a Styrofoam tray, ten rows of five, rattling gently together. "Took me a couple hours per box, but the stuff you give me was primo, so it wasn't as hard as I thought."

Even in the store's dim light, the silvery sheen of each cartridge tip was obvious.

Martin took out his wallet and laid it on the counter. "Looks like a nice job, Rag. Thank you."

Rag smiled again. "Not to be nosy, but what are you hunting, anyway? Maybe that werewolf that got on the news a couple years ago? The werewolf of Oconomowoc, they called it on the silly news."

"Werewolf, huh?" Martin laughed. "No, nothing so bizarre. Actually, it's a gift for a very special friend. I thought the silver bullets were good for a joke. My friend, he's a big Lone Ranger fan."

"Really? I grew up on the stuff, man. Jonah Hex, too. Hey, I hear they brought Jonah back a couple years ago."

"Yeah?" Martin examined the other box of reloaded ammunition. "So what'd I end up with?"

"I coated every slug with the silver, like you wanted. Double-jacketed and split the top, so you should get quite the expanding effect. Loads upped to fifty grains, too, so you get more bang. I was gonna try it out, but we're talkin' almost four bucks a shot and I had just enough silver, so I didn't. You let me know how they handle, okay?"

"You bet." Martin thumbed the release and swung out the cylinder. "Can I get a bag for all this?"

"Sure thing." Rag turned around and rummaged on the workbench.

Martin waited until Rag's head was turned, then he glanced at the front of the store. No one was in sight. He slid a single silver round into the cylinder and carefully closed it, snapping it into the frame so that the cartridge he had inserted sat squarely under the hammer. He cocked it back with his thumb.

"Can you recommend some oil to clean it with?" His words masked the hammer's buttery *click*.

Rag nodded. "Got just the thing," he said, turning around to face the bench.

Martin reached out, rested the muzzle lightly on the side of Rag's head, and jerked the trigger.

The explosion slammed into his ears and the recoil drove his hand up and nearly ripped his shoulder out of its socket.

"Ouch."

Rag's head deflated like a balloon, blood and cranial matter smattering the workbench and back wall. His body spasmed just once, his bowels let go, and then he sprawled on the floor, out of sight.

Martin gagged momentarily at the smell, but he recovered quickly and scooped up his own wallet, the handgun, holster, and two boxes of ammunition. He filled the paper bag Rag had just set on the counter.

He glanced at the front of the store. Still nothing. Things were going well, according to his plan. So much depended on luck, even in a perfect plan, and luck was with him—no customers for Rag today. But then Martin had spent enough time with Rag to know that his few customers were so regular that he didn't have to worry about running into them. And Rag's walk-in traffic was nearly nonexistent.

Martin reached over the counter with a handkerchief in his hand and slid open the display case door, which Rag hadn't yet locked. He scooped up the Glock and the four spare magazines neatly lined up next to it. Then he ducked below the gate, inhaling deeply of the cordite smoke that hung in the air. He grabbed two handfuls of 9mm ammunition boxes from the wall case, and with his foot slid the metal footlocker out from below the workbench—Rag's box of goodies. He threw open the lid, his fingers still covered by the cloth, and made a quick selection. Two UZI submachine guns ("the full-auto kind," Rag had said once, showing him how to cock the stubby thing), a tiny MAC-10, a bundle of spare thirty-round magazines, and a dozen grenades strung on a webbed belt so they resembled a bunch of green metal grapes.

This ought to do it.

Martin unfolded a cloth shopping sack from under his jacket and stuffed it with his new acquisitions. He shoved the locker most of the way back under the counter. Then he felt under the countertop for a lever, felt it and pulled it toward him, and a metal box swung down and out and into his waiting hand. Rag's paranoid distrust of banks and the government had led him to believe his money would only be safe where he could protect it himself. The cash box was ingeniously hidden but unlocked, and Martin helped himself to Rag's life savings. He didn't bother to count it—Rag had once told him he had set aside twenty-five thousand dollars. As Martin stuffed the cash into his shopping bag, he reflected that it did feel like about twenty-five thousand, if not more. It made his score all that much higher, and it killed two birds with one bullet, to paraphrase one of Rag's favorite distorted clichés. Now he wouldn't have to arouse suspicions with further bank transactions.

Less than thirty seconds later, he strolled out the door of the shop and onto an empty sidewalk. Human ears rattled once as he eased the door shut after wiping the handle and jamb as best he could, and then he was walking slowly away. A dumpy woman climbed out of a minivan a few doors down and glanced at him briefly. He smiled widely—not a care in the world—and nodded in greeting. Her features softened and she smiled back.

By then, Martin was crossing the street.

The blood and cordite smelled sweet in his nostrils, and he couldn't help but grin and hum a nonsense tune in his head.

Chapter Eleven

JESSIE

Circle Moon Drive was deserted. It felt almost abandoned, as if everyone had disappeared in the middle of supper. Like that English colony, what was it? Roanoke? Her history lessons were a jumble of useless and disordered trivia, but she prided herself on occasionally chancing upon the perfect one to describe something in her life.

Jessie Hawkins turned left onto the frost-wedged remains of the blacktopped road and shifted down, slowing to let the Pathfinder negotiate each pothole one at a time. All around, white and jack pine rose impossibly straight and tall, like organ pipes waiting for a musician's loving touch.

The Schulze mailbox was shot full of holes again, Jessie noted, as was their cheery *Welcome!* sign. The stop sign at the intersection had sported three dimpled bullet holes as well, but Jessie thought she might have seen them already, on her last visit nearly a month ago. Vilas County Sheriff Bunche had cleared out most of the ruined signage just last year, but the local itchy trigger fingers continued to claim their flat victims.

"Might as well paint a target on these damned signs," Bunche had commented with a snort while a crew worked to extract a gun-shot road sign from the shoulder.

"Maybe then they'd miss," Jessie had pointed out, dragging a chuckle out of the serious lawman, whose laugh lines belied the tension his job brought during spearfishing season, when blaze-orange-clad locals took to the protest trail while tribesmen took their quotas of game fish at spearpoint, leaving the sheriff and his force of six deputies to defuse each and every potentially flammable situation. It was a job Jessie appreciated, and she never avoided reminding him.

Bunche had laughed heartily, trying unsuccessfully to pull his pants up around his widening belly while a holstered pistol applied opposing downward pressure. It was obvious Bunche liked Jessie, everyone in town did, even if she did practice on the Reservation. That fact alone might have doomed a lesser individual, or a lesser general practitioner and sometime marriage counselor. Jessie had grown up in the controversy of a mixed household in a mixed county, and the tensions here between Indians and locals went deep enough to cause occasional feuds and violence, but never so much that a forest fire couldn't be fought by the cooperation born when the regular volunteers accepted the aid offered by a couple companies from the Reservation. After such an event, the beer frankly tasted the same no matter who was buying, and Jessie tried to turn each uneasy occurrence into a low-key lecture on cooperation and good-neighborliness. The trick was not to get caught lecturing.

Now that the Reservation elders had voted to build a casino, things would get even uglier and stranger here, as the res would probably get rich off the local morons who'd gladly stuff the slot machines for the unlikely possibility of a big win.

Serves them right!

She laughed once, bitterly, as she pulled into the driveway at the 1090 Circle Moon Drive marker.

Nothing was ever as easy as it seemed. Take, for instance, this property of hers. For forty years it had been her father's, a getaway far from the usual getaways, and now it had become her side income, a long-term rental property that required relatively little upkeep besides the usual winterizing and opening or closing as the seasons changed. Boats in the water in spring and out by mid-September.

After a storm as violent as the one that had rocked the woods the night before, though, all bets were off. Indeed, before Jessie could reach the cottage, she rolled the Pathfinder to a stop inches from a toppled pine trunk that angled from out of the woods. It had been snapped like a twig a few feet above the roots and lay across the narrow drive, effectively blocking access to vehicles. It was too large and heavy to drag off the drive without chains, and its trunk was so well threaded between living trees that she couldn't risk damaging other living trees.

"Shit," muttered Jessie, though she was not unused to the mysterious ways of the woods. She took an axe from the back of the truck and went to work, knowing that—based on her calendar and a phone message left on her machine—her tenant would be driving up to the cottage sometime either today or early tomorrow. She swore again as the sweat started to form on her forehead and drip, and she put her back into it, wishing she had her chain saw.

She'd charge Nick Lupo for the time and labor, she decided, and make him pay before the end of his next little vacation. That way, she reasoned, she could deliver the bill in person. Any excuse would do. She smiled, then swung her axe again, relishing the exercise. But she'd find *some* way to make him pay.

KLUG

Wilbur Klug wriggled his big toe into the leather stirrup and kicked open the cover of the rusted Coca-Cola bottle cooler he kept on his porch. He dunked his bare foot into the cold square opening and grabbed the thin neck of a Rhinelander bottle between his big and second toes, relishing the nip of the cap's sharp little creases.

One of the pleasures of life, he allowed, as he drew his foot close enough so he could transfer the bottle to his eager hand. Now unburdened, his foot kicked the cover closed. Rust flaked off the side of the cooler and disintegrated, falling on the bare wood planking of the porch. He pried the top off on a bent nail head and took a long swallow, fighting down the burp that was already working its way back up, letting it build and then escape in one glorious explosion. He smiled and chugged from the bottle.

Wil's day was already turning out to be a keeper. First old man Brawlings had called to bitch him out for screwing up the deliveries last week, threatening to cancel his standing order for Wil's services—*Fuckin' dink don't deserve a job well done*, Wil figured after getting his ear chewed for ten minutes, before hanging up on the old bastard and canceling his own services, *thanks a fuckin' lot to your sister, too.* Lost a two-bit job, maybe, but here he was, barely ten in the morning and a cold one going down, and others near at hand.

Then there was Shelly. Oh, yeah, she'd held out her wifely duties long enough, and this morning was one of those days a headache just didn't cut it, no sir, and that had made his early-morning rise-n-shine a *real* riser. Woman was still in bed, crying about how he'd hurt her, but hadn't she been asking for it, with her innocent as an angel routine? What was it, a month since he'd last cajoled some decent sack time from his timeworn better half, groveling for it like a starving beggar and having to make do with the crumbs she saw fit to toss his way? Was that any way to love, honor, and obey? No sir, it hadn't been. But she'd seen the light today, that was for sure. He had finally entered that holy orifice, the same one that Shelly had sworn he would never breach. He relished the memory. He had paused at the puckered entrance to her anus and then, holding her down forcibly and with little interest in her comfort, had thrust his engorged penis into her over and over with no lubrication, skewering her pride along with her flesh until her cries were drowned out by his bellowing surge of orgasm, the force of which sent his semen squirting half in and half out of her bowels to dapple her inner thighs along with the blood drawn by his savage entry.

He giggled and snorted at the memory, then sucked another long pull from the bottle.

Yup, the day was looking up. If he drank at just the right pace, the cooler's stock would last at least until Kenny and Buck found their way back with reinforcements. And maybe some entertainment. Right now, they were both scraping by on some stupid job that barely kept their asses covered in denim and their palates coated in beer, but soon they'd be able to afford better.

Much better, actually, because Wilbur had a plan he wanted to share with the boys, after the first few bottles had been emptied. He'd been working on this plan for almost a year, using his jack-of-all-tradesman's connections to nail down some particulars that he could hold in his head. Or that they could hold in theirs—hell, if he was a dense know-nothing, what did that make his friends? He chuckled. Let them think of him any way they wanted.

He hit bottom and immediately felt the need for another.

A cool wind suddenly picked up dead leaves in the yard and whipped them into tiny tornadoes, then rustled through the trees at the edge of his property. It made a high-pitched, mournful sound, and it set his teeth on edge. Like a voice he didn't want to hear, or a thought he didn't want to think. It was like something had come to visit, come to stay, and it made goose bumps rise on his bare skin.

He shook his head. Fuckin' weirdo shit was more like Shelly's thinking than his. He could still hear the wind's voice as it swirled between the tall pines, and he saw the upper branches swaying in unison above.

Shelly's sobbing from the window just behind the ratty old armchair seemed louder somehow after the wind had died down.

Eat me, he thought as he maneuvered his foot into the cooler. Then he thought, *Yeah.* As his hand grasped the neck of his next cold one, he felt the need building up again in his loins. He let the cooler slam shut, then gathered his legs below him. Moments later, he was entering the dark house, his hand caressing the bottle.

Yessir, Wilbur Klug had a plan. But first he was not done celebrating yet.

Not by a long shot.

CHAPTER TWELVE

MARTIN

His usual refuge, the coffee shop, was one of those chain diners that attempt to capture true diner status without going the extra mile. Chrome and Formica, yes, but no real jukebox. Greasy breakfasts and specials, but all done exactly alike, thanks to corporate schooling. Uncomfortable booths encouraged quick dining and even quicker exits. Most foods came prepped from the freezer. Tired waitresses dished up stale donuts and rolls from fly-speckled serving plates. Strung-out customers regularly clashed with the drunks, and the semihomeless nursed endless cups of black coffee, their gnarled hands wrapped around chipped mugs.

Martin eyed his late-night company warily. This was no place for a writer. He grinned. Here the charade had brought him better-than-average service, as both aging and barely pubescent waitresses hoped to influence, or at least witness, his creative process. Martin's little act had a kind of sitcom flair, and he was pleased with it. Even if there was no need for it, it had become comforting in its routine.

Martin sipped his scalding coffee and eyed the congealing remains of his hamburger. This wasn't true food, not enough to sustain him mentally and physically on his quest, but it would have to do.

Martin turned and surveyed the scene in the wall mirror, which ran the length of the room. The tired, the drunk, the strung out. Working class. Underclass. No class. It was pathetic. He was clearly above such a place, if only because of his education. If only because of his intelligence. His presence here was a fluke, an accident of nature, a strange cosmic coincidence. There was no one here he could relate to, nor anyone he would have wanted to.

Martin smiled, remembering why he was here. What he was slowly maneuvering into place. The enormity of his knowledge both ate at him and amused him.

His hands were steady. The day's events had not changed him, not that he'd expected it. He'd had his share of practice, even if it had been a while since he'd used a firearm.

There was a dark shape at the door of the diner. He was not surprised to see the woman come in out of the thin drizzle that had begun shortly after his arrival.

She was almost attractive enough to be legitimate, a woman waiting for her boyfriend or fiancé. Dark blond. Black leather skirt. White blouse under a thin brown leather jacket. Was that a fashion faux pas, wearing two different shades of leather? Martin could only wonder as she slid into the booth next in line to his, in the seat facing him. He was granted special privileges because of his notebooks and large tips, he knew, but she seemed undaunted by the ubiquitous signs that announced: TWO OR MORE CUSTOMERS PER BOOTH. She made a gesture at the elder waitress and was brought coffee with hardly a look to spare.

So, now Martin was interested. A hooker, certainly. Awaiting a customer? Taking a break? Going on strike? He let his eyes roam over her features boldly.

This was, after all, his style. And one must live up to one's style.

The hair seemed natural—no bottles for her. Nose, long and straight. Nose job maybe, he thought. Eyes set wide, clear and intelligent. Cold, maybe. Calculating. In fact, they had already picked him out across the ten feet that separated their two booths, and were even then boldly measuring him while he measured her. Nice cheekbones. High. Simple earrings, though three adorned one ear while only one hung from the other. Chin jutted just a little, witchlike, but not enough to cause a problem. Lips, well, her lips were wide and full—and of course were the feature at which he most wanted to stare. So he did, and he was sure she smiled slightly as she dug into her tiny purse and wrestled out a compact and a pager. She pretended to check her makeup while eyeing him over the little mirror, and Martin smiled at her attempt to seem nonchalant. Just a break, then, after all. She took a silver canister from the purse and held it up in front of her face, staring at it as she slowly twisted it and raised the lipstick from its recessed compartment. She held it there for a few moments, bobbing it in front of her lips, the corners of which were slightly curled in obvious enjoyment.

Martin squirmed in his seat. He felt the mug almost slip from his fingers and brought it down to the table carefully, never taking his eyes off her and her tantalizing ballet.

Fully aware of his gaze, she slowly let the lush red tip of the lipstick rest against her lower lip before dragging it left, then right, from side to side. She took the lipstick from her lower lip, let it hover momentarily, then repeated the process on her upper lip, taking an impossibly long time and staring right at him. She pursed her mouth, checking her image in the mirror but positioning the compact so he could see, then slowly inserted the tip of the lipstick between her red lips, withdrawing it ever so slowly. She smiled and put the lipstick down.

Martin felt the pen bend in his hand. A sheen of sweat cooled his forehead, and a vague sense—no, more than a sense—of hatred flowed like liquid mercury through his veins.

Does it ever end?

His mind screamed incoherently as his hand dropped the pen and the images came unbidden, faster than he could have imagined, faster almost than he could begin to assimilate. Not that he wanted to assimilate, but his head swelled with the balloon of knowledge, of dread, of hate, of love, and then he was nine again, and his father was rummaging in the purse and Martin was young, but he knew that what was coming was going to be very bad.

Martin's eyes closed momentarily and he was no longer here, but there.

If you love me, his daddy was saying, if you love me . . .

Thing was, Martin *did* love his daddy. A whimper escaped his lips. He had always loved his daddy a lot.

If you love me more than mommy . . .

His daddy had begged him to keep their love a secret, because mommy and Carrie would get jealous if they knew, and even though Martin was bursting with the joy of how much his daddy loved him, he kept quiet. He noticed that mommy had recently developed a habit of staring at daddy while he faced a different direction, engaged in some daddy-like behavior. Mommy wasn't smiling as much these days as she had just a year before, and Martin could see that daddy was right. She was jealous of the time the two of them spent together, the same time she was spending with Carrie these days. Carrie, who was four years older and always moping around the house. Carrie, who never talked and who gazed at everyone through hooded eyes. Martin had noticed these things, and thought they helped explain why daddy loved him all the more now.

The first time daddy showed Martin how much he loved him was a day mommy had taken Carrie to some appointment, to see someone who was supposed to help Carrie stop moping. So it was just Martin and his daddy in the big old house, and daddy said, *let's play a game.* Martin nodded quickly, before daddy could change his mind. Daddy smiled. *For this game, we have to play in our underwear.* Martin had never heard of a game like that, but he was more than happy to learn a new one. By the time mommy and his stupid sister came home, Martin had learned the game real well, but he remembered not to say anything. It was strange, what daddy had called a game was something he had heard some kids talking about, and they talked about it as if it were something only adults could do. Martin decided he would keep playing as long as his daddy wanted to, but he would pay attention to what his friends said, too.

At this point in the memory, Martin shuddered. He watched the blond woman across from him as she powdered her cheeks lightly, patting them with the round applicator from her compact. The silver lipstick canister stood on the chipped Formica table in front of her, and he was sure she could see him staring at her and at the canister. Beads of sweat collected at the sides of his forehead and trickled slowly down his cheeks, causing a cool itch that he ignored.

Martin had played the underwear game with his daddy for almost a year, until daddy didn't seem to enjoy it anymore. Martin was still enjoying it, he thought, because he was spending time with his daddy that no one knew about, and he felt special (especially since mommy and daddy didn't seem to ever play *their* games anymore). But daddy was getting bored. Until the day he first rummaged through mommy's purse while she was off somewhere with Carrie, finding the silver lipstick canister and a tiny bag of other jars and things that mommy wore to make herself pretty. Daddy's eyes lit up . . .

Martin felt a shiver at the clarity of the memory.

. . . as he removed the items from the purse one by one, standing them up on the kitchen table. Daddy twisted the top off the canister and watched the colored tip emerge from hiding, then he looked at Martin. *I just found a new way to play our game,* he said, one hand holding the lipstick. *Do you want to see?* But Martin backed up a step. He wasn't sure why, but he felt suddenly uneasy about the game and what daddy wanted him to do. It was as if some kind of line had been crossed, and now things were different. Martin liked playing the game with daddy, because it was Martin's time and no one else's—because he liked sharing the secret. Because daddy wanted him and nobody else. But suddenly, with the things from mommy's purse between them, Martin could see that daddy really wanted mommy, and if she wasn't there then Martin would do just fine, but he had to be *like* mommy. And something in his spirit rebelled at the notion. Before he knew what he was doing, he had run out of the kitchen screaming and crying and howling so loudly that daddy was after him with lightning in his eyes and an upraised hand, and then daddy caught him and the hand came down once, twice, and Martin cried, but there was nothing he could do except play the game daddy's way.

In the kitchen again, daddy held his head with one meaty hand and carefully filled in Martin's lips with the other, the silvery canister flashing in the light over the sink. The tip was purple and smelled sweet, and it made his lips sticky—he could tell that daddy was putting on more than mommy ever would, but that didn't seem to bother daddy. His breath came in short, quick gusts, as if he'd been running, and Martin could smell the stuff his parents called Scotch. When daddy was done, they sat in the kitchen and played a new version of the game— messy, like finger painting.

And from that moment on Martin decided he hated daddy, though a part of him still enjoyed the game they played—first with mommy's things from her purse, and then with things that daddy brought home and hid in his tool chest. Things he hid even from mommy.

Now Martin wiped at the drying sweat trails on his face, drank from his cold mug, and pretended to write in his notebook. He turned to wave at Linda, but she was already crossing toward him with a coffeepot in one hand.

"Top that off for you?"

He nodded. "Thanks." Out of the corner of his eye he watched the blonde react to Linda, who seemed to be thrusting her breasts at him. Now, was that really the case, Martin wondered, or was he just filling in the spaces where there was nothing? He stared at Linda's pierced nostril for a second, at her pink lips, at her smile—the smile reserved for the restaurant's very own writer. He nodded again, saw Linda hover as if about to ask him something, or as if waiting for him to say something—that was it, waiting for *him* to make some sort of move—then he took his mug in one hand and crossed over and stood next to the blonde.

"Mind if I sit?" he asked. She merely shrugged, and Martin slid in across from her, his hands wrapped around the now-hot coffee mug. He was vaguely aware of Linda's shape in the background, staring at him disapprovingly. He shrugged his own shoulders. Such was life, after all, with winners and losers. "Cold night, what with this rain," he said.

"Yeah," said the blonde. She watched him drink some coffee, then sipped at her own mug.

Martin stared at the red half-circle she left on the rim of the mug. He smiled. "Got anything doing tonight?" He was taking a chance, he knew. This was a new experience for him, but he was curious to see if he had read the woman's movements correctly. He wanted to expand his arsenal of knowledge, he told himself as he waited for her response.

She smiled crookedly. "Nah, I'm pretty well free for the rest of the night. So to speak."

Martin felt his lips curl up into another smile. He narrowed his eyes slightly, watched her lips from the slits his eyelids made. "Care for some company?"

Her fingers thumped the table. A nonchalant gesture. "I could be persuaded."

"Can we get out of this rain pretty fast?"

"I'm just around the corner," she said. She scooped her pager and other things back into her purse. Martin watched the lipstick container disappear. "Care for—a nightcap?"

He nodded. She was already shrugging into her thin leather coat and dropping a dollar on the table. Martin reached into his pocket, drew out some crumpled bills and selected a five, dropped it onto his own table with the check, then picked up his notebook and followed the blonde to the door.

Linda's eyes bored into his back, and he could feel her displeasure.

Winners and losers, he thought as he held the door for the woman and followed her out into the cold drizzle.

Her apartment really was just around the corner, and they walked in silence until reaching her front door. A sort of pseudo-brownstone, he decided, recently redone to play up its antique wrought-iron railings. She let him into one of the ground floor flats, six steps up, and took his coat.

"I, uh, didn't expect company." She gestured toward some clutter on the table, clothes strewn on the tiny sofa.

"It's okay," Martin said. He was looking at her face, noting how her own lighting made her lines softer—her chin wasn't as pronounced, for instance, as it had been under the fluorescents—and how her hair seemed even more golden. He stared at the dark gash of her lips, feeling himself respond to the musk she now exuded. He fumbled with his wallet, then she laughed and reached for his belt.

She took his trousers down and gently placed her lips around the head of his penis, which was outlined under his briefs. He held her head as she licked him through the thin cotton, her lips leaving wide red streaks on the fabric as she worked on him, her eyes fastened on his the whole time. He squirmed as the warmth and cold engorged his penis further and he thought he would burst from the cloth. She started to reach into his waistband, but his hand stopped her.

"What's wrong?" She stared up at him, surprised at his interruption.

Martin remembered to breathe. "More lipstick," he whispered, hoarse. "You need more lipstick."

She held his stare just a few moments longer, then shrugged once—a twitch. *Hell,* her gesture seemed to say, *I can do* that.

Her purse was within reach, on the floor. She dragged it closer and found the silver canister. As Martin watched, enraptured, she continued kneeling before him and repeated her slow replenishment of the dark red lipstick, first her fleshy lower lip and then her upper lip, her eyes still boring into his.

"Like this?"

He nodded. "More."

She smiled. She went over each lip again, and the gash of her mouth seemed almost black in the near-dark. Martin could tell that she was an expert, because she didn't stray from the outside edges of her lips at all. But the cosmetic itself was now a thick layer on both lips, and Martin could feel the tip of his penis moistening the fabric of his briefs.

She learned fast. Her lips went around his glans again, smearing on the white cotton, and her tongue snuck into attack mode. A minute later, she paused and applied more lipstick before taking more of him between her lips.

Martin couldn't hold on, and he felt himself shooting into the fabric and through it, into her mouth, where her tongue lapped at the filtered thick liquid. Martin's hands pressed on her ears and held her in place as she cleaned him without once coming into contact with his bare skin. She looked up and smiled, her teeth shining amid the smeared skin around her lips.

Martin nearly collapsed on top of her. In a haze, he felt her cool fingers removing his soiled underpants and then she was removing her clothing and he was being used, but he barely felt it because in his mind there was nothing but his penis and the lips and the lipstick.

He asked her twice more to retouch her lips, still not knowing her name, and she did while he watched. At one point she held the canister out to him and he helped, drawing carefully around her lips as if worried that someone would take his coloring book away if he went outside the lines. She massaged him with lips and fingers until he was hard again, then she drank from him as if he were a faucet, until he sank down and licked his semen from her lips and the inside of her mouth, the thick and aromatic lipstick smearing both their lips. The heady smell of cosmetics twirled in his nostrils, and he reveled in its cloying sweetness.

When they went again, it seemed to Martin that she was suspending him from her lips, his penis the only connection that sustained him and kept him from falling. The slick coloring changed in his eyes like a kaleidoscope as he whirled through the air dangling from her mouth, until she was licking his semen from the corners and sides of her lips again.

Now he felt some of the memories of daddy's game slip away, while others still ate at the edges of his consciousness. He licked at her lips and she laughed, wiping his face, and for a while he was just Martin, not a fake writer in a restaurant, or someone who had *played* with his daddy and liked it. Just Martin, not Martin the murderer.

Later, when she slept and he could have easily killed her with one well-placed hand, he found himself looking at her with a strange fondness.

He dressed, left what he thought was an appropriate

sum, and walked into the night, where the drizzle had turned to a downpour that rustled through the trees. His diner was open, and he ordered coffee from a weary graveyard shift waitress he had never seen.

She had nice lips, he thought as she brought him his mug, but she wasn't playing them up as well as she could have.

Martin smiled. *Today.* Today was the day he would tighten the pressure on Lupo. He had just the way, and he was eager to get on with it.

He gazed across the street from his usual booth. Lupo's lights were still off.

Sleep well, my friend. He drank some coffee. *Sleep while you can.*

A sense of power surged through him.

He reached into his pocket and felt the two metal canisters clink together. His fingers gently traced their outlines and he shivered with joy.

One was the woman's red lipstick, a memento for his collection. The other was a silver-jacketed .44 Magnum cartridge.

CHAPTER THIRTEEN

LUPO

Lupo shuffled the report into a pile of indeterminate file folders again and rubbed his eyes.

"I'll look at it later," he said. "I know what he did to her. I saw her, remember?"

"Look now, Nick." Ben used his right hand to sweep off some space on his desk. "You were supposed to look at it yesterday."

Lupo made no move toward the folder.

"Dammit, you're just as stubborn as your old man. Okay, I'll tell you the part you should know about. She'd had sex before he, uh, committed the crime."

"No shit." Lupo couldn't stop himself from being flip. "The pictures told us that. He got his jollies, then he killed her."

"You should read the damn report. She also had sex *before* the guy in the pictures. Twice, both vaginal and anal. Lab says the semen tests out differently for both of those, so there were two different guys within half a day before time of death."

"One of those might have followed her into the bathroom after she left the guy in the photo booth, right?"

"You'd think it's possible. Our male model's semen tests out differently from the other two. Based on scrapings from the inside of her cheeks and palate, he only had oral sex with her."

Lupo ran a clawlike hand through his hair. "So there's less chance our perp's the first or second guy."

"Right, but one of them coulda hung around waiting . . ."

"On the other hand, why would Number One or Number Two leave behind pictures of her with a stranger, our Number Three? They weren't just missed, they were left intentionally."

"Got me. Same goes for Number Three. If this was the guy, the same guy in the pictures, why leave them like that? Why leave something that might be traceable?"

"Good point," Ben conceded. "But there they were. Maybe they appealed to his sense of humor."

Lupo winced.

"Sorry Nick," Ben said. "Keep forgettin' you knew her, is all."

"I know. It wasn't like we—I mean . . . we really were just friends. But she was better than the streets, man. She was better than, than *that*." He gestured at the report folder.

Ben nodded. "Either way, I say we look for two guys now. I'd eliminate the guy in the pictures just because they're too obvious."

"Three," Lupo said. "Don't eliminate him at all. He's our best bet. Ben, an innocent guy would've taken the pictures. As a souvenir. A trophy. Something to flash the guys on poker night. *Look at what I did the last time I went to the mall!*"

Ben nodded. "Point again. But he wouldn't have been so innocent, our innocent guy."

"No."

Lupo leafed aimlessly through another folder, without seeing any of its contents. He realized he wasn't really handling Corinne's death very well, but he couldn't help feeling useless and way too late to do anything.

Anything except catch the sonofabitch responsible.

"There's one more thing I can't make any sense of," Ben said. His voice was clearly hesitant, the volume down to a mumble. "May be nothing at all, but it's a little weird."

Lupo cocked his head. He felt the blood pumping in his veins as clearly as he could hear the squad room clatter. Something about Corinne and him? Something about him, or perhaps his unique condition? Ben was usually less circumspect than this, and Lupo couldn't help wonder why the hesitation—what could be so strange that it would make Ben uncomfortable?

"Okay, it's a lot weird. According to the report, there were traces of certain chemicals, animal oils and dyes in her, you know, in her genitals."

"Dyes? What the fuck?"

"The lab says they're all ingredients of lipstick. There were traces of lipstick in her mouth and in her genitals. Her anus, too." Ben shook his head and looked down. "Sorry, Nicky, had to tell you."

"Another woman? We're looking for a woman?"

"Don't forget the semen traces."

Lupo pondered a moment. "One of three men . . . and a woman? How likely is that? And in a photo booth? Come on, Ben, get real."

"The booth pictures only show oral sex, and there ain't enough room for anything else there, I don't think. That might mean they started their little party elsewhere. I got uniforms canvassing all the nearest hotels, swanky and fleabag both. You never know, might get lucky."

Lupo stared out the window. The day had turned gray

after a hint of sunlight, taking his mood with it. He had slept little, felt watched all night, and jumped at every sound his old flat conjured up for his entertainment. So when he had come into the squadroom and seen Ben's rested face, he had started barking at his partner and anyone else unfortunate enough to get within range.

"Did you check out the rest of the girlfriend's statement?" Ben said from right behind him.

Lupo shook his head. He hadn't even heard the big guy approach. This was ridiculous—Corinne barely gone and he was losing his perspective already.

Had she meant this much to him? And if she had, why the hell hadn't he realized it long ago and gotten her off the street?

Lupo shook his head again. "No," he sighed. "I missed a chunk of it."

"Upshot is, she wasn't just doing her usual gig with the service."

"Oh, yeah?" Lupo perked up. Was Ben leading him somewhere with subtlety? It wasn't Ben's style, feeding him bits and pieces and stringing him along. What was wrong now? Was Ben walking on proverbial eggshells around him? Was anyone else? Suddenly Lupo felt very uncomfortable in the big room, and wished he could duck out. Actually, he wished he could just climb into his car and drive due north—only there could he find total peace, and it beckoned him with a siren song no one else could hear.

He shook his head. He wanted to shake the thought away. "So, what else was she into?" He would just have to forget she was his friend—concentrate on her as a victim and do his job to locate the murderer. Still, a big part of him just wanted to block all the details before they reached him.

"According to the friend, Corinne was doing some proamateur porn out of an office studio south of downtown. I might have the address."

"Might have it?"

Ben grimaced. "It was on a list we saw just a couple weeks ago, a list of new ventures. Remember it?"

"Nah. But I'll take your word for it. What the hell's proamateur porn?

"Well, the real amateur stuff's just your basic ma and pa—they get bored, buy a camcorder, suddenly they're hotshot porn-mongers."

Lupo snorted. "Who'd buy *that* stuff?"

Ben pointed a stubby finger at Lupo's face. "You'd be surprised."

"Oh, yeah, I forgot *you're* ma and pa's age. And you got a camcorder." He winked.

"Leave my private life, such as it is, outta this. So anyway, real amateur stuff is just that. Then there's the proamateur stuff. Real tricky deal. Pro-am's a small-budget pro production shot to look like amateur and marketed that way for people who want ma and pa in theory, but for real they'd rather look at someone beautiful."

Lupo whistled. "How the hell did you get so wise to this?"

"Went to a vice seminar last month. Hey, a seminar on vices, that was just what I needed."

"Like a second head." Lupo smoothed some piles of paperwork before him, still avoiding the lab report. "So, Corinne was moonlighting, huh?" He was half whispering, and only half aware of it.

"She ever mention it, Nick?"

"Nope. Pretty sure. I'd remember an explanation like you just gave me." *Damn it, why hadn't he noticed?*

"Yeah. Anyway, the girlfriend laid a studio address on me and it's the same place. After I get a cup of that crap they call coffee around here, we're gonna go check it out." He headed for the coffeepot and swished the liquid around with a frown before pouring.

Lupo felt certain the guy in the photographs was the

one they wanted, as certain as he'd ever been of anything.
A sort of alternate sense had told him this right from the
beginning. It was *too* cool, too calm and calculated, the
way the guy had just stood in the photo booth a few feet
away from a crowd and the way he took measure of his
victim. Oh, no, it was the guy in the photographs. Lupo
would have staked his miserable life on it. Where the
other possible suspects—and a woman—fit into this, he
wasn't sure yet. But he had learned to heed that alternate
sense when it tingled, and now it told him that the first
two guys were like decoys. *Maybe she'd been on a movie
set until early that morning?*

"Ready?" Ben held a travel mug full of watery brown
liquid.

Lupo grabbed his coat and followed Ben out the door.
He would read the lab report as soon as they returned.
He'd be ready then.

In the many years since becoming accustomed to what
he thought of as his *condition,* Lupo had spent time re-
searching what all the books had to say. None of the
sources, serious or otherwise, ever mentioned his alternate sense, the innate knowledge that struck at him from
out of nowhere, often with physical force, but that did not
make it any less real. In fact, finding aspects that hadn't
been dealt with in some low-budget horror flick was a
positive, because then he could attempt to convince himself that he was no monster.

Regardless of Caroline Stewart, and what he had done
to her when she had tried to help him.

How could he not be a monster, when the one he had
loved deeply and completely—long before Corinne—
had suffered terrible pain at his hands and died, a sacrifice to the beast that could never be renounced? The
thought stung every hour of every day.

Lupo let Ben lead him out onto the dim sidewalk, on
their way to visit ma and pa and their camcorder.

The address led them to a converted warehouse in the trendy Third Ward, an area that had seen much urban renewal in the last decade.

Restaurants and clubs, high-ticket shops, chic vintage boutiques, and numerous residential buildings offering New York–style lofts at inflated but still Midwestern prices had been carved out of an area that had seen the city's long and colorful labor movement struggles. Largely abandoned for several decades, the area had lost its railway lines and, with those, its relevance in today's suburban-oriented society. That is, until someone had noticed that under the sloppy tile and drywall lay the beautiful Cream City brick, the tan bricks that characterized a whole generation of Milwaukee architecture. Newer generations had simply and condescendingly covered the bricks with the cheap and inelegant, perhaps hoping to erase the blue-collar past.

Then renewal had struck full force, and the Third Ward was reborn as a high-priced southern extension of the lower East Side—it was adjacent to the old Port of Milwaukee, and just minutes from the downtown bustle.

This building near the corner of Buffalo and Milwaukee Streets was one of a dozen in which relatively recent refurbishing had not yet been completed. Indeed, several contractors' vans lined the sidewalk along one side, and painting activity seemed to be taking place in one of the street-level shops.

A phone call had netted Ben further information he had been reluctant to share with his partner. Now he led them to an anonymous side entrance, the inside of which was a tiny lobby that smelled of fresh paint and wood varnish.

"This is one of the shoots going on right now," Ben explained in a whisper. "I dropped your friend's name and my source confirmed this operation—we'll see if it's any good."

They flashed their badges at the bored muscleman whose seated bulk guarded the inside door. He waved

them in and returned to his weight lifter's magazine. They
trod the narrow staircase up to a dingy second floor that
had not yet seen much refurbishing, went through an un-
painted door, and then through a doorway blocked by a
black curtain.

"You studied up on this stuff, huh?"

"Hey, it was a seminar," Ben said. "Got to see movies."

"You made contacts."

"And learned a lot."

"Let's do it—I want to learn too."

When they walked into the shoot, a slick-haired cameraman stood in one corner fooling with his camera
while a blonde with dark roots crouched on a bed in front
of a naked man, her head bobbing quickly.

Ben nudged Lupo. "It's never too late to learn."

A sound guy was wiring a mike under the bed—to capture spring action, Lupo guessed—and another blonde
was diddling herself on the bed, a bored expression on
her face. Umbrellas hovered over her, giving off heat and
white light.

The outside window was blocked off, and a short man
stood in front of it studying a thin dog-eared script. His
hair was tied in a straggly ponytail he seemed to caress
constantly with one hand.

"Anybody know where Tara Lace went?" he shouted in
a nasal voice.

No one answered.

As Lupo and Ben approached the bed, the actor
moaned and rapidly patted the fake blonde's head with
both hands.

"Hey, cool it," the ponytail man said, running up and
pulling the fluffer off the actor, causing her glittery-pink
lips to smack as he came loose.

"Sorry," she mumbled, letting a line of drool slip down
her chin. Her eyes were glazed and bloodshot, and her
lids drooped.

"Ashlyn, darling," he said, patting her cheek, "the point

is to get him ready for the money shot, not to eat it yourself. Remember?"

"Yeah, Vic. I just got carried away. When can I screw on camera, huh? You said soon."

"I did, babe, and soon it'll be. Now go fix your lipstick and stay ready. Okay?"

" 'Kay, Vic." She shambled off in search of a mirror.

Vic looked down at his leading stud, whose penis still stood at attention. "Where's Tara? Where the fuck is she?"

"How the hell should I know?" the actor whined. "But if she don't show soon, well, I'm gonna—"

"Just put the squeeze on it until we find her, got it?"

Muscles rippled as the stud reached for himself and held on.

"Sal, I'm gonna lose my shirt on this if we fuck up," Vic said.

Sal found that funny, or the coke made it seem funny, and he giggled like a kid. He held on to his crotch for dear life.

Vic became aware of his visitors just then.

"Yes? Do you have a pass? This is a closed set."

"I bet it is," said Lupo.

"Will this do?" Ben showed his badge. "Milwaukee Police, homicide squad. We're Detectives Lupo and Sabatini. We got a few questions. Take a minute."

Vic pursed his lips. "Sure, what the fuck." To Sal, he said, "Would you please find your costar, get her problem taken care of, and get her back here in five?"

"Sure, Vic." Sal strutted off, still holding himself, totally unself-conscious. The muscles in his buttocks rippled with each step.

"I remember you," Vic was already saying to Ben. "That informational program for the cops—you set it up."

"Yeah. It was helpful and informative, Vic. I had a hard-on for a week."

Vic smiled. "Then my work was done. What now? You in need of another hard-on?"

Ben's eyes narrowed and his frown was ugly. Vic seemed to get the message, closing his mouth with an audible snap.

"See, Vic, what I got is a hard-on for somebody who just offed a local girl. You mighta read about it, if you can read."

Vic looked hurt. "I read *The New York Times* and the *Wall Street Journal* every day."

"Sure you do, but how much do you retain? Anyway, you know the chick I mean?"

"Yeah, I think I do. Hooker that got whacked at that mall on the other side o' town, right?"

"You knew her?" Lupo spoke for the first time. His tone was less than friendly.

Vic hesitated. "I don't—"

"Don't fuck with us, okay, 'cause our mutual friend Dillie D'Amato already told me you told him you wanted to dick her bad, so don't waltz us around."

Lupo glanced at Ben but kept silent.

Vic crossed his eyes for a second. Then he glanced toward his crew, who were sitting on the bed whispering and laughing with the blonde. "Look, I knew her. Corey Diamond. Least, that was her name with us, if you know what I mean. Did three, no four, pro-am features in the last couple months. She was too good for us, you know, really knew acting. We do fuck films, but she coulda done real legit adult stuff."

"Did she work for you recently? Here?"

Vic looked down and sideways. "Yeah, the night before she got— Before she was—"

Lupo felt his rage building. Not so much at this worthless little man, whose only knowledge of Corinne had come from the sleazy end of his camera, but at the system that made people buy into this lifestyle.

"How well did you know her?" Lupo interrupted, his voice almost too calm and friendly. Scary.

Vic shivered visibly. "Look, there's a strict policy here.

We—we stay away from the talent. Me and the crew, I mean, none of us ever gets involved in a picture. Other guys in the business like to film their own blow jobs, okay, but we don't do that here."

Maybe the vibes Lupo gave off were going right to the jerk's head—Vic was sweating under Lupo's intense gaze.

"How about the others? Who else was in on this shoot?"

"We shoot simple, okay? Me, a cameraman, a sound guy who does second camera for close-ups, a makeup girl, and usually two or three chicks. Maybe four if it's a budget-buster."

"How about the guys?"

"Yeah, two or three. Sometimes five or six. They come cheap, you know, cause most of 'em would do it for free. At first, anyway."

Ben spoke, gesturing. "Who worked with the Diamond girl on this video? Any of these people?"

"I don't remember. I mean, no, none of these people. There was a few different people for each shoot. I can't memorize—"

"But you could find out, right, Vic? You have records somewhere?" Lupo leaned in closer.

Vic backed away. "Sure. I mean, I got files. Releases. I could give you names." He wiped his forehead, which was shining under the umbrella lights.

"That would be good," Ben said. "Very good." He gave Vic a card, which Vic took with a shaky hand. "You'll call us this afternoon with names, right? Anyone who worked on this recent video. You got any copies of this immortal work?"

"Yeah, I could get you copies."

"Good. Send them over to us at the station. Today."

"And names, Vic," Lupo said. "Don't forget to call with names."

"Now you can continue with your little blue movie."

Vic nodded. His ponytail bobbed. It didn't look as if he could continue with anything. But then Sal walked back in, still holding his member, this time dragging a thinly beautiful woman whose hair was shower-wet and whose breasts glistened with water droplets.

Vic spotted her and forgot about his police troubles. "Tara, where the hell have you been?"

"None of your business, you slimy little faggot. Now one last time, I don't do anal, and that's that. I'm not gonna have this gorilla stick that telephone pole up my ass, got it?"

"But baby, your contract—"

"Stuff my contract up *your* ass, Victor. God knows *you* can take it." She grabbed a purse from beside the bed and started to walk toward the door, still naked.

"Aw, Tara," Sal said, going after her all the way into the hall. "You'll ruin my first big movie!"

Just then Ashlyn burst into the room. "I can do the scene, Vic. Let me."

Vic stopped. Then he spread his arms. "Ashlyn, babe, come here."

She cooed and he swept her into an embrace, his hands roving over her buttocks as she squealed with delight.

"Let's get outa here," Ben said. "I feel a strange urge to take a long, hot shower."

MARTIN

This mall was another perfectly sterile place, and Martin smiled at the thought of someone finally bringing color to its drab walls and dirty tile floors. He smiled at the thought of being the one to do it, and he smiled at the thought of making his friend Lupo wallow in that smelly, sticky color until the son of a bitch acknowledged what he had done. Acknowledged his guilt.

"Come on, it'll be fun."

She hesitated. "I don't know. It's a little too—"

"Dangerous?" Martin supplied. "Look, I'm paying, right?"

"Yeah, I know."

"This is just part of the thrill, you see. You'll earn your money and have a little fun just a few feet away from all this wholesome family stuff. It can't be any worse than some flophouse somewhere."

"Well, yeah," she said, licking her lips.

Martin liked that—had liked that about her from the moment he'd spotted her at the bar and interpreted the signs. He was getting better at it.

"Yeah," she continued after making her lips glossy again, "it could be worse, 'cause they arrest people who do stuff like this *here*. They don't bother with the flophouses."

He took her arm. "I'll double your going price."

"Well . . ."

He led her to the escalator, and she let him. Martin had won, as he had known he would. He was God. He could manipulate anyone into anything. His voice was silk. His personality was strong and forceful, but likable enough to smooth over people's doubts. And what doubts could this hooker have, anyway? What thoughts crossed such a mind, a mind and psyche suited only to giving pleasure and receiving payment? What doubts could someone like her exhibit, once having chosen such a career path? Martin smiled. He liked analyzing things, and this girl on his arm was both an enigma and an open book to him—he knew what drove her, and what would make her happy. He knew what he could tell her, and what she would say. He knew that nothing he requested would be out of bounds, now that he had forced his will on her once. The giving in had unempowered her—the payment, a double payment, was all she thought of, all she needed. She was putty in his hands, as the old cliché said, and he could feel a tingle where his skin touched hers.

He looked at her face as they rode upward, toward the mall's upper level, where the fast-food eateries lined up like carnival booths. She was also an enigma, for he did not quite understand how she had come to be this way.

She was pretty, in a blank sort of way. Her hair was blond, but dark roots gave her away. Her eyes were a clear blue, but vacant—distant and lost, maybe drugged. Her nose might have been perfect with the exception of one small ridge that a plastic surgeon could remove in mere minutes. As it was, her nose was her weakest feature. A strong chin and high cheekbones perfectly set off her best feature, and the one on which Martin had first focused—her lips, ablaze in a shiny pink cream and covered in a clear gloss that shimmered under the mall's natural and fluorescent lighting mix. Martin was aware that men on the down escalator beside them watched her with open lust. He smiled at them. *See what I have that you don't?* It was part of the game. And he knew that they were watching her so intently that not one would remember his features. In fact, had he really been *with* her? Dredging their weakened memories would bring up the fact that he was standing one or two steps below her on the moving staircase, not exactly *with* her. They would be confused; cut him out of the picture completely.

Martin knew he was right. He was always right.

They reached the top floor and she looked to him for guidance. But he knew where he was going, and he led her there after a nod in the right direction.

The photo booth was tucked in a corner, near two rows of tables. Interspersed among the tables were several large potted figs and swing-topped refuse pails. A half-dozen people sat alone at tables, eating fast food quickly—*so much shopping to do*. One small table was overwhelmed by a family, whose various children ran to and fro amid a tangle of parental hands and feet, packages and bags piled high enough on the table to make Martin wonder where they would set their food once the various orders were taken and a parent had set off to fulfill every wish.

As he stepped past these people with the blond

woman not quite on his arm, he noticed several heads turn and glance at them—two men with open lust, one woman in apparent disgust (his companion's cleavage was rather indelicately displayed, after all), and several of the children with open, though fleeting, curiosity. Then they were past the tangle of tables and entering the tiny booth, and Martin was drawing the black plastic curtain on both sides.

She sat on the stool facing the camera eye and the mirror, and Martin stood beside her. He knew their feet were visible beneath the edge of the curtain, but he didn't mind—the knowledge made the game all the more fun. Couples took lovey-dovey photographs in these booths all the time.

He slid the paper bills into the slot, waited for the light to signal the camera was set, then turned to his companion. His throat was dry, and he had to clear it, dredge up some saliva. This was always the most exciting part (well, almost the most exciting part), and he wanted to enjoy it.

"Would you please refresh your lipstick?" he whispered, hoarse with desire.

The blonde knew what he wanted. It wasn't a typical fetish, but not altogether unknown. Anyway, there was a reason she played up her lips—they were perfect, full, wide, and as sensuous as any famous model's. She applied her lipstick, neglecting the unneeded mirror to instead watch Martin's obvious pleasure as she smiled and pouted for him.

When he unzipped his fly and slipped out his erection, she was ready. Her velvety lips stretched over its length and she went to work, visions of double pay perhaps dancing in her head. Martin flicked the button and heard the camera start to whirr. Vaguely he could hear the chatter of children, the steps of an adult considering a choice of tables, the sound of plastic tableware hitting the inside of a refuse pail, someone coughing uncontrollably. Ice clinking in a plastic cup. But then his father was speaking to him, urging him to play the game *right* with his daddy, groaning as Martin tried—

as Martin tried to please his daddy, whose desires became more and more difficult, and whose groans seemed to fade in and out, and blend in with Martin's gasps as

—she tried to please him while the camera took one, two, three shots and then he was spurting into her mouth and onto her lips and chin and the camera was clicking one last time, a perfectly timed encounter, and she was licking him clean and he was zipping up just as a mall cop stuck his head inside the booth.

"Everything all right in here?"

Martin faced him and hid the woman's face from the cop with his body. He could sense her hand busily wiping the evidence from around her mouth.

"Couldn't be better, Officer," Martin smiled. "Just taking some pictures for the folks back home."

Thirties and bull-necked, the cop was flabby in the middle but not much, like a weight lifter who's been laying off the weights and eating double breakfasts for a year. But his eyes were hardened and knowing, and he tried to look around Martin. "You all right, miss?"

"Yes, Officer," she said from behind Martin. She pushed him aside gently and looked at the cop, batting her eyelashes. Martin glanced down at her. She looked like the girl next door now, with barely a smudge left on her cheek and no lipstick on her mouth. He could see a paper hanky balled up in her fist. "Everything's fine."

"Wanna see the pictures?" Martin asked, smiling more widely now, pushing his envelope of margin, basking in the knowledge that he could do no wrong, pushing fate beyond where most would dare. He heard the woman gasp slightly and hold it in, unbelieving of his courage. His gall in cheating capture so cavalierly.

"Nah," said the cop. "Just wanted to make sure you're okay in there." His head retreated, and Martin followed to retrieve the strip of pictures from the little tray on the outside of the booth where it had curled up, offering a hint of pink and white to anyone who bothered to look closely.

Martin watched the cop's back as he stalked past the diners and the noisy family, some of whom had watched the exchange silently and perhaps with more than a flicker of interest. *At least two of those people are aware of what went on here,* Martin thought. He smiled at them. He watched the cop disappear around the bend—*idiot! How easily fooled was the moron!*—and then ducked back into the booth, where she was once again applying lipstick. She looked up at him. The question was plain— *When do I get paid?*

"Don't you want to see our pictures?"

She shrugged. It wasn't like this guy had invented film or video, for Chrissakes. He could hear her thoughts almost as clearly as if she had spoken them. "Okay, whatever."

He handed her the strip.

She curled her lips, smiling. "Hey, these are great!" A little enthusiasm, after all. "You know just where to stand, don't you?"

Ah, yes, even the most vacant of brain could sometimes make connections unwanted and unwarranted. Still, the local police had not released all the details of the previous death to the news media, so this particular indulgence of his was still unknown by the general public, though he wondered if area mall cops wouldn't have been alerted. Perhaps it was time to move on to phase two, and be done with it.

He tucked the colorful strip into his shirt pocket and led his companion to the other side of the mall, where he knew the least-used washrooms were likely to be empty at this time of day. "I'll pay you in the washroom. I have to dig into my money belt for the cash. Plus, I have a little blow we can do."

She accepted the explanation. "Why didn't you say so in the first place?"

The tiles in the washroom were dirty white with a fleshy pink trim, and when he turned and keyed the door locked behind them, her eyes widened.

"Friend of mine's a security guard here," Martin lied, thinking of the janitor he'd tied up earlier. He smiled and took a glass vial out of his pocket. He watched her pour some out onto her little mirror, which she'd taken from her purse. He backed her into a stall and pushed her down onto the toilet, where she sat with her legs spread and maneuvered a thin white straw into the powder on her mirror. She inhaled noisily, then fixed him with an angry stare.

"This isn't—"

By then Martin was taking the knife from the sheath that pressed into the small of his back. Her eyes widened as the blade danced before her.

"Hey, come on now, mister, you got what you wanted and it was on the house, okay, no charge."

Martin shook his head and clucked his tongue. His fingers shook around the knife's hilt—it was a flexible cutting knife, almost a straight razor, and he handled it carefully. A thin voice made its way from between his lips. It didn't sound like Martin at all.

"Why, mommy, why didn't you do something? Why were you almost always gone, huh, mommy? Why did I have to play mommy for daddy? Why did I have to do those things for daddy that you should have done?"

"W-what? Mister, I don't know w-what—"

"Shut up, mommy!" He motioned with the blade. "You should have been there. You should have done all those things for daddy. Not me."

He slashed out with the blade.

Heard her skin zip open like a piece of cheap clothing.

Scream cut off as he clapped a hand over her mouth and held it there as she spasmed.

Tiles, turning red.

He let her head go.

"Not me!" he screamed into her wide-open mouth, staring into the dead eyes.

He still had work to do, and he set about it with the usual efficiency.

All the while, he muttered.

"Not me. Not me. *Not me.*"

From the Journals of Caroline Stewart

October 12, 1971
It's hard to pick up a pen again after so long, but now that I seem to have found a new life I can't bear to avoid the old one. I wanted to continue writing in my beautiful set of matching diaries, the set my mother gave me while I was still in grade school and which managed to last me all through high school (those hellish years!), but they have long since disappeared. My brother took them, probably, as he took so much from me over the whole of our lives together. Or maybe it was my father. It occurs to me that I still have a bunch of unpacked boxes in storage here at the Whitman dormitory, so maybe I'll get lucky and find the diaries there. I just don't want to wait—I want to start writing of my new life as it happens, not as I remember it!

Maybe it took two and a half semesters, but I seem to have found my calling. After taking the Intro to Psychology and Intro to Sociology survey courses, I found that everything I read seemed to make sense to me. That was a first! God, I've hated the math and heavy science courses (except the geology survey—I found myself relishing the quiet dignity of ancient rocks and minerals!). I've never been any good at math and sciences, and any interest I may have shown when I was little was eaten away by my family life (see early diaries, if ever located!). So finally finding myself nodding and smiling as I read about human behavior surprised and delighted me.

Unless something even better comes along, I can see myself as a psychiatrist or psychologist like my uncle, drawing people out of their shells and fixing whatever's wrong in their lives. I wish someone could have done that for me, and I hope to God I would have the compassion to help others cope with the kind of things I faced. Maybe I'll teach, or maybe both practice and teach! Wow, I can't believe I'm being so decisive. Now if only I could go and study for that German midterm! It's going to be a bear, and I don't want to repeat the class.

December 15, 1971

Classes are just about done—only finals left to study for—and already I'm obsessing about going "home." I can't really explain it, but I don't want to see anyone. My aunt and uncle are nice people, but there's just too much history . . . God knows, all this psychology I've been reading seems to be right on target. I'm nothing but a case history! Hell, my entire family is made up of case histories . . . my brother's never likely to get out of that "institution" he's in (and thank God for that!), and I'm never going to get out of therapy—I'm fucked up enough that I want my classes to teach me how to be normal! If they weren't closing down the dorms for a month, I'd stay here. Donna did invite me to stay with her family, but even though we're pretty close as roommates go I'm not sure that it was a sincere invitation. A nice gesture though. I've talked a little about my family, usually after a couple of pitchers at The Gasthaus, the pub in the basement of the Student Union—it's dark and the booths seem kind of anonymous, and the beer seems to bring out an urge to spill all my deepest se-

crets. If only she knew how much I've left out! She would definitely not invite me to share in her Currier & Ives Christmas . . .

I may just take a little vacation on my own. My job at the library brought in enough that I can probably manage to spend a decent month at a motel off the freeway. I may have to diet, but I can stand to lose fifteen pounds anyway—the dorm cafeteria food is outrageously fattening! The more I think about it, the more I like it. Even if I will look like some tramp, staying at a motel by myself. I'll have my psychology textbooks, and who needs anything more? Ha!

February 20, 1973

It's nuts that the more I learn, the more I would like to psychoanalyze my brother, the creep, to find out what made him the way he was. Sure, part of it was my father's abuse. I didn't know how bad that was until much later, but that was because I was too busy dealing with what my father was doing to me. Of course, my father blamed my mother for his "urges" (that's what he called them), but that was just his excuse. Still, why did my brother become murderous, when all I did was withdraw? What made his wiring go all berserk, while mine held up so much better? I mean, I know I'm fucked up, but I don't want to kill anybody. I wouldn't even have killed my father, even though I hated him. And my mother, well, I blamed her when I was little, but I know she was just another victim, really. I think the males in my family got the bad genes, that's all. All this psychology I'm taking is really opening my eyes, and it's helping me. I'm sleeping better than ever now, and I'm not taking Uncle's prescriptions anymore. Hey, and I'm learning to relax and have a good time. Last night I said the hell with studying and Donna and I went bowling in the Union. I don't like bowling, but I had fun anyway! Maybe there's hope for me yet . . . Brother Martin, though, I don't think there's any hope at all for him.

August 17, 1979

Office hours loomed long and boring today. After all, it's almost the end of the summer session, and barely a half dozen students have ever broken the silence here at Johnson Hall. I guess the weather's just too nice to worry about grades. Maybe if I didn't have to be here I'd be down at Bradford Beach, too, taking in the sun. Most of the students think summer sessions are more relaxed because they're compressed, but they'll be surprised to find out that the test next week is no different than the test I always give at the end of a semester, and if they haven't kept up on their own, well, I'll be seeing them again in the fall.

One of the few students who has bothered to come in and discuss his grades and his problems showed up again today. He's an earnest young man, and intense—though I sense he's what I might be tempted to describe as "distant" in his intensity. It's almost as if he's afraid to get close to people, and I mean physically as well as socially. Dominic Lupo is one of the few who seems truly interested in the subject matter—not just for the sake of filling out a major, but because there's something he's seeking. He told me so today, though he was evasive as to what he'd like to find. I confess that he actually scared me a little, coming in as he did with a three-day stubble and unkempt hair. But he spoke well, and softly enough, and he seems to understand the course material well—better than his classmates, the majority of whom sit with wide-eyed glazed expressions through my lectures and appear to awaken only when the minute hand approaches the hour of dis-

missal. I guess I wasn't too much different from them myself just a few years ago, but this Lupo kid is so different that he threw me for a loop (ha ha, no pun intended).

I admit, I found myself inviting him back to discuss his interests during my next office hour—I hope I wasn't too obviously coming on to him (was I? maybe I was!). It's a cliché to say he had haunted eyes, but there's no other way to describe the look. Like a deer caught in the headlights, I guess. Actually, I know the look well, since it took me years to get away from it myself. I have no doubt that during my first couple years of college people saw that haunted quality in me, and if they only knew how much they would have crossed the street to be away from me—as I did with my own past.

I'm rambling now, but it's not often an interesting student comes along. And I might as well say it—a good-looking one, too. Maybe I've been teaching too long! Or maybe it's just been long enough since they tried to take my soul—now that it's mine I can choose to give it to whomever I please.

More on Mr. Lupo later, as I learn more. IF I learn more.

CHAPTER FOURTEEN

LUPO

He held the door for Ben, who hustled past him and across the hall to the detectives' squadroom.

"You sure you don't want those headache pills, Nick?"

"Nah, you go ahead in. I'm gonna hit the can."

Lupo pushed into the men's room and leaned over the counter, into the mirror. He stared at his own eyes, wondering. Wondering how things might have been different if his friend Andy had just not—

No, not this again. Some things you can't change. Things go to hell on their own. Andy got something from some wild animal and he bit you and you caught it. It's that simple. Corinne was a hooker, for better or worse, and was targeted because of me, but if she hadn't been an escort he wouldn't have had it so easy. Corinne had also splashed herself across videotape and DVD. Just one more thing you can't change, no matter how much you try. There's no going back, Nick Lupo.

He'd always wondered about his name. Lupo. *Wolf.*

Had he somehow been destined to become what he was? Could he have changed that destiny, perhaps by leaving home earlier, at a younger age? By changing his name? Not that it mattered—like Corinne, it was too late now.

Lupo felt the hairs on his hands prickling. It was a sign that he needed to head north, out of the city. He needed space, woods to roam in. He needed to let his true nature out for a walk. He felt this way just before the full moon, but the feeling intensified because of Corinne's death. She had been more than a friend, more than a lover might have been. The nagging sense that he should have been able to deduce the killer's identity haunted him. It was someone familiar, someone who knew *him*—the bloody message on the wall made that clear enough, even if no one else got it. But should Lupo know him? How many petty crooks and crackheads had he put behind bars? Had he pissed off any mobsters lately? Whoever it was, he had a twisted sense of humor as well as a huge shoulder chip and a tub of pent-up rage.

What connection was there between the gruesome murder of Lupo's friend and his past? Or between her death and his true nature?

A toilet flushed behind him and he jumped. He hadn't noticed anyone in the washroom, but now a stall door swung open and a young cop named Keeler came out.

"Hey, Nick, how's it hangin'?"

"Okay." Lupo looked at Keeler in the long mirror. "You?"

Keeler didn't bother to wash his hands, but he did slick back his hair and check out the results.

"Everything's cool," he said. "Hunky-dory, know what I mean?"

Lupo nodded and turned away. Keeler wasn't very well liked. Maybe the kid spent too much time looking at himself, or maybe he was just too hip. Most likely it was because he seemed to have gotten his street-smart attitude from watching too many *gritty* cop shows.

"Hear you got another homicide?"

Keeler was a day late and a dollar short, as always. Lupo turned and fixed him with a stare. "The Devereaux murder was yesterday, Keeler. Get with it."

The cop smiled widely. His teeth were uneven, like kernels on a corn cob. "*You* get with it, Lupo. I ain't talkin' about the hooker. Haven't you heard about the gunsmith?" He shook his head and made a face. "Where you been all day, anyway?"

As the door slammed behind Keeler's bulky body, Lupo added today's encounter to his list of reasons for not liking the jerk.

When he stepped out of the washroom, he was cornered by Ben.

"They assigned us another one, Nicky. The bastards. But we're not gonna cut back on Corinne, don't worry about that. We can head over there—the lab boys are still at the scene."

"A gunsmith?" Lupo snorted, pointing at Keeler's back. "The stock's probably been depleted by a hundred percent. Like we need more damn guns on the street."

Ben handed him his coat. "Funny thing is, the way the beat guys reported it, it looks like a couple things are missing, but there's still a shitload of stuff on the racks."

Lupo raised an eyebrow. "So they were interrupted. Cash?"

"Plenty there, I gather. They're not sure what to make of this one."

"Maybe working on something else will shake something loose on our other guy."

"Pretty soon we'll get a fix on the possibles. Probably wake up with it, at some point."

Lupo stopped in the doorway. Ben bumped into him.

"What did you just say?"

"I said we'll be sleepin' and it'll come to us. Happens to me all the time."

Lupo felt that something, something important, had just happened. A clue? *No. More like a feeling, or hunch.*

Something that should have set off alarm bells, but instead it was just a little irritating dinging. He shook his head and led the way back out into the afternoon's chilly springtime air.

Rag's Gunshop was sealed off with a length of yellow tape, though there were no crowds to keep away from the doors and windows—in this neighborhood, regular citizens would cheer Rag's sudden closing. Anything to keep a few guns off the streets. Though businesses such as this had once formed the backbone of American society, they now seemed to hide in the dark—abandoned by everyone but the very dedicated. Lupo wondered if there'd been any legit business for old Rag at all lately, or if he just sat around with his friends and reminisced, toasting the good old days.

The photographer's camera flashed as they walked past the door guard, and the first thing Lupo saw—illuminated as it was by the brief light that banished the natural cave-like appearance of the back of the store—was the wall-mounted rack crowded with high-powered bolt-action rifles, semiautomatic military style assault rifles, shotguns, and the occasional war relic.

In a corner stood one sorry-looking piece Lupo could have sworn was a Mannlicher-Carcano identical to the one found in the Dallas Book Depository. M-16s, Russian AK-47s and Chinese copies, an older M-14, a WWII BAR, a gangster-style Thompson, complete with 100-round drum magazine, and other historical pieces shared space with several fine Weatherby sporting rifles, as well as a dozen standard Remington deer rifles.

It was a true arsenal, with plenty of ammunition nearby, and it was all still in place, apparently untouched. The thief or thieves must have been disturbed. Unless there were a few high-dollar pieces missing and it was a quick job, the place having been cased first.

Ben and Lupo donned latex surgeon's gloves and made

for the camera flashes. Lupo peered over the counter to where the photographer crouched, reloading his camera.

"If you want to take a look, Detective," he said to Lupo, "go ahead, before we flip 'im."

Lupo nodded. He came around and held the door panel for Ben, who stepped behind the counter and frowned.

Lupo felt dizzy, the blood-smell clogging his nostrils. And maybe something else? His head began to ache, as if—*as if what?* he asked himself. The dull throb had begun as soon as they came within sight of the victim's body. It was bad, that was certain. It was as bad a mess as Corinne, except that here the guy had not played games with the victim's blood. But it had been a messy hit. Lupo could see Ben's reaction. *No matter how often . . .* Still, Lupo wondered as he pressed a hand against his right temple, why the sudden headache? Blood aroused many different feelings and senses, but never pain.

"Who is this?"

"The uniforms say it's Rag Johnson, the owner." Ben shook his head. "Somebody did a number on him, all right."

Rag—if it was indeed the gunsmith himself—had suffered a gunshot wound to the head so massive that the top of his head had caved in on itself when the bullet and everything else had exited.

"Geez, Nick. Looks like a .357, or a .44 Magnum. Not much left of the guy."

Lupo nodded. "I'd say .44, close. Very close. Powder burns on the skin of the right temple, all around the entry wound. Guy put the piece right on him, maybe even touched the bastard's skin, then blew him apart. This was no kid looking for a quick score. He's done this before. Or visualized doing it for a long time."

"He likes it."

"Maybe." Lupo examined the rear of the counter.

"How about the interruption theory, though. Kid comes

in, wants some guns, Rag here says no, kid panics and puts the gun up to his head. Not knowin' how bad it'll look, you know. Then, when he offs the guy, the kid freaks at all the blood and shit and takes off. He took the piece with him, so that mostly rules out a pro hit. Mob pro, anyway."

"Yeah, that could swing." Lupo was leaning over Rag's right hand now, as if he was following a bug. "A pro shooter wouldn't use such a cannon. This is just too big a piece." He brought his face even closer to the right hand. "There's some shiny stuff under his fingernails."

"What is it?"

Lupo was about to answer when his hand began to throb, then suddenly shooting pains traveled up his wrist and forearm. He had almost touched the victim's fingers, but even from inches away the pain was acute. He knew what it was, and he moved his hand away, feeling the pain recede like a soothed burn.

It was *silver.*

Pure silver, from what he could see, in the shape of filings or slivers or particles under the gunsmith's nails. Lupo's neck hair bristled ever so slightly. He felt dizzy.

He raised his head and shrugged. "Before they bag his hands or move him, I want an extra series of shots of his fingertips," Lupo said to the photographer. "And make sure the lab takes an extra look at his fingers first thing."

The photographer nodded and got to work.

Lupo rocked back on his haunches, sweeping the area with his well-practiced gaze. The dizziness diminished and faded.

"Anything else?" Ben said, shielding his eyes against the flashes.

"Another piece missing out of the display case."

"Yeah? How'd you figure?"

"There's a space where a handgun would have been, middle of the top shelf."

"That's good, I see that." Ben nodded. "But maybe that's the gun does the hit, right?"

"No. That whole shelf is either 9mm or .380 semiauto-matics. Piece that did this was a revolver, .44 like we said. A 9mm wouldn't have made this much of a mess."

"Could have been one of those old Auto-Mags," Ben sniffed.

"Could be, but how many of those have you actually seen since *Sudden Impact?* Aren't that many around."

"Okay, so the guy takes a piece off the top shelf, a semi-auto. Before or after the hit?"

"After. See the blood on the outside of the glass door—the one our guy left open? The guy pops Rag, then he slides the door open, blood and all, and takes the one piece. Maybe another 9mm."

Ben sighed. "So we got a shooter armed with a .44 *and* a 9mm. Great, Nicky, just great."

"Maybe more." Lupo straightened and nodded at the photographer, who stepped back as a technician moved in with two uniforms and started to flip Rag over. The smell of Rag's last bodily function wafted up to them and Lupo turned away. "There's a big footlocker down here. Looks like it's been moved recently. Tracks in the dust."

"Prints?"

"We can only hope."

With the latex gloves covering his fingers, Lupo lifted the locker's cover and held it open.

Ben looked inside. "Whew." It was halfway between a whistle and a sigh.

Lupo lifted out a half-dozen UZI submachine guns, all coated with heavy grease for long-term storage. He wiped off the breech of one and pointed to its markings. "Israeli issue. These are full-auto. No import tax, no FFL, no paper of any kind."

Ben was reaching in and coming up with a homemade wooden rack and the four tiny weapons it held. "Old but very well-kept MAC 10s. Why're they still here and not on the street?"

"Good question. But let's count our blessings."

The rest of the weapons included two dozen exotic military pistols, including Russian and Chinese makes, and spare magazines for them. At the bottom, among several belts and cartridge cases, was a rounded object. "Yow," Ben said as he held up a live grenade. "Whole new ball game."

"Damn it, there were probably more in there." Nick took the grenade from his partner's hand. "Probably stolen from an armory. Something we can check, anyway. The question is, how many did our guy lay his hands on?"

"And what else?"

"We're ready here, Detectives." The uniform's voice interrupted them, directing their attention to Rag's body, which had been turned over. The photographer was taking additional pictures. Then the hands were bagged in paper, the better to preserve any clues. Plastic bags didn't breathe and could cause alteration of evidence, besides speeding up putrefaction.

While Ben examined the body further, Lupo turned toward the workbench behind the counter that spanned the width of the store. Several vises gripped weapons in various stages of assembly. A reloading press took up a third of the space. Lupo leaned over the workspace, which was illuminated by a magnifying work light, and felt the same heat-pain in his skin. His head spun.

Shiny filings lay scattered on the flat work area.

Lupo had no need to wait for analysis to know that the material was more silver. The lab people would confirm it, but his own senses were attuned to the feel of the element—just as popular myth would have it.

He had no idea why his condition followed so closely the rules set forth in B-movies, but it did. He remembered well his first encounter with silver, on the day his mother had bought him a silver chain—all the rage in the seventies—and he had begged for her to exchange it for a gold one. She had been hurt by his irrational behavior, but would have been shocked at the lesions the silver left on the skin around his neck, lesions that took almost a year to heal completely.

Why would a gunsmith work with silver?

Lupo let the truth wash over him. He had suspected it since feeling the presence of the metal, but the workbench clinched it—as did the proximity of Rag's reloading apparatus. A small smelting setup was probably on the premises, too, maybe in the back room. It had to be a professional setup, due to silver's high boiling point. That silver had been used in reloading was obvious. A number of slugs had been either coated or filled with pure silver, then loaded into brass cartridges. They had been filed or notched then, to increase impact. A custom order. Rag had to die after filling such an eccentric order. And after providing an appropriate weapon with which to fire the silver slugs. Whatever else had the guy made off with—grenades? Submachine guns?

HERE'S ONE FOR YOU, NICK!

This time his message was Rag himself, and the silver slug that had taken off most of his head. Lupo was sure of it. And there was no way he could tell Ben, or anyone else, because the only connection between Rag and Corinne was Lupo himself. And the silver.

Beside him, Ben had turned his attention to the counter and was scraping the filings onto a sheet of paper. He wrapped it in a druggist's fold and slipped it into an envelope.

As the photographer's flash turned the scene into a strobe-lit nightmare, Lupo wrestled with the facts. Someone knew enough about his condition to know that silver could hurt or kill him. And that someone had a grudge. Now, if only Lupo could figure out who.

Before anyone else is killed, or he kills me.

For the first time since he had acted against his father's wishes and become a cop, he felt vulnerable to something other than his own bestial urges. For the first time, he felt as if a target was painted on his back.

*   *   *

Lupo turned in early but couldn't sleep.

His tossing allowed him more than sufficient time to examine both his life and the case, this damned case which
was more than that—it was personal and it brought pain
because Corinne was gone, and he had so few friends
that the loss of one caused a huge impact to ripple
through his life. He felt the selfish thought wrap itself
around him like a blanket and allowed it—what else were
sleepless nights for, if not for selfish thoughts we try to
cover up and suppress in daylight?

He felt the exquisite pain of his loss and let himself wallow in delicious self-pity. Sometimes it was therapeutic to
allow such thoughts their space, letting them chip away at
his stoic resolve when he could at least hide his emotions
from others, especially other cops. But not Ben. No, Ben
understood. Lupo was certain, and he felt thankful for a
decent friend among the strangers with which he worked.

Lupo had always been different, and the different attract few friends.

Lupo flipped over and felt comfortable for a minute, letting his body sink into the mattress, but then his muscles
tightened and signaled the end of this attempt. He gave
up and lay on his back, watching the vague gray smudge
of the ceiling hover above him as he started to go over the
facts of the case yet again.

The combination of Corinne's murder, the gunsmith,
and their obvious connection was one of the obstacles
impeding his rest. That he couldn't tell Ben or anyone
else about the connection rankled too, but not as much.
The identity of the murderer was his first concern, since it
had to be someone he knew—someone with a grudge,
real or imagined, against Lupo himself. He scrolled
through a mental film of faces—perps he'd arrested and
convicted, one or two he'd shot with official justification
and their angry relatives, the occasional fight, and the
few personal grudges he could remember. Fact was, Lupo

lived a solitary life. He'd avoided attachments—since Caroline, anyway—because of the unpredictable nature of his disease.

He did think of it as a disease, and he always had. At least until recently, when faced with the possibility that he could learn to control his transformations. He'd so feared the lunar cycles and their effect on him that he had hidden himself away during the full moon—in his specially altered condominium apartment, or, better yet, upstate in Wisconsin's sparsely populated North Woods, where he could allow himself to prowl the national forest and hunt with little chance of discovery.

In the twenty years since he had become a cop, the only control he had been able to exert on his wolf's form was an extreme type of suppression, which covered for him in emergencies, but for which he suffered almost unendurable pain. His time at the police academy had been keen torture, as he had been forced to suppress the changes he called *episodes* almost right up until the full moon—graduation had been on a Thursday and the moon turned full on Saturday. He had become accustomed to the accelerating changes and minor episodes, such as inadvertent growls and sporadic hair growth, which occurred with alarming frequency during the last few days of his training. He had suspected, on the other hand, that his condition also increased his physical abilities enough to win him class honors in required tests—he found to his surprise that at lifting, running, jumping, and climbing, he was by far the best of the forty cadets.

His childhood had never been particularly sports-oriented, since his parents were Italian immigrants who didn't much care for the strange American sports they saw. They never discouraged their son, it was true, but they never encouraged him either, and he had grown up blissfully unaware of baseball and basketball, enjoying only the calculated bursts of violence he saw on the football field (though not enough to risk true participation beyond the occasional school-yard game spurred by the success of the Green Bay Packers, the best home team ever). Therefore, his newfound physical abilities had surprised no one more than the young Dominic Lupo himself.

If only he could *command* it. But he could not, and he had often nearly run afoul of his father—whose silver-loaded shotgun seemed to shimmer in the gun cabinet. No, Nick knew from an early age that he was now a target—his father's cure would also kill the patient.

These realities had left him with little choice but to hide in misery and shame and read, read voraciously from endless library shelves on the occult in general and the phenomenon known as *lycanthropy* in particular. He knew now what he was, but he also knew that there was little he could do to change his fate—the sources, both fiction and nonfiction, seemed to agree that the only way out was death and that silver was a potent weapon against him in any form. And his mother's gift—the necklace that had burned into his skin—had only proven the delicate balance between life and death by skewering his altered nervous system with such pain that he knew without a doubt that death would be only moments away in the presence of any amount of the forty-seventh element.

The lesson had been valuable, helping to delineate his limits. A few years later, Caroline Stewart came along to help him discover more limits, and to point out more positive aspects he had never considered. And it had been Caroline who helped him decide to break with his father's wishes and become a police officer. Then she had helped him cope with the pain of his condition during his training and rookie years.

And he had repaid her love and trust by ending her life on a blood-soaked bed he could never quite forget—he saw it, felt the wet sheets, *smelled the blood,* whenever he closed his eyes.

Lupo rolled over, watching the images come unbidden into his head—like a never-ending film loop playing in his mind whenever he let down his guard enough to let it begin by threading the spools of his stricken conscience.

Caroline ("It's pronounced Caro-lynn!" she'd said in class) was almost ten years older than Nick, and had already earned a doctorate in psychiatry and started a private practice by the time he stumbled into her at the state university, where he floundered amid various courses dictated by his father's wishes for his life, and where he studiously applied himself to one course—the Psychology intro course that held his interest because it dealt with human weaknesses (of which he felt he had many) and because it was taught by the lovely Caroline Stewart.

There was little doubt of Caroline's beauty—every male student eyed her chestnut hair, wide expressive mouth, and dark soulful eyes with a combination of doleful adoration and undisguised lust. Nick Lupo was hardly an exception, but his questions into the duality of human nature obviously intrigued her, much to the envy of the rest of the men in the class, who viewed Nick as the one class member who was obviously headed to the place to which they all aspired—her bedroom. A frequent visitor to her tiny, cubicle-like office, Nick actually only aspired to be where he was—in the presence of an intellect that engaged him by helping him explore the questions he had. Still, the other aspects were difficult to ignore, and he also felt the sexual force pulling them together despite all logic and common sense.

Though at first neither had acted on the mutual attraction, Nick's course was set and his outstanding Psychology grades demanded several follow-up seminars. He registered eagerly for any course she taught, and their bond grew until the inevitable happened and the whispers—which had never stopped—finally gained substance.

On that day, Nick came to her office with the half-formed thought of confessing his problem. He had considered long and hard, deciding that if he could share his secret with anyone, Caroline Stewart had to be the one.

She was patient and understanding. She was intelligent. She had spoken of a partial belief in the supernatural—or at least the paranormal—and had mentioned research she had done in the occult sciences. Given his condition, Nick thought, could a more open-minded person be found?

He knocked on the door of her office, hoping no one would see him in the hallway. The building was nearly deserted, but he really didn't want anyone to feed the rumor mill.

"Walk in." Her voice was slightly husky, as if she'd just awakened. Her male students loved this characteristic, and Nick was no exception.

"Hi, Dr. Stewart," he said as he opened the door.

She tossed her hair and nodded him into a chair. "I've told you before, Nick," she scolded. "You may call me Caroline. Okay?"

He nodded. Maybe it was time he listened. "Okay, Caroline." He tried out the sound of her name on his lips and rather liked it. "Are you busy?"

She spread her hands over a pile of term papers, rolling her eyes. "Yes. But I need a break."

"Are those ours?"

She smiled and nodded. "Don't worry, I haven't done yours yet."

He shook his head. "That's not why I'm here. You remember some of those discussions we've had about duality. About repressing another self, a darker side of ourselves?"

"I do remember. Interesting stuff. Quite a lot of research is being done now, with all those multiple-personality cases showing up on the news lately."

Nick paused, not knowing how to proceed.

Should he blurt it out, and let her disbelieve? *Well, Caroline, it appears that I'm a werewolf.*

Yeah, *that* would work.

Should he dance around the point, further gauging her

position on the possibilities? How subtle should he be? How blunt? He chose subtlety.

"What if I told you I have personal knowledge of a serious case, and that both the person and I would like you to examine him—or her? Would you do it?" He winced at the sound of his awkward lie.

Caroline seemed not to notice. She tilted her head slightly and stared at him. "You mean step away from the theoretical?" He nodded. "Well, yes, I suppose I would. Though it's highly irregular, you've hooked me pretty well. I guess I could try a diagnosis, if this person actually wanted to talk to me, and maybe refer him—or *her*—to the right specialist. Would that satisfy you?"

He was thrilled at her interest. Now, how could he lead into his questions? How could he tell Caroline about a condition most people would consider a fantasy, something out of a cheap Creature Features movie, or one that Elvira giggled and mugged through the parts that brought agony to Nick's soul? How did one approach something so bizarre?

Nick knew that his grandmother would have believed. There was little doubt in his mind, because such things were not unheard of even in the North of Italy, where she had grown up and poverty was not as widespread as in the South, stories and legends entwined with truth and facts until the result became a whole new legend. Nick remembered how his grandmother had often spoken of the witches she knew who practiced in her hometown. He also remembered how her stories haunted him after Andy had passed his dark legacy on to him.

Maria Saltini had seen *things* in her life. He had heard her hushed whispers to other grown-ups over the years. He remembered the story of a suspected witch who was forced by townspeople to attend holy mass in the village church only to break down into hysterical fits when given Communion, then spitting out the sacred host while shouting obscenities in French, a language she couldn't know. He wasn't supposed to have heard that story, of course, but he'd been sneaky.

Grandma also told the story of a village witch who sold love potions and revenge spells, and what the Italian partisans had done to her when they accused her of betraying their leaders to the Nazi occupiers. They had "passed her around," Grandma said, until she was torn and bloody, then they had decapitated her battered corpse and buried it in two graves filled with salt and holy water. Everyone knew that witches could transform themselves into other creatures, so you had to make sure they couldn't come back to their bodies. While as a kid he hadn't been sure what "passing her around" meant, he was sophisticated enough to let his imagination do the rest.

But now this was Caroline Stewart, his young professor, who'd set aside her grading chores to grant him her entire attention. After closing the door to her tiny office—legs touching as she edged past him to reach the doorknob—she faced him and he fell into her eyes.

"You were saying?" Her voice was full of amused curiosity. "About your friend's case?"

"Huh, yeah," Nick stammered. "It's a unique case, I'm pretty sure. This friend that I mentioned seems to be, uh, two entities. Totally separate personalities. One is human and the other—"

His lips froze. How did one explain this?

"Go on," she prodded. Her serious attitude reassured him further, and he launched into a carefully edited version of his story. At least, as much of his story as he could bring himself to reveal.

"My grandmother believed that all sorts of strange things happen whether or not people believe in them, and that sometimes strange things happen *because* people believe in them. Kind of like voodoo." He stopped for a breath and waited for her to interrupt, but she didn't. Reassured, he continued. "She—my grandmother—grew up in a mountain village in Northern Italy, where people were superstitious and very practical. They were Catholic, but they had no problem borrowing talismans and good-luck charms from other European cultures." He glanced for a sign that she wanted to stop him, or interject. Her eyes were alert and focused on him and his every word, so he continued. "They were afraid of Gypsies because it was said they harnessed dark powers, but the people actually bought Gypsy good-luck charms and love spells and whatever else seemed to be a cure for what ailed them.

"I heard her stories when I was a kid, even though I wasn't supposed to. Stories about curses and horrible things that happened to people who dabbled in the forbidden arts."

He heard himself sound like a voice-over, but she didn't seem to mind. She leaned forward slightly, her hands nestled in her lap. Her lips were parted slightly, provocatively, though he had no doubt she was unaware of it. He stretched back a bit, intimidated by her closeness. Her scent was intoxicating in the close quarters. The ends of his long hair brushed the back of his chair and he felt electrocuted, melted to the spot.

"What I'm trying to say is that I've been conditioned to believe the bizarre and the impossible, see? Like what happened to my friend—what I came to talk to you about."

He found her gaze too intense and let his eyes roam over her cluttered office instead. Her bookshelves reminded him of his own, every space filled with books facing every which way and the narrow space in front of the books cluttered with toys and knickknacks meaningful only to her. He liked that. The bottom shelves were obscured by stacks of books that would never fit.

She waited for his eyes to find hers again. "Go on."

"My friend thinks—this is hard to say—he's pretty sure he's a werewolf."

Nick couldn't stop himself from just blurting it out. And he couldn't avoid cringing, either. It sounded ridiculous, even to him.

To her credit, Professor Caroline Stewart didn't laugh. "A werewolf . . . Let's see if I can dig up something on *lycanthropy*." She pushed her squeaky swivel chair toward one overcrowded bookcase and searched with a fingertip. "Here's one book we can consult. How long has your friend been lycanthropic?"

Nick squinted. Still no sign of ridicule. This was unexpected behavior.

Nice, but unexpected.

"Uh, since he was bitten by a German shepherd–like dog. Maybe three, four years. Is it . . . Is it possible?"

She raised her eyebrows. They were delectable. "Well, anything is, really."

Nick followed those eyebrows down to her high cheekbones. He opened his mouth, but couldn't make a sound. He stared at her full lips, against which she was tapping a chewed-up pencil. Nick never wanted to leave.

"Here's another book you can look at. It's a definitive study of lycanthropy, and it groups together many of the myths and tales that go hand-in-hand with shape-shifting."

"Myths?"

"Anything we don't quite understand we explain away as mythology. For instance, Atlantis. I believe that one day we'll locate ruins that prove the place was no myth. It's just a matter of time. The literature of too many cultures has references to this city, and that can't be an accident. In the meantime, those of us who keep open minds look like fools to some." She smiled. "But at least we're keeping our minds open."

"Like with UFOs," Nick muttered. He was entranced by her smile, but she took his reticence as doubt.

"Right! Why be so conceited as to think we're the only ones in this universe the size of which we can't even conceive? I've never seen a UFO, but I'd like to."

Nick tried not to narrow his eyes at all. He'd sought understanding, but had he found a kook?

Professor Stewart was still ruffling through the pages of

the book. She looked up suddenly and her hair fell into her eyes. She swiped it off absently.

"I'll be happy to let you lend this book to your friend, but you'll have to take responsibility for it. It's not something I can find at the corner drugstore."

"Uh, that's okay, I'll be glad to sign a note or something with my address on it."

"That's all right—you're on my class list, and so is your address. Computers, you know." She smiled again and held out the book. His hand brushed hers as he took it, and he blushed. She looked right at him, and he thought he saw the ghost of a strange loneliness, or something darker, hovering just behind her bright eyes. He roused himself before becoming impolite.

When she ushered him to the door, he saw another student waiting outside. She'd let her appointment wait while talking to him! Her words washed over him and he nodded his thanks even though he couldn't have repeated any part of what she said. Then he was heading down the hall, the book clutched tightly in his hand, her gaze a memory he could not erase.

Later at home in the dingy, barely furnished apartment he shared with a rugby player and a fellow "undeclared major," he snatched one of the last beers from the fridge and turned off the lights in his room. The headphones brought him the buzzy Moog synthesizers of Rick Wakeman's "Myths and Legends of King Arthur and the Knights of the Round Table" as well as a sort of peace. Tears came during the tragic climax, the fall of Arthur's realm. They always did. This time, the face of Caroline Stewart shone like Guinevere's out of the darkness, which enveloped him with the memory of her scent.

He read the book quickly and returned it, saying his friend had also read it. She burrowed a few more out of the barely organized piles in her office. They chose to discuss the books only after they'd both read them, so their out-of-class meetings were brief and impersonal. Even so, Nick heard whispers in the lecture hall. He sensed that some of the other male students had picked up a subtle difference in Professor Stewart's demeanor—she nodded eagerly when Nick made a point, she put him in charge of a study group, and she handed him outside reading materials. At any time somebody might complain to the dean, Nick knew, but he couldn't bear to distance himself from her now that they'd been drawn together by his research.

Nick had relayed some of Grandma's stories as Caroline listened intently. At first they met only in her office, but one fall day they walked to the library together and it was only natural then for them to amble to the student union.

"How about coffee—or a beer?" Nick's sheepish grin countered his brazen invitation.

"Down to the Gasthaus? I haven't done that in a while. Why not?"

"You've been there?" He hurried to catch her at the stairs to the basement.

"Nick, I skipped my share of lectures while sitting in the corner booth—you know, the really dark one."

In that very booth, after two draft beers and a basket of salty popcorn, they broached the subject of Nick's "friend."

"Has any of the material helped your friend?"

Caroline's dusky voice had softened with the beer, and Nick wished somebody would kick the plug out of the jukebox so he could hear her better. Besides, he didn't consider The Cars *real* music. New wave was a fad, nothing more. He leaned in conspiratorially.

"I think he'd really like to find someone to prove himself to," Nick said. "Prove that the whole thing isn't in his head—that it's real, even if it does sound like a bad horror flick."

"Well, maybe I'd be willing to be that person," Caroline said around a mouthful of popcorn.

Nick had hoped she would volunteer, but now that she

had he didn't know how to proceed. How does one confess to such a long list of lies and half-truths?

"I'll be sure to ask him," he croaked weakly. Under the table, he bent an index finger all the way back to his wrist—punishment for his weakness.

"Good. I'm curious about his condition. I mean, I have to remain skeptical, but I want to believe. I'd like to prove all the stuffed shirts wrong. Something like this, properly documented, could revolutionize modern psychology. Or zoology, I guess. Thanks." She picked up the plastic cup Nick had refilled and drank. She smiled a lot now, and waved her arms.

Nick wasn't sure how it happened exactly, but it was several hours later and she had just closed her apartment door behind him. He swayed just a little, but he was sober enough to know that everything—his entire life, in fact—was about to change.

Caroline shot the bolt and turned around to face her student, and before either of them could say anything she had drawn his face closer to hers and gently placed her warm lips on his. And then each action achieved a response, their passion exploding into a series of firm, probing kisses that shocked them both, leaving them breathless.

"I shouldn't—" began Nick.

"I didn't mean to—" Her words collided with his.

Their lips joined again, this time with fierceness. Nick felt her hands caress his body as no high school girl's ever had, and he let himself be led to her bedroom, where they fell atangle onto the brilliant white bedspread.

There was no time and there was no pressure.

There was only passion, and this they shared equally.

When Nick awoke hours later to find Caroline tucked into his arms, he realized the enormity of what had happened.

But it was too late.

Nick Lupo and Caroline Stewart were lovers.

He couldn't help wondering, though, why there were still traces of tears on her cheeks. And why, at one point during their lovemaking, Caroline had let out a scream and a whimper that sounded more frightened than aroused.

They tried to keep their affair secret, but there was no mistaking Professor Stewart's new "glow," or her obvious enjoyment of Nick Lupo's presence in her classroom. He became a staple visitor during her office hours, bringing her a deli lunch on those days she could not schedule a long enough break.

The university frowned on such relationships, but sexual harassment had not yet entered the public consciousness and both were aware of numerous professor-student liaisons occurring throughout the psychology, English, music, and art departments. Therein lay their safety net— a bold sweep of these inappropriate relationships would surely decimate the Humanities faculty, not to mention the graduate school, and no dean could weather the ensuing political storm.

For all intents and purposes, no one could touch them as long as they didn't flaunt their connection, make love in public, or lead anyone to believe that Nick's grades would improve dramatically. Ultimately, they realized there was no human way for them to stay apart, and their acceptance of the fact seemed somehow to satisfy others who might have objected. The occasional comment that made its way to Nick's ears tended to involve envy and awe, not anger or bitterness.

Sometimes after the last office hours Caroline closed her door and took Nick into her arms, ravishing him with body, hands, and lips. Their passion transported them far away during these brief moments, and invariably she wept whenever it seemed to veer out of control.

"It's nothing," she replied when Nick once inquired about her sadness. Her fear.

"Whenever you're ready to talk about it, I'll be waiting."
He wondered if the same would be true when he finally
disclosed his own secret.

Nick knew that Caroline had decided to treat his
friend's story as fixation, and his long and involved de-
scriptions as symptoms of that fixation, but he hoped to
prove his earnestness to her soon enough—perhaps at
the time of his next change.

*If only he could figure out how to do it without endan-
gering her life.*

For now he contented himself with their passionate
unions and with the notion—newly formed—that she
might need him every bit as much as he needed her. He
heard her weeping in the darkness, as always after inter-
course, and so secretively.

When alone, Nick thought of her sadness and wore out
the grooves on ELP's *Works, Volume One,* in which Greg
Lake's baritone drew emotion from his soul with no apol-
ogy. Nick foundered amid the tragedy of his love and of
whatever secret ate away at Caroline, but the music kept
him from drowning.

Other times she grabbed him as he walked past,
cradling him gently until he was ready and then ravaging
him with lips and searing fingertips. Then clothing would
be shed and they celebrated their love as long as their
stamina held.

But Nick felt the heaviness of something dark lying in
her past, something hinted at in her eyes. Sometimes he
looked there and felt an irrational fear, seeing a reflection
of his own demons. Then all he saw was passion. She
would only let her guard down for a few moments before
shoring up her defenses and deflecting his curious gaze.

The feeling of a shared bond continued to torment
Nick after each liaison. While he wanted to share his own
secret, he also understood that he could not do so
easily—it was too fantastic, and traumatically so—to
share with anyone. And he knew that as much as he

wanted her to share her secret with him, she would view hers in exactly the same way. Still, this similarity *was* the bond, and Nick was intelligent enough to catch the irony.

Within a year Nick had moved into Caroline's East Side apartment, a cavernous space of white-painted woodwork and shiny wood floors, where they grew closer even as they deftly dodged discovery by relatives, friends, and colleagues. Nick's name no longer appeared on her class lists, however, so the intensity of an illicit relationship no longer hovered over them.

Lupo threw off his blankets and snarled. It was impossible to keep the images from his mind. No matter what abstract terms he used in his head, the visuals always began with her face and ended with her mutilated remains.

Blood.

It had splattered everywhere.

He had awakened thirsty as always, mouth coated in blood. Human flesh. His head ached so hard it seemed as though it would burst. And the body next to his, what was left of it, was Caroline's. It was as if he'd torn her apart, a crazed Jack the Ripper. He choked back vomit and tears, realizing that it was too late for that, too late for anything but covering up, trying to escape with his life, trying to move on without her, the one thing in his life that had made sense.

He whimpered and cried all day, but he wiped and cleaned and removed every bit of his life from her surroundings, thankful now that they had never added his name to the lease. Yes, they would know she'd had a lover and there would be a description, but no one would connect him directly with her, would they? It had been years since he'd been her student, and the university faculty had turned over somewhat. No one would remember that she'd been rumored to have slept with a student, and so many profs were doing it that no one would have mentioned it if they did.

Nick Lupo had managed to disappear from Caroline Stewart's life, but she could never disappear from his, haunting his existence with the guilt he would always feel, knowing what he had done.

To this day, Lupo's sleep was affected by the memories of Caroline, and now he had to add a new name to his list of failures. *Corinne*. The woman who could have replaced Caroline was gone, too, and he surely shared in the blame.

He cried in his sleep, wishing away his cursed existence.

CHAPTER FIFTEEN

MARTIN

He awoke with the *Feeling*.

His eyes were still closed, but he came awake with the same unaccustomed suddenness.

Sounds squeezed into his head. Someone shouting in the hallway. A door slamming. Footsteps past his door and down the concrete stairs.

None of it mattered. Not with the Feeling rapidly making its way through his body.

The itch in his hands burned with the intensity of a propane torch, as if the blue flame were licking his skin and charring it in the most delicate way possible. It was a sensation he had come to both dread and savor, in the way of most things in his life.

The cheap alarm clock on his nightstand kept time with a loud, inelegant clacking. He had bought it when the other alarm clock proved too difficult to program, like a damned computer. This one was old-fashioned—big black numbers on a white face, with big knobs on the back. Sometimes he thought the sound of it rattled in his brain, and sometimes it seemed so far away it was nearly muffled by his own breathing.

He catalogued each tiny nuance of the *Feeling* carefully, keeping track of any new ones. There had been no new nuances since his time in Cincinnati, which probably meant he was due for something new.

The itch in his hands was driving him insane and, by this point, his erection was rock-hard and straining at the single sheet that covered him. Sweat broke out on his forehead and dribbled sideways down his face and into the pillow. He handled himself, gently at first, then more roughly, the itch driving him on until he could wait no longer.

He opened his eyes and turned his head far enough to look at the ancient chest of drawers near the bed. On its scarred top sat the Case. Old-fashioned, covered with a fading flower print. Safe. Exactly the way it was on the day he had taken its possession. He flashed back, for a second, on that first blush of ownership—how he had caressed and fondled the Case long into the night, driving himself beyond any hope of return, and how he had finally accepted what *the Case* meant to him, and the perfection of the way in which he had gained ownership. As he thought about that day, he felt himself surrendering to the memory fully and without restraint. He held himself as he stared at *the Case,* mentally preparing for the next part of his ritual.

Slowly, but without effort, Martin sat up in the bed and let the sheet slip off his loins. He felt slick there, his hand warm and comforting. Without taking his eyes off *the Case,* he slid out of bed and slowly approached the bureau. He reached out and put his hand on *the Case,* fingering the cylinders inside through the thinning fabric, a quiver running through his belly and below.

His eyes roved upward and met those of the Martin in the mirror. They were the same, Martin and he, but only to a point. Martin knew that the other Martin pushed him

farther than he wished to go, that the other Martin sometimes dictated his behavior. But he also knew that he often liked the direction the other Martin pushed him.

It had served him well in the Institute, his skill at playact-
ing. He had played the Martin-in-the-mirror game with
them until they believed in his belief without reservation—
that a version of himself which resided only in mirrors
could force him to act in ways generally not associated
with his own behavior patterns. In that way, many of Martin's more outrageous actions could be written off as the influence of Martin-in-the-mirror. He had found himself so
adept at acting out this delusion that, after a dozen years,
he sometimes wondered whether it was acting, or had always been true, or whether he had made it *come* true.

*What is this? What have you done, Martin? Oh, my God,
you've soiled your sheets again! This is intolerable. I'm going to tell Dr. Berthold! I just can't trust you to keep yourself
clean, can I?*

I'm sorry, Miss Dievers, Martin whimpered. *I had to go,
but he wouldn't let me! He told me I had to just do it here
or burst!*

*The teenager pointed at the bureau mirror, and the nurse
found herself looking into it as if there was a chance she
would see Martin's tormentor somewhere inside, but all
she saw was her own nose and mouth wrinkled at the
smell that came from the boy's bed and had now permeated the whole room and her clothes and ruined her dinner, which sat half-eaten at her station (just waiting for her
to return so she could toss it into the wastebasket—like
most of her meals when she was assigned to this floor, she
suddenly realized). She rolled her eyes at her own image
and got to work, gathering up the bedclothes and fussing
the boy until he was heading for the bathroom down the
hall. She would check on him in a minute, to make sure he
was scrubbing off the half-dried patches of his own waste.
She would throw out the now-unappetizing remains of her
meal and then write up a Martin-in-the-mirror report for*

Berthold to go over in the morning, the day's fifth. She wondered, briefly, just how real this imagined Martin was to the young man who claimed he was forced to do things by this image only he could see. Well, that was Berthold's problem. His territory, his patient, his problem. She just wished she could have been transferred out of the chronic wing, so she could at least have some respite from the loonies.

After she had remade his bed and disposed of the ruined sheets, she checked on him as he stood in the trickling shower. She stepped back, startled, when she saw him handling his engorged penis, the whole while carrying on a conversation with no one—there was no one else in the communal shower. Wait, no, that was untrue. She stood half-in and half-out, watching Martin talking to his own image in the full-length mirror bolted to the wall that faced into the shower room. Martin wasn't standing in the spray, because then he couldn't have seen himself in the mirror, but he was naked and fully engaged in self-pleasure. Despite herself and her long experience, she felt a blush creeping up her features.

Yeah, I know Dievers has beautiful lips, Martin was saying to the mirror, and I really like when her lipstick is so dark and wet, and almost purple. But I don't think she's interested in me at all, I'm just another weirdo. I know she's not that old! Yeah, and I know she'd probably love to take my thing in her mouth and get lipstick all over it, but I'm just not gonna ask her, okay? I don't care how much you beg me, I'm not gonna ask. You come out of that mirror and ask her yourself, you want it that bad!

Nurse Dievers had put a hand to her mouth in shock and bewilderment, and now she looked at her fingers and saw the streak of mauve on her skin. That was it, no more lipstick while on duty! And this would have to be another Martin-in-the-mirror report, and she would ask Berthold for a new assignment again.

In the shower room, the nineteen-year-old Martin was caressing himself to orgasm, looking straight into his own image in the mirror and grunting with animal satisfaction.

*Was there any way to change this boy's behavior? she
wondered, slowly backing out of the steaming room.*

*She didn't see the smiling Martin turn his head toward
the sound of the door clicking softly closed.*

Now he smiled at the memory. He never knew how she
felt as she spied on him that night, but she had stopped
wearing lipstick and, three weeks later, she had left her
job for good. Martin had merely filled in the gaps in his
knowledge and formed a fully rounded memory of the
event. He enjoyed reliving that half hour from her point of
view, but he did feel regret that he was never able to determine whether she would have placed her lips on him if
given the opportunity.

Martin unzipped the makeup case—

(his mother's makeup Case; *the Case*)

—and rummaged through the canisters, knowing that
he would recognize the one he needed now as soon as he
saw it.

It was a shade called Berry Mauve, and it came in a
white container. He separated it from the other white canisters and set the Case aside, then he uncapped it and
slowly, tantalizingly twisted the bottom.

He felt a delicious shiver stir his genitals as the rounded
tip came into view. A tiny purple phallus growing in
length until his trembling hand conveyed it to his lips and
he began to draw, as carefully as he had learned (no, had
been *taught*), filling in his lips until he pursed and—for a
second—saw Nurse Dievers in the mirror. Then it was just
Martin again, or Martin-in-the-mirror.

He inhaled deeply, enjoying the chemical cosmetic
smell of the lipstick under his nostrils. Slowly, he wiped a
finger across his upper lip and smeared the mauve coloring
onto his cheek. With a shudder, Martin climaxed. He had
not touched himself further. As always, there was no need.

Nurse Dievers had missed out on this action, but she
would live on in Martin's memory. And in his memory she
always came back for more.

Martin sat on his bed and felt the need wash from his body. And the itch in his hands had stopped, for now. If the pattern held up, he would not feel the itch for another day or so. In the meantime, he could concentrate on other matters.

Without bothering to shower or dress, or wipe his lips, he turned to the Office Depot desk in the corner of the room. He took Volume Six from the pile and opened it flat, starting to read the smooth, right-leaning cursive.

Tears formed at the corners of his eyes, and he blinked them away. He always cried when reading Caroline's words.

Sweet Caroline.

He hummed a few bars of the song, then dabbed at his eyes again and turned to the text, the part he hated most. This was his sister's very first mention of the bastard, and already she was smitten. Every time Martin read the passages he felt the anger rising through his veins like boiling acid. Now he smashed his fist down on the desk and felt the rickety furniture wobble.

He opened the vinyl-covered diary again and lowered his nose to the yellowing pages, inhaling deeply, imagining that he could smell her scent, and picking up the smell of his lipstick as well, and in his fantasy this *was* her lipstick and he was with her, and they were doing what his father had taught him to do, except that now she was doing it—*the way it was meant to be,* said the voice in his head, the crazy Martin-voice he so hated—and she was good at it because their father had taught her, too, and she knew no better than to try harder to keep the blows at bay.

Aroused again, he decided to deprive himself, reluctantly closing the book and refiling it in order. Even though he knew well enough what came next in the two dozen journals, and the details his sister would divulge, it was still this volume—Caroline's first innocent mention of Dominic Lupo—that drove him to the red-framed rages his doctors had been unable to comprehend. He hadn't allowed them to comprehend. Hadn't wanted them to.

With a snort, Martin returned to the bureau and shakily refreshed his lipstick, making sure it was layered on heavily—*like a common whore,* his father would say, and then bending over to retrieve the duffel bag from near the bed. He reached in and took out the .44, caressing its cold metal with infinite tenderness.

Then, while staring at himself in the mirror, he slowly inserted the muzzle between his painted lips and did what his father had taught him to do. Martin watched the lipstick smear onto the gunmetal blue and felt himself rock-hard and ready to burst once again. The flat heads of the cartridges blunt in the cylinder, visible in their tiny vaginas, peeked at him like clitoral protrusions.

He ignored the tears that ran down the bloated face in the mirror and sparkled on the glossy painted lips. That was Martin-in-the-mirror, and what happened to him had nothing at all to do with what happened to Martin.

He wondered just how much pressure it would take, as his index finger caressed the trigger.

Afterward, he threw up until he thought his guts might well dislodge and spew out in great gouts of blood. But, as always, they didn't.

LUPO

Sitting in Ben's cluttered dining room, Lupo felt a little homesick. It reminded him of his parents' house—the religious painting on one wall, the crucifix on another. A flickering candle in front of the brownish portrait of a great-uncle lost in the last war. "Lost somewhere on the Russian Front," Ben would often say. "Most people don't even know how many Italians got killed there, coverin' Jerry's ass. They were betrayed and cut off so Hitler's bastards could live to fight another day, may the assholes rot in Nazi hell."

Marie, Ben's wife of nearly thirty years, would shush

him then, pointing at the youngest of the children, whose
ears extended like antennae around grown-up conversa-
tions so that he could echo their words at school the next
day. "Yeah, yeah," Ben would say with a gesture of dis-
missal. "He's gonna learn it anyway, he might as well learn
it from his old man."

This was ritual, as were the several glasses of potent red
wine that preceded dinner. As always at the Sabatini dinner table, Lupo was starting out half in the bag. He'd had a
full glass since walking in the door an hour ago, and as
much as he had knocked back, his glass still seemed to
be topped off. It was like some secret of invisibility—
someone filled the glass without Lupo ever seeing it happen. He *was* beginning to see double by the time Marie
smoothed out the tablecloth, rearranged the settings they
had brushed aside, and began serving the men and the
three youngest Sabatini children.

Given Lupo's mood that evening, seeing double was—
somewhat desirable.

They had spent the afternoon running theories on the
gunshop case, all while further tests were conducted by
the ballistics lab and by the ME. Everything was being
tested, it seemed, and nothing was going anywhere. Vic
had failed to call as promised, so they planned a visit to
his set early in the morning. Lupo really looked forward to
that, he pondered as he sipped the wine. He marveled at
how the ruby liquid looked like blood in the right light,
and how it lapped at the rim of the glass—filled again by
some unseen presence. He shrugged and drank some
more, letting the sweet liquid caress his palate.

"You gotta come over, Nick," Ben had said. "Marie's
been givin' me hell about not inviting you over. I keep
tellin' her it's you don't wanna come, but she don't believe
me. And me, I got to protect your reputation, Nick, 'cause
why would you keep turnin' us down?"

Lupo had smiled and nodded. "I'd like to see Marie and
the kids again," he said. But inside he felt caged, tethered,

leashed to the cases that were piling up on his desk—
taking his attention away from Corinne, where it belonged. The moon was nearly full, and the call of the
woods formed a powerful urge into an obsession. He
wanted to drive north and shed his humanity, shed his
anger in the cold woods and satiate his hunger for raw
flesh. He wanted all this, but it would be another day before he could take the time off. He had called his landlord
at her reservation office and left a message saying he
would likely be using the cabin this weekend, and now he
wanted nothing more than to be there.

Well, he would have traded that pleasure for one crack
at whoever had killed Corinne. Even if it cost his badge. He
hoped it would, so he wouldn't be bound by the ever more
constraining rules that seemed to hog-tie his every move.

Marie set a huge ceramic bowl of ravioli in the middle
of the table, and even Lupo—whose taste ran to rare red
meat—had to admit the vapor was tantalizing. This was
delicate ravioli, only about an inch and a half square, unlike the monstrous-size version available in most restaurants. Not only homemade, but infinitely better tasting.

Fortunately, he had talked the Sabatinis out of laying
out their best silver for the meal. The pain would have
driven him from their home. They had substituted a
bland stainless-steel pattern, not at all sure they understood his quirks but letting him have them and giving in
graciously.

Lupo swallowed deep red wine and surveyed the elab-
orately set table and the spread-out food. This was too
much. *Too much like home.* Maybe he would call his parents one of these days, see if his father would still refuse
to talk to him. The food was a concrete reminder that he
was letting his heritage slip away, and he felt a vague
shame reddening his face. Maybe the wine was to blame,
he thought, but there was definitely something else there.
Maybe it was the fact that he hadn't seen his parents in
years. Lupo watched Marie, Ben's wife, and saw his

mother reflected. Marie was a plump, handsome woman whose chestnut hair was just now beginning to gray. And gracefully enough, too, as Ben used to say while rubbing his bald spot wistfully.

MARIE

Having Nick over for a meal was wonderful! They were so preoccupied, so serious. She wanted nothing more than to please them, and her children, with the comfort food they all loved.

She had done her best as a cop's wife, learning to live with the hours and the waiting and the uncertainty. Fortunately, the city was far from violent (if one didn't count occasional gang executions and drive-by shootings), and cops had always for the most part felt safe walking their beats. It was a deceptive safety, perhaps, but better than the outright danger of the Chicago streets from which she had come. So she thought nothing of the call when it came, taking it as she cleared away the remains of the first course. She had a platter of delicately stuffed Cornish hens waiting in the kitchen, and two bowls of mixed vegetables, but she let the men talk and laugh as she picked up the extension near the refrigerator.

"Good evening, madam." The voice was even, smooth, confident, and charming. "I'm sorry to bother you in the middle of your meal."

A polite police caller! Marie wondered at the possibility this was a joke. But no, it sounded like Detective Bialek.

"It's okay," she said as she hovered over her next course, ready to serve it as soon as this interruption could be handled. "You need Ben, right? I'll get him."

"No, dear lady. Actually I need to speak with Detective Lupo. Do you think you could ask him to take this call?"

Marie frowned. Bialek had never been so polite. So . . . mockingly urbane. That was it, she was picking up a hint of humor in the voice. It made her uncomfortable. Usually these calls meant Ben would leave for the rest of the night to help locate spent brass on some street corner, or speak to countless defiant witnesses regarding the body as often as not spread like a limp rag on a bloody sidewalk. This call sounded different.

"Yeah, I'll get Nick for you," she said into the phone.

"Certainly, Mrs. Sabatini."

Something cold seemed to trickle down her back. "Just a second, okay?"

She pushed the swinging door aside and caught the tail end of some off-color joke. She frowned at the three children, two boys and a girl, who were nodding and giggling even as their father repeated the punch line, exaggerating it for effect.

"Nick."

He turned. "What is it, Marie?"

Apparently, Ben felt it too. He waved the children's laughter down and stared at Nick for a second, then at his wife.

"Telephone. It's for . . . you."

LUPO

When she handed Lupo the receiver, its cord stretched through the door from the kitchen extension, Lupo wondered for a split second if her hand could be trembling. Plus, something in her voice tripped an inner alarm.

"Detective Lupo here," he barked into the phone. Chances were this was just somebody calling to tell him there was a new report to consider. Or maybe a new murder?

"Well, well."

The voice was quiet, almost hushed, but Lupo heard it perfectly. And he knew that his mysterious foe had tracked him down. He knew it as surely as if the man had identified himself. But the voice said nothing, choosing instead to wait.

"Yes?" Lupo snarled into the silence. "What is it?"

"You know, it's a cozy little gathering there at the Sabatini homestead. Touching, really. You seem to have so little by way of family life, Nick."

"Who are you?" Lupo didn't expect an answer, but he had to begin stalling. He gestured to Ben—*trace the call, use your cell to call in!*—who stood up quickly and knocked over his chair. The children caught the serious intensity and jumped up nervously, but Marie whispered soothing words, quieting them down. Her eyes followed her husband out of the room.

The voice spoke in Lupo's ear. "Why, I thought you'd know me by now. I'm somewhat miffed at your selective memory, Nick."

"Give me a hint."

"*This one's for you, Nick.* How's that?"

"That wasn't in the paper," he growled. Helpless stalling.

"That's right. So I must be a real-live suspect, right?"

"Why did you kill her?" Lupo felt his hand tremble, so he switched the phone to his left. "What was the point? What did you prove, you—"

"I killed her as a warm-up, Detective Lupo. A milk run. An opening act, if you will. Now there's been an act two. But you, you're the main event. I just want to lead up to you and you can be the climax. That should suit you."

Lupo let that sink in for another stalling beat. "Why?"

"Don't let your Cornish hens get cold, Nick. I don't feel like ending the game just yet. Keep in mind, though, that I will get around to you. Eventually."

As soon as he heard the click, Lupo was up and at the door and passing through into the living room.

Ben was babbling into his cell phone. Then he slammed it into the couch and looked at Lupo, shrugging. "Not fucking long enough. And they're pretty sure it was a goddamn cell."

Lupo nodded. He'd thought so. There had been a metallic echo in the quietly mischievous voice.

"I think there may be another body. For us to find, I mean. He said Corinne was the opening act, and now there's been an act two. Call it in, have patrols check mall bathrooms."

Ben nodded and dialed.

Damn this savage asshole to hell. Now he was playing his games in the open. Who the hell did he think he was, calling Ben's house like that? Scaring his family.

Of course, that was the point. He had succeeded, if Marie's expression meant anything.

Lupo returned the phone to the kitchen.

"Don't let your Cornish hens get cold, Nick."

Lupo heard the words in his mind just as his eyes swept across the counter and he saw Marie's platter of hens. The second course.

"Damn it," he shouted, and then he was at the back door, his Glock in hand. "He was calling from here, goddamnit!"

MARTIN

He tiptoed to the back of the driveway. The house was a typical Milwaukee bungalow, with the kitchen in the rear, the dining room in the center, and the living room up front. He was lucky this wasn't gravel, or his little game might have been more dangerous, and maybe not worth playing.

Ever since he had seen Tim Robbins employ this same maneuver in *The Player,* Martin had planned the day he too could so coolly rattle a victim while watching. He *liked* to watch. The cellular phone still had some blood marring its sleek black lines, but he had managed to wipe most of it off, and now it rested easily in his hand. The wife was a wise one, that he could sense right away. The way she read his voice. It was uncanny. And Ben had seemed less like an old man and more like a cop as he went from room to room with the phone in his hand, working on a trace that could never be. The children were easily scared, and Martin carefully filed away their faces. Just in case, he thought, even though he had no quarrel with them. Still, one never knew when pawns might become necessary.

But Lupo. Lupo was cold on the phone, maybe not quite catching on at first. But making up for it fast. Martin said his words, his watch up near his eyes so he could see the second hand sweeping across the face.

Why pretend?

Well, because it's fun.

Because he wanted very badly to drive Lupo to something unthinkable. Might the cop take advantage of his *condition* here and now? Martin doubted it, but half wished he would. The weight of the Smith & Wesson in its holster gave off strength, power. The silver loads were a hedge, really, in case all that folklore bullshit was correct. But he trusted his sister, his lovely sister, and in her own words she'd described what the cop could become. She had also mentioned that at least one myth, the deadly quality of silver, was true.

He'd used the Cornish hen reference just to test the odds, to challenge himself. He chuckled as he set the cell phone on top of the Sabatini mailbox and disappeared into the shadows of the neighbor's overgrown hedges.

This little gambit had been too easy, and way too much fun. The fun was addictive, and he hoped he could have more before he ended the game.

LUPO

His nostrils flared in the chill of the night.

Damn it, the sonofabitch had stood right here, a phone in his hand.

"Shit!"

Lupo could smell him, could sense the lingering presence of the man he'd stalked in the tunnel at the mall. The same man who had been through his trash, and Corinne's.

And now the man who had offed some poor bastard for his phone, Lupo thought as he picked up the cracked plastic instrument with a clean handkerchief.

He considered attempting a controlled Change, but only for a moment. Ben was huffing down the driveway, pistol in hand. The time wasn't right for a face-to-face. Not yet.

But soon, Lupo promised the night air. *Soon enough.*

Then he remembered Rag's silver slugs.

He shivered.

MARTIN

Later, he replayed the scene in his mind, imagination furnishing those delicious details that he had missed because of the dangerous location and the fact that he was well aware it wouldn't take long for Lupo to catch on. He had been confident in his ability to outwit the trace Lupo's partner would attempt—after all, that was why he had gone through the trouble of obtaining a cell phone with a current account—but he had imagined that Lupo would catch on almost immediately. So Martin felt surprise—and some disappointment—that Lupo's long experience as a cop hadn't kicked in and led the freak detective out of the house earlier.

Martin had enjoyed the catch of fear he heard in the old Sabatini broad's voice when she realized that he was not the usual police caller. He had also enjoyed the freak's wary tone as the woman had handed him the phone, and Martin would have given anything to have been there when the old cop realized that his sainted family was now in danger. Marked by a dangerous criminal such as himself. God, how he enjoyed the fear his victims felt when they first realized they were about to become his playthings—their fear would build nicely from there, of course, but nothing would ever match that first quaver in the voice, that verbal question mark hovering just this side of the all-out terror Martin would induce. Fear was delicious, he had realized at an early age, and a weapon to be feared. He loved the paradox.

Now he sat in the center of his large downtown loft apartment.

Well, not *his,* exactly. It belonged to the old man he had strangled and whose body was folded into the coffinlike freezer Martin had ordered and had delivered a day after. The old man was Dr. John Freiburg, a name from the past. Freiburg was Martin's uncle, his mother's older brother, and a psychiatrist though he had recently retired. Martin suspected that their uncle's profession had had something to do with Caroline's choice of career. When Martin showed up at his door, the old man remembered Martin quite well. After all, the juvenile Martin Stewart had killed his parents, one of whom was the old doctor's sister. He should have slammed the door in Martin's face. But Martin had played the card of his release from the Institute, and played it well. Freiburg was a true believer. He had staked his life on therapy and his psychiatric studies, and Martin was so clean-cut, so eloquent, and so quietly innocent, that the doc was bound to accept that Martin's years under psychiatric care had indeed rehabilitated him. After a long and emotional session, Freiburg had consented to take Martin in as an assistant, especially when Martin had explained how he too was writing a book about his life in therapy. This had tickled the old doctor, who was writing a book on some syndrome or other. Martin's acting had never been so convincing.

The old man had no living relatives, which suited Martin just fine, but he did have neighbors—well-off neighbors he only saw occasionally, but nonetheless people who would likely see Martin. Considering the history of Martin's family, Martin had little trouble talking the old man into introducing him as the doctor's newly hired home-care giver. Martin, good old Martin who could be anyone, had looked the part—devoted home-care giver—with little or no effort. A pressed white shirt, buttoned to the collar. Shined shoes. Hair less than medium length and neatly combed. He was a poster boy for either home care or for Jehovah's Witnesses. The old man had taken him in eagerly enough (maybe because Martin was sure he'd been gay and Martin reminded him of a lost lover) and within days had given him the run of the house, introduced him to the two neighbors who mattered most in this old loft building, and shown him where everything of value was stored. Everything else Martin found for himself.

Then Dr. Freiburg had "taken ill" and the neighbors saw only Martin, who did the old man's laundry regularly and made sure he was seen carrying prescriptions and food and other home medical goods to his "patient." Martin had strangled Freiburg in a most matter-of-fact way. Like the cell phone guy and Rag the gun dealer, the old man meant nothing to him. He wasn't even a connection to Caroline. He was just something in the way that had to be moved (or *removed*) and then Martin could carry on with the rest of his plans. He took no real pleasure in *these* acts of violence. They were necessary, and he tried to remain pragmatic about them. Now, the hooker in the photo booth, that was fun. In some ways that had been even better than Lupo's friend Corinne. He thought it was because they'd almost been caught. He wondered why they hadn't found the woman yet, but it didn't matter. They'd find her soon now.

Before killing him, Martin had forced Freiburg to send e-mail to his friends and colleagues to tell them that he would be traveling abroad for a year. Martin learned how to forge Freiburg's signature, took control of the old man's finances, then dyed his hair a blond shade that seemed a closer match to Freiburg's license photo. He added clear glasses bought from a Walgreens store, and—outside the building—began to live Freiburg's life, turning it into his own. He told Freiburg's building manager (with the help of a letter from the doc himself and a five-hundred-dollar "tip") that his uncle would be residing in a clinic for a while and that he was homesitting. Slowly sinking into his Freiburg/Freiburg's nephew persona, Martin now drew cash from the old man's accounts, into which mutual fund and stock dividends poured automatically along with pension and royalty checks. Martin's forgery of Freiburg's signature allowed him to access the checking accounts he'd opened at different banks, and to access the rest of the accounts he found that the bank card worked quite well at ATMs, which couldn't detect his more intense Freiburg disguise when he used them at night. For all intents and purposes, Martin had become both Freiburg and Freiburg's nephew, as well as his home-care giver. Martin was thrilled with the acting job that went along with the various personas—he'd built a career out of playing parts, and this allowed him to stretch himself as an amateur thespian.

He found that sometimes he talked to the old man, his uncle. He'd open the freezer and slap the old man's ice-crusted head like one might a small child's or a dog's. "Hey, Uncle," he might say, "you should see what I did today! Thanks for giving me another chance!"

"You're welcome," he'd reply for the old man, who clearly was in no mood to talk. "You're such a good boy! Such a good example of the power of therapy!"

"Yes, Uncle," he would say, closing the freezer. "Don't go anywhere!"

He enjoyed his new life, Martin did, because it allowed him to become so many new people when he needed to.

But right now, in the loft, Martin wanted to enjoy the afterglow of his visit to the Sabatini household. *Oh, yes, Uncle! That was a beauty!* He steeped in the memory of the fear he had induced. The remote control held in one hand and the flickering screen before him, only six feet away.

On the screen, limbs were sweatily entangled in a tableau that the bright lighting eventually revealed as three persons, two male and one female, engaged in various sexual acts of the sandwich variety. Martin thumbed up the volume slightly, smiling at the throaty moaning that came from the blond woman, whose extremities were being penetrated by one male's aroused fullness and the other's slithery tongue. While one male thrust rapidly in and out of her loins, the other smothered the blonde's mouth with his, lipstick smearing on the skin of both.

"Corey Diamond" had made this video only two months earlier, according to the Certificate of Compliance printed on the box. It was a local production, but there was not much in its eighty-seven minutes to prove it. All the sets were generic interiors—an office, a hotel room, two bedrooms, and a variety of cheap fantasy stages constructed in the Third Ward suite that housed Luxury Productions, Incorporated. The plot, such as it was, consisted of a woman's search for an elusive diamond stolen from a museum, and allowed her to bed a variety of cops, security guards, private eyes, insurance investigators, chambermaids, thieves, and even several museum patrons at once. This was one of Corinne Devereaux's pro videos, one of the better ones. Martin had stacked some others near the flat-panel television and VCR/DVD cart—the room's only other furniture, which he'd bought to upgrade his uncle's ancient television. Martin forwarded the disc at 2x speed, slipping back into regular-speed Play when the two museum guards positioned Corinne between them and began to perform what the industry called a "DP," a double penetration, which had become a staple of the porn world. Here the cinematography was crisp and unflinching, switching between two cameras to capture the physical aspect of what was happening to Corinne and her facial responses as recorded in close-up by a third camera just inches from her sweat-slick face.

Martin stopped the disc in Still mode when the image was of Corinne's face bloated with lust—lids half-closed, mouth open halfway between a moan and a scream and with pink lipstick smeared in blushing lines across her chin and cheeks. This was his favorite spot on the video, and he couldn't get enough of it. The director was clearly a man whose tastes meshed perfectly with his. Balancing the remote on the arm of his chair, he picked up his hand mirror with one hand and the open lipstick, an expensive Revlon pink, with the other. Eyes shifting between the frozen image on the screen and his own magnified reflection, he applied the lipstick. The result was a pouty look not unlike the one Corinne had worn at the beginning of the scene, until one guard's erection had been pushed into her mouth and dragged across her willing face.

Martin watched the frozen image and remembered his father's games, flashing into some of the games he himself had played in the last year. And he also remembered Caroline, whom Dominic Lupo had taken away from him. As he remembered, he massaged himself with long, oily strokes.

He watched and remembered and worked himself into a frenzy of lust and anger and anticipation. He shuddered in waves and then it was over.

When he was finished, Martin sat in the dark and let the harsh colors of the television screen wash over his own distorted features. His shame and disgust were matched only by his anger and lust for revenge.

He smeared the lipstick onto his chin and cheeks until his face resembled Corinne's after the two men were finished with her and she was covered with globules of semen. For a second, Martin identified with her to such an extent that he might as well have *been* her—he could almost see his own face there, on the flickering screen.

And one of the two men, now busy stuffing himself back into the cheap guard's uniform, was his own father. Yes, Martin remembered well the games his father had taught him. They still brought him the only relief he could find.

Damn his father. Damn his mother. Damn them all.

He felt the tears course down his smudged cheeks. He hadn't felt them squeeze out of the corners of his eyes, but he felt them now as they slowly ran through the sticky streaks. The Martin who resided in the hand mirror cried too.

Very soon he would tighten the screws on Detective Dominic Lupo once again.

He forced himself to smile, to will the tears away.

For the first time that night, Martin's smile finally reached into a well of sincerity and his mood was past. There was planning to do, and now was as good a time as any. He started the disc again and got dressed as the late Corinne Devereaux aka Corey Diamond stared into the camera and pouted after her partners had evidently brought her to orgasm. Her face was beautiful, bathed in thin strands of pearly semen. She looked into the lens and smiled right at him, licking her lips seductively.

He smiled back.

Video was just like being there.

LUPO

The blood on the cellular phone belonged to one Harry R. Singer.

At least, that was the assumption. No one had heard from Mr. Singer for two days. Known to spend weeks at a time traveling on business, his absence had not yet raised suspicions when Lupo and Ben traced him through his cellular phone number. Unfortunately, no other calls had been made from his phone recently.

The lab had picked up a perfect set of prints, but like

GET UP TO 4 FREE BOOKS!

You can have the best fiction delivered to your door for less than what you'd pay in a bookstore or online—only $4.25 a book! Sign up for our book clubs today, and we'll send you **FREE* BOOKS** just for trying it out...**with no obligation to buy, ever!**

LEISURE HORROR BOOK CLUB

With more award-winning horror authors than any other publisher, it's easy to see why CNN.com says "Leisure Books has been leading the way in paperback horror novels." Your shipments will include authors such as RICHARD LAYMON, DOUGLAS CLEGG, JACK KETCHUM, MARY ANN MITCHELL, and many more.

LEISURE THRILLER BOOK CLUB

If you love fast-paced page-turners, you won't want to miss any of the books in Leisure's thriller line. Filled with gripping tension and edge-of-your-seat excitement, these titles feature everything from psychological suspense to legal thrillers to police procedurals and more!

As a book club member you also receive the following special benefits:

- **30% OFF all orders through our website & telecenter!**
- **Exclusive access to special discounts!**
- **Convenient home delivery and 10 days to return any books you don't want to keep.**

There is no minimum number of books to buy, and you may cancel membership at any time. See back to sign up!

YES! ☐

Sign me up for the Leisure Horror Book Club and send my TWO FREE BOOKS! If I choose to stay in the club, I will pay only $8.50* each month, a savings of $5.48!

YES! ☐

Sign me up for the Leisure Thriller Book Club and send my TWO FREE BOOKS! If I choose to stay in the club, I will pay only $8.50* each month, a savings of $5.48!

NAME: _____

ADDRESS: _____

_____

TELEPHONE: _____

E-MAIL: _____

☐ **I WANT TO PAY BY CREDIT CARD.**

☐ VISA   ☐ MasterCard.   ☐ DISCOVER

ACCOUNT #: _____

EXPIRATION DATE: _____

SIGNATURE: _____

Send this card along with $2.00 shipping & handling for each club you wish to join, to:

Horror/Thriller Book Clubs
20 Academy Street
Norwalk, CT 06850-4032

Or fax (must include credit card information!) to: 610.995.9274.
You can also sign up online at www.dorchesterpub.com.

*Plus $2.00 for shipping. Offer open to residents of the U.S. and Canada only.
Canadian residents please call 1.800.481.9191 for pricing information.
If under 18, a parent or guardian must sign. Terms, prices and conditions subject to change. Subscription subject
to acceptance. Dorchester Publishing reserves the right to reject any order or cancel any subscription.

JOIN NOW!

those from the gun shop they seemed to be a dead end.
Lupo had not officially connected the gun shop murder
to Corinne's, and he hated considering the possible slay-
ing of Harry Singer a third connecting point. It might raise
too many questions about his inside knowledge. No one
but Ben really knew Corinne had been his friend. The
bloody message on the wall was directed at him, but the
word was out that Satanists were involved. Ben probably
suspected the original message was meant for Lupo, but
he hadn't said a word. Now that Ben had been dragged
into it, maybe somebody would spot the connection, but
for now they were playing it as if the psycho knew they'd
been assigned and was pulling a Jack the Ripper, goading
the police. If Lupo stated the gunsmith's murder was connected, what then? Surely no serious cop would see the
significance of the silver bullets. Or might someone? It
seemed that someone already had.

And what about prints? This guy made no effort to keep
his prints off crime-scene items. Obviously, he didn't have
a record, or he had found a novel way to hide one. Lupo
had to admit, he was stumped. Not only because the guy's
identity was a mystery, but also because it seemed unlikely that someone could kill so easily, so enthusiastically,
without having done it before. And if he'd done it before,
then there should have been a record of it. Somewhere.

Lupo sat at his desk and doodled on a legal pad. His
drawings all had a tendency to turn into guns or
airplanes—it had been like that since his childhood. His
grandmother had always said that he'd become either a
soldier or a pilot, though she would have preferred a
priest.

*Ha! Hell of a priest I'd have made! Half of my friends are
misfits and rejects, and the other half spend most of their
time chasing down the first half.*

Almost incongruously, the ELP song "Welcome Back My
Friends To the Show That Never Ends" popped into his
head. If only he could think.

How might there *not* be a record of the perp?

He fashioned a Luger P-08 pistol into a supersonic jet fighter and then back again, with the addition of a shoulder stock. Guns and planes, planes and guns. Maybe he did have a one-track mind. But then, perps didn't usually leave messages for the cops, except in cheap B-movies. That is, unless you counted bullet-riddled corpses and blood splatters as messages.

Secret messages, that only cops could read.

Secret messages.

Lupo found himself doodling the figure of a man in a trench coat. He drew in dark glasses and scrawled FBI underneath, then added an arm carrying a manacled briefcase. The other arm he added held a silenced Walther PPK in its surrealistic fist. The figure was just enough out of proportion to be funny, almost like a caricature, but Lupo wasn't laughing. It had just occurred to him that federal intelligence agents might well have their prints kept off the record, and it was a cinch they *loved* your basic torture and murder scenario. Lupo snorted—every fed he'd ever met had given him the creeps, like when you pick up a rock in the park and there's something dead smeared under it and insects are crawling all over the dead matter, and you drop the rock because you don't care about being macho, that stuff's just too damn disgusting to look at.

Too far-fetched. His guy wasn't a fed gone rogue.

Who else? Who else could keep his prints off the record?

Lupo smiled grimly. If it wasn't intelligence or law-enforcement agents, what about people who had friendships or connections to such agents? He drew a line from his FBI caricature to a shadowy figure he concocted out of squiggly lines, and whose face he obscured with a cartoon cloud. Witness protection programs had been known to harbor criminals who were still a menace to society after their identities were changed or buried. Some became an even greater menace precisely *because* they were thus protected, and the system often granted them immunity. Lupo scrawled "WPP" with a question mark under his unknown-man caricature, then he drew another line from the FBI agent and sketched in a raincoat and bowler hat–wearing figure brandishing a closed umbrella—diplomatic immunity? A renegade foreign diplomat? Possible, but not likely. He hadn't actually *felt* the aura of a cover-up, at least not yet, and something like this would have left a vacuum as the lid was pushed into place. No, that scenario was no more than a remote chance. It was another bad movie script, not everyday reality.

There had to be other habitual criminals who had somehow wiped their prints from all known databases. It was just a matter of time, and running down all the possibilities. But he had to do it without revealing what he knew, or what the perp seemed to know.

Lupo checked his watch. It was almost time for their appointment with Lieutenant Bowen. The lieutenant had been in his office all day, a steady stream of visitors—mostly suits from city hall—slithering their way in and out in unusually quick shifts. Lupo wished he could peer through the closed blinds behind the old-fashioned reinforced glass of Bowen's door.

He glanced across the squadroom at Ben, who was standing still for a change, staring out a window at the gray spring day as if somehow frozen between two activities. Ben seemed to be moving even though he stood immobile, his implied forward motion not so much muscular as neurotic.

Just hours earlier, Ben had been visibly shaken by the assault on his home and family. Lupo understood. Ben considered the smug phone call from the driveway an assault, and his request for a day-and-night police patrol was quickly and quietly granted by Lieutenant Bowen. Lupo had slept on the Sabatini couch, his Glock cocked on the cocktail table only inches away from his hands.

Marie Sabatini had seemed flustered the rest of the evening, and the children were subdued until they had kissed their uncle Dominic good night before heading off to their beds.

"Thanks for staying the night, Nicky. I really appreciate it." Ben had worn a somber look as he shook his partner's hand. "If I ever get a hold of that sonofabitch, I'm gonna cut his balls off. Sitting in the driveway like that, staring in at *my* family, my *kids,* scarin' my wife to death. He's a real sicko, and I'm gonna take him down if it's the last thing I do."

Lupo just nodded, knowing words wouldn't measure up against Ben's fear and anger. Ben jacked a shell into the Remington pump he kept for home protection. Lupo figured there was no way the guy would return—his goal had been accomplished—but the shotgun would reassure Ben.

Now Ben came over to Lupo's desk. "I sent Marie and the kids to my brother's farm out near New Glarus. I think it's best they're out of here. My brother works at home, and he's well-armed." He looked at Lupo. "No way this jack-off is getting near my family ever again. My kids are too young for this. I'm hopin' they're not traumatized by what happened."

Lupo almost spoke in agreement. Instead he grunted as a picture formed in his mind. He looked down at his doodles. Too *out there*. But Ben had said "Too young . . . I hope they're not traumatized . . ." and the words flipped a switch in Lupo's brain.

"What about a juvie?"

Ben froze. They knew they were butting heads with a brick wall for suspects, but obviously he caught the meaning immediately. "Sealed records?"

"You got it. Might explain why killing's not new to him, but there are no records."

"Fuck! I'll get right on it and run a database search. How far back?"

Lupo thought. "Go back a long ways. Thirty, forty years."

"Nick, some of those records won't be converted to machine-readable form yet. They're working backwards. I think they're up to the mid- or late seventies."

"It's a start. Maybe we'll get lucky."

Ben nodded and hurried off.

Minutes later in Bowen's office, Lupo once again found himself staring at the dozen or so framed color photographs the lieutenant had placed on his paneled walls. An avid outdoorsman and hunter, he had recorded some of his most treasured kills with the careful fastidiousness of an artist. Each photograph showed Bowen as the victor, but left the victim with a strange kind of dignity. For instance, though he had won his contest against a ferocious-looking grizzly bear, Bowen had somehow managed to capture the beast's awesome majesty—even in death. And the way Bowen cradled the antlered head of the elk spoke of the love Bowen had felt for the beast.

Just before blowing it away with a .458-caliber high-velocity fully jacketed slug from his prized Weatherby rifle.

It was a whispered joke among homicide squad detectives that if Bowen had loved the beasts as much as the photos showed, he wouldn't have killed them in the first place.

It was also understood that if the Tac Team ever needed another sniper, Bowen's name was on the short list of those who would get the call. Behind the stock of a rifle, Bowen was the best. And his photograph collection drove the point home again and again. Rumor had it he'd learned sniping as a Green Beret toward the end of Vietnam and liked it. Everybody believed the rumors.

Lupo hoped Bowen never had a chance to hunt wolf. Every time he had the thought, he felt the shivers creeping up his spine. Now it brought him back into the conversation.

"What I'd like to know is why you haven't been able to

match any prints," Bowen was saying. He had a gravelly Robert Mitchum kind of voice, a voice that went with the image. Maybe a little too well. Too studied. But it fit, and that was the bottom line.

"Nobody has him on file," Lupo said. "We've lifted pristine entire sets, but it's a no-go. The Bureau, Interpol, the Yard—you name it. I've sent e-mail to all my contacts, with attached files explaining what we need. Nothing, so far. That's probably why he's never made an effort to hide his prints."

"And what does that mean?" Bowen glared at them until Ben cleared his throat.

"He's either a first-timer or he's got some way to alter his prints, which ain't likely."

"Or he has friends in high places," Lupo said, surprising even himself for stating this thought half in jest. He didn't want to mention the sealed records just yet, and he'd convinced Ben to go along.

Bowen nodded. "Maybe. But he's sure as hell no first-timer. He likes it too much. These acts are obviously related. He's on a mission. You just need to figure out what it is."

Without making myself a suspect, Lupo thought. *Or getting myself killed in the process. No sweat. What the hell does the perp know about me, and how?*

"Have you gentlemen made some time to speak to the doc about this? Seems to me that should have been one of your first stops."

Ben and Lupo looked at each other and shook their heads.

"So, there you are. See her today. *Now.*"

Lupo sighed. This was a waste of time. Meanwhile, somewhere out there, the guy was thumbing his nose at him.

He was glad he had buried Corinne's letter, and that Ben was willing to cover up Lupo's connection to her. He glanced again at the photographs on Bowen's wall, at the way Bowen's hand and eyes caressed the dead animals.

Lupo hoped he never saw the same kind of concern in the lieutenant's gaze for *him*.

"Come on, Nick, let's get this over with." Ben stood in the open doorway, disgust written on his features.

They left the office without a second glance at Bowen, who snatched up a stack of color-coded folders and followed them out, then beelined down the hall.

Lupo waved Ben over to his desk again. It was piled high with manila folders and textbooks. Some time before a coffee cup had spilled, and it still sat in a congealed brown stain. They slouched into the two squeaky chairs.

Ben waved a folder he carried. "The filings at the gun shop were silver, just like you said. How'd you know?"

"Instinct."

"Ah, so," Ben said with a smirk.

"What do you think?" Lupo cocked his head at Bowen's door.

"Bowen's a dork," Ben said from a sideways slit in his mouth. "We smeared shit all over his desk, he'd still have to taste it to figure out what it is."

Lupo grinned without humor. "Still, he's got a point about the doc. We should have talked to her already."

Ben rolled his eyes. "I tried to make us an appointment yesterday—"

"Without telling me?"

"I'm telling you now. But her schedule was *full*. She wouldn't see us until sometime next week, the uppity broad."

"Great." Lupo tossed his clipboard onto the desk and strode off down the hall. "Let's move up on her agenda."

"Good luck."

A dozen offices down he stopped and rapped loudly on a closed door. The hallway traffic flowed around him without slowing down as he stared impatiently at the frosted glass. The woman who opened the door several inches moments later was severely dressed in a gray wool suit, her gray hair tied in a tight bun. Her lips were a red gash, slightly askew. A pair of gray wire-framed glasses seemed to float above her forehead.

"Yes, Detective?" Her tone was curt, barely polite.

"Doc Barrett." Lupo nodded and came right to the point. "Bowen wants me and my partner to consult with you on this murder at the mall."

"The prostitute?" Her distaste was palpable.

Lupo swallowed his anger and nodded. "I have the report on her, and it looks like some pretty weird shit went down after he killed her. We want to start getting a handle on this guy before he finds he really liked it and goes out to score again."

"Do you make him out as a potential serial?" She held the door so he couldn't see inside her office, as if she wanted to hide the person who was sitting inside with her. He could make out a trousered knee and a nervous hand resting on it.

"I think it's a possibility. We may need a task force," he added as an afterthought, to sweeten the deal if she had political aspirations.

Dr. Barrett seemed unimpressed. "Yes, I told your partner to make an appointment. I'll be glad to sit down with you and sort this out, but I have a tight schedule."

"What about today?" Lupo pressed. "It'll only take a few minutes."

She stepped through the tiny gap and stood in front of the door. Lupo took advantage of his greater height to attempt looking over her head at her guest, but she was too quick, and then they were both in the busy hallway, dodging the stubborn foot traffic that never seemed to abate during prime time.

"I'm afraid I can't be interrupted today. Send me an e-mail and we'll make an appointment for next week, and I'll be glad to help you then."

The door was closing in his face before he could respond, but his right foot shot out and stopped its arc. She glared at him but he didn't remove it, and her insistent pushing made no headway.

"I certainly don't mean to clutter your busy schedule, Doctor," Lupo spat, "but more innocent people could die if this jerk thinks he's getting away with it."

"I sincerely doubt any woman like that is innocent, Detective, and I'd guess they know the risks every time they climb into some john's car or shimmy into some hotel room, not to mention spread out on a cheap motel bed. Now, if you'll excuse me, I have a prior appointment. Surely Lieutenant Bowen would not want to hear of this harassment, if I make myself clear?"

Astounded, Lupo stepped back and watched the door slam. He stood for a full minute, ignoring the stares as people passed, letting his anger come down from full boil. He found it difficult to avoid pounding his fist on the doctor's door, but somehow he was able to channel the fury he felt into a long, low growl, which sufficed as an outlet. When he turned, he saw Ben smiling crookedly at him from down the hall. He squeezed past his partner and reached his desk in quick strides, then spent another thirty seconds rearranging the clutter with a sweeping hand until he had cleared a space large enough to accommodate a legal pad. Lupo rarely used his desk to work, preferring its unending storage potential.

"What'd I tell you?" Ben said from across their desks. "She's got some broomstick up her butt, and I'm not sure she doesn't enjoy it."

"Let's get out of here. I was going to put a note on her door, but I've got better things to do than start a war." He held up the pad, where he had scrawled: *Do not disturb the fucking doctor.*

Ben nodded wisely and walked away. "Better you than me, my friend."

"Whatever *that* means," Lupo muttered, following.

*   *   *

Ben drove, because he pointed out that Lupo was so upset that he would certainly break some minor traffic law and some rookie street cop would pull them over.

Without discussion they headed for the Third Ward again, driving the brief stretch of freeway and getting off at the Lakefront exit. Ben steered Lupo's Nissan Maxima through the decorative arch that spanned the revitalized road, announcing their entrance into the historic section of town. Within minutes, Ben pulled in behind a customized van and parked, a half block from the set of Vic's latest opus.

"How official is this?" Lupo said.

"How official you want it to be?"

"We don't have a warrant."

"We could get one, we ask nice."

Lupo grimaced and nodded. "We could probably find something to charge him with, without looking too hard."

"I bet."

Lupo sighed. "Much as I don't like the sleazebag, I don't think Vic's the murderous type. And if we pull him in, we might screw up enough to send the real guy packing to another state."

"We're on the same page, partner." Ben took a stick of cinnamon gum from his pocket, unwrapped it, and pushed it into his mouth.

"Assuming the real guy is somehow connected to Vic," Lupo mused.

"Like, a costar? A camera guy?"

Lupo wiped a hand over his mouth, feeling the bristly hairs scrape his lips. None of this sounded right, and it felt as if they were just going through the motions. "Maybe" was all he said.

The same burly doorman waved them through without a glance at their badges. "Camera's on," he muttered, fulfilling his duty admirably.

Lupo and Ben stepped inside. The center of the room was ablaze with impossibly bright lights humming on

stands and tripods, all aimed at a low bed frame. Two cam-
eramen were simultaneously recording the action from
different angles. Panting and a low moaning came from
the bed, which was half surrounded by sound technicians
with microphones, and other crew members. Vic stood off
to one side, his hand rubbing his chin absentmindedly.

Lupo could see that two performers were sprawled on
the bed, one atop the other, with a third about to step in.

"All right, Dick," Vic began. Somebody snickered, and
Vic shot the perpetrator a deadly look. "And . . . enter," Vic
said with complete seriousness. The chuckler struck
again, but no one seemed to care. The third actor lowered
himself onto the couple, impaling one of them—Lupo
couldn't tell which one—and soon all three were swaying
together in a chorus of moans.

It was hot in the room, due to both lights and sexual en-
ergy, and Lupo felt desperately in need of air. He'd seen
porn before, had even enjoyed it to some extent, but here
the act's mechanical nature—as the actors stopped while
someone snapped stills—and the crew's leering faces
and surreptitious groin-groping, and the memory of
Corinne's sideline all combined to produce a throbbing
ache in his head.

And in his heart, he realized.

Thankfully the scene was soon over, and the three actors
headed for the shower, sweat and semen shining on their
slick bodies. Vic saw to the stowing of the cameras person-
ally, then pretended to notice them for the first time.

"Detectives," he said by way of greeting. "Hope you enjoyed that as much as I did."

Lupo and Ben kept quiet, Lupo hoping their silence
might put him on edge, maybe enough to make him slip
and reveal something—anything—that could help in
their investigation.

"I can tell you, Detective, your friend Corey loved that
kind of scene. It was her favorite—couldn't get enough."

Lupo blinked, and when he opened his eyes it was as if

Vic were covered in a red haze. He felt the growl building way down in his throat, and he struggled to suppress it. He felt Ben's hand on his arm and let himself breathe slowly again, hearing Vic's words in midsentence.

". . . was going to bring them by, but since you're here I'll get them for you." He plucked a plain brown box from a nearby cocktail table and held it out. "Corey Diamond's only pro-am work for us, as well as the list of everyone who worked on them. As you requested. I hope you have DVD—we don't use much VHS anymore."

Lupo made no move to take the package, so Ben did, tucking it under his arm. "Anything else you have to tell us?"

Vic started shaking his head, but then thought better of it and nodded. "Yeah, one thing. I got this from one of the crew. Corey had been asking around for somebody to put up a Web site."

"A Web site?" Lupo asked.

"Yeah, you know, something like *www.coreydiamond. com* or whatever. A presence on the Web. Place to sell her videos, pictures, have her panties sold off to weirdos with fat wives, that kind of thing. Oh, and probably live video so guys could dial in and tell her what to do and watch her do it on a webcam. Most of the porn stars and wannabes have these sites. I think it would have been her next logical step in this glamorous career."

Lupo felt the rage simmering. Vic lived off them and bad-mouthed them in the same breath. Ben touched his arm and brought him back a little.

"Who gave you this information?"

"Soundman named Carter. He's gone home, though. Caught a flight to LA. I can get him back for you."

"Maybe later. Did she get beyond just asking around?"

Vic beamed widely. He had very nice teeth. "Very *good*, Detective! You beat me to the big announcement. Yes, Corey did find somebody and Carter knows him. I'll get you the name as soon as I can." He waited for a response. "You're welcome."

Ben pointedly avoided thanking Vic, who grinned too widely.

"Can I get back to work now?" Vic said with a smirk.

"Knock yourself out." Ben half-pushed, half-pulled Lupo along toward the door.

When they were standing in the stairwell, Lupo let out a long breath—as if he'd been saving it up.

"I'm no prude, Ben, but that guy . . . that guy makes me crazy. I don't know what it is."

"Heh, I got a word for it. Scum. That guy is scum."

"Maybe so. Let's get this over with."

"Yeah, this is the only kinda homework I'm ever gonna like."

Lupo made to punch his partner in the arm, but he was too slow. He dreaded what he'd see on the discs, what he would have to force himself to watch. For the sake of closure, if nothing else. And there might be a clue, something they could use.

Lupo felt the hairs on his back rising as if to meet the moon. In a way, that was exactly what they were doing.

CHAPTER SIXTEEN

MARTIN

When the doorbell pealed its one note, *Dr. Freiburg* opened the door.

The young woman who stood in the hall was stunning, but then he'd known she would be.

"Please come in," he said, stepping aside and closing the door, noting that no one was loitering in the hall. She smiled—a mite sadly, he thought—and then visibly put her training and experience to work. He smiled too. "I'm glad you could come."

She wore a leather skirt barely covering her coltish thighs and a gold lamé blouse cut dramatically low. Her hair displayed the studied disarray that appeared to be accidental but wasn't, and her makeup was exquisitely done. *Dr. Freiburg* stared at her lips, perfectly shaped and nicely glossed in a fresh, hot pink with sparkles that caught the overhead light when she smiled. Her lower lip was full and delicious, and the doctor wished he had more time.

"My name is Stacey," she said, her voice sweet and melodious. She was among the best, that was certain.

"I know," he said, nodding. "I requested you. That is, I think it was love at first sight . . ."

"Oh? Have we met?" She scrunched up her cute nose in concentration, biting her lower lip.

"Yes, we have." He waved her toward the side of the foyer and saw her notice the loose hundred-dollar bills in the fruit bowl. There were five, her specific price for an all-nighter. She smiled, more seductively this time, because the money was reassurance and because he was doing everything right. Cops couldn't put out money without possibly facing entrapment charges, so he must be on the up and up. These thoughts flickered in and out of her eyes, and then she turned to him and leaned close.

Dr. Freiburg met her lips with his and crushed her face to him, feigning passion. He *would* have felt passion for her, had he not been strapped for time. The locale was also not of his choosing, so he lingered in the embrace, inhaling the scent of her and the feel of her lipstick on his lips, enjoying her probing tongue.

When she tried to pull away, doubtless to begin the doctor's engagement, or perhaps to start removing her clothes, he clutched her all the harder. He watched her eyes widen with surprise, then flash quickly with fear, and then his hands were around her throat like pliers, cutting off her air supply. His thumbs found her larynx and he applied pressure until she began to turn blue under her off-season salon tan. She pushed against him and smacked at his face with her arms, but she was already weak and all she managed to do was knock his glasses off. Her legs gave out from under her. She tried to swing at him again. Her tiny purse raked across his forehead, but he never loosened his grip and he stared into her eyes as she went from surprise to fear to panic and, finally, to half-unconsciousness. Her attempts to breathe resulted in convulsions, which he contained by slowly lowering her backward and to the hardwood floor, straddling her struggling body and holding her air passage tightly shut until she collapsed completely and he felt her throat give. Her eyes rolled up into her head and he continued applying the pressure for minutes, squeezing with determination, driving her loose-limbed body downward below his own until he was certain she was gone.

Her lipstick streaked her chin now, her tan pale in death. He wished he had the time, for he was quite aroused by now, even though he had not used his favorite blade. But he couldn't afford blood here, not now.

He waited and waited, but her breathing never resumed.

When the phone rang, as he had expected, Dr. Freiburg explained that the escort he had hired had not shown up, and he would not be calling this service again.

He carefully folded her into the huge freezer. "Uncle, meet Stacey," he said, chuckling. Frost almost obscured the old man's features, but his wide-open eyes seemed to be measuring Stacey's beauty. "I'm sure you two will have lots to talk about. Don't do anything I wouldn't do, Uncle! Enjoy your new friend . . ."

Martin had a little trouble closing the door, but some manipulation of her left arm did the trick and he left her in the old man's frozen embrace. He would have loved meeting her in a photo booth and letting her go down on him as the camera rolled, but he had to assume that by now the cops had considered watching most mall booths. Unless they hadn't found his previous *greeting* yet. Or maybe they had found her but weren't saying.

In any case, Stacey Collins could finger him, so she had to be removed from the board. Chances were no one would look in Dr. Freiburg's deep freeze, not until well after Martin was long gone.

Martin whistled a tuneless melody as he cleared his foyer and prepared for the next step.

BUCK

Buck Benton had earned his nickname after slicing open three other men's faces with his old Buck knife. The tag was inevitable. Three men in one day, even if it had been years before, when Buck was still in his twenties and spry. He loved his knife, and never went anywhere without its scarred leather pouch on his belt. The knife's weight was comforting, riding there on his hip. It was a friend a man could count on, even more than his buddies. It never laughed at you, or called you names when you went to piss out all the beer you had drunk. It never called you stupid, or told others of the dumb things you had done while drunk.

Buck savored the smooth way the blade swung open under his thumb—old-fashioned, but sturdy and worn smooth where his thumb and forefinger had so often caressed its metallic sheen. He gloried in the feel of it, and had added to his own legend willingly by using the smoothly worn weapon whenever the chance presented itself.

For instance, that very morning.

Insults were often lost on Buck, since his schooling had ended one day in the seventh grade when the police had come to greet him and offer him some educational alternatives. Juvenile corrections had been less interested in correcting his lack of intellect than his budding sense of social injustice. Even then he had begun to hone his lightning-quick response to any slights—real or imagined—and being called a *shithead* certainly applied, yessir, and he had dealt with *that* problem.

The dink who had called Buck a *shithead* today was a fat-ass two-bit lawyer, an ambulance-chasing bottom-feeder stuck in a one-point-five-horse dump of a town. Yes, Smiley R. Jamieson might have done well in a city big enough to pay him little attention, but here he hadn't done so well, was in fact barely tolerated by the locals. So when he snorted the word *shithead* in reference to an admittedly unoccupied and unemployed Buck Benton, the latter felt he had more than enough reason to unlimber his weapon and commence amateur surgery upon Jamieson's features.

Buck's efforts to that end were interrupted not by a benefactor, exactly, but by another complainant looking for the honorable Mr. Jamieson, who saw in Buck's knife attack the opportunity to draw blood for his own satisfaction. The new player quickly gauged Buck's intentions, plainly written as they were in the thin lines of Mr. Jamieson's blood, which ran down into his withered collar while Buck prepared to slice again.

Harve Billings, Jamieson's visitor, speed-dialed Sheriff Bunche's number on his cell phone even as a startled Buck grunted in surprise at the interruption, widened his nostrils, and smashed through Jamieson's first-floor window to take off down the street.

The wounded lawyer flopped and rolled on the worn carpeting, emitting a loud series of squeals.

Billings took the opportunity of Jamieson's currently noisy indisposition to rifle through the lawyer's files, a stack of which lay invitingly on the cluttered desk, even as he described the lawyer's attacker over the phone. On the floor, Jamieson continued to scream and spray blood.

While Buck's description—hardly necessary, since everyone in town knew of him—was read by the dispatcher to a cruising Sheriff Bunche, Buck himself was already availing himself of the complete bar services of Jerry's Pub and Grub, which had just opened for business that day.

JESSIE

Jerry's Pub and Grub was coincidentally Jessie Hawkins's destination for a quick lunch. She was on her way to meet her tenant, who would be up today. She steered her

Pathfinder into the gravel lot at the same time as the sheriff's own 4-by-4 squad car, a brand-new TrailBlazer.

So Jessie was present when Sheriff Bunche slapped cuffs on Buck's bony wrists, his thin voice reedily exclaiming his innocence even though fresh lawyer blood stained both his denim work shirt and the blade of his knife.

Not one to waste an opportunity, Sheriff Bunche immediately turned to Jessie. "Doctor, can I ask your professional help in visiting our wounded victim over at his office? I got an ambulance on the way, but they been running slow lately."

Jessie nodded. "I have a bag in the truck." Further preparations for her tenant's arrival would have to wait.

When they reached Jamieson's office, where Billings seemed to be standing guard over the flabby lawyer's bloated corpse, Jessie glanced out the broken window at Buck, who was handcuffed and chained in the backseat of the sheriff's truck. He was looking right at her with vacantly hostile eyes and an open-jawed grin that nearly unhinged her even though she knew she was safe.

That's one local I don't want wandering the streets at night, she thought. *Here or on the reservation.*

Then she turned her attention to the lawyer, who was apparently not dead at all, and who had begun groaning and wheezing. The ambulance—late, just as Sheriff Bunche had assumed—pulled up outside as she bent to examine Jamieson's wounds. Now Jamieson was crying and muttering incoherently.

"—walked in just as that creepo was cutting Mr. Jamieson here with this huge knife," Billings was saying. "I scared him away, then I called you and tried to keep the patient comfortable."

Jessie couldn't see the results of any attempt to keep the lawyer comfortable. He lay where he had fallen, his back soaked with blood and his face slashed to ribbons. As far as she could see, his eyes had survived the brutal attack, and that was in itself a small miracle. She opened her bag, donned latex gloves, and set about checking him for serious damage. Jamieson still whimpered softly, and she handled him gently while dabbing at his wounds, which appeared to be shallow and clean.

By now the paramedics had entered and, seeing her already on the scene, unlimbered a stretcher nearby. She supervised their efforts in loading the heavyset lawyer onto it and walked along as they wheeled him out to the lot, whispering and holding his hand—which felt somewhat like a dead carp. He was in shock, mostly blubbering helplessly and staring through widened eyes.

Sheriff Bunche left Billings for a moment and spoke to her quietly as the medics loaded their burden into the back of the ambulance.

"How is he, Doc?"

"He's in shock. His wounds are relatively minor, but they are painful and will take a long time to heal. He'll recover, but he'll need a good plastic surgeon to repair the muscular and nerve damage." She glanced at Buck Benton, who was staring at her through the 4-by-4's window, the tip of his tongue protruding from between his yellow teeth. She shuddered, fingering the faded line of the long, jagged scar that curled around her left ear and across her neck to disappear into the darkness of her hair. "Was he definitely the man?"

Bunche seemed not to notice her gesture.

"I have the knife bagged," he said. "The lab in Minocqua will have to confirm it, of course, but the blade's still slick with blood. I doubt Jamieson cut himself shaving."

Jessie shook her head. The blade that had done the cutting was long and curved, exactly like Benton's Buck knife, and she would most likely be able to identify it from the wounds in Jamieson's face. Buck Benton's career as a thug would come to an end, if she had any say in the matter.

As the ambulance pulled away, they went back into the building. Bunche pointed at several manila folders Billings held in one hand. "So what are those?"

"Files I was bringing Mr. Jamieson, Sheriff. I guess I'll have to hang on to them now."

Jessie stood looking at the stained flooring, and at the window, and Bunche and Billings's conversation became a low buzzing drone. From outside, Buck Benton scrunched up his features so that he resembled a wrinkled gorilla, alternately gloating and leering at her, and then sticking his bloated tongue out and wagging it obscenely, his eyes spinning around in his sockets.

She frowned and turned away, leaving the building and entering her SUV. She saw Buck start laughing uncontrollably.

The inside of her Pathfinder suddenly reeked of decaying copper, and she realized she was still wearing the latex gloves, which were encrusted with Jamieson's coagulating blood. She stripped them off carefully and dropped them in the trash bag she kept in the back. The smell was pungent, and she rolled down her window.

When she drove past the sheriff's truck, Benton appeared to be laughing hard enough to choke. She felt a shiver trickling down her back and tried to forget his distorted features.

To clear her mind, she reminded herself that her favorite tenant would arrive soon. There was that to look forward to, at least. She was glad she had finished clearing his driveway earlier. She popped an Alan Parsons CD into the slot and hummed along as she drove back toward Circle Moon Drive. She'd have to make do with something from the fridge for lunch.

Jessie's father had bought a half-dozen lots on what would become Circle Moon Drive over a half century before, when land was cheap and plentiful and the nearest neighbors were likely to be ten miles away. There was no town then, just a jumble of county roads wiggling along the shoreline of the dozens of long, narrow lakes and the short channels that connected them. As often as not, the roads formed jagged boundaries between white people's land and the various reservations created in the latter part of the nineteenth century to get the Indians under control somewhere whites wouldn't have to worry about them. Circle Moon Drive had been nothing but a dirt road servicing two dozen parcels of wooded land, almost all of which overlooked either a lake or a narrow, tree-shaded channel. All six of Mason Hawkins's lots overlooked such a channel, so that at night sitting at one of his campsites would be pitch black because of the tree line on the opposite bank. By the time Hawkins had built three of his six cottages, others had purchased lots on Circle Moon Drive, and a small union of friends had begun to take cocktails together and watch the sunlight slowly disappear behind the uninterrupted line of pines just across the channel.

Jessie had grown up in the woods around their land, burying treasures here and there, secreting tiny boxes of meaningful trinkets in each of the tidy wooden cottages that sprang out of the gentle hillside that rolled to the banks of the channel, now dotted with the piers of other hidden properties.

Now that her parents had retired to the big city, closer to the hospital for which Mason Hawkins occasionally consulted, they had left their remaining four cottages to her management. She supplemented her meager reservation salary by living in one cottage and renting the other three. All were winterized, so she could usually find renters for each season or even the entire year. She ran an ad in several local papers year-round and so always managed to catch at least a few short vacation rentals. Painters and writers often used the still-quiet area, the rustle of the water in the channel, and the slurp of boat wakes against pier supports to give their work a less urban feel.

One cottage was currently unoccupied, but two couples from Milwaukee were to drive up soon and spend a week lazing. One was rented by a writer she suspected had written his last book, for he seemed to spend his days bobbing on his rented pontoon boat, moored and in no danger of going anywhere, a blender-full of some icy drink always in hand. The last cottage was tucked into a grove of middle-aged jack pines and nearly hidden by undergrowth her oldest tenant would not let her clear.

"I love the shade and the solitude," he always said whenever she mentioned the subject. He was not old, this tenant, but he had rented from her the longest of anyone, so she thought of him as the "oldest." The rough barrier of wild ferns and overgrown alpine currant bushes occasionally insulted her sense of order and cleanliness, and she would itch to just go ahead and clear it when he wasn't there to stop her. But then she would realize two things that always stopped her—first, as her oldest regular tenant, he deserved a little slack, and second, he was the only tenant who wanted the place year-round even when he couldn't use it, and who was willing to pay more than market price for her to do the necessary upkeep inside and out. Short of clearing out the old brush, of course. He'd made her put the promise in writing, half seriously and half in jest. Jessie knew very well that for what he paid her in rent he could have bought a newer, larger cottage of higher quality than hers, so she bit her tongue and allowed him to dictate when it came to "his" place.

As far as she could tell, he used the place for all of a few days a month, not necessarily weekends, and occasionally a week or two in the summer. Sometimes a few days over deer season, when so many other cottages in the area went to the hunters who streamed in not only from Milwaukee and Green Bay, but from all the southern and southwestern cities. Given the money he forked over in half-year increments, and his dark good looks, how could she avoid letting him walk all over her? Hell, she rather *liked* it, she joked to herself.

Jessie smiled as she parked the Pathfinder in front of his garage. She thought of it as *his* rather than hers, and that was symbolic of how long he had been her tenant. She shivered a bit, thinking of his arrival, of his looking at her with that dark-eyed intensity, some sort of tragic and horribly sad events in his life giving him an almost poetic look, as if he routinely fenced with his soul and often felt the piercing of his heart as the thin blade slid into his body.

She shook her head. *Such a romantic fool.* Where did she get that? Surely not from her father, the crotchety old res doctor.

She sat for a moment and inhaled the clean, woodsy air. The freaky emergency involving that fool Benton and the lawyer had made her feel tired and sluggish all of a sudden. This was no way to prepare for Nick, whose presence always livened up her life despite his frequent and sudden disappearances even when he *was* in residence. If she hadn't known that he was a police detective, she would have suspected criminal activity. Such were the mysterious ways of life in the North Woods. An hour farther north and you'd be in Michigan's Upper Peninsula; not much farther than that in Canada, and the history of the area included plenty of criminal activity of the smuggling kind. Not to mention the Chicago gangsters who had all owned or frequented retreats in these woods. Some had even hosted shoot-outs against the much less politically correct police of the past.

She finally climbed out of the SUV, checking his mailbox and taking a stack of junk mail and shoppers' pages to the door. She struggled with the stubborn key before letting herself into his cottage from the upstairs rear, where the bedrooms lined the hall. She headed down the stairs and added the new circulars to the heap on the rough-hewn dining room table just off the kitchen, wondering why he allowed mail to be delivered here at all. God knew, by the time he saw it, it was always outdated and somehow stale, as if it had sagged from the heat or lack of attention. This time, though, a plain white security envelope slid out from between hardware store and gun shop flyers. She wasn't what one might call nosy, but as she put her hand on the envelope to slip it back into the pile, she couldn't help but notice the return address. It was the same as Nick's address, so this letter had come from—his neighbor? And it had been mailed three days earlier.

She shook her head violently, ashamed of herself. She had pledged never to speculate about his life unless he invited her to, and how likely was that? She placed the envelope with the rest of his mail, but in the middle of the pile, so it wouldn't look as though she'd singled it out. She chuckled at her own latent sneakiness. Why, she might as well steam it open if she knew how to cover her tracks so well.

Chuckling, she set about her tasks—waving away the occasional cobweb, firing up the furnace and checking the temperature of the water heater, making sure the appliances were all plugged in and operational, and generally making the place seem less abandoned. She opened the sarcophagus-shaped freezer, which always reminded her of some fifties science-fiction monster movie, and peered inside through the wisps of fog. The usual packages of white-wrapped steaks and chops, separated in a dozen neat, orderly piles. A few frozen pizzas. A couple tubs of ice cream and frozen yogurt. Not much else. She wondered what he would think if he knew she had checked out his eating habits. Well, she had to check the appliances, didn't she? She paused with the cover open—who ate that much red meat these days? Not a chicken or turkey breast in sight among the neatly labeled packages of roasts and steaks, and no vegetables, either. Talk about meat and potatoes, hold the potatoes! Maybe he bought all fresh produce at roadside stands on the way up. Whatever else she could say about Dominic Lupo, she sure couldn't argue about his health. He was one of the most robust men she'd ever seen. He wasn't overly muscled, but he gave the impression of quiet power and controlled grace.

She stopped in the bathroom and carefully applied a light lavender lipstick while smiling at herself in the mirror. Why not? If you didn't count knife-wielding weirdos and malcontents, her social life was nonexistent. She admired her new and improved look and slowly put the canister away. Damn it, there was nothing wrong with feeling a little sexy! A shower, clean clothes, and a touch-up—and then she'd pay her special tenant a visit. Meet him at the cabin as he drove up and give him a warm welcome. She laughed a cartoon maniacal laugh. A warm welcome! She'd have to plan her outfit carefully—sexy but practical.

She hummed "Games People Play" as she dusted the paneled living room and bar area. She couldn't help grinning like a fool.

BUCK

Jessie Hawkins wasn't receding from Buck Benton's memory. Not yet. He sat in his cell, massaging the bulge in his oily jeans.

I gotta get me some of that.

He knew the sheriff and his dinky-doo deputies could see him if they looked through the Plexiglas window set in the door that led to the cells. He didn't care, hoping they'd see him rubbing himself. He was totally taken with the madam doctor, yes he was. He'd have to talk some at Wilbur about her, see what could be done about her damn nice ass.

Thinking about it now, Buck reached into his belt-less jeans and hoped they'd come see him right then.

CHAPTER SEVENTEEN

LUPO

At home, he didn't procrastinate. He'd been doing just that, but now he needed an exorcism of sorts. He had to step back just a bit and say good-bye to Corinne, the woman he might have found—had he looked. Her death would forever be on his conscience, albeit once removed, but he would always know he'd let her down.

So he stiffened his resolve and placed several of Vic's Corey Diamond DVDs into his changer, skipping ahead through the "safe sex" warnings, Certificates of Compliance, and "coming attraction" ads. He skipped through the credits, launching immediately into a sex scene, but the woman was a brunette. Then a redhead and a blonde and an Asian girl. Then he clicked to the next chapter and there she was.

Beautiful, vibrant, Corinne Devereaux. She drew the camera to her even though she wasn't the star. She seemed to suck in the lens, which saw through the home-spun qualities Lupo had always known and right into her dark corners, for where Corinne ended and Corey began was apparently a latex and leather sort of place, where rubber sex toys and genitalia mingled with oiled, sweaty bodies in every sexual permutation Lupo could imagine, and then even more. Corinne/Corey at first seemed a mere participant in the scene, but soon it became obvious that she was in control. Her voice barked orders everyone else obeyed, and she took her pleasure from a variety of acts she demanded.

When the scene ended, Lupo's skin was sweat-slick. The Creature stirred beneath, aroused by the animal sexuality on the screen and by Lupo's reaction to it. He was aroused, and he felt guilty. The guilt made him blush—heating up his cheeks—and his breathing increased its tempo.

Corinne's dominatrix scene was the only one on that DVD, so he shuffled to the next disc and located her much sooner in the mix—maybe her fame from one production had raised her casting level in the other. Here she was almost sweet, a girl-next-door type who started out naive only to be corrupted by neighbors and friends until she became wanton and predatory. Again she soaked up the camera's attention and became the single most convincing performer, featured in all but one scene. She began as a makeup-free natural beauty, but by the end she had graduated to the made-up look of the hooker, her level of sexuality rising accordingly. Lupo sweated through the whole disc, alternately missing Corinne his neighbor and lusting for Corey the porn starlet. The paradox made his head spin. His animal instincts seemed confused, too.

He took a half-dozen aspirin with two pints of cold water from his fridge and flicked to the third disc, which was far more hardcore. Here he watched his friend step out of herself and blossom into a supercharged erotic vixen who coupled with men and women, single and double and triple and in group settings, letting them use her like an erotic toy. When the plot line veered into bondage and domination, and the sex became increasingly raw and painful, Lupo shut it off.

He sat in the flickering light of the blank screen, the last image one that would remain with him forever—Corey Diamond, sandwiched between three willing male partners and in the throes of lust. He knew this ritual would allow him to say his final good-bye to Corinne.

Layers of guilt ate at him like acid.

The traffic was light on I45, and Lupo maneuvered around what little there was, making up time before being limited to the two-lane county highways that would take him to his refuge in the North Woods. It was still early enough in spring that few people were likely to brave the cool days and frigid nights, unless their cabins were winterized. Weather was immaterial to Lupo, but he could look forward to less traffic on the roads, less hikers, no hunters, and very few nature lovers. Spring up north blooms late and often unfriendly.

Lupo gripped the wheel with both hands, his mood grim. He'd had just enough time to throw a bag in the trunk and head for the highway, after attending the funeral he'd arranged for Corinne. It had been a stark, quick last-second service—presided over by a priest Lupo had known all his life and who was not against doing friends personal favors. Lupo had explained the situation, and Father Richard Fellows had come through, never mind that Corinne hadn't seen the inside of a church for years. Lupo's call to Corinne's escort service had yielded several girlfriends and her boss, who turned out quietly dressed and clearly upset. He was surprised the friend who had been with Corinne at the mall, the one they had interviewed at the scene, hadn't come. Stacey. Maybe she was still shell-shocked.

Eileen Edwards had owned the Roxanne escort service for seven years, she told Lupo, and nothing ever happened to any of her girls.

"Which is barely any comfort at all in this situation, I know," she had added quickly. Her wide, clear eyes and generous mouth made her look like some famous television or movie star, maybe a few years past her prime. A Jaclyn Smith or Cybill Shepherd. She seemed genuinely distraught.

Lupo frowned. "Was there any sign, any sign at all that she was being stalked? Did she seem afraid?" If Eileen Edwards knew about the four letters Corinne had received, she would say so now. She had been interviewed by detectives before Lupo could reach her, but he'd seen the report and she hadn't mentioned it to them. If she hadn't known about Lupo's friendship with Corinne, she did now, and he hoped she'd have some information he'd missed.

"She did seem on edge lately," she said, her eyes unfocusing for a second before fixing Lupo squarely again, "but she wouldn't talk about what was wrong. I thought it had to do with her family."

"What about her video porn work?"

She stepped back and half-smiled, but only for a second. "You don't pull any punches. But, then, I understand why you wouldn't. I was fond of her, too."

"The porn?"

"Yes, well, that was her side business. I had advised her against it—ask any of my girls, I always do—but people do what they want despite the advice they're given. She hadn't done all that much work yet, I think. Mostly with one or two production companies."

"Can you point me in a specific direction? Names?"

She shook her head. "It was local, I think. Corinne hadn't made the jump to the LA scene yet."

"But she would have?"

Eileen Edwards smiled, and she was indeed beautiful for her age. "Oh yes," she said with a sure nod. "She had sexuality that oozed from her like sweat. She was bisexual, you know, and I tell you—Corinne could have turned me with just a look."

It was more than he really wanted to know, and she smiled at his discomfort. "I hope I've been helpful."

He gave her his card. "If anything comes to mind."

"Of course."

He'd watched her walk away sadly, and then all Corinne's coworkers headed off as a group. Lupo had spoken for a moment with Father Fellows, thanking him for his compassion, then had stood awkwardly at the foot of the open grave. Cemetery workers hovered in the background, waiting for him to leave.

"Damn it, Corinne," he whispered. "I could have prevented this." He felt a tear form at the corner of his right eye and left it there to blur his vision, as if it represented some promise to his friend's ghost.

He sensed that someone else had approached and turned slightly. It was a young priest, head bowed, deep in prayer. Lupo was glad there'd been a few people to say good-bye. He said his own farewell under his breath. Though he'd been taught all sorts of prayers, he had learned early that they were meaningless. There were more appropriate, meaningful words in his progressive rock music collection. Lupo nodded at the priest when their gazes met.

Then he'd walked away and taken the highway out of town. As the city gave way to farmland, he dialed his cell phone.

"The autopsy report is due day after tomorrow, Nick," Ben reminded him. "Or sooner."

"I'll be back maybe tomorrow or the next day at the latest. You'll just have to cover for me with Bowen. Tell him I'm working an angle."

"In Eagle River? What angle? Angling, maybe? I don't think he'll fall for it."

"Try."

"I wasn't gonna tell you, but there's more."

"More?"

"Yeah." There was a long sigh over the cell phone's dead air. "We found another girl an hour ago. Different mall, same deal. Just like the guy said."

"Fuck!" Lupo pounded the wheel.

"No shit. You comin' back or you want the details?"

"Details."

"Well, it's the same guy. A real sicko—no doubting this one. Prelim shows an exact match. He did her up the same way, complete with the photo strip of him getting his blow job. She's wearin' a lot of hot pink lipstick in the photos, and the guy's equipment seems to match. The lab's comparing the two right now, but it's the same guy."

"Yeah," Lupo said. "It's not Stacey, is it? Corinne's friend?"

"Nah, we're running her ID. So he somehow gets her into the can and slices her up good. Same again, with one exception. Wrote 'For Nick' on her forehead with her lipstick. Everybody's still gunning for the Satanist angle, and I let 'em. Anyway, he did her after she was dead, the fucker, and really messed up what he left behind. Locked the door and put a maintenance department Out of Order sign on it, so nobody found her. Maybe a couple days. Like maybe he did this right after the other—uh, after Corinne. He's one lucky sonofabitch, 'cause he should have been covered with blood spatters, but nobody saw nothin'. So, you turned the car around yet?"

"Too late. I told you, cover for me."

"Damn it, Nick, you know Bowen's got a hard-on for you! And the psycho-doc hates you, too. They might get those little Nick references, they think hard enough. You're just like your father, more than you know! Stubborn as hell and so set in your ways it's makin' me crazy."

"Don't forget to check on those juvie records."

Ben growled and muttered, then clicked off.

As he drove, Lupo pondered Ben's outburst. He knew

Lupo had issues, as they said in therapy-speak, with a domineering father whose love was difficult to express. Even long before the Andy Corrazza *incident,* Nick Lupo had navigated his father's orbit with difficulty and mixed emotions.

Taciturn and stern, Frank Lupo had seemed impossible to please Nick's entire life. He suspected, and his mother had once confirmed, that it was a combination of a life wasted in the service of others and the loss of Nick's sister, Carla, when she was just a baby. Nick barely remembered the sister he'd had for such a short while, but the anger and resentment and hurt caused by her death had been like an arrow through the heart of the Lupo household, and therefore the marriage.

Lupo himself had been rebuffed when, as a young adult, he'd tried to learn the details of his sister's death in order to clear the air. He had read that airing grievances and heartaches was best, but in his family the way to deal with crisis and deep feelings was to shut everyone out and keep silent. In fact, he and his father had almost come to blows over the elder Lupo's unwillingness to speak of whatever incident had claimed his daughter's life. Frank Lupo had turned Nick's childhood and his own marriage into some sort of silent hell. Nick had no idea how his mother had coped, but her sad eyes and weakening body told the story all too well. When Nick had challenged his old man's behavior, a rift opened between them—a chasm that no amount of openness could heal.

Finally, Nick had felt he had no choice but to cut off his father altogether—the result was years of bitter silence and hurt feelings, resulting in a strained relationship worsened by Nick's decision to become a cop. Nick had learned long ago to live with the fact that for some reason he was a deep and bitter disappointment to his father. He had asked his mother outright whether he himself had been responsible for his sister's death, but all she would say was, "Don't talk about it. It upsets your father."

The frustration had driven him farther and farther away, until the sexy academic Caroline had come along and rescued him from the darkness of his family—and almost from the darkness of his disease, too, if only he had been able to control the wild monster that had gorged on his personality from the inside.

Now he pulled into and out of Three Lakes, Wisconsin, only twenty minutes or so from his destination. The trees had changed from mostly deciduous to almost all evergreens in the last hour and a half, but the transition hadn't made him as happy as it usually did. Still, the smells of the woods entered his nostrils in a rush, and he knew that the Creature already looked forward to scampering in the wild. He hoped he could control the Change as he had in the service tunnel. This weekend would serve as a test; he needed to prove to himself that he could repeat it anytime. He hated leaving Ben to handle the case on his own, but he had no choice. If he could take control of the Change once and for all, then he would no longer be a slave to the Creature's whims.

Besides, he wondered if the Creature under his control could help his police work. If not to catch criminals, then at least to track them. The Creature's heightened senses had helped him already, but once completely harnessed they could rewrite his approach to investigations. It was a fantasy, perhaps, but he sensed that Caroline would have approved. Maybe Corinne, too, if he'd ever had the chance to tell her.

Three Lakes lay behind him now. Both sides of the road were lined with sentinel-straight tall stands of spindly pines, behind which peeked the occasional boarded-up live bait shop. Too early for the fishing, but only a few weeks would turn the area into a quagmire of tourists and renegade boaters. Lupo took the snaky turns off the main road and followed the signs past dormant resorts and summer retreats behind winding wooded driveways.

Soon he was nosing onto Circle Moon Drive, past the corner house with its aggressive Doberman—a year-round annoying resident—and past the six other neighboring homes that lined the outer edge of the Circle, three of them with channel frontage. The middle of the three was his permanent rental, a wood-sided cottage forty years old, nestled onto a gentle slope leading down to a recently rebuilt dock that jutted into the shallow channel. The narrow waterway stretched between two medium-size lakes, roughly in the center of the long chain of elongated lakes that ringed the town of Eagle River, four miles away.

Lupo pulled the car up to the garage recently added behind the main house, slipping in between an old Evinrude tri-hull on a rusty trailer and the Pathfinder that belonged to Jessie Hawkins. He turned the key and rolled down his window, letting the chill air sweep through his nose and hair. And the quiet. There was no sound but the rustle of a breeze through the pines, and the occasional bird call. It was serene and it was exactly what he needed.

Cold still gripped the woods at night, but during the middle of the day an active person could generate enough heat to counteract the chill. From Lupo's experience, there would be a good two months yet of the cold, as the calendar slowly edged into late spring and finally early summer. It would warm up in July and August for a few short weeks, and then the chill would set in once more.

The cottage's back door opened and his landlord stepped outside, waving.

For a second he was entranced. Her sinewy body, tall but not gangling, was superb in the khaki shorts and light brown suede shirt she wore loosely tucked in at her hips. Her dark hair cascaded over her face and hid everything but her eyes, and he saw the smile in them and reacted the same way.

She stopped before his car and tossed her hair aside,

revealing a wide smile that matched the one in her eyes and made his heart beat a little more rapidly.

It was almost like going home. He felt the woods welcoming him like a loving parent. Some of the sadness left him, and some decided it would let him be for now.

"So you decided to drive up all of a sudden, just for a night or two?" Jessie Hawkins asked, opening the garage door for Lupo before he could do it himself.

"Yes, I need a hideout for a couple days!" Their longstanding joke was that he needed a place to lie low, like a mobster.

He watched her as she muscled the cranky door that often gave him trouble and surprised himself by smiling widely. He wiped the smile from his face before she could see it and ask him why he looked so silly. The fact was that he had forgotten both how much he genuinely liked his Up North landlord, and how attractive she was in her outdoorsy outfit.

He waved again as Jessie stood aside and allowed him to drive into the garage. He was taking his duffel bag from the car when his senses overloaded with the scent of her, a slightly sweaty and healthy outdoor smell that encompassed both her femininity and the smokiness of the crisp air surrounding them. Almost an autumnal scent, reminding him of fireplaces and cozy Christmases he'd never had. He turned and greeted her again as she approached him.

"Greetings!" he said, then kicked himself mentally. What kind of idiot says *Greetings?*

She laughed with her full throat, and he joined her, appreciating the sound. Sanity amid recent insanity.

"Greetings, Earthling!" she said, attempting the Vulcan salute and settling for a rough version.

"I don't usually say that!" He laughed again and noticed how her hair bobbed around her features.

She closed the distance between them and extended a slim, strong hand. Her handshake was firm but delicate.

Only then did he realize how truly happy he was to see her.

MARTIN

Martin nosed the old man's inconspicuous Buick into the turnoff for Circle Moon Drive. Seeing Lupo's car enter the tree-lined driveway, he slowed and hoped the bastard was too busy to notice him. He drove past slowly and parked a ways down the curving asphalt road, which really was a circle. He flicked on the car's flashers and risked a short walk to the edge of the driveway. Through the straight trees, Martin watched as Lupo climbed out of his car and shook hands with a stunning beauty.

What's this? How many women does this asshole have?

Caroline's old journals mentioned his hideaway in the woods, and how he'd learned to get away from the city and let his monster side out. But Caroline's tight hand had hidden any knowledge of a woman. Martin wiped sweat from his forehead. Was he hallucinating? Caroline's journal was years old. This woman would have been too young to have known the cop or his secret. No, she was a more recent development.

An *interesting* development.

From here, the sight of her made his palms itch.

Martin returned to his car and quietly drove off, following the circle until he was on the main road again, about a mile away. He saw the historical marker just in time to turn in and park where a narrow path disappeared into the woods. Just another idiot tourist.

He slid the heavy .44 Magnum into the holster he wore, locked the car, then headed back the way he'd come. Martin had a curiously developed sense of direction, a fact that often served him well. After a short hike, he was again in the center of Circle Moon Drive, near Lupo's hideout. Enjoying the midday warmth, gnats of some kind buzzed around him, but he ignored them as he gently made his way through the undergrowth, following the gentle contours of the hill. A swirling flash of glinting sunlight told him there was a lake or river down there. Not that he cared. His target was the dense woods on one side of the picturesque cedar-sided cottage. Windows lined that side, and he hoped his luck held. After all, he could have lost the cop on the way up here and wasted his trip. Instead, it appeared he was about to be rewarded for his patience.

Yes indeed.

JESSIE

"I just finished opening up for you," Jessie said, lingering in his handshake. It seemed he didn't mind. "It's still cold at night, so I turned on the furnace and made sure all the appliances work. Checked your mail, too, Detective Lupo." She smiled. She wasn't about to tell him about the tree she'd had to hack up, or her run-in with the local village idiot.

"Thanks! But you didn't have to go to any trouble." He turned to glance at the cottage. His image was distorted in the back door's glass panel, rendering him into a black-clad blur with shoulder-length dark hair. A very nice blur. "Really, I'm just here for some good nights' sleep. And after all these years, you're supposed to call me Nick!"

She blushed. "No trouble at all, Nick, and I was going to open it next week anyway, so . . ." She kicked herself. *I sound inane.* "I heard about the murders in Milwaukee. Two women now, isn't it?"

He grimaced and she saw pain and rage, and maybe something else there.

I shouldn't have asked.

"Yeah." He stood, still as a wooden post, and she

thought he was just going to dismiss her and slam the door in her face. Then he half-smiled, as if making a decision. "Want to come in? I could use some coffee. And a set of ears."

What a curious way to invite me in. She was through the door before her brain knew she'd made her own decision.

He rifled through the mail stack and thoughtfully separated out the same long white envelope that had caught her eye. She was surprised when he slit it with a sharp fingernail. He slid out the single sheet, unfolded and read it, folded it again, then carefully set it on the table.

"How about some coffee, Dr. Hawkins?" he said, looking up, embarrassed at his instinctive slipup.

"My God, call me Jessie! Or Jess! We've known each other for, well, a long time. And I'd *love* some coffee, Nick. You know, why don't I make it?" she added, not waiting for him to argue.

"Hi, Jessie or Jess," he said, almost shyly. "Nice to meet you." He didn't bother to argue, instead taking cups and saucers off the cupboard. Creamer from the counter and sugar. Spoons.

She noticed that he scratched his hands a lot, as if he'd been bitten by a swarm of mosquitoes. It was too early, though, wasn't it? No, she'd seen some already. *Have to warn him about the West Nile virus, in case he doesn't know.* She made coffee while he perused the rest of his mail. The quietly domestic situation surprised and thrilled her. She hoped he noticed how much she enjoyed it, but he seemed preoccupied.

After the coffee was poured—a rich Arabian blend she'd taken the liberty to stock for him—they sat not quite across from each other and she sensed that he wanted to talk. That a part of him *needed* to talk. It was the same intuition she had used in her practice for so long, a sort of sympathetic understanding that made people comfortable around her and willing to open up (even uptight young tribesmen and their old-fashioned grandparents).

Jessie looked into his eyes and saw the troubled past written there. There *was* something else. Fear. A sense of loss. *What else?*

"The first of the two women killed was my friend, Corinne," he began. And he nearly broke down.

The story poured from his own lips, confirming some of the details she'd heard on the radio. What the creep had done to the poor woman and how he'd arranged the corpse. Taunting the police with the photo strip. He told her that they hadn't released that information yet, hoping it would confirm any confessions, but no one had taken credit for the murder. *Credit,* he growled. His left hand seemed to be scratching his right hand below her view, under the table.

Jessie's eyes filled with tears. She *felt* his loss, the pain and the guilt at not thwarting the killing. He mentioned the bloody message—he knew it was meant for him, he said—and she sensed that this blurting out of information wasn't like him at all. He seemed to have dropped all his defenses. She felt a shiver, as if someone were watching her.

"The police psychologist is MIA in this one," he said. "She should be profiling, but I think she's having an affair or something. And she hates my guts. No help at all. I think this guy's after me. He's killed a friend of mine and he's threatened my partner's family, but I can't tell anyone about our friendship or they'd pull me off the case. Ben knows, but he'll keep it quiet—he wants me to stay on. I really think we need that profile, something to get a line on this guy. By the time I get back, there may be a task force."

"Is he a Dahmer or Ed Gein copycat?"

"Ah, the famous Wisconsin Duo of Death. If you drop in Chicago's Gacy, the three make up what I call the Midwest's Bermuda Triangle of serial killers."

"And Richard Speck? Doesn't he make it a rectangle?"

He was ready for that one. "Speck was a spree killer or

mass murderer, not technically a *serial* killer. So my triangle of death holds, except this guy's trying to add his mark. He's got a definite, uh, style."

"What about the way he stages the crime scene?" she asked.

His eyes widened. "You know a lot about staging?"

"You forget, my father was assistant coroner up here for about thirty years. After I finished med school, I assisted for a while in an almost official capacity here and in Minocqua. I've worked for Sheriff Bunche a few times, too, when they needed a medical opinion. Or a coroner's opinion without a coroner."

He nodded. "Okay, you pass. Besides his hatred for me, I'd have to say part of his staging and the other connecting link is, well, lipstick. There's evidence he needs heavy use by the women, according to what's on the photo strips. Plus he seems to apply some on them, uh, after he's killed them."

Jessie felt herself blushing. She felt the sticky lavender lipstick she had applied before his arrival, and the slick gloss she'd rolled over it. There was a violet half-moon mark on her mug.

"He's clearly fetishized the cosmetic," she said. "He must be terribly excited by it, though I doubt it's the *reason* he's killing . . ."

"I'm the reason," Lupo said.

She nodded, thinking. "But the lipstick must be important to him. Can I ask if there's a specific color he's using?"

"Corinne was wearing a light purple, I guess. My partner says the second victim had on a hot pink. But maybe that's just what they had."

She considered his words. "True, but I wonder if maybe he's just not as turned on by earth tones. You know, maybe the brassier, less natural colors are his thing . . . Oh, I didn't mean . . ."

He waved a hand. "No, no. I know what you meant. What might have made him want to use so much after they're dead? It's as if he's masturbating with their made-up lips."

Her thoughts raced. Leaning over, she rummaged in her purse and took out her lipstick, blushing again as she handled it. "See how phallic the tip is when I twist it open?" She demonstrated.

"Damn it, I do."

"Watch." She applied some of her Wet Shine Diamonds without a mirror, monitoring his expression. A light layer on her bottom lip, then the top lip. Then she repeated the process, leaving a much heavier than usual layer of shimmering color behind. She leaned the rounded lavender tip on her full lower lip for a few seconds, emphasizing her point.

"It's pretty erotic, right?" She felt uncomfortable, but secretly glowing.

"Uh, yeah." He shifted in his seat, maybe unconsciously.

"And the picture strips show him being fellated by his victims?"

"What I've seen, anyway." He nodded, following.

"He's obsessed with oral sex."

"Aren't most men?" he asked, clearly still ill at ease.

"I imagine. But he's tied the sex in with his revenge on you, and maybe women. He knows you and hates you, for some reason, but he also has a hatred for oral sex."

"Whoa," Lupo said, caught by surprise. "*Hatred* of oral sex? I thought we agreed he *likes* it."

Score one for me! a voice in her head couldn't help but shout with glee.

"I'd say he's obsessed with it, yes, but that doesn't necessarily mean he likes it. I'm no profiler, but he strikes me as someone resentful of it, of the sexiness. He's resentful of the women too, and certainly of the mouth as a sexual hotspot. There has to be a reason for that." She sipped from her cooling cup. "Do you know why women use lipstick?"

"To make themselves attractive? To stand out from the crowd?"

"Yes, but also there's something called 'body mimicry,' a theory I guess, that says women of most cultures unconsciously make their mouths resemble their aroused vaginal lips when they use lipstick and gloss. Which is supposed to make them more erotic and therefore more attractive to prospective mates . . . It's a primal urge to attract mating opportunities, though we've outgrown the desperate need our ancient ancestors had."

She realized how flushed her face felt again. What had *she* done shortly before his arrival, after all?

"I guess that makes sense, but I never thought about it."

"For most women, the theory goes, it's happening at the subconscious level. They just think of it as making themselves prettier or more presentable usually, except if they're making up for a special date or something. I bet most men who react to it don't even know why. But there's something wrong in this case, as if it's inverted or something. Do you know anything about this guy's childhood?"

"No, if we did we might be able to figure out who he is. My partner's checking juvie records, but most are sealed."

"Well, you can start by checking into court records on abused children—*victims*—and see if any connection can be made to cosmetics. Maybe he was forced to . . ." Her voice faded. The silence between them seemed to rise in volume.

"And that would cause him to kill like this?" Lupo couldn't tell her about himself, but he wanted to pick her brain.

"No," she replied. "From my reading, I'd say a bad environment magnified the effects, but he was probably miswired from birth. I think his oral sex fixation may tie in to what happened to him as a child, but he was probably ticking before that."

Lupo grinned suddenly, but there was no mirth in it. "Damn it, Jess, you've given me a whole new angle with the lipstick fetish. And there's something else I can't quite remember . . ."

LUPO

But he *did* remember.

It was sudden, like a head-on collision on the freeway in a dense fog that had suddenly lifted.

He remembered Caroline Stewart's youth as she'd described it. *His Caroline had been abused.* Caroline had suffered at the hands of her father and then, in an absurd twist of fate, had suffered even more at the hands of her younger brother. *What was his name?* Lupo remembered more now, could almost see Caroline, lying in bed, opening up and replaying all the evil to which she'd been subjected by a crazed father whose wife would not consent to "dirty" sexual favors, and so who'd rationalized he'd been driven to sate himself on his teenage daughter. But then the elder Stewart, *sick fuck that he was,* had slipped off the edge and begun abusing Caroline's younger brother the same way, except even worse because of the boy's resemblance to his mother.

And as sick and twisted as that story had been, Caroline had capped it off with the revelation that her brother was jealous of their father because he, too, had loved her. And he too had molested her, even though he was younger. "I was so mixed up then, Nick," she'd said, tears running down her cheeks. "I could have stopped it, but for a long while I didn't know how. My father scared me physically, but my brother—he scared me even more, as if the evil in him threatened to engulf us all. When he molested me, he would wear lipstick—just like my father made him wear when *he* was molesting *him,* because I wouldn't. My brother made me—he put it on his penis. He would rub it all over me and pretend I was our mother, probably because that's what my father did."

Lupo had just held her until she stopped crying. "I can't figure out who was worse of the four of us. My mother for denying my father and turning a blind eye, my father for abusing us, my brother for using his experiences to make mine worse, or me for being a stupid victim to both of them. My brother loved me, he said. He loved me so much, he killed our parents and they locked him up for it, but as a juvenile. He's at the Stevensen Institute, where he can't hurt anyone, but if it was up to me, they'd have put him to death. *There was so much blood.* Not that I ever had reason to mourn my father, the bastard, or my mother, who let him use us. At least, I blamed her when I was a kid, but now I see that she just didn't know how to stop their evil. I hated all of them at the time. I just wanted to get away and forget they existed. And I know they're the reason I wanted to learn psychology like my uncle. Oh, Nick, I thank God you walked into my classroom, because you're the only one who could possibly understand me. You and I are similar in many ways. You have your secrets and I have mine."

He had cried, too, and held her, and then they'd made love.

Later, she had whispered to him. "I hope they never let Martin out."

Martin.

Martin Stewart.

He remembered a photograph she had shown him of her brother, but the face was fuzzy. Only a few years younger than she, that made him a couple years older than Lupo. Was he still locked up in the Institute? First chance he got, he'd call and give Ben the word, but Ben would have to pretend he'd found it. Bad enough Lupo was connected to Corinne, but his connection to Caroline had to be kept secret.

He snapped out of the reverie. Jessie looked at him, curious and concerned. He'd gone away for a minute, and it must have looked strange—he could almost feel his own vacant expression.

"Can I borrow your computer tomorrow?" he said. "I want to run a Google search or two, and log on to the department database through the Web."

"I have a brand-new Mac on a cable modem at the office. Just stop by and it's all yours."

"Thanks," he said. He wished he could recapture the feeling they'd shared a few minutes before.

JESSIE

The sadness rolled off him like sweat she could almost see. She sensed deeper-than-surface feelings and she understood that Nick Lupo had lost some kind of soul mate in Corinne.

My God, she was a call girl and yet I'm convinced there was some sort of bond between them that even he couldn't explain to me. But there's something else, something that made him sad even before this murder. In fact, Nick Lupo has been sad as long as I've known him.

His back was to her as he fiddled with the miniature stereo while she poured more coffee. He dug into a CD case and selected something she'd never heard before, something that sounded like a cross between Celtic and hard rock. She examined his square shoulders and his posture and sensed that the music was important to him, that it soothed him in ways she couldn't quite understand. But then, she knew how much her music soothed *her,* and she smiled because it was a quality she really liked in a man. Emotion based on art—that was a real turn-on!

When he turned back, they resumed their conversation, but she could tell some connections had been made in his mind or his memory.

"I hope you don't mind the music," he said.

"Not at all. It's nice."

He nodded. "It's a Scottish guy named Fish. Sometimes

music's the only thing I can hold on to." He shook his head sadly. "If you had a chance to profile my guy, where would you take it? I mean, do you have any other insight?"

"What about the photograph strips? Anything else stand out, so to speak?"

"Well, it appears the guy's bland-looking. His clothes are nothing fancy or flashy. Off-the-rack Dockers stuff."

"My guess is that's how he gets close to people. He's a bit of a chameleon, maybe, something of an actor."

"Hmmm."

"You know, like the William Goldman novel they made a movie out of with George Segal and—what was her name? Lee Remick. And Rod Steiger."

"You mean *No Way to Treat a Lady?*"

"Yes! Remember, Steiger's a serial killer who was an actor, and he could be a handyman one day and a priest the next. And I think he painted the women with lipstick, too. He gave them fake red lips on the forehead. But they were older—mother figures. He was obsessed with his mother. What's the matter?"

"I'm an idiot, that's what's the matter!" he said, smashing his hand on the table and making their cups bounce. "A priest. I think he came to Corinne's funeral!"

"You mean this guy came disguised as a priest?" She felt her pulse racing a little. It was scary to think that someone you ran into—even a priest—could be a serial killer.

"I think it's possible, yeah. He's got it in for me and he'd want to stick close."

I think he's figured out who this guy is, but he's not telling me.

Lupo set his coffee cup aside with a distasteful look, as if it had soured on him suddenly. He rubbed his eyes and scratched his hands, then caught himself and hid them out of sight below the edge of the table. She had the distinct impression he was still scratching them, however. He noticed and brought his hands back out onto the table.

Before she could think and overthink it, she laid her

hands over his, letting her warmth penetrate his rough skin. Then, while he looked down as if trying to determine what she was doing, she leaned close and tilted her head just enough to let her lips meet his. Her eyes were open, gazing into his and registering the surprise there, the shock, and then suddenly the welcome. Their lips opened at the same time, and then they were kissing passionately, tongues exploring and tasting, as if the end of the world had been declared and time were running short. Into each other's eyes they gazed, openly and without embarrassment, with no hesitation and no turning back.

Their hands clasped and unclasped, but then he raised his away from her grasp and instead took her flushed cheeks into a gentle grip and she was sure she felt some sort of shiver run through his body, a ripple of—what? Feelings? Fear? Expectation? She couldn't be sure, but the sweetness of her first tentative kiss had given way to passion, and she felt herself respond, becoming aroused even as they clutched at each other like lovers caught in a gale, fighting the wind that would tear them apart.

I had no idea he was so passionate, she thought, giving herself over to the heat. She wanted to cry, sing, smile, and cheer all at once, because this was something she now knew she'd wanted for years, but that something had kept her from expressing. Something had plagued her with doubts, something dark and twisted within her, inhibiting her from exploring her feelings about him all this time. Sure, she'd had her share of bad or simply static relationships, but this one had tickled at her until she'd suppressed it and made damn sure she dealt with her city detective on a business-only level.

Until now. It was as if she'd sensed he was vulnerable and swooped in like a great owl looking for prey.

It didn't matter! Her heart screamed at her and reminded her that she was overdue for some tenderness, and right now his hands on her cheeks and his lips pressed tightly on hers supplied just the right amount.

Her hands went looking for a place to rest, finding his shoulders and feeling his muscles roiling under his clothing, almost as if they were under there knotting and changing, and in shock she took her hands off and broke their kiss suddenly. She gasped. But then he covered her lips again and she responded and nothing else mattered, and whatever was happening to his shoulder muscles had to do with the tension he felt, the sadness, and now the suddenness of their passion, finding themselves so starved for each other.

Jessie abandoned her professional side altogether and lost herself in Nick Lupo's embrace, and for a second there was nothing at all wrong with the world.

MARTIN

After maneuvering around the cottage, contending with bushes and the woodpile under the overhang of the large deck that surrounded three sides of the house, and almost losing his footing on the steep hillside that swept down to the water's edge, Martin had finally located a place to hide that gave him a view of the bastard Lupo and his woman.

He peered through the glass pane and open blinds, past a long wooden dining table and into the small kitchen, where they were seated next to each other at a small round table with three chairs around it. The table was like an afterthought in the kitchen, which was open on all sides and flowed into the paneled living room and its rough-hewn bar down the opposite wall. Had the lighting been different, Martin wouldn't have been able to see them at all. But he was watching as they drank and talked and drank some more, and he was getting bored. He fleetingly thought about killing the woman as soon as she left Lupo's place—another message. He'd either not heard of the other hooker yet or had ignored it and driven north to let the old fuck cover his ass, Martin figured, and he knew damn well why the cop had left the city. Martin knew how to read a calendar—it was the full moon, and Caroline's journals made clear what happened to the fucker during those times.

It was during one of *those times* that Dominic Lupo had killed his sister, tearing her apart like barbecued pork and—

He'd gotten away with it, the bastard, but he wouldn't escape Martin's wrath. Martin caressed the .44 Magnum revolver in his jacket pocket. It was loaded with six of Rag's best silver-jacketed bullets, and Martin knew damn well he could just burst into the cottage right now and kill the two. He could empty the gun into them and worry about the full moon later—most likely the bullets would just kill the bastard anyway, and if the silver was needed, well, it was there. In fact, the temptation was so great that he drew the revolver and cocked it silently. Rag had taught him that, unlike what all those stupid suspense books said, revolvers *don't* have safeties. He was ready to go, just kick in the window and start blasting.

But then the two leaned toward each other and started kissing like teenagers in heat.

Martin's rage was suddenly matched by his lust. What harm in watching for a while? The woman was a beauty. He'd seen her very clearly earlier. Her eyes, her hair, her cheekbones, and best of all, her lips—on which she'd used some subtle mauve or wine shade—they'd all thrilled him. And now that she was in a clinch with the cop, he was aroused by what he saw, and by knowing that they didn't see him. He very badly wanted to fuck her painted mouth, then her corpse. Then maybe her mouth again.

He uncocked the gun the way Rag had shown him and tucked it away. Then he reached inside his pants and felt his warm stiffness there. He started massaging, thinking that this was almost as good as how he would feel when he killed *him*. No, *them*.

LUPO

The shock of her lips on his melted immediately, and Lupo surrendered to the feelings it released within him.

He'd been alone since Caroline, whom he had loved beyond words and time and space. Yet his feelings for Caroline had not been able to keep the Creature within him at bay as she had thought, and as he had relented and agreed to the test. The test had gone awry—he had somehow willed a Change, but the Creature's hunger and frustration had overridden any control Lupo had been able to bring with him through the Change, and he had murdered Caroline.

Now it had to be her deranged brother, returning to extract a price, and the first payment had been the life of Corinne, another woman who'd snuck into his life without his even realizing it. He knew now that he'd loved Corinne, that on some level he had loved her from the moment he had met her, despite what she was and what she did. Her personality really had nothing much to do with her work, at least he hadn't thought so, and he had fallen into a comfortable relationship that maybe someday would have revealed itself to them both. But that possibility was shattered, taken from him as her life was taken from her, and it was because of *him*. Because of Caroline. *Because of him and Caroline.*

Now here was Jessica Hawkins, Dr. Hawkins, his straightlaced landlord and casual friend, suddenly melting into him with a passion that threatened to overwhelm both of them, and through her soft, willing lips he could feel her loneliness and her long frustration with regard to her feelings about him, and he felt himself respond, understanding that—like Corinne—Jessie Hawkins was a person he could have fallen in love with and whose love could have helped dispel his fears and self-hatred about Caroline, but that he'd not allowed himself to notice these feelings. He'd suppressed them for years.

Their passion increased and their tongues tested and tasted and tangled, and the fragrance of her was heady and he looked into her eyes and felt years of self-pity wash away in mere moments, knowing that here, perhaps, was the home he had longed for, the place he wanted to be, and the person he wanted to be with.

His arousal struck him as almost sinful, so pure were the feelings in his heart at that moment. But his body would not be denied, and he abandoned his attempt to suppress, instead leaning into it and feeling her respond even as they came closer, their chairs scraping the wood floor as their knees touched and electricity coursed through him . . .

But then he felt an intrusion. *Two intrusions.*

One was the Creature, whose essence was being drawn out by the full moon that would rise soon—*was it dusk already?*—and claim it and his body for its own. Lupo felt his muscles begin to warp as if beginning the Change, moving liquidlike, *flowing* under his skin like molten rivers of animal blood and sinew, and he knew that hair had begun to sprout on the backs of his hands and up and down his spine. He took Jessie's face in his hands so she wouldn't notice, but then she put her hands on his shoulders and he could see in her eyes that she felt *something*—

But it was as clear as the lancet scent of ammonia, and it entered his nostrils and jabbed his heightened sense of smell like a poison. The other intrusion was a hint of something he'd smelled before, the third thread from Corinne's apartment, where the guy—*was it Martin Stewart?*—had been. The knowledge flooded into Lupo's brain that it had to be Martin Stewart, because that explained the fourth thread, what he couldn't place before, but what clearly had been the scent, no *her* scent, in the Creature's memory. *Caroline's scent.*

Suddenly, Jessie pulled away and their kiss ended, leaving an aching loss in his lips and in his heart. He could still taste her on his lips and tongue, a very desirable sweet-tartness. Inside, the Creature boiled just under the surface, torn between Lupo's interrupted passion and the scents that were arousing anger and hatred and huge wells of sadness.

Jessie sat back in her chair, still staring into his eyes.

What does she see there? He suppressed any other thought along those lines and tried to imagine where Martin could be. Was he outside, as he had been at the Sabatini house?

She was breathless, but then so was he.

She reached out a hand and started to wipe her lipstick from his lips, but he stopped her gently. He wanted to smell her on him. The only good thing he had to hold on to at the moment. Especially if Martin Stewart was lurking outside.

Could the Creature be wrong?

He kissed her fingertips tenderly, and enjoyed the smile that curled her smeared lips.

My God, he thought, *am I really that different from Martin right now?* His arousal was plain to see if she glanced downward.

"That was very, very nice," Jessica Hawkins whispered, still smiling, suddenly becoming aware that he was staring at her lips. She reached up and wiped along the top of her upper lip and below the edge of her full lower lip, seeing the color there on her fingers and blushing again. Remembering their conversation.

"Yes, it was." He wanted to say more, to shout and laugh aloud, but it took a lot of his concentration and skill to suppress the Change he felt wanting to crest. Was the Creature making his presence felt because of the coming moon, or to protect him against Martin's apparent presence? Perhaps both.

Either way, the nearness of the Creature frightened him, for he might come to the fore and hurt Jessie. He couldn't live with another Caroline on his conscience.

"I—" she began.

"I think—" he began.

They chuckled, as in a silly TV script. He deferred to her with an overdone chivalrous wave. She fake-curtsied.

"I'd better get home. I'm supposed to be on call tonight, and I don't have my cell phone. I—I really had a good time, Mr.—uh, Nick. I'm sorry—"

He cut her off. "There's nothing to be sorry about, Jess. We're both adults, and I think there's something here we need to . . ."

"Explore?" she finished for him.

"Yeah, *explore*. That's it. I want to. I have some things to get over. I'm—you know, Corinne was my friend, nothing more really, but I owe her finding the man who killed her, and the others, and helping to get him what he deserves." He hoped she couldn't sense the finality and hatred in his words. "He wants *me* just as much, though, and that means I'm dangerous to be around right now." He hoped this oblique reference would be enough to make her understand without his having to be specific.

She nodded.

"There's a lot about you I don't know, isn't there?" she said, standing. "Don't worry, I don't mind that. It might be fun to learn it all." She laughed, probably at his stunned look.

He hoped she didn't find out under the wrong circumstances.

He walked her upstairs and to the door, then to her SUV. He sniffed the cold night air but couldn't quite grasp any scent. The moment had passed. Or the breeze had carried it away. Or he'd been wrong. Or the Creature had hunkered down, out of sight. In any case, they seemed alone again.

He held the door for her and she climbed in, then leaned out and suddenly pecked at his cheek. "I want to explore a little more like we did tonight," she said, a wicked little smile on her lips. "Very soon. Lunch maybe? You think about that." She started the Nissan and started to back out.

"I am thinking about it," he said. "Believe me."

"Good."

"Jess?"

"Yeah?"

"Watch your back. This guy's dangerous."

She nodded. As she pulled away, he heard early Alan Parsons Project coming from her speakers.

Damn it, something else we have in common!

He walked out to the road, watching her taillights redden and then fade between the pines. His breath fogged in front of his face. It was cold, and getting colder fast as darkness fell. He shivered, but walked the whole of Circle Moon Drive, finding no other car, but a set of tire tracks that seemed to indicate that someone had stopped a ways down the road. Was the scent there? He thought so, but he couldn't be sure. But his instinct said yes.

In the cottage, Fish—once the lead singer of Marillion—was on the stereo singing about seeing his life as a shadow play.

Lupo had to agree.

JESSIE

"Damn it, girl! I can't believe how you threw yourself at him!" she said to herself. She giggled a little. She'd lied about being on call, but she had sensed that they both needed a little time to figure out what had happened be-

tween them. Tomorrow was another day. Maybe some
fresh bakery for breakfast and some of her own jelly pre-
serves. And some fresh fruit. *And no sports bra.* She giggled again.

Her house was only a minute away by car, at the other
end of the snaky Circle Moon Drive, so she was almost
there.

In the speakers, Eric Woolfson sang about how time
was flowing like a river to the sea.

She shut it off in midsentence, one of her favorite
songs, but suddenly afraid of its irony.

CHAPTER EIGHTEEN

MARTIN

The Days Inn just outside Eagle River had one dingy little room left and he took it, stale smoke and all, sweat still clammy on his back and the wet spot inside the front of his pants congealing in a cold, smelly mess that both aroused and disgusted him.

He needed a shower. Then he needed a drink or two. He'd passed a half-dozen cowboy-type bars. Apparently, Up North meant redneck, if the number of muddied Rams, Rangers, and Silverados meant anything. Maybe what he needed was right here, and maybe this would be the best way—and place—to do it. Now that there was somebody else in the cop's life it meant a bit of a detour, but that was okay. For Martin, the journey was going to be every bit as wonderful and exciting as the destination.

He put the Smith & Wesson on the bed as he stripped. It would have been too easy. Just like sitting outside that cop's house. Why do anything the easy way? Where was the fun in that?

What he really wanted, Martin realized, was to kill the freak while making sure he knew *why*. Martin wanted to see the freak do his wolf thing, if it was real. If Caroline hadn't hallucinated the whole thing. No, she believed it, and after reading her words, so did he. He knew exactly what he needed.

He hummed some song in the shower, a melody he'd heard that evening out of Lupo's stereo that he couldn't get out of his head.

LUPO

If it is Martin Stewart, he knows everything about me. My condition. Everything.

Caroline had written about it, and her journals had disappeared. He'd wondered at the time who had taken them, and worried about it. Now he knew.

Jessie Hawkins. Could he love someone without hurting her? Without killing her, as he had Martin's sister?

He decided to break off anything that might be happening between him and Jessie, for her own safety.

He would tell her tomorrow. Right now, he had other responsibilities . . .

The moon called from far away.

The Creature began to surface.

His body changed, and he let it.

KLUG

Wilbur Klug had been waiting for Kenny for an hour. He was on his second beer, almost ready for a third, and he contemplated taking his anger out on one of the waitresses. Suzie was her name, if you bothered to read the plastic tag she wore pinned to her left breast. He flashed for a second on what he could do with that pin on soft, creamy flesh. Her nipples stretched out the t-shirt nicely. He must have been staring, because she caught him at it, her eyes widening at his brazen leer. *Give me five minutes, Suzie-Q, and you'll see what I been savin' for you.* He raised his bottled Bud in her direction and the fake toast settled her enough that she gave him a half-smile and went about her rounds, stopping at a large table of drunken frat boys.

How did the wench know I wasn't asking for another beer?

Wilbur stared at the strapping young men, taking the measure of each. That one was overfed. The greaseball next to him was a pretty boy. The third guy was muscular but clearly weight-room muscle-bound—he'd fold in thirty seconds flat. The thin, Irish-looking guy next to him seemed deceptively calm—he'd fight dirty and with little regard for himself. Wil figured the guy'd go five minutes before a broken limb would shut him down. The fifth guy was a wideboy who probably carried some sort of con-cealed weapon—a boot knife, a set of knuckles—but he wouldn't know how to use it. Wil fingered his own Bowen knife belt and remembered the look on the late Phil Car-son's face as the slightly curved blade had sliced open his belly like a scalpel parting salted lard. That was a moment you wanted to remember forever, to call up whenever you were down. He loved the way old Phil's tight little fists had become splayed hands as he tried to hold his greasy guts inside his split belly, while the blood seeped like petro-leum through his fat fingers. Wil had told Buck about that and enjoyed Buck's jealous rage at having missed it. Wil imagined himself giving the fifth guy here the same busi-ness. They had some dumb bastard from Rhinelander in the slammer for Phil's bye-bye, and last Wil had heard, he was being passed around for more than just tea parties. Wil laughed at the notion of the wrong guy getting the shaft while getting shafted.

The fifth guy, obviously drunk, reached up and touched

Suzie-Q's breast as she zipped by. From across the room Wil heard her gasp and saw her step back, fist poised overhead. The guy laughed and waved her off to gales of laughter from his crew. Wil glanced at his watch. Kenny was very late, but maybe he could amuse himself for a while. He drained the rest of his beer and straightened, scraping his chair back. Anticipation coursed through his veins and he allowed himself a moment to enjoy it—lust mixed with adrenaline. Blood pumping so strongly to his limbs that muscle and sinew seemed to sing with the tension. Wil felt his neck and shoulders tighten and the bulge in his groin grow, as if a beautiful buck had just ambled into his crosshairs. He wished this moment—this first bodily preparation for battle—would last forever. It was more intoxicating than any brew or distillate.

By now Suzie had returned with another pitcher of pissy beer, and the fifth guy took the opportunity to torment her again, this time pinching her buttocks and lifting her apron to examine her muscular and well-shaped thighs and buttocks. He laughed the wide-open-mouth laugh of the bully, the slow-witted kid who shakes down the weak and frail for their lunch money. He showed his horse teeth when he laughed, looking around with beady eyes for the approval he needed. His buddies gave it to him, while others in the room concentrated on ignoring him lest his wrath turned on them.

He was just like Wil, except Wil was smarter. And on home ground. And Wil didn't appreciate the competition. *No fuckin' way, college boy.* Wil headed for the kids' table and seemed to materialize there, bottle held innocently in hand. One second there was no one, and the next there he stood with a smirk on his face.

"Hey man," Wil said softly, "I think you're bothering the chick."

The tormentor was facing away at that moment, and it took him a few seconds to turn and stare at Wil. His lips formed a sneer. "Take a hike, Helen," he said. Then he turned to his little group and put a hand on his forehead. "Not tonight, honey, I have a headache." He laughed so hard he splashed spittle all over the table. One of his friends gushed out beer and let it spill all over his shirt. Mirth was their middle name.

Without a warning or a moment's hesitation, Wilbur slashed the beer bottle across the back of the frat boy's head hard enough to shatter it, then raking it back just as quick as a blur so the jagged shards would do their thing in the back of the jerk's skull.

The frat boy screeched and blood flew as the bottle completed the arc of its return trip and gouged flesh and bone from the boy's skull, and then Wil was jabbing the glassy remains in the face of the overfed one, who crumpled with a snootful of glass, bone, and teeth while his fat fingers tried to hold his face together as blood squirted between them. Wil was turning to face the rising body-builder type before anyone noticed that he'd sucker-punched Pretty Boy and nearly downed him with nary a whisper. When the bodybuilder presented a wide enough target, Wil's pointed and steel-toed motorcycle boot shot out and put a major hurt on the muscleman's groin. The dude dropped like a sack of rotten potatoes—with a *splat* in the blood-beer-bile-bottle combo below—and then it was just the Irish lad and the original bully, who'd managed to ignore the gore oozing from the back of his own head *(tells you where his brain ain't!)* and was now gathering himself for some kind of defense. Wil dropped the remains of the Bud-swill bottle and reached into his back pocket for the special length of carved pool cue he kept there. It was cut down to about twelve inches and years ago he'd lovingly embedded four rows of lead shot in the compass points of the last five inches, so that when he swung it at the Irish lad—who proved his loyalty and stupidity both by advancing without recon—the weight took out half a jawful of college-boy teeth in yet another gush of blood and, this time, puke.

Then he was facing the original bully, the fifth guy, the guy whose horse teeth reminded Wil of—well, horses. *Fuck this,* he thought. *Time to end it.* The guy roared once, his voice full of pain and rage—or outrage—and charged Wil, who neatly sidestepped and watched as he flew past in a blur of blood and windmilling limbs to land on the filthy beer-encrusted floor. Wil stepped up immediately behind him and planted a booted kick in the guy's lower back, putting his entire weight into it almost as if kicking a field goal. The guy screamed in pain and half-crawled, half-rolled away from Wil's foot, scampering over the blood- and debris-covered floor to the side of the room.

Wil didn't bother to follow. Only a few patrons had stood to watch the fight, one-sided and brief as it was, but most of the clientele had watched from their seats. Wilbur Klug had a bit of a reputation in the department of kicking college butt, as Buck Benton once put it—a reputation that more college kids should have heeded before placing him in the position of proving it, Wil thought. Problem was, no one knew which drinking establishment might be the recipient of Wil's attentions, and those college kids who learned about him during one of his sessions invariably never returned to any local watering hole.

Somebody bought him a beer. When Kenny finally showed up, he was just in time to see damaged or groggy college kids taking themselves very quickly out the door, heading for campus health services for stitches and plenty of gauze. They wouldn't be back tonight.

No one had called the sheriff. Wilbur Klug's occasional outbursts were considered to be for the common good—after all, they served as an outlet valve for his aggressions. College kids from the nearby state extension school were barely tolerated, so the occasional beating went unnoticed. Now college girls, however, found themselves welcome just about anytime and rarely witnessed Wil's kind of public purge. Had his friends Buck and Kenny been present, they might well have given the college boys a little more of their hospitality, but as it was, Wil was thirsty and alone, so he let them off easy.

He grabbed the Bud and guzzled it. Free beer was free beer.

Kenny nodded apologetically. "Sorry I missed it all, Wilbur! I'da kicked me a little college butt too."

"Sit the fuck down and let's us figure out a way to break Buck outta jail, Kenny. No bullshit."

"Break him out? You nuts?"

Wilbur chugged beer and tried to put into words what had occurred to him. It was difficult, because the key to his earlier thoughts happened to be the fact that Mrs. Klug was now chopped into white, roast-size packages stored in his venison freezer in the basement. Bits of bone and flesh were still wedged under his nails. He had burned out the small chain saw halfway through the job and put his hacksaw set to work, then he'd buried the tools out in the vegetable patch. There were a couple more recently dug holes in the vicinity, but he'd checked and they seemed to have held up pretty well over the winter. It really *was* time to get the hell out of Vilas County, if only because his tale of Shelly's departure wouldn't hold more than a few days.

She'd fought him when he went back in to reclaim his new prize. She'd kicked and scratched and threatened to call Sheriff Bunche if he went near her, which of course infuriated him no end and pretty much meant he *had* to subdue her. Shelly'd grown up tougher than most, but he would not be denied and he'd taught her the lesson again and again, not realizing until it was too late that one time he had held his hands around her neck too long. By then the bruises had begun to come up, and he'd had no choice. No choice at all. Well, they wouldn't look in his venison freezer for a while.

He'd had a grand plan—the three of them could have masterminded a small crime wave, given what he knew about where several local businesses kept their petty cash stashes. He'd been in the middle of fantasizing about how he and Buck and Kenny could avail themselves of his knowledge when the unfortunate accident with Shelly forced him to rethink portions of the plan. And then Kenny'd called with news of Buck's arrest, and the weekend 'd gone to hell before it had really started. He had wrapped his blood-flecked, meaty hands around the phone while talking to Buck, and had figured that part of his plan was now shot. But not all of it. They could still handle the cash stashes, once Buck was free. The only thing was, they couldn't follow his original plan and stay, no sir, his stupid fuckin' wife had seen to *that*. Getting herself killed had put a major damper on his plan, but maybe it also gave him the opportunity to split this backwater and find more suitable digs elsewhere.

Now he tried carefully to put his ideas into words for Kenny, not the sharpest knife in the block, sure, but they'd bullied their way through grade school and a prolonged tour of duty in high school, and frankly no one else would have listened and obeyed half as well.

Wil said, "Buck and me—and you—we been here all our lives. We spend our money here, fuck our women here, drink our beer here, and do what all else here, and nowhere else. I figure it's time we moved on, but first we need some capital. Buck knows a couple places we can get that capital, and so do I. Then we can head outta here and start over somewhere else."

Kenny had drunk some beer and listened to the grand plan, and Wilbur could see that he wasn't all the way happy about how things were going. That was too fuckin' bad.

"What about Shelly?" Kenny asked with a whine.

"Shelly's gone. Left me. Headed back home, far's I know. I don't give a good fuck, you know? I took a lotta shit from that woman, and I ain't sad a 'tall to see her headin' for the horizon. I'm a free man, Kenny! And when we get Buck out, then we're all gonna be free. We get enough cash, I'm thinking we head for Chicago first, then

New Orleans. Think of all that titty hangin' out during Mardi Gras. You seen that *Cops* special, ain't ya?"

Kenny nodded and Wil could see how he was considering it, wrapping his head around it. Kenny would go along.

"Or, hey, we could head for Canada. The mountains. Never find us there! Yeah, the mountains . . ."

"I don't know, Wilbur," Kenny said. But his voice was shaky. He'd never let his friends leave him behind. He had nothing else.

Wilbur chugged his beer and smiled. Maybe things were looking up after all.

MARTIN

The man was a one-person dynamo. There was no describing it. It was like a scene from that old seventies flick he'd once seen in the Institute—what was it? *Billy Jack*? In which the guy went wacko on a group of bad guys and *kung fu*-ed them into blubbering idiots because they just made him "go berserk." Martin had come into the North Woods Bar and eaten an incredible double cheeseburger while seated at the long wooden bar. The burger was loaded with grease and fried onions and Martin had squirted a huge amount of mustard all over it. It was heartburn in a basket, but it had taken the edge off the empty-stomach gnawing he'd felt ever since seeing the freak cop and the woman making out like children. They had what he wanted, what he once had, and now he was an empty vessel all because of Lupo. The weight of the .44 was comfortable in the concealed holster, and the weight of the greasy bar food seemed to compensate for the emptiness inside, at least for a while.

He'd been about to move on to some other dive when he'd noticed the college kids bothering the waitress at about the same time he noticed the mountain of a man across the room. He'd stared at the waitress himself, seeing that all her lips needed was a heavy coat of classic red to break out her fragile features from the delicate porcelain skin. She reminded him a bit of his Nurse Dievers, and he flashed into a fantasy about her—better yet, the two of them—locked in a smeary embrace. Then there'd been some sort of a barometric pressure change in the place and he'd felt the air alter around him as the guy approached the kids and, seconds later, laid them all out without even breaking a sweat. Martin had seen some amazing brawls at the Institute, and he enjoyed this one. He asked the bartender about the big guy and got only a name and an elaborate shrug. Afterward, Martin sidled to an empty table near the man and his jumpy friend, a raggedy-looking wino-type whose nervous eyes roamed all around.

The big guy had a look in his eye that reminded Martin of his father's sadistic glee as they played their games. He shivered, though he couldn't tell if it was fear or expectation.

Martin heard enough of their conversation to allow himself a smile. It was serendipitous, coming here. He felt the pieces falling into place.

KLUG AND KENNY

At first the bland-looking city guy who came up suddenly looked like a cop. In fact, Wilbur thought he saw the outline of a piece under the quilted jacket. His hair was too short, too neat. He seemed both square and twisted at the same time, but it was the eyes that gave him away. There was nothing but emptiness there.

Wil saw himself reflected in the stranger's eyes. *This guy's no fuckin' cop.*

"Gentlemen," said the stranger. "Are you by any chance looking for employment?"

Wil stared a moment longer. "Might be. What kind of

employment?" He slitted his eyelids. The stranger had seen him dispose of the queer quintet, but he didn't seem intimidated, and that was interesting. His eyes were blank—as blank as his overall appearance. He could have melted into a wall.

"My name is Martin Stewart. I have a proposition for you."

"Sit," Wil said. "I'm listenin'."

The conversation lasted over an hour. Empty beer bottle ranks took up the table's center. Some of what the Martin dink said was strange and kinda funny. But he had money, one thing Wil figured he himself was too short of now, given his situation, and the story included a couple perks that he might find interesting. Mighty interesting indeed. And all they had to do was off a city cop, and hunt this wolf the guy was obsessing about. Yeah, he said the guy *was* the wolf, but obviously that was bullshit made up to get them interested. Wilbur didn't need any of that crap to know he was seeing an opportunity better than the string of robberies he'd planned. No, this was better because there was a chance they could pry some of this Martin fella's cash from him, too, along the line.

Wilbur Klug listened, and when the name of the reservation doctor was mentioned, he smiled.

Better and better.

The images he saw in his mind were more than enough to convince him. The cash now and later was the gravy, but the meat looked pretty good, too, nice and edible.

Oh, yes.

CHAPTER NINETEEN

LUPO

The moon rises high in the night sky, its halo tinting the treetop edges with a silver-black glow.

A slight, cold breeze ruffles the uppermost branches of the straight pines and rattles the hardening leaves of the undergrowth below.

The moon's glow is dulled by clouds, draping the woods in a white snowlike mantle. The light seems to pulsate while the clouds race from one side of the sky to the other in stop-motion. Beneath the dark trees, the Creature stares upward, entranced by the moon, held prisoner by its power, held prisoner by its presence.

The Creature's breath puffs in front of his muzzle.

A growl escapes the Creature's throat. Hunger drives him forward, toward the human's dwelling. There is a fence around the house, and within the fence he smells various animal scents. Pets, any one of which would sate his hunger, have wandered the space between the house and the expanse of chain link, but now the Creature can sense that there is nothing. Even though he is within sight of the dwelling's entrance, which is lit by a softly glowing globe, the Creature knows there will be no meal here. He will not take a meal in such circumstances.

About to turn away and follow another path, the Creature stops and sniffs the air. A rustle from behind alerts him to the approach of some small night animal, perhaps a raccoon or badger, or even a fat rabbit, who hasn't caught his own scent yet. He samples the frigid air carefully and knows it is a rabbit, its fur packed with succulent flesh. The Creature knows there are flying predators around who would take his dinner from him, so he sets off immediately and stalks the hapless morsel. The prey has now frozen in fear, aware of danger but unable to determine its source. The indecision is fatal, for the Creature pounces and soon there is bloody flesh between its pointed jaws, his front paws helping to hold the still-squirming body while dipping his muzzle into the warmth of the rabbit's stomach and delighting in the delicacies to be found there. Minutes later, his nose wet with warm redness made black by the dim moonlight, the Creature abandons the remains of his feast to the scavengers who wait for their turn in the wings. They are afraid of the Creature, but they have seen him kill before and there is always a meal for them afterward. When the Creature disappears in the darkness of the woods, they will approach and quietly stuff themselves on the leftovers. They will remain subservient to the Creature who comes only at long intervals but whose scent, or some mysterious element in his scent, makes them nervous and skittish.

The Creature hears their squabbling over the bloody fur and few bones he left behind, but now he heeds only the moon's call and cannot be bothered with his fellow carnivores. In a few moments, he is running through the night, the cool air caressing his fur and cleansing his whiskers. Though he avoids low-reaching branches with little effort, occasionally leaves brush across his back and rustle above him as he runs headlong into the moonlit night. He is so happy that a joyous howl escapes his throat before he can stifle it, and then a second quick howl. And still he runs, his callused pads treading the fine green needles and the occasional patch of icy snow left from the last fall.

Another howl escapes him, and somewhere deep in the recess of his brain, the Creature knows that he should control himself. But the running feels so good, and the full stomach, and the blood tang in his throat, that he cannot. And he wonders why these doubts plague him even during the best running, after the best meals. He senses there's a reason, but instinct overrules these strange feelings. He continues running, stopping only to void his bladder and mark his territory. In the last few hunts he has smelled the scent of a newcomer from a new or foreign pack, a full-grown male who has been tapping the local pet population to fill his belly. The Creature avoids doing so, but lusts for a snout-to-snout meeting with the interloper. It will happen someday, but for now he romps happily and without bothering the humans. He knows there is a reason for not hurting humans, but it's still locked behind a gauze curtain in his brain. He knows that he's on the verge of understanding, but can't worry about it yet.

For now, there is the pleasure of running free and the fresh blood.

The moon calls to him, and he answers.

SAM WATERS

He came awake with a start.

His heart raced faster than normal. That was his first observation. As if his dreams had been somehow disturbing. Or frightening.

His arm hurt. Rheumatism, arthritis, whatever it was, the joints hurt as he moved it and laid his fingers across the vein in his neck, taking his pulse. A reflex. Was his heart finally giving up?

Before he could find the pulse and gauge the situation, he heard the howling again, and he knew without a doubt that it was responsible for his awakening, and perhaps also for his state of heightened anxiety.

Even as he pondered this fact for a few seconds, another long and plaintive howl echoed through the forest outside his window and drove him deeper under the quilt.

"Lord God," he whispered hoarsely.

It was back.

A third howl seemed to answer him, and he shivered. It was cold in his bedroom, but not that cold. He knew that fear chilled his heart now, not illness. At least, not yet.

He gathered up his courage and touched the top of the nightstand for his glasses, finding them in the usual spot. With them perched on his nose, the clock was no longer just a red glow. The numbers coalesced into the time, 1:15 A.M., mocking him with the blinking colon. Sam half-raised himself and turned toward the frosted window. The register below kicked out warm air and kept the glass pane above both foggy and frosty, depending on the weather outside. A bit of cold wind whistled through the gaps in his old storm windows. The calendar lied; even though it was nearly spring, the weather was pure winter minus some of the snow, which had melted in the January thaw.

He knew he would have awakened in about an hour anyway, so he might as well get up and see if there was more howling to come. Usually, there would be a howl just before light, as if the animal were saluting the coming day. Or decrying it, whatever.

"You're an idiot, Waters," he said to the darkness. "Just an old fool with childish fears."

But Sam Waters knew that he was only trying to fill the room with the comfort of his own voice. He had noticed long ago that there was a pattern to the howling, and therefore to the animal's presence. And he had fallen asleep with a vague thought on his mind, mindful of the fact that the moon would be full this night.

He swung his thinning legs from the warmth of the bed and searched with his feet for the sheepskin slippers below. He'd been a barrel of a man, huge and tree-trunk strong in his youth, and he'd acted that way. But now the muscles were softening and every day brought more reminders that his health was something to worry about, not disregard. He hated thinking about it, because he'd always been scornful of people who were wrapped up in themselves. But daily aches and pains eventually added up to the point at which he realized why those others complained. Pain really could make you lazy and self-pitying, and he supposed whining, too. Good thing no one but he had to listen to his bleating. Everyone he knew thought he was stoic, but he complained plenty, in private.

Within minutes there was hot tea bubbling into a mug and he had added a few chocolate chip cookies to take the edge off his fear.

He made his way to the window overlooking the tiny private cemetery, where the love of his life called to him more and more these days and nights. Sarah Waters had been dead almost fifteen years, and in all that time he had promised her that he would face his fear and hunt the monster. It had been his promise from the day the disease had taken his son from him. His son Michael, whose remains now lay beside Sarah's, had been killed in the southern part of the state, shortly after infecting a young boy in the city with the disease. Sam never told Sarah that it was he who had followed his son to the city and, to his shame, killed him when he was unable to control him or cure him from the ravages of the disease. The killing of his own son had ruined Sam for life, and he had spent years sulking in fits of guilt. Until the creature had somehow returned to the area, and a grisly murder in Milwaukee had reminded him of how the creature killed. Sam had realized then that the beast he sometimes heard in his woods was the one who had butchered the woman psychologist in the city. He suspected that the disease had passed either from his son to the new victim in the city, or somehow to someone else first. He had vowed to himself and Sarah's memory that he would face that creature one day, but had grown old and tired.

Lazy, you mean.

Yeah, lazy.

It had grown easier to let the creature be. Once a month, perhaps nine or ten months a year, Sam could live and let live. Whoever had the disease now was careful never to kill humans. Sam had followed the news, both official and unofficial, with great care. He knew the local journalists and he knew the local medicine men. He had connections in state government, at the Department of Natural Resources and at the Bureau of Indian Affairs. Plus, he had friends on the elders' council. He knew those who dared speak of the creature, and he knew what they thought in private. He had become convinced that whoever carried the horrible disease now was less dangerous than the one who had infected his beloved son.

But in the last several months, the monster's kills had become more daring. Instead of wild hares and other animals, people on the res and off had reported losing livestock and pets. Maybe it had been naive to think that the beast, whatever it was, would avoid humans forever. Maybe it was time to fulfill the promise he had made long ago, to his dead son, to himself, and later, to his wife.

He ate his cookies and drank his tea as he stared outside, seeing through the pines the headstones marking the graves of the two people he treasured most, both of them gone. The disease should be stopped. He had put it off long enough.

He went to the gunrack and took down the side-by-side, a splendid Beretta, a gift—for he could never have afforded such a weapon—from a long-gone friend. He cradled the sleek stock and caressed it. No, it was much too beautiful. He swapped it for a Remington semiauto, then loaded the magazine with five shells filled with buckshot from the "special" batch he'd had all these years. He didn't look forward to it, but tomorrow night he would be on the hunt.

In the meantime, he selected a DVD from his small collection and popped the cap on a Corona—the two vices he allowed himself—and settled down to watch his favorite movie, *The Graduate*, for the twentieth or thirtieth time. As he lost himself in the Simon and Garfunkel songs, he could not help caressing the Remington's stock with his gnarled hand.

He dozed, and remembered. It was all too clear in his mind, how his friend had rejected white man's society after being let go from yet another job. He remembered how Joseph Badger, a priest and shaman of the Ojibwa tribe, had begun to seethe in his hatred of whites. He had wallowed in despair, but then Joseph chanced upon some European magical texts, some ancient alchemy rituals, and some of the writings of Aleister Crowley, the Beast, who had practiced sex magick and other arcane arts, and a plan for revenge against the whites became his obsession. Sam and other elders had attempted to discourage their distraught friend and respected medicine man from polluting his soul and therefore his medicine, but it was too late.

One day Joseph's experiments in native witchcraft rituals, vision quests, and peyote ingesting converged with his dabbling into the European Black Arts and sucked away his soul forever as he altered his body structure and became a massive black wolf. In that form, he would ravage herds and pets and even maul the occasional farmer, taking his revenge out in the warm blood of innocents. Only when drunk and stoned on peyote and various hallucinogens had he confessed to his former friend, Sam Waters, who had then informed the tribal elders and requested a cleansing. Unfortunately, after being banished,

Joseph Badger blamed Sam for turning the council against him.

First he had convinced Sam's son, Michael, that there was power in his blending of the Old World and the New World magicks, managing to alienate son from father. Then, in the form of a wolf, he had bitten Michael and passed the disease on to him, hoping to start an epidemic that would rid the state of whites. But Sam had done his duty, tracking his old friend and finishing him the way the European werewolves were killed, with silver. The element silver symbolized purity, and Joseph had confessed that his experiments proved it was the only metal that could harm such a creature. Though other parts of the mythology had turned out to be inaccurate, Joseph had proven that some characteristics were all too true. Sam had shuddered at the thought of the kind of experiments Joseph had been up to. Eventually, Sam had been forced to track his own son in the city and end his life, but only after he'd apparently already bitten someone. Years passed and he thought the nightmare was over, until some years ago, when the monster returned to the North Woods and that woman psychologist was murdered down south.

Sam sat up and recalled his years and his losses. He hugged the shotgun close as the movie came to an end. It was a downer, even though it ended with Benjamin getting the girl. You could almost guess that they'd never stay together. That life without their families would be too tough for at least one of them. That their counterculture gesture had been for naught. He always cried at the end of that one, so he chose a different DVD from his stash. *Thunderball*, another favorite. Out of print. James Bond was one of Sam's weaknesses. He had read the books, the novelizations, the scripts. He had read about Ian Fleming's life, Sean Connery's, Roger Moore's. You name it and Sam knew it, if it was part of the world of 007. Mindless entertainment, yeah, but it was what he needed right now, as dawn approached. He lost himself in the Caribbean setting and slept a little, dreaming of sharks in a tank and wolves in the woods, and a colorful Carnival in which blood gushed from the throats of innocent young men and women.

When Sam opened his eyes, the sun was well above his roof and it all seemed foolish. Until he went for a walk and found the remains of a butchered rabbit barely a hundred yards from his window.

CHAPTER TWENTY

MARTIN

Just before the bar closed, Martin staggered outside after saluting his two new friends. Employees. Comrades.

Whatever.

He didn't like beer. Never had. He remembered the yeasty smell and taste of it on his father's breath and—*down there, too, because his father was always interrupting their games to use the bathroom*—it triggered more memories he didn't want. But he could drink it, especially if he was in character. What had he been tonight? He'd actually loosened his tongue a bit too much, telling them not so much that the cop he hated was a werewolf, which would have made them snort with derisive laughter, but that maybe the cop *thought* he was a magical creature, that he *acted* like one, and that he should be put down like a rabid dog even if he wasn't a wolf, dog, mutt, or puppy.

Martin chuckled as he thought back. Sure, they obviously thought him stupid, and the cop a total wacko, but

Wilbur Klug had laughed and said, "I'm gonna get to use them old wolf traps I got rustin' out in the garage."

Dumber than doornails, no doubt, but they were extra guns in a hunt. Now they wanted to bust their friend out of jail. Martin made it clear that if they were caught, he'd never heard of any of them. He was willing to let them bring in their idiot friend, but if they got themselves tagged, he was outta there. He made sure he told them. A dozen times. Finally, Klug had threatened to rip his tongue out with red-hot pincers.

Martin figured he half meant it, even though he smiled when he said it. His teeth were like fangs, but browned by tobacco, coffee, or both.

Some retainer cash changed hands, and then they'd downed another half-dozen Buds each to seal the deal. They stayed behind to plan their mission, while Martin headed for his motel bed.

He squinted in the pale lamp light and he still could barely make out the different shapes in the gravel lot that spread out in a U pattern around the tavern (which, he now realized, itself consisted of a double-wide trailer on a cinder-block foundation with a rough wooden porch wrapped around three sides). All around stood the thick black line of ramrod-straight trees locked in one long rank. Martin looked up and realized with a start that the lamp light was really the full moon, partially hidden behind trees and fast-moving puffy clouds.

A chill wind swirled through the trees and made them shimmer in his vision, their shadows lengthening and shrinking rhythmically. The rustling through the leaves and needles was loud and eerie, and an owl's hoot sent a shiver down his spine. He realized that he was the only person outside, and that the tree line was closer to him than he was to the bar. The car wasn't far, but he suddenly felt stalked. Spied.

Were those eyes, luminescent eyes, glowing like red coals just over there, in the pitch-black shadows under the pines?

Before he could reassure himself, a howl echoed through the woods and seemed to reach down into his groin, squeezing his testicles like lemons. His knees shook. He reached for the gun, but then the howl faded away.

Martin unlocked the car and prayed it would start. It did, then he spewed gravel and gunned it onto the dark road, heading for his fleabag a few miles out of town. The dark woods on either side of the road spooked him and he imagined werewolves running parallel to the car, waiting for him to stop so they could tear him to pieces like Caroline. What if there were more of them?

For the first time since he'd started his vendetta, Martin felt fear.

KLUG

Customers left the bar in groups, nervous in the spooky light of the rising moon. Klug and Kenny plotted (Wilbur plotted and Kenny nodded) until closing time, at which point they stood carefully and made for the door, the beers and shots they'd had apparently slowing their progress considerably.

At the door, Wil reached out and patted Suzie on the ass. She whipped around to slug him, but his fist caught her hand in a steel grip and he grinned as pain crossed her features.

"Is that any way to say good night?" he drawled, letting his words slur a bit more than they should. Wilbur liked playing at being drunker than he was, because it made other men underestimate him. In reality, he wasn't that drunk at all.

Suzie realized it just as she opened her mouth to speak. Without breaking his grip, Wil leaned in and plastered his saliva-flecked lips over hers.

"Mmmmmm!" she screamed into his mouth as she tried to pull away, dislodge, unbalance, or otherwise disengage his disgusting grasp. "Mmmmmm, let go!" she mumbled loudly onto his lips.

"Problem over there?" Harry North called from behind the bar. His name provided the establishment with the pun on the sign outside, but he was damned if he'd let this backwoods Romeo manhandle his waitress like that.

"Keep your drawers on, Harry!" Wilbur said, laughing as he unsmacked his lips from Suzie's and watched her gag and spit to get the taste of him out of her mouth. "I'm headin' home to the little woman."

To Suzie he said, much more softly, "You an' me got a tad unfinished business, don't we? I'm gonna want those lips of yours to show me some lovin', and it's goin' to be pretty soon. I know you cain't wait, but I'll be back for ya, Suzie-Q!"

He left, Kenny in tow, laughing as she recoiled with disgust.

"What'd you do that for, Wil?" Kenny whined, once out on the porch.

"Quit your bitchin' and just remember our plan, got it, Kenny-boy? We're gonna get Buck outta that jail cell. Then we're goin' huntin'."

Theirs was the last car and truck in the lot, Kenny's tired old Trans Am covered in primer, and Wil's battered Dodge Ram pickup. As they separated, a series of howls ripped through the night.

"Fuck is that?"

"I think that's our guy's little wolfie," Wil said, his voice a bit uncertain. Wouldn't do to seem frightened in front of Kenny. In the truck, he had a sawn-off shotgun, and that helped him feel safe.

"Here, wolfie. Here, little wolfie!" Wil called out softly. "Come to Wilbur, boy."

His eyes widened in anticipation.

CHAPTER TWENTY-ONE

LUPO

Lupo awoke in the bushes behind his cottage. He was used to it. Though he had managed to reach home all right and the Change had caught him at exactly the right time, he saw from the position of the sun that he had slept much too long. His muscles were sore from the running, and his throat was a parched desert. He found the key in its hiding place and let himself in after collecting his hastily piled clothing. He caught a glimpse of himself in the hall mirror and shuddered. His face and chin were bloodstained, as were his hands. His hair was a matted mess full of twigs and pine needles. The hair that magically grew during the Change had left no trace except its traditional itching. He stared at himself and scratched his cheeks.

Jesus Christ, what a sight!

He made a beeline for the refrigerator. It took a full bottle of water to wash the taste of rancid blood and raw animal flesh from his palate, and a second bottle to quench the thirst he often thought of as unquenchable. In the early days of the disease, he would vomit until his throat was raw, but he had since become accustomed to the bits of flesh that remained from his hunts. Then he washed his hands and set about showering and washing his hair, hoping no one would come visit soon. He half-hoped he would have one specific visitor, however, and it surprised him that he so looked forward to the visit. Nearly noon, he noted with a little yelp of panic, and Jess Hawkins had mentioned checking to see if he wanted lunch today, a near-date he hadn't been quick enough to get out of and that he hadn't really wanted to.

He toweled himself dry and allowed that he felt almost human again.

He barked a laugh. *Almost human!* He hadn't felt human since before Andy Corrazza's completely instinctive attack. Lupo didn't really hold it against him. He'd probably been frightened to death, finding himself altered and in such a strange body. Lupo knew well enough by now what it felt like.

He brushed his teeth three times. Suddenly, he sat on the edge of the old-fashioned tub. Dizzy, he grabbed the vanity and waited until the spell had passed. But with the spell came a strong memory, a certainty, from his romp in the woods. A memory that made his neck hairs tingle. He felt the growl in his throat and suppressed it. It was him. He—Martin Stewart, if that's who his enemy was—had been here. At the cottage. Last night.

Last night.

All at once, memories of his outing crashed upon themselves and overloaded his circuits, making his head spin. Could it be that he'd made another breakthrough? Could control over his Change be far behind? But before dealing with these greater questions, he needed to sort out the animal-like memories, half image and half impulse, that bunched together into packets of raw data. All he needed was the key to unraveling it. He stood and stared into the foggy mirror. The haze seemed to help, and he listened to what the Creature wanted to tell him.

The scent was present all around the cottage—the one that included the scent from long ago. *Caroline.*

There was also the scent of another predator, a male wolf who must have wandered south from the Upper Peninsula. He was an enemy, too, aware of Lupo's scent and challenging his dominance. He would have to be dealt with.

Lupo pondered the other wolf's presence. The UP was where a couple packs had sprung up after efforts to restore the wolf population eradicated by farmers in the previous hundred years.

Why'd you have to choose my woods? Lupo thought. Of all places . . . As if he didn't have enough trouble.

Someone knocked at the door and Lupo swore, dropping his towel. He fumbled with his fresh cutoff jeans and hurried to the door, still wet.

"Rise and shine!" Jessie Hawkins said, holding up a wicker basket. "I have handmade muffins!" Then she realized that he was barely out of the shower and giggled. "You really take your vacation seriously!"

He noticed she was checking out his physique and waved her inside. "You don't know the half of it," he muttered. He sniffed the cold, pine-laden air outside and shivered, then closed the door. "Let me, uh, get some clothes on."

"If you insist."

Pondering the meanings layered there, Lupo finished drying and dressed in long pants and a loose shirt. As he thought of her, standing in his doorway with a basket of baked goods and a smile on her open, wonderful face, all his resolve seemed to dissipate. He wasn't sure he could fend off her charms, and he decided that was no bad thing after all.

"Did you have a good meal last night?" she asked from the other room.

He nodded. *Very satisfactory.* "Yeah," he said for her benefit, then rejoined her, fully clothed and groomed.

She smiled again at the sight of him. "I was going to bring you some fresh food, but I don't eat that much meat and I figured you'd have a steak or something."

"Yes, I like meat. Very rare."

She let that go, and he wondered if she'd looked in his freezer. Of course she had—she'd have to, to make a proper appliance check.

"I bribed my assistant into keeping an eye out at the clinic, but I'm on call if they need me."

Lupo thanked her. Her smile had him nearly tongue-tied, and certainly flustered. *Like a schoolboy with a crush.* He hoped the Creature was indeed asleep.

He set the table awkwardly, barely remembering where anything was. She watched, amused, but didn't offer to help. She seemed to be measuring him, or weighing her options.

Tension increased within him, and by the time they sat to eat, a cold glass of white wine from her basket before each of them, Lupo thought it would drive him crazy.

He'd put on a CD, the romantic side of Emerson Lake and Palmer's *Works, Volume One,* and Lake's edgy ballads swirled around them.

They chatted about the weather and the season to come, and he muttered a few words about Corinne, but his lack of enthusiasm for the subject cooled them a bit. Then Jessie relayed her encounter with Buck Benton, which concerned him a great deal.

"This guy sounds like big trouble."

"He's been one of those troublemakers you just expect to read about every other day. If there's a fight or an assault, he's bound to be there. If there's a car theft or some pot confiscated, he's nearby. If there's violence against native fishermen, he's one of the ringleaders. Him and this Klug guy he hangs out with."

"How do you know all this?"

"Well, I'm the res doctor, so I hear about all the misbehaving. And these trailer-trash whites are always stirring up trouble around spearfishing time, so everybody knows their names. It's never anything good, though. Always some negative deal in which somebody got hurt. They're the reason redneck stereotypes exist up here."

"And elsewhere," he pointed out.

"Right! These guys think they're in the bayous or something. They want to be, pardon me, backwoods assholes. Klug's been up on charges for beating his wife, but sure enough, she stays with him. He's a monster. This Buck guy's not married, but I know Sheriff Bunche wanted to arrest him on some rape charges last year, but no one would testify. Buck's the name of his knife, see, and—"

"Oh, I get it. How original! He must be some piece of work. Forgive my saying so, but it's even worse in the city. And now they've got us watching for terrorists, so petty crimes seem to go unnoticed."

"Shame," she said, as she held out her glass for more wine. "Might as well drink more! What else can we do?"

He poured the sprightly Zeller Schwarze Katz for both of them, finishing the bottle—and letting her question hang in the air between them.

He wasn't sure how it happened, or exactly when, but like teenagers in a parked car, their chairs seemed to edge closer together, until either the wine or the tension or the combination brought their lips together again.

He tasted the chilled sweet grape on her lips and felt the passion rising in his loins. There had been so much sadness in him for the last few days, and so much unresolved sexual and emotional longing—he knew that now—for Corinne, sweet Corinne, who was gone, that he began to feel as if he would burst. They kissed passionately, intensely, for a while, and when they adjourned to the floor it was as much a surprise as it was inevitable. On the warm rug spread in front of the silent fireplace, they slowly undressed each other like gifts, accepting the beauty and joy of the moment with no restraint.

He nuzzled her lips and nose, and then her downy neck, his tongue leaving a hot-cold streak behind until he found her hardening nipples and tasted them one at a time while she purred her pleasure at his touch. His hands caressed and massaged, and his lips brought her to the brink, and then he moved lower, opening her and tasting of her secret folds while she touched his head gently, allowing him this most intimate of moments.

Lupo felt a rainbow of emotion as he raised her to a fever pitch. He felt a repressed lust, a love he'd not known was there, and a fondness for her he had to suspect had been there all along, and—

fear

—for what if he did to Jessie what he had done to Caroline?

He felt so much a prisoner of the moon . . . Was he wise to engage his lust so thoroughly when the Creature roamed so close to the surface? Was he tempting Fate, gambling with Jessie's life? His hands and feet itched, but he ignored them and concentrated on the soft, warm body beneath him until her voice rewarded him with the sounds of her pleasure and she melted completely and without restraint at the tender touch of his tongue.

Then they shifted and he looked into the dark pools of her eyes, seeing that she saw *something* in his, but the moment passed and she slid down along his tense body and they tangled again, but now she took him between her lips and maneuvered him slowly into hot and cold regions, using her tongue to test, taste and judge, caressing him with a firm, wet gentleness until he was ready to burst.

But they dissolved and recoalesced into a different orientation, and when he entered her his passion grew fiery and she matched it stroke for stroke, until they rose together and crested the wave, their mouths locked and their voices speaking in tongues together, rising in volume, riding the lovely turbulence in joyous tandem as if it were an endless waterfall, roaring in their ears until their need finally began to ebb. They coasted in mutual satisfied silence, content in each other's arms, the sweat drying coolly on their skin in the afternoon chill.

"Mr. Lupo," Jessie murmured into his neck, "I think you're trying to avoid paying the rent."

"I thought you were absolving me," he whispered back, and then they laughed, because it was more the way they were used to speaking to each other. But there was no denying that the nonverbal communication between them had been stellar the last half hour.

They held each other for a while, breathing rhythmically as one, enjoying the closeness.

Greg Lake was on Repeat, singing "C'est la Vie" with Emerson's evocative accordion solo, and it was the most romantic thing Nick Lupo had ever heard even though he knew this album very well. Jessie seemed to feel the moment too, and the music made them one again. And as the disc hit Repeat for the third time, they melted together in a Repeat of their own.

Much later, in front of the crackling fire Lupo had started, he tried to tell her that he would have to be alone in just a few hours. And for the first time since Caroline, he considered confessing why.

"There's something I have to tell you," he began.

"Is it a secret? I know you have secrets."

"You do?"

"Yes, but I haven't been a snoop, really. I just—I can sense it. I've always sensed it, with you. There's a part of you that you don't share with anyone." She chuckled. "Not the part you're thinking of. *That* you shared to my great satisfaction."

"Then what?" Lupo looked at her in the dim lighting. She was an exquisite creature, full of the outdoors and tough and tender, and he wondered at the Fate that had brought them together. *For how long?*

"Well, I don't know, Detective Lupo." She paused. "Your name means *wolf* in Italian. But you know that . . . Do you speak Italian?" She nuzzled his shoulder and licked at his sweaty skin.

"Sí," he said. *"Parlo Italiano molto bene."* He wondered what connections she'd made.

"Very sexy! We've had wolves here again, did you know that?"

"Again?"

"They'd all been killed off by the idiot farmers and ranchers. The native wolf population was down to zero for a long time. But then they were reintroduced and I guess they've been doing well, mating and running in packs. Not so much here, but further north. Also in Minnesota. But we've had a wolf here for years. I think they never got him, and he's almost—almost comforting, I guess, because he seems to appear almost once a month, you know, when the moon is full."

"What do you mean, *appear*?" His breathing had gone very quiet, and the itch in his hands and feet intensified.

"I don't mean *appear*. I've never seen him, but you can hear him at night, howling. It sounds lonely and tragic, and it seems as though he's running. Maybe running away from something or someone. Maybe he knew they would have killed him if they'd caught him taking the livestock."

Lupo wanted to tell her. He'd never taken livestock. He *knew* he only tracked wild animals during his hunts. But he wasn't sure how he knew.

He felt the Creature straining to leap out of him. The timing was all wrong. He should have been alone, waiting for the Change. What was he doing? He felt that he was developing feelings for this woman, and yet he was jeopardizing her life, in more ways than one.

The fear grew inside him even as the clock wound down toward nightfall, and he felt the Creature stirring just beyond his reach. The sexual emotions had echoed deeply inside him, and he felt that the Creature was aroused, too. Lupo held his new love and choked back tears.

"Secrets," she whispered. "We both have secrets."

Dusk entered the windows, and Lupo almost began to speak.

But he didn't.

When he took her again, this time from behind and not as gently, he wondered if it was him or the Creature. And he cursed the side of him that could hurt her.

They writhed together in ecstasy until, spent, he lay across her back and wondered what she thought of this last coupling, where its implied violence had come from.

MARTIN

Safely tucked inside several leafy arborvitae bushes that hugged the side of the cottage along the hillside, Martin couldn't help himself. He blended well into the dark shadows, and the black lipstick he had rubbed football player–like over his cheeks helped him avoid reflecting light from inside. His hands stayed busy, watching those two. He wanted so badly to kill them, but he wanted to torture them, too, and there was plenty of time for that. Besides, he wanted to know whether this Lupo fucker was really a werewolf, as his lovely sister Caroline had believed. Martin believed the cop had killed her, but he still harbored doubt as to whether he had used teeth or some sort of destructive device.

Watching these two go at each other like rutting animals, though, he could almost believe that they were *both* supernatural creatures.

He sated himself twice at their expense, his seed pooling in the dirt below the windowsill, then very quietly extricated himself from the bushes and made his way out to the road. Shadows were lengthening, and he sure as hell didn't want to get caught out here, silver bullets or no. When a dog tied up behind one of the houses began to bark at him suddenly, his bladder almost emptied from the shock. He glared at the invisible dog somewhere behind a stand of pines and bushes, wishing he could choke the life out of him. What if Lupo heard all the barking and decided to investigate? Martin hastened to his car and drove off as quickly as he could. He'd wanted to see her again. He would enjoy doing her in the same way as the others, but he might well use her as a bone for the guys first. *His guys*. From what he'd gathered, they would be very grateful.

Almost as grateful for this as they had been when he'd given them the box from his trunk.

Right now he aimed the car south. There was a loose end in Milwaukee, and he felt an obsessive need to tie up loose ends.

Martin loved loose ends.

He sang his tuneless ditty as he drove into the night.

LUPO

When the barking began, he wondered who might be calling. But then the thought hit him that it could just as easily be somebody leaving. Somehow, the Creature's senses were manifesting themselves—he thought he'd picked up the guy's scent, even here, inside the cottage, even with the fireplace smell and the lingering remnants of the sweat and sex smell they'd produced together so often in the last few hours.

He looked at Jessie as she slept peacefully in his arms. Who could have imagined her unbridled passion, even toward the end, when his need had become more physical and more aggressive? Her repressed sexuality had overwhelmed him—maybe her, too—and he'd reveled in it because of *his* repression. Maybe it was time to let himself go, enjoy what he could in life, instead of doing penance forever. Now her eyes were closed and her hair spread silkily over the rug and his shoulder, and her lips curled upward in a little satisfied sleep-smile that made him want to kiss her and awaken her desire again.

Instead he shifted and watched her wake up, and kicked himself for what he was about to do.

"I'm sorry to wake you, Jess, I really am, but I need to leave for a while." He managed to hide the urgency he felt.

Her eyes opened wider, then settled into a slight glare.

"More secrets?"

He nodded. "I'm afraid so. Not happy about it, but kind of stuck. Maybe someday . . ." He let the possibility hang. He hoped she wouldn't end it right there.

She gathered herself and stood, naked and glorious in the glare of the fire. "Okay, Detective Lupo. I can take a hint. But I'll want a rain check." She started to gather her clothes.

Lupo wanted to say more, but his insides were screaming. His extremities itched. His senses boiled.

The Change was not far off, and this time he felt as though he was seeing through two sets of eyes. *God, not yet!*

The scent of her was exciting, but there was another scent that played under his nostrils, and the Creature wanted at it.

JESSIE

Driving home didn't take long, but her mind raced so quickly through feelings that the ride seemed to last a century.

She still tingled *down there*, where her policeman from the city had reawakened her senses and they had explored each other over and over, without hesitation or embarrassment. It was really remarkable, she thought, that she had been so liberated, so free with herself, so giving. And so willing to take. Even at the end, when he'd become more like a beast than a man, and she'd accepted and even enjoyed it, though it was rougher than she was accustomed to with her infrequent lovers. She had been shocking, she knew. The sweet scent of their sex still lingered in her nostrils, on her lips, on her fingertips.

And I'm in love! She giggled.

He had been gentle when it counted and rougher when she was ready for it, when she'd indicated she wanted to shed inhibitions like shower water. He had been a thoughtful and caring lover, if a bit hesitant, as if he didn't share much of himself with anyone. He had a dark past, she understood that, with secrets of some sort. She even thought he might have some kind of power over her, or over others, some kind of magic. She wasn't sure how she had come up with that, but then she'd always been sensitive to other people's secret sides. She'd sensed a depth of rage and anger in him, which was understandable because of his friend's murder and her *career* and all his repressed feelings toward her. Jessie understood that some of his newfound sexuality may well have been directed at the memory of this friend who'd been killed, but she also knew the connection she herself and he had made long ago and how they had sparred with the possibilities for years.

And now I'm in love! She couldn't help herself.

Even when the reality of the darkness that surrounded him came back to her, she still had to figure that as an adult she had the choice to either explore this relationship or let it fizzle, and she had already chosen.

Jessie Hawkins had been married once, to a perfectly stable man with a decent job and no real black marks against him.

Except that he had been passionless. Somewhere along the line that had been their three-year marriage, she'd realized that their biggest hurdle was the strength of her passions and the utter lack of Paul's. He barely tolerated sex, and then only if she initiated. This had eventually infuriated her to the point that she no longer initiated—*begged*—at all, preferring to seethe as he cruised through life apparently none the worse for wear without the sex life so many other men craved. She had divorced Paul with an almost businesslike coldness, and he had moved on, apparently neither broken up nor angry. *Passionless*.

She was not passionless. She'd had a few affairs, a few "dalliances," as they used to say. Her job kept her busy, and she did feel guilty about letting it slide the last day and a half, but she really did have a sick friend, as she'd told her assistant and the nurse down at the clinic. Jessie liked to think today had gone a long way toward healing that sickness.

She still tingled, and the feeling was so prevalent that she almost considered turning the Pathfinder around and surprising him. She slowed, in fact, and waited for a set of headlights behind her to pass, thinking she would make a U-turn and head back. What man could resist a wanton, willing woman on his doorstep?

She braked, checked the mirror, and began to swing around. But after a couple feet she braked again.

"What am I doing? He wants to go slow, and there's nothing attractive about a desperate woman looking for a sex handout!"

She straightened the SUV and headed home, still happy, and now more settled. She hummed the instrumental from Alan Parsons *Gaudi* album, wishing she had it with her to play. Ian Bairnson's Flamenco-style guitar solo would have fit her mood just fine right then.

She drove on, unaware that the car which had passed

her a few moments before had now pulled over and waited in darkness for her to pass again.

Moments later, Jessie Hawkins pulled into her own cottage's driveway.

As she climbed out of the truck, she swore she heard a wolf howl in the distance. It was that rogue wolf again! She shivered a little, but felt excited, too, wondering at her strange, sudden mixture of feelings.

CHAPTER TWENTY-TWO

LUPO

The Change had come upon him quite unexpectedly, in a sense, because it was early. The moon still hid. He shed his clothes just in time, and then—*just like that!*—he was over and the Creature was aware of his confusion. As if to respond, the Creature seemed to pass on the scent—*yes*, that scent—so that Lupo the man could understand.

And then on four strong paws he had gone bounding out the door and into the evening dusk, scenting the tied-up dog who suddenly wanted to go inside, and then catching the scent again of the man who had been at the window. He cautiously approached the spot through the bushes, smelling the man's seed that had been spilled into the dirt and wrinkling his snout, growling.

Inside the Creature's head, Lupo regained enough control to find himself thinking about Jessie Hawkins, and what this discovery meant.

The Creature howled and headed off in the same direction the man had taken, to where a car had been parked.

Then he entered the woods and crept through the under-growth, aware that the scent of another male wolf was lingering, too.

Lupo's awareness grew and he became aware of it and suddenly he commanded the Creature to stop. And it did, sniffing softly at the base of a tree he had marked the night before.

Mark, Lupo commanded.

The Creature lifted its leg slightly.

No, stop!

The Creature stopped.

Lupo wanted to laugh with glee. He was conscious inside the Creature's head! He was able to tell the Creature—himself—what to do and what not to do.

Then the Creature marked the tree.

Well, there was something to be said for instinct.

He bounded off in search of food, Lupo aware and feeling as though a weight had been lifted, a burden removed. Could his feelings for the beautiful doctor have helped clear the logjam?

He set off in search of the interloper. Not the human, not yet. *The other one.*

KLUG

He had finished packing the things he would need, taking a few boxes out of the sportcab on his truck. Wilbur Klug hadn't owned much. A few tools, some clothes, a safe full of guns, and some small, rickety furniture. He was leaving the furniture behind, along with Shelly in the freezer.

He chuckled.

Yessir, he was going to leave this place with a full band playing some loud song, that was for sure. He couldn't believe what the city boy had given them, and the promise of more, just for—for what? Another murder. A cop. *Big deal.* If the guy was like a monster movie, then he'd deal with that, too. First there was Buck to bust out. He'd learned that they'd be transferring him from the lockup at the sheriff's office to the courthouse the next night for an arraignment two days hence. Yes, indeed, it was time to get rolling. He owed Buck for a couple things, not least of which was a throat-slashing that had saved Klug's life once, years ago.

He stacked the boxes in front of the great tarp-covered hump that sat like a black wart beside his ramshackle garage. When he was finished, he climbed the six-foot rickety stepladder he had built out of used two-by-fours back when he'd had his half-assed business idea, the same idea dumb-fuck Shelly had shot down so many times that finally he'd given it up. He climbed the steps and stood on the swaying platform, reaching out to grab hold of the heavy tarp and pulling it until it slid off the vehicle that rested underneath.

It was a 1944-model DUKW, otherwise known to everyone in Wisconsin as a "Duck," an original US Army amphibious vehicle in better-than-average shape. It was Klug's proudest possession, and he had dreamed of operating it like the legendary Wisconsin Dells Ducks, which gave tours up and down the Wisconsin River in the Dells, an area of unusually beautiful sandstone rock formations in the center of the state. Klug had bought the vehicle for a song from an old soldier who'd managed to salvage the beast after it had been used in the WW2 invasion of Sicily, and he had intended to operate his own tourist business. But Shelly would have had to provide the rest of the capital and she had steadfastly refused, forcing Klug to seek the money elsewhere and, when no one ponied up, having to abandon the idea.

The 32-foot long, 7-ton Duck could be driven on a highway, on a dirt road, on a path, and then directly into the ocean or a river. Its 270-cubic-inch engine generated 100 horsepower and could drive the monster 50 mph on a road or 7 knots in the water, where a large propeller engaged by the driver would take over the propulsion duties.

Wilbur Klug had learned to drive the metal beast from the old soldier himself until he died, and then had hired one of the Dells' drivers to teach him further tricks. After Shelly had killed his dream, though, Klug had used the Duck only as a self-propelled duck blind (*ha ha*) during the legal season, and more often than not as a hunting vehicle during the "off-season," when deer-shining became his friends' and his favorite sport. The spotlight he'd installed near the driver's seat was specifically to catch the deer unawares, and he'd eaten a lot of state-duty-free venison because of it.

Suddenly, a howl split the night not far away, and it made Klug's flesh crawl. He looked around for a weapon, but realized that he had left everything on the ground near the steps.

Klug had heard the howling before, of course, every few weeks as if the wolf were some sort of tourist. But he hadn't ever thought of hunting it. When Martin Stewart had mentioned his wolf hunt, Klug had immediately flashed onto the use of the Duck as a platform, sort of like an elephant on a tiger hunt in India. The height of the vehicle would likely prevent the rogue wolf from springing up and attacking them, while they could shoot it at their leisure. Klug wanted the wolf, now—it was a matter of pride.

But then a second howl came from a different direction, and a series of growls. *What the hell?* There were *two* wolves out there, and from the sound of it, they were going to slug it out.

It was illogical, going hunting after what he and Kenny and the city boy had planned for Buck's release, but he'd glommed onto the idea and now he wouldn't have given it up for a lifetime's supply of Rhinelander.

He listened as the wolves tore into each other out there, somewhere in the cold, black woods.

Klug knew that he'd take down the winner.

CHAPTER TWENTY-THREE

LUPO

The Creature stalks the interloper tree by tree, following his trail in the cold woods and preparing for a fight. Riding along, his awareness greater than it has ever been, is Nick Lupo, who finds it easier to let the Creature's instinct take control than attempting to give it direction. But he has learned that his will can influence the Creature, defying instinct and making the animal more subservient. Part of his brain is occupied still trying to understand why the Change came earlier, but the rest is tasting all the Creature's senses and learning to enjoy the steady stream of information— the cold breeze ruffling the hair on his back, the prickliness of pine needles under his pads, the pungent scent of the other wolf's urine, and the night sounds that seem to quiet at his passing.

He lopes within scenting distance of a few human dwellings, knowing the smells—places he has visited before—and willing the Creature to move on, to pass them by. He knows this one has pets, who now cower inside their master's sleeping room, while that one feels great fear. And this one, this one smells like danger, raises the hair on his neck, reminding him of someone, long ago, someone he thinks he should remember, but he does not. He gives this house a wide berth, too, sensing that its owner knows too much and wants to use his knowledge. He growls slightly at the danger behind those dark windows, knowing there is someone there, watching him, taking his measure, and he remembers something that came before his own memory, but that he is aware of nonetheless. He backs away from the windows, from the gaze he feels on his fur, and from the feeling that the human behind the glass knows far too much.

It is an elderly man, the Creature can smell this and his fear, too, but also the knowledge that makes him so dangerous. There is silver here, and it is for him. He knows this, and he retreats, as he has so many times before.

When the house is out of sight, hidden among the trees, the moon's rays give him the view he has sought. The interloper wolf is there, waiting for him, fangs bared and fur ruffled upward like a porcupine's quills. He approaches quickly, without trickery, letting the interloper smell his magic and his strength. The other won't back down, however, tilting his head a bit and letting out a challenging growl.

The Creature responds with an unearthly growl of his own, then quickly crosses the ground between them, lunging for the interloper in a flash that startles the opponent and leaves him unprotected for the Creature's jaws. The Creature's snout seems to grow in size as his jaws grasp the opponent's neck and bite down, tearing, while the other's claws slash harmlessly at the air around them.

Snarling and growling, the two bodies hurtle toward one side of the clearing, the Creature's controlling their flight. His jaws rip and shred the other's throat without mercy and suddenly the other seems to surrender, going limp in submission, as if hoping the Creature will slacken his attack.

But the magical Creature presses his attack and tears out the other's throat with one last twist of his clamped jaws. Blood sprays into his throat. The other whimpers as he sees the light in the Creature's eyes, realizing too late that he has challenged something other than a fellow being.

The interloper dies, his throat and neck a bloody mess. The Creature's snout is blood-flecked and his fangs continue to rip and tear until his enemy is hardly recognizable.

I am greater than you! As he feeds, he now realizes that he the Creature and Nick Lupo can nevermore be separate . . . they are one, together, inseparable, and dominant. These woods are his to control and to protect.

Nick Lupo feels the thrill of the kill, the blood tang arousing his lust. He is completely aware, awake now inside the Creature, in tune with its instincts and its needs. He howls, long and loud in triumph, then lowers his snout. Much later, when he is done feeding, his paws find the way home unerringly. But it is Nick Lupo's feet that cross the threshold of home just as dawn begins to lighten the tops of the trees.

SAM WATERS

Hugging the silver-loaded shotgun, the old man listens as the fight progresses not far from his boundary.

The two wolves snarl and growl, and he can imagine their slashing jaws and knife-sharp fangs glinting in the fading moonlight. Then in a huge crash of bodies and growls and whimpers it appears to be over, with one the winner and the other—the other dead, apparently. No quarter given. The old man knows it's the monthly visitor who has won the contest, and he shivers a bit. Yet his instinct tells him not to worry, that the Creature out there even now tearing into the carcass of his enemy is not concerned with humans here in these woods, at least as long as humans aren't concerned with him. Sam wonders whether it's true. Whether it was the other wolf who took the pets and livestock. Whatever the case, now there is only one.

Sam falls asleep, conflicted at the rush of his thoughts. As if his fear has been squashed by a new, disturbing feeling of kinship and understanding, as if the Creature is more friend than foe. His sleep is not restful. Not at all.

JESSIE

She tossed and turned all night long, her thoughts leaping from dream to nightmare and back, but Dominic Lupo dominated both, seeming to be at once dangerous and yet protective.

When she awoke near dawn, she felt as if she'd had an orgasm. Touching herself, she was surprised to find wetness. The sheets were a mess, sodden with sweat and her essence, and her fading dream memory included a gigantic wolf defeating another in mortal battle.

Where in the hell did that come from? she thought, trying to catch her breath. It was as if she had been lying in a lover's arms all night—all right, in Nick Lupo's arms!—and only now took the time to rest and let her body slow to a normal rhythm, coming down from the fever-pitch of an orgasm she could sense but barely remember.

This is weird, she thought just before falling asleep contented and smiling, the image of her new lover as clearly in her mind as if he were there with her. Pleased, she rolled gently into sleep.

BEN

"Hey, Nick, you there? Pick up. Okay, you're not there and your cell's dead, too. I *hope* you're having a good time while I'm slaving away. Listen, I got a hit on the juvie search. Jackpot! They just finished converting the records or whatever for that year. That's why it took this long. Anyway, I got Judge O'Hara to open the file for me—guy owes me, so he moved his ass. Name of Martin Stewart mean anything to you? Seems to me you might remember a Caroline Stewart, used to teach at the university, got herself killed years ago, maybe 'bout the time you were a rookie. Butchered, but her brother was already in a mental ward, 'cause he'd killed their parents and abused her when she was a kid and, you name it, this wacko's done it. Anyways, your fuckin' tape's gonna cut me off, so call me back—"

Chapter Twenty-four

LUPO

His whole body tingled.

Was it love? Or was it the unprecedented control he'd finally achieved over the Creature? Was it the triumph of the kill? He remembered the night's events, the fight with the other wolf, his dominance, his awareness. He remembered it all.

So, the Creature and I are even more linked now than ever!

He'd wanted to sniff out the fucker, Martin, if he was here, but the other wolf had taken his attention and lured him away.

Damn it!

He drank a second bottle and rinsed out his mouth. His jaws ached from the battle.

But why did his body tingle so much?

He'd been tired, but he still looked forward to seeing Jessie Hawkins. His groin ached with desire. There was no other way to put it, as if the night's events had somehow affected his libido. He had to have her again. He ached for the tenderness, and some of the repressed sexual aggression they'd both felt. He wondered if the Creature's needs weren't getting a bit crossed with his own. How dangerous was that?

Then the phone had rung and he'd let the machine take it.

Now that Ben had spoken the names, he wondered what could result from all the strings hanging out there, connected in plain sight. Could he withstand the scrutiny? Corinne *and* Caroline?

He called Jessie and left a message, figuring she was either in the shower or off to the clinic. He tried to warn her about Martin without letting panic creep into his tone. He mentioned his suspicion about having been followed, begging her to keep an eye out for herself, that the guy was dangerous. "Until we meet again, Doctor, and I for one hope it's very soon." Well, for *him* it was tender. Too late to take it back or add a more appropriate ending after the long pause. He hated fucking answering machines, because you never got a second chance. *No spellcheck.*

He would try to catch her later, either at home or at the res medical center. But he had to try tracking down Martin Stewart first. Lupo couldn't be in two places at once—and there was a fifty percent chance he'd be wrong at either place. Jess could take care of herself, and Stewart was most likely going to attack him here. Maybe he could provide Jessie a police guard. He could call the sheriff here, what was his name? Bunche? He'd call Bunche and explain, see about getting a deputy assigned to her doorstep. The decision made him feel better, even if the timing didn't. Corinne's body, as he'd seen it in death, haunted him.

As did the fear that he would find Jessie the same way.

He *had* to find Martin Stewart first.

JESSIE

She awoke with the vague echo of the phone in her ears, knowing the machine had picked up and that a message was left, but not willing to part with the covers. Now that the sweat had dried and she was snuggled underneath, there seemed to be no reason to get up so early. She had made arrangements at the clinic—again! They were going to *kill* her if she didn't go in one of these days!—and had planned to maybe see Nick again before he left.

She tingled at the thought, sure enough, both physically and emotionally.

I've got it bad.

Late thirties and desperate?

No, late thirties and finally able to converse with someone, joke with someone, laugh with someone, then screw someone's brains out in a most unladylike manner! Score!

She smiled into the pillow. She opened her eyes and saw a lavender smudge on the cotton, and suddenly she remembered everything they'd talked about.

Groaning, she tumbled out of bed and let the cold caress her skin as she made her way toward the phone and machine on her desk in the living room, half of which she used as a wide-open office.

Grinning, she pushed the button. Nick Lupo's terse voice spoke to her, and her smile turned quickly to a frown.

Jesus! As if it weren't enough that her mind was playing little tricks on her, making her think Nick had some sort of magical power, now she had to worry about the murderer who had it in for him? She wasn't sure whether to worry more for him or for herself, so she decided to make coffee instead.

Fresh coffee would stimulate clear thinking.

She realized she was still naked and wondered at the

changes Mr. Nick Lupo had already wrought in her life.

Shameless!

She smiled and enjoyed the feeling. It really had been too long since she'd felt this way about anyone, and now she wasn't going to let some whacked-out wannabe Hannibal Lecter ruin her life.

She whistled a melody out of the Parsons canon again, about the same old sun shining tomorrow. That was strange, she thought. Why so sad a song? Try as she might, she couldn't quite get a happy song in her head, only sad or cynical ones.

She showered off the negativity, then she had coffee.

BEN

The empty house reminded him so much of his wife and kids that he felt a lump in his throat.

Marie and the kids were safe near Madison. He'd called again to check on them. He stopped in the kitchen and contemplated a soda in the fridge, but decided against it. Damn carbonation would really get to him later. He settled for a long, cold swallow from the water pitcher, a practice for which Marie would have scolded him. But there were perks to *batching it,* as they said. Still, he felt lonely. If she'd been home, she would have given him his choice of freshly baked *biscotti* or maybe some *ciambella*—pie—one of her specialties. Marie reminded him a little of a TV mom also named Marie, the one on that Raymond show. The good parts of her, anyway.

Ben smiled at the thought and stepped into the bedroom.

Strange, he thought, *it looks like Marie's in bed. On my side.* When had she come home? And why?

"Marie?" He approached, alarmed. "For God's sake, what's wrong? What's happened?"

The shape under the sheet muttered softly and moved, trembling.

Concerned, Ben laid his hand on Marie's soft hip and—

—with a sudden twist, the shape rose up screeching and reached out for Ben's hand, which he was too startled to pull back.

The first slash severed the main artery across his wrist, sending a geyser of blood spraying upward as he reacted and finally pulled his arm back. The blond man with the sheet over his head screamed again and the bedroom light glinted off the sharp blade he held.

"You! You're Martin—"

Right-handed Ben fumbled for his Glock with his un-hurt left hand, getting caught in the folds of his jacket just as the blade swished past him again and he thought he had stepped back far enough, only to realize that a long gash had slit open his left forearm. Blood soaked his sleeve and weighed down his efforts to free the pistol, while he felt his life's blood spraying the walls from the slash.

The fucker was filleting him like a fish, and all he could do was babble incoherently and whimper as the pain finally hit his nerve center and he screamed, his hand giving up its hunt for the pistol and now his brain reversing his every motion in an effort to retreat away from the madman with the blade before the remainder of his blood could be spilled.

In a flashing strobelike split second Ben saw that the man's lips were painted a deep purple color and he *knew* without a shadow of a doubt that he was in the presence of the very madman they were seeking, Martin Stewart, the master of disguise and killer of girls in photo booths. Now, cop-killer.

Ben Sabatini's mind processed the information at su-percomputer speed, passing the fastest Intel or Motorola chip and yet giving him no time at all to do the one thing necessary for his survival, which would have been to make his legs move against the forward momentum still carrying him forward even after his initial backward recoil once he'd unmasked the assailant.

The blade sank deep and true, slicing his throat open from side to side, severing the larynx and Adam's apple and releasing a great gout of blood outward as the words or curses or pleas died on his lips like bloody bubbles and he died with them, his feet still trying to engage reverse even though the toes were now scrabbling into the stained hardwood floor as if he couldn't wait to enter the ground.

His mind formed one last coherent word, which could not travel to his lips, even though in his mind he saw his wife.

"Nick!"

Then the void opened up and Ben Sabatini entered it and the pain was flushed away like his soul.

MARTIN

Humming a tuneless ditty, Martin bounced off the soaked bed and was glad he'd kept the sheet wrapped over himself. The old fuck's blood was still spurting, though less so now that he was about squeezed like a lemon.

Martin giggled.

He brought a hand up and absentmindedly smeared the lipstick, enjoying the intoxicating smell on his skin and under his nose.

Well, that was easy.

He was surprised to learn they knew his name, though. That he hadn't expected, not so soon. Somebody had managed to unseal his records. Oh, well, he was ready to end it all, anyway. Wheels were rolling. It was too late to pull back. And anyway, he'd wanted Lupo to know eventually. Revenge was no good if the victim didn't even know the reason he was targeted.

But now Martin was torn. He'd wanted to leave a personalized wall note here for the bastard cop, *writ in blood*, as they said. But the old fuck had come home later than Martin expected, even though he had left a message at the office that Ben's wife was ill and at home. Maybe the old bastard didn't even know. That was possible. Maybe his showing up at home at lunchtime was just a lucky coincidence. Still, he now had to drive like a maniac to make the trip Up North to end it all.

He would call Klug and his idiot sidekick while on the road, then stop at some sort of department store for the supplies they'd put on the list. Fortunately, they'd already made their plans, and all they had to do was carry them out. He'd leave immediately—he had a lot of traveling to do before he and his two new guys got to work together, but it wouldn't be long. There was just enough time to go through the plan once more, and then they were on.

Martin surveyed his work here and found it good.

Very good, indeed.

Chapter Twenty-five

LUPO

He was naked.

He had to determine how far he had come.

The growl worked its way up into his throat and he gave himself over to his anger. The doors were locked and bolted, the windows barred. No soundproofing here, but there was no need. Nick Lupo pushed—in his mind, it was like pushing against a wall and feeling a whole building move.

Lupo pushed.

Harder.

And then he was Over again, just like that—*a fact, Jack*—he was Over and on four paws, his gigantic muscular body hurtling through the room and scrabbling at the door, the scent of his enemy in his nostrils and the hatred, ten times—no, a thousand times—worse than the hatred he had felt for the interloper wolf, the hatred coursing through him like a poison and adrenaline and kerosene cocktail.

Lupo and the Creature howled madly.

And this time, Lupo knew he was in control, for he felt the Creature respond to his thoughts.

Maybe he had needed Corinne to bridge his worlds, but he would never know. Now it seemed his rage and hatred and sadness had formed a Force he could control.

Lupo thought in the Creature's head, and the Creature in his. For the first time the thoughts were lucid in both directions.

He gobbled down a pile of raw meat he had ladled onto a dish, relishing the protein—the blood—and then he lapped water from a bowl, knowing that his wolf side felt insulted by this treatment. The Creature wanted to roam, to hunt, to bring down prey, to tear flesh from carcass and to swallow fur and bone and skin. The Creature loathed being treated like a dog, and that was why Lupo did it.

Because he could.

He pushed again, pushed hard as if trying to move the building back, allowing himself an almost *orgasmic* effort, as he thrust and folded himself back into human form, leaving the Creature behind.

He tried forcing himself to not fall asleep this time. He needed to get out and follow that scent, his enemy. He hoped control nulled and voided the need for sleep. But not his need for water. He took a cold jug from the fridge, his hand suddenly heavy with fatigue.

Control. He drank.

Then his body betrayed him, and he slept on the floor.

He dialed Jessie Hawkins's number, not sure why, perhaps looking for an antidote to the sour liquid that sloshed around in his stomach along with the raw meat, but got only a ringing.

Ten, twenty, thirty rings.

No machine.

That was strange . . .

"Sonofabitch!" he growled.

He was still naked, still feeling the aftereffects of the Change he had brought about intentionally.

He was out of time. He'd gambled and lost, Fifty percent.

He dressed quickly in jeans and layers—a t-shirt, a thin Kevlar vest, a heavy denim shirt, and a brown leather bomber jacket, then stopped long enough to grab extra ammo clips for his Glock and a second handgun, a stodgy short-barreled .38 Smith & Wesson Model 10 in an ankle holster, a sling of full speed-loaders and a box of extra semijacketed hollow-point cartridges from his duffel bag.

Once in his car, he debated. No one at Jessie's meant she would be at work. He scoured his memory for the road to the res. Not a religious man, yet Lupo prayed he was in time for whatever was about to happen.

Suddenly, he felt as if *control*—the very control he had just gained—had slipped through his fingers like grains of sand.

KLUG

At about dinnertime, Sheriff Bunche and one of his deputies drove the TrailBlazer right up to the back door of the county courthouse, where a tiny exercise yard and a loading dock sat side by side next to a row of industrial-size Dumpsters and chain-link fence protected air-conditioning units.

The handy little radio on his belt squawked. It was Martin, calling with the other radio from the matching set they'd bought at a Target store barely an hour before. The whole thing had come together last minute, but it was solid.

Oh, yeah, it was solid.

"Yeah?" Wilbur Klug hissed into the radio dwarfed by his meaty fist.

"The road's clear."

The sheriff's office and jail was only a mile away, down a stretch of Highway 45, and the city boy had followed their departure from there.

Looking at the deputy, Klug thought it was Wes Norman, a little snot he remembered beating up repeatedly just off school grounds years before, now all grown up and tidy in his precious uniform. While Wes stood guard looking bored, pump shotgun cradled loosely in his arms, that fat-ass Bunche pulled Buck none too gently out of the backseat. Buck wore the prisoner's orange jumpsuit and chains.

Fuck! Klug hadn't figured on that. How did the sheriff's office get so much money for all the updates? The new squads, new weapons, the jumpsuits. This was bullshit. Did they think they were gonna face terrorists in this backwater half-assed resort town? Klug grinned and decided that it was the perfect way for him to blow this popsicle stand. Not only would he and his buddies break their ties with the past, but they'd make CNN and probably even the network broadcasts. Maybe O'Reilly would get to rant about them. Klug had few illusions about fame. You had to kill somebody to have it, and he'd passed that milestone with Shelly. They were so close to the Canadian border here, only an hour to the UP and then nothing but forest and a line on a map. They'd be in Canada's mountains long before anybody even figured out who they were. It was better than heading south, his original plan.

Meanwhile, this Martin would get his stupid cop up here, with their help, of course, and they'd do the guy and pocket the twenty grand he was offering. Maybe they'd screw the city boy out of a few more grand, maybe do him just for the fun of it.

Klug nodded to Kenny, who sat in the cab of the garbage truck they had commandeered from the crew, who now lay in back with the garbage and shit, tied up and gagged, probably wondering whether the crusher was going to come to life any second. Klug thought it was a done deal—he was curious to see what the machine would do to them.

Kenny started the rig and ground the gears. The cops turned to look at them, but didn't really *see* them, just a garbage crew. After all, they had jumpsuits, too, almost the same shade as the city's. From a distance, they'd be right on.

As Klug hopped up on the moving truck's sideboard platform, he unlimbered the UZI strapped around his neck and pulled the bolt back, letting it snap into place cocked and with a round in the breech. Fuckin'-A UZI submachine guns, the city boy had given them. Two of 'em with plenty of clips full of 9mm military ammo. It was like a candy store! Klug hadn't believed what else the guy had pulled from the trunk of his rental car. A half-dozen fucking grenades, the pineapple kind you saw in the movies. He and Kenny now each had three hanging off their gun slings.

Kenny drove the truck haltingly toward the Dumpsters, which would take them right behind the Trail-Blazer and block its path in case it tried to back out. The nose was too close to the loading dock, so there would be no maneuvering.

Kenny was sweating profusely, his jumpsuit already soaked. He was way out of his league and they both knew it, but Klug figured he'd stick with the two of them because he was a born follower, with not a creative bone in his pathetic excuse for a body. Buck he didn't have to worry about, because Buck was a sadist through and through. He'd have eaten this up.

Wilbur Klug wasn't even nervous, and the fact pleased him mightily. "Stop!"

The truck's brakes screeched and the sheriff looked their way. Somehow recognition flashed through his eyes and he started to wrestle the cranky Buck back into the Chevy while shouting something incoherent at his deputy.

Now.

Klug leaped off the sideboard, his UZI chattering and bucking in his hand as he tried to hold it muzzle-down, which was easier said than done.

Hot spent brass spewed out of the UZI and slugs splattered into the sheriff's new Chevy, taking out half the windows.

One of the slugs must have caught Wes, because he spun and went down, his shotgun flying out of his grasp and exploding harmlessly into the side of the building. Klug kept shooting, letting the clip drain and digging the cordite cloud around him like an opium haze. He suddenly realized that he was shouting and laughing incoherently and he didn't care.

Meanwhile, Kenny squeezed off a few rounds from his UZI, then pulled the pin on a grenade and tossed it in the general direction of the sheriff's car, behind which the sheriff was drawing his service pistol.

Klug screamed at Kenny, but it was too late, because the grenade exploded with a *crump* that blew out half the windows in the back of the courthouse. Some shrapnel must have found its mark, because the sheriff went down and out of sight behind the vehicle. Buck was squirming around inside the Chevy, probably wetting himself.

"Don't be killin' Buck you shithead!" Klug shouted as he slid another clip into the UZI's handgrip and cocked the gun again. His first burst tore through the Chevy's hood and front tires, while his second trailed across the building's back door, which had started to open. Bailiffs probably. *Fuck 'em.* The gunfire caused them to step back and close the door, and that was when Klug took the opportunity to run toward the Chevy, screaming "Cover me!" to his idiot sidekick and hoping he'd live through this caper but digging every second of it. Hell, he should've stayed in the damned Army when he had the chance! The blood rushed through his veins like a mixture of rocket fuel and cocaine, igniting every limb with the tingling excitement

of an all-body orgasm. He was so hopped up on the feeling, it was amazing he could think at all.

He reached the Chevy and found Sheriff Bunche sitting up behind it, holding a blood-spattered arm with his other hand. There was a bloody hole in the side of his uniform shirt, but he was otherwise all right, breathing fast and looking at Klug through slitted eyes. His pistol was nowhere to be seen. Wes was moaning softly on the other side of the Chevy, crying and sniffling like a girl. Klug spat.

Kenny came up behind Klug. "Keep an eye on the door and the alley," Klug told him. *Shithead!*

"You all right, Buck?" Klug called out to the prisoner.

"Yeah, you all right?" Kenny echoed from a few yards away.

"No thanks to you motherfuckers," Buck hissed. He had cuts on his face from the exploding car windows, but appeared otherwise unhurt. "Get these fuckin' things offa me!" He held out his arms.

"You heard the man, Sheriff," Klug said. "Where's the keys?"

Bunche seemed about to defy them, but then he winced and gave in, just like that, deflating to about a third his size. He'd never dreamed anything like this could happen in his little corner of the North Woods, no sir, and now all he wanted to do was survive so he could get these bastards.

Klug knew what went through the sheriff's mind without any doubt.

Bunche handed Klug a set of keys, which he tossed to Buck, who had clambered out of the Chevy. He went to work on his chains and cuffs.

"You know, you can still get out of this without major charges," Bunche began, talking slowly and enunciating carefully. Probably the way they taught hostage negotiation, Klug figured.

Klug nodded.

Bunche nodded, too.

"Nah," Klug said, suddenly, and squeezed the trigger of the UZI. "Too late for that shit."

The dozen rounds tore through Bunche's body and jerked him to a half-standing position before slamming him against the sagging Chevy in a bloody heap.

Klug walked over to Wes, who was crying softly, and rolled him over with one foot.

"Wil—"

Klug smiled encouragingly and shot him once in the head. *Hard to believe the idiot had that much brains in his skull.*

"Let's get outta here, man!" Kenny called, his voice shaking.

For once, Klug figured Kenny was right. He pulled the pin on one of his grenades and tossed it into the bloody, shot-up Chevy, then ran for the garbage truck.

"Where you goin', man?" Kenny called out as he and Buck raced toward the car Martin had just driven up.

Klug didn't answer. He hopped up into the truck's cab and pushed the lever that operated the crusher.

Then he headed for Martin's car, laughing as the muffled screaming started from the rear of the truck.

CHAPTER TWENTY-SIX

SAM WATERS

Sam approached the well-tended cottage-and-a-half on the back part of Circle Moon Drive, hoping the doc would be home. Her Pathfinder was parked on the slab in the rear, and a space had been cleared for another car.

Sam wondered about that, but he wasn't the nosy sort.

He rang the bell twice, trying to avoid being jumpy and annoying as neighbors could be, but he knew what he looked like. An old man with a long ponytail, wearing cowboy boots, a leather vest over a denim shirt, and carrying a shotgun would probably raise a flag in anybody's mind. But he'd heard the radio calls and he knew what was up, so he was armed, for better or worse. He wished he'd dug his old Army footlocker out from under the bed and stuffed a handgun down his back, too. The shotgun was for the wolf, or whatever he was, but would serve just as well for escapees or terrorists, or whoever the hell had taken out half the police force and courthouse.

Doc Hawkins opened the door looking flustered, almost ready to be pleasantly surprised and then unable to cover her disappointment.

Oh, well! Once you got old, they *all* looked at you like that . . .

"Doc," he started, making sure he kept the shotgun aimed safely downward. "You remember me, don't you? I'm your neighbor from the other side of Circle Moon, and I'm an old friend of your father's. Sam Waters."

"Of course I remember you, Mr. Waters! You always gave us the best candy at Halloween!" She rewarded him with a full smile, tempered slightly at the sight of his shotgun.

"Sorry about the weapon, Doc! I don't know if you're plugged in on local events, but I just heard on my scanner that there was some sort of terrorist attack at the courthouse—"

"What!" She opened the door fully and waved him in.

He surveyed the driveway, then nodded and ducked in. "Much obliged."

"What happened?"

"Bad news. It sounds like the sheriff was killed and maybe one more fella, a deputy, though I hear a couple county workers are missing too. They bombed the squad car and took out a guy they had in lockup, a Buck Benton. Sort of a local lowlife . . ."

"My God, I didn't drive in to the clinic today and I'm not on call, so I don't have my cell phone on. The sheriff's dead? This is horrible. I'm going to grab my bag and go see what I can do," she began.

Sam waved her off, asking her to listen to him. "Sure, but keep this in mind, it's too late. Sounds as though they were dead at the scene. The county ambulance and EMTs have already been there, and I hear they've got word out to the peds already, what with the explosions and machine guns. The mayor moved pretty quick, for once."

"Jesus!" she said matter-of-factly.

"My very thought." He nodded. "I came by to talk at you

about somethin' else altogether, though I think the things might connect somehow."

She waved him toward a worn leather sofa and he sank into it gratefully, leaning the shotgun with care against an overstuffed bookcase, one of a half dozen that jockeyed for space in the paneled living room.

"Something to drink? Soda? Beer?"

He nodded his thanks, but refused. "Carbonation! I have to pick my times."

"If you change your mind," she said. "What did you want to talk about?"

"You're going to think me strange," he began, "but have you noticed the wolf population lately?"

Her surprise was obvious. He'd come in talking about terrorists and a gun battle, and now he'd switched to— *wolves?* He gestured to beg her understanding. "This is difficult for me, but I have some knowledge about a wolf, a specific wolf, who's ravaged our area for quite a while now."

"Ravaged?"

The way her voice rose, he realized that her thinking followed along the same lines as his. Or perhaps she was suspicious, if not a believer.

"Your father will vouch for my education and abilities, Doctor. It seems outrageous and far-fetched, but I know that the wolf we have had in this area is not one of the survivors of the repopulation project. You are aware of our Native American legends, are you not?"

"I'm part Ojibwa," Jessie said softly, almost whispering. "My mother's side."

Had she ever acknowledged it? Sam let that go.

"As I thought," he said. "Then you know that the wolf is a powerful totem within our tradition. Indeed, it's one of the most important, along with the fox, owl, and beaver. You also know that the shaman practices a certain witchcraft, mostly good. Functional, you might say."

"Yes, my mother spoke of it, too." Remembrance dotted

her features, as she recalled things she'd learned as a child. Maybe things forgotten on purpose. *Good.* He didn't have much time to make his case.

"When I was much younger, however, we had a shaman—he was named Joseph Badger—who hated whites for what they had done to our people. Of course, many of our people share this hate. But Badger allowed his hatred to cloud his judgment . . ."

Sam Waters quickly recounted the story of Badger's dabbling with the whites' black magic, Aleister Crowley's *magick* and the European black arts, mixing his evil with theirs to make a new, never-before-seen evil.

"You see, Badger blended the European werewolf mythology, the disease called *lycanthropy*, with the many wolf-oriented stories of magic native to our tribe and others. Europeans feared their so-called werewolves and demonized even normal wolves, killing both animals and people they thought could transform themselves. There were hundreds of witchcraft and werewolf trials in the Middle Ages, and over eight hundred executions. Here, on the other hand, the wolf represented heroic figures and was revered as a powerful totem. Joseph Badger concocted or learned enough rituals from both traditions and spent years perfecting them and creating his own. His rituals worked, apparently. He must have tapped into some of the native magic we all know has lingered in these woods for centuries. It's the magic heard in the whispering of the trees and the birdcalls, but it also seems to run through the water and ground itself. You feel it, too, don't you?"

She hesitated, then nodded.

Sam continued. "It's hard to believe, but Badger became able to transform himself into a werewolf. Enough of our people saw him do it that it cannot be doubted. He chose to pass on his evil to others, an evil of which my own son was a victim." He decided to gloss over all the pain, for what was the point of sharing that? Then he went on. "I vowed to avenge my son and eradicate this evil, and I managed to complete the first part of that quest, but eventually I gave up . . . I became old and frightened, and I chose to sit by while the wolf returned among us, bearing his disease."

"And now, now you want to kill him?" Her tone was anxious.

He paused. "I did," he confessed. "But I've done a lot of thinking in the last few days, and I believe the creature we have here might be more akin to our traditional wolf— heroic, a defender of the tribe and our lands. I can't put my finger on it, but it's as if it has spoken to me. I no longer hunger for its destruction, though I'm ready." He pointed to the shotgun. "He is vulnerable to silver."

"That would be a . . . European trait?" Jessie asked.

His eyes lit up. "Yes! A blending of the traditions. Both Badger the shaman and my son succumbed to silver, so I know it's not just a legend. Though they say Hollywood created it, it must have been based in truth. I'm ready for him if I'm wrong, but I think he is special and may need to be protected. Don't ask me how I know. Perhaps these are thoughts my Sarah has passed on from the grave. God knows, I've been thinking about her a lot lately. So here we have this wolf, maybe a werewolf, who has never taken a human life around here. But now another wolf, a natural wolf, challenged him last night, and our original wolf was victorious. I heard them fighting in the woods. It was very frightening."

He smiled sadly. "Though not more frightening than having armed murderers roving our forests."

"No, I suppose not." Thoughtful and clearly unwilling to show whether she believed or not, Jessie asked him pointed questions, which he answered truthfully. Yes, the so-called disease had spread south to Milwaukee, where it had been passed on to a boy, who had in turn passed it on. No, he had not learned of this new carrier until much later, when the wolf arrived. Yes, there had been one or two murders in the city that were possibly his doing, but not as many as one would have imagined for a creature that would need much protein.

"Protein?" she asked, startled. "Red meat?"

"Mounds of it, if he's not eating large animals. I believe he subsists on small game—rabbits, field mice, and the like. He's probably staying away from deer, now that wasting disease is killing them all anyway. And no pets. I don't sense that this wolf has ever taken a pet anywhere in our area, but I don't know how I could ever prove it."

She nodded, deep in thought. It was all Sam Waters had wanted to achieve.

"About the armed men . . . The local news radio labeled them terrorists, but I'm not convinced. Anyways, who knows where they are? And the wolf thing—it's keeping me from my usual deep sleep. I don't want to kill it, but neither do I want to be attacked. Hence, the shotgun. Do you have one? I can give you some shells filled with silver pellets, just in case."

"I don't have one," she said, lying. Sam could see an old-fashioned gun rack in the other room, and among a handful of long guns it contained a shotgun nearly identical to his. "I don't go out at night, lately. And . . . Well, I'm not really a believer."

Somehow he could tell that she was lying again, or at least not voicing her doubts. *She knows or suspects something, but won't say what it is.*

"Very well, Doc, I just wanted to fill you in on my thoughts," he said. "I should be going now."

She offered him something to drink again, almost reluctantly, but he refused, saying he wanted to be home before dark.

"The full moon's waning," he said. "But I don't know enough to not worry about it."

He let himself be maneuvered back into the small foyer and out the door, his shotgun at the ready. "I hope you'll think about what I said," he reiterated, still not sure he knew himself exactly what he was telling her and why. Then it hit him. "Perhaps we are pawns in a game of destiny, and we must come to the aid of our protector." He looked down at his weapon. "That's a far cry from what I thought even an hour ago, but there you are. Maybe Sarah put that thought in my mind. Maybe the great Manito speaks through the wolf and I've just figured it out. Maybe both."

She nodded. Too quickly. "Yes, Sam, I think you may be right."

She hurried him out, and he knew he'd gone too far.

Damn it! He would have to find the wolf himself and test his theory. Then he would either kill it, or give it his blessing on behalf of his people. Whether or not the blessing was his to give.

He wished he could be watching his favorite DVD, drinking a smooth Corona with a twist of lime in the bottle and the hell with the gas. "Plastics!" he said to the swishing tree limbs above him, quoting the movie. *If only it were so simple.*

He went into the woods, where shadows were beginning to lengthen.

JESSIE

She closed and bolted the door, shaken at the news. Sheriff Bunche, dead? Could it be? She felt tears begin, a natural reaction. She would make some calls, see if the county needed her help, or the clinic's.

What about all the magic stuff?

She pondered a bit. It *was* far-fetched, of course. But it fit the thoughts and feelings she'd been having. And Nick's frozen meat selection was so much larger than even the most avid red meat lover's. But wasn't that ridiculous? Wasn't she just seeing it that way because she wanted to?

Damn it, Nick Lupo. What the hell are you?

MARTIN

The fucking vehicle was too loud, its huge engine rattling like a helicopter. But Wilbur assured him it was muffled, so it could have been even louder a clatter. He'd expected a large and unsightly piece of olive-drab equipment, of course, but not that it would be so, well, *massive.* He rode shotgun to Wilbur's driving, while Kenny and Buck sat just behind them in the first of the ten seats Wilbur had left of the original twenty. Uncomfortable school-bus seats, their vinyl was torn and tattered as if by generations of unruly schoolchildren bearing switchblades. The remainder of the open cabin consisted of bare, rusted metal flooring now covered by several crates of supplies.

The engine's rattle made talking nearly impossible, and Martin didn't think he cared all that much, because he had nothing to say to these three.

This was an unsophisticated end to his plans, which he had so carefully laid out and nurtured. The murders, the personal messages, the losses Dominic Lupo had suffered, even if he wasn't aware of them yet. It was all very sophisticated, until it led here, to the place Lupo called his own. Martin had wanted to claim his prize here, doubly so since he had witnessed the cop's attraction for the lady doctor bearing fruit of the forbidden kind. He'd thought hooking up with Klug and his cronies created a fine final phase for his plan, but now it would have to be improvised, spur of the moment. He'd considered the woodsmen perfect—hardy hunters he could trust in a pinch to live off the land and help him trap the cop if he could really turn into a wolf as his sister had so carefully documented. But now he wasn't so sure.

Wilbur Klug was a bully whose sole interest in life appeared to be the intimidation of others and maybe drinking, not always in that order. His buddy Kenny was an ignoramus who followed because he had not a shred of imagination, and who also ranked drinking highly as a hobby. And Buck Benton—well, Martin would have cheerfully blown off his head mere moments after they had freed him, had he not needed all three. It was too late to change horses in midstream, Martin figured. He was stuck with them. *Make the best of it.*

Suddenly, Wilbur crashed through the Duck's gears in a noisy downshift that included a short revving of the engine with the accelerator, and pulled them slowly onto Circle Moon Drive. Martin held up his hand and Wilbur applied the screechy brakes.

"We're here," he said as Wilbur shut down the engine. "The rest on foot. Don't wanna get heard."

He waited as they gathered up their guns, then they clambered off the Duck using a battered aluminum ladder.

Chapter Twenty-seven

JESSIE

She thought she heard the doorbell ring again while in the bathroom washing her hands. Normally, she would have peeked through the gap in the curtains of the side window to see who stood on her porch. Even though she had spent most of her life in the rural regions of what locals called "Up North," she had also spent enough time in the city with her big-time doctor father to know that trust could so easily be fragile and, therefore, broken.

But she had just watched Sam Waters leave a few minutes ago, and she half suspected Nick would make an appearance soon. Not that she considered herself so irresistible, but what they'd shared had so much altered her perception of day-to-day life that she hoped that his had been altered as well. She couldn't wait to see him.

So she ran straight toward the door, wiping her hands on her shorts, intending to throw it wide open.

And realized immediately that she was in deep trouble.

The door suddenly burst inward, exploding jagged

wooden spears from the shattered jamb. The inset glass panel also shattered when the door reached the end of its arc and rebounded. In the meantime, the imposing barrel-chested man who staggered inside from the top of the steps set his gigantic booted foot inside the doorway and jammed the door wide open.

Jessie leaped back, surprised but also quick-acting, and went for the police tactical baton she kept on a ledge near the door, but a ham-sized fist closed over her wrist and stopped her cold before she could reach it.

Still silent—not a screamer Jessie Hawkins, and not accustomed to asking for help, self-sufficient to a fault—she twisted out of the grasp and, finding her way out the door blocked by other bodies, thrust herself in the direction of the gun rack in the den. But the big man who'd invaded her home was already on her heels, and she heard the others following with a loud clatter. She never reached the rack, but found herself flipped onto her face by the man's ankle tackle. She barely avoided smashing her nose on the hardwood floor by falling hard on her forearms, and her attacker immediately began to reel her in.

Just as quickly, she twisted her athletic body out of his grasp again and lashed out with a moccasin-clad foot.

Damn it! she had changed out of her Timberlands.

Still, her deadly toe-jab connected with the giant's nose and he grinned through the sudden curtain of blood. Nevertheless, his hands became a vise around her foot.

"A wildcat!" he shouted, speaking for the first time as she thrashed in his grip. "I like that."

Jessie grunted. She wasn't about to waste her breath on screams or insults or inane questions, knowing instinctively that these were the men Sam had warned her about. Why hadn't she prepared more?

Because she was distracted with Nick, that was why.

She concentrated on her resistance, realizing way

down deep in her gut that her life had suddenly become a fragile construct.

Literally in his hands.

He turned her slowly, like a bird on a spit, twisting her resisting body back against her efforts, so that she had no choice but to lie belly-down on the floor again. The ragged fringes of an area rug filled her mouth with yarn. Her kicking radius was shortened to only backward and upward, which her attacker contained with ease using only one massive hand.

"Oh, now, I like *that!*" he said, laughing and surveying the view of her buttocks and lower back.

She realized that her thrashing excited him, so she relaxed her muscles, sagging to the floor as if surrendering to his will. Suddenly, she surged with all her strength and tried to stick her foot in his face, but he had foreseen her attempt and he foiled it easily, driving her toes so hard into the floor that she screamed in pain.

"Behave!" he warned, doing a bad Austin Powers voice. No one laughed.

Sweat rolled down her forehead and into her eyes. She turned her head painfully and blinked, seeing them all clearly for the first time. The big guy leaning with all his weight on her legs, a sleazy-looking one in a bright orange jumpsuit—*him* she recognized—a dumb-looking one in another gray jumpsuit that matched the big guy's, and a casually dressed blond man carrying a huge revolver. Two of the others held UZIs. She knew her guns and had seen plenty of UZIs in gun books and at gun shows—it's not a weapon easily mistaken for another. Were these the terrorists? Why here?

Why her?

"Nice rack," the big guy said, and she wasn't sure whether he meant her or the guns just out of reach against the wall. Shivering, she realized he probably meant both.

They were all looking at the selection of shotguns and deer rifles nearby, but then they all stared at her.

Like a pack of drooling hyenas.

Shock set in and she began to tremble and hyperventilate, her breathing ragged and much too quick to replenish the growing vacuum in her lungs.

Tears squeezed out of her eyes, but she fought them and brought herself under control, trying to slow her breathing. Survival required she play the game smart.

But it wasn't a game.

The thought hit her all at once that this invasion was no accident. These weren't a couple of county escapees holing up in a cottage, hoping to elude a dragnet. Well, maybe they'd try eluding the dragnet too, but she knew that there was more to it than that.

It was the blond man. He didn't fit in. Not at all.

He's the murderer who's after Nick, who killed his friend.

Looking at his smarmy, smirky smile, she knew she was right. Whether she could use that knowledge or not, that was the question.

As if he realized her thoughts were on him, the blond man spoke.

"All right, gentlemen, let's take what we came for and head out. I'm certain our friend will be after us soon. I left a couple personal messages for him back home, and after what I saw going on near here, he's gonna come looking." He pointed at the big guy. "You have a place staked out like we planned?"

The big guy's hands on her legs didn't move. "Yeah, I got the place. Not much to it. It's isolated, but it ain't far from here as the duck paddles."

Jessie felt his hands begin crawling along the backs of her legs. Struggling didn't help; his grip was just too strong. He stopped when he reached the bottom of her buttocks. He squeezed her there, as if he were checking out produce.

"Tell your Rottweiler to get off me!" she shouted at the blond man, surmising that he would try to maintain his control. What had they come for, anyway?

The other two laughed, especially annoying honking laughter coming from the Buck guy she'd seen carted off to jail. "Wilbur, you're a dog!" he hooted.

The big guy didn't respond, but his grip grew stronger and one of his hands wandered under the hem of her scrunched-up shorts. Had she gone too far?

"Let's get going," the blond man said tersely. "I'm paying the bills, and you guys are going to be all over the news. You don't have time to play with your toys, Wilbur."

Now she made the connection. She hadn't really recognized Klug yet.

Wilbur grunted behind her, his fingers touching her panties, his breath wheezing over her back. "Okay, okay," he said finally. "But this is mine later on, when we get there." He unstraddled her feet and dragged her into a kneeling position, then up on her feet. His dumb-looking friend gave him a pair of handcuffs and before she knew it they were snapped around her wrists, behind her back.

"Kenny, grab a couple of these fine-looking weapons," Wilbur said.

"Okay!" Kenny set about his quest with gusto, raiding Jessie's father's beloved gun rack. "Hey, lookie here!"

Everyone turned. Kenny crouched to rummage below the row of long guns. From a special cradle he took a Saxon hunting crossbow with fiberglass cut-out rifle stock, its frame fitted with a quiver of twelve wicked-looking hunting bolts.

"What a toy!" Kenny said with reverence.

"You don't even know how to load that thing," Buck called out, snorting. "Give it here!"

Jessie understood then that Kenny was used to being the token idiot, the dumb guy follower who'd get in trouble with his buddies because he wanted their respect, but who would never have it because they *had* to be better than *somebody,* after all, and why not him? Kenny mumbled a few words below his breath, but he gave Buck the crossbow without argument.

"Buck, you get to carry the bow. Are you happy now?"

Martin Stewart's voice approximated a whine, and she sensed that he felt his control unraveling. He waved the revolver. "Let's go!" He spotted the phone and walked up, scratching his chin. Looking around as if about to ask a question, instead he unplugged the phone from the answering machine and let the cord dangle.

Wilbur growled. "Kenny, carry out them guns. Buck, find some fuckin' clothes that don't make you look like county butt-bait, okay?" He shoved her roughly toward the door, where they waited. She felt his hands on her buttocks and recoiled, but he held her close by the handcuffs. Buck returned a few minutes later and picked up the crossbow again, having found some of her father's jeans and a shirt-and-sweater combination she'd given him as a Christmas gift, and a light parka.

"Where are we going?" she asked.

"You'll see, babe, you'll see," Wilbur whispered in her ear through her hair. His tongue left cold slime on her earlobe.

Jessie Hawkins vowed right then that if she had a chance, she would kill him. She had cared for people and saved lives her entire career, but he represented everything about human life not worth saving.

Martin kicked over one of her bookcases, spilling dozens of medical and science books. "Just in case your boyfriend doesn't get the message."

Wilbur took one hand off her and aimed the UZI. A short burst nearly blew out her eardrums and shattered the television. Hot brass danced on the floor.

"Never anythin' good on, anyway," Wilbur shouted.

When they dragged her out into the evening darkness,

she felt the cold immediately. "Can I have a jacket?" she asked Martin.

He looked down at her shorts and shook his head. "I think you won't be needing too many clothes at all."

And the chill in his words canceled out the cold night air for her.

PART THREE
PAVANE

CHAPTER TWENTY-EIGHT

LUPO

He knew he was behind, being jerked around like a puppet by this bastard, Martin, this *growth* that had to be excised. He'd been behind from the start, when Corinne's death had been dangled before him like an evil clown's toy.

Jessie hadn't been at the clinic all day. He'd been about to leave when the call had come in and he'd heard all about the so-called terrorist attack.

Now Lupo smacked the steering wheel. Damn it, why had his instincts failed him? He'd luxuriated in his new ability to control the Creature, and he'd just thrown the dice cold.

He knew what else. He'd been too close to it all to see the infamous big picture, the forest instead of the trees.

He speed-dialed his cell. Ben's machine picked up, but did that make sense?

He redialed and listened to Ben's outgoing message again. "Hey, Benny, pick up if you're there, man. Pick up!

I'm gonna need some help up here. Are you there? All right, I'll call back."

Blessed with a good memory for numbers, he dialed Jessie's again, but again there was no answer and no machine.

He felt like a rubber band in a child's game, being pulled in both directions.

The squadroom phone was answered by a gruff Sergeant Kosko, a friend of Ben's. "No, Nick, he ain't here. Thought he was out in the field with you."

"Fuck! Listen, Sarge, there's somethin' going on—"

"Hell yeah! You hear about Eagle River? All hell's breaking loose up there! Sounds like terrorists broke some scumbag perp outta jail, had grenades and full auto guns."

"Yeah, I'm heading there now," Lupo said. "Rag's gun shop!" He shook his head. Why hadn't he seen the connection? "We figured they got grenades and more, Sarge. Listen, you better send a squad over to Ben's and check on him. I need him to call me, but he's not answering. I'm—" His phone emitted three short beeps and went dead, its battery drained. He tossed it aside in disgust.

Lupo drove on, his mind screaming.

JESSIE

She had pulled a rough wool blanket over herself and no one had stopped her. The night was darkening, and there would be frost. Her breath reminded her of how cold it was every time it puffed in front of her face.

She'd been amazed—shocked, really—by their getaway vehicle. She'd been to the Dells in central Wisconsin, so she knew damn well what it was. She'd just never expected to be whisked away in a Duck, for Christ's sake!

She knew now that she was bait.

Maybe Nick Lupo would be able to help her. No, they

expected him to follow her so they could kill him. She couldn't think in straight lines anymore. She remembered what Sam had implied Nick was. Some creature out of mixed mythologies. Would he be able to track them here, on the river? As a wolf? Was he a wolf? A *werewolf?* At this point, she would have welcomed him as any monster, because in his arms she had found more than she ever had, with anyone. If he was a monster, then monsters were misunderstood. That was for sure. Because he had been gentle, loving and caring, and what they'd shared had renewed her love of life, not that she'd ever really lost it. Now she wondered if he was bounding through the woods, a black wolf looking for her. She remembered a romantic movie about a wolf and a hawk. The music seemed familiar. Her mind wandered again.

They had driven around Circle Moon Drive to the Rivkin house (*she'd always laughed at the name, Rivkin, the infamous serial killer . . . Little did the old folks who lived there know how their neighbors chuckled every time they passed the mailbox on which it was prominently painted*) and entered the narrow driveway, and then she'd realized what they were doing. The Rivkins owned a private boat launch, a wide concrete ribbon that disappeared into the dark waters of the channel. Sometimes their friends and neighbors launched there for free, though tourists had to pay. But the big guy, Klug, had driven straight toward the ramp and after a great gnashing of gears he slid a shift lever all the way forward and engaged the propeller in the rear of the squared-off chassis. The great vehicle rumbled and trembled as it went through its transformation, then slid into the water with a great splash as the snowblade-shaped front end hit the surface. Its momentum carried it out into the channel and then the spinning prop got a grip and the Duck waddled toward the center of the current.

She shivered now, having been nearly drenched by the cold sheet of water that had soaked through her clothes. Only the blanket kept her teeth from chattering aloud.

They didn't talk much, but she felt Buck Benton's eyes on her the whole time. They'd stationed Kenny aft, to stand guard and watch the rear. Martin Stewart sat next to Klug and occasionally spoke to him in low tones. But Buck sat in one of the seats closest to where she lay, in the seatless empty cargo space. Every time their eyes met, he licked his lips lasciviously.

"I'm going to kill you, you bastard," she mumbled through slack lips. He couldn't hear her, and the threat made her feel better.

"We're almost there," she heard Klug tell Martin.

The shiver she felt was not so much due to the freezing night air.

LUPO

Just outside Eagle River's business district, he found a phone. It wasn't a booth, for they had disappeared in the face of the cell phone's onslaught, but a cherry-red bubble covering a battered phone. He dropped a handful of quarters into the slot and dialed the squad room, hoping to speak to Ben.

Kosko was still on duty.

"Sarge, you have any word from Ben yet? We were supposed to touch base, so he can't have gone anywhere—" He didn't know exactly why the thought hit him, but suddenly he heard the silence at the other end of the line speaking volumes. "Something's happened to Ben, hasn't it? You better fucking tell me!" he growled, losing the thin veneer of civility that covered up his *rough spots,* a term Caroline had coined for him many years before. She had theorized that *rough spots* were a near-surfacing of the Creature within him. His hair grew in tufts, his hands and feet itched, and under stress he could barely control his growling. Now he must have spooked Kosko.

"Ben's dead, Nick," Kosko said quickly. "I'm sorry, man, I didn't want to tell you like this, but—"

He felt deadened. "How?" His facial features turned to marble. Blood chilled his veins. The Creature howled within. "Tell me, dammit!" he snapped.

The sergeant relayed the squad's report. "And Nick? I been reading your file on Devereaux . . ."

"Yeah?"

"There was purple lipstick all over the pillow."

Lupo swore and hung up.

There was nothing left to say, no one to call or tell.

This was between Lupo and Martin, Caroline's deranged brother.

Jessie!

I'm coming, you bastard.

BUCK BENTON

Goddamn, she's a prime piece of tail, layin' right here at my feet. Wilbur's got dibs, I know, but goddamn it all, this is enough to make a man's pecker stand up and sa-lute! Only thing I'd like better woulda been to cut off Bunche's balls with my Buck knife. Fuckin'-A, I shoulda got to shoot him myself, the bastard. Fuck, she's just prime. I seen you around, little lady, I seen you givin' me the stink-eye all the time you been over there, on the res, makin' them headdress-niggers all better and battin' your eyelashes at them tourist fucks. I seen you, and I think you're gonna see me hangin' in your face pretty soon, so you better get ready . . .

Buck's mind wandered from topic to topic, but always returned to the doctor covered in the wet blanket a few feet away. He bet her nipples were nice and hard, like buttons, under that suede shirt she was wearing. He bet they'd taste right nice, and so would her bald beaver. He didn't know if she was bald, but he figured she was just the kind of cunt who would shave like a cheap whore.

He looked forward, past Wil and the city fella, and into the night sky. It was gonna be cold and clear. Oh, yeah, he was happy in the parka he'd gotten from the doc's house. Warm as hell and smelling of sweet pipe tobacco. What a shame he'd be getting blood all over it. But after she watched the fat-ass Bunche put him in the slammer, all he could think about was slicing up that soft, firm flesh of hers one inch at a time, making it last.

Oh, yeah.

Buck Benton was in his element now.

KLUG

He hadn't been out on the lakes since—well, since years ago, when he was practicing for his dream business. Until Shelly'd killed it right before his eyes. He was happy to be rid of her, and he'd enjoyed doing the sheriff and his pal, too. Wilbur had never thought of himself as violent, but now he had to admit, the genie was out of the bottle. Something in him had snapped and he wasn't at all eager to fix it, whatever *it* was. Maybe it was all those years with that lack of respect. His daddy hadn't given him none, and his mama had run off with some trailer trash dude. But then the dude, he'd ended up in prison and when he got out he wasn't so kind to mama no more, and that was why Wilbur had worked out until he was big enough and then he'd gone to the trailer trash dude's place and beaten him silly with a baseball bat and a tire iron (Wilbur wanted to experiment and see which weapon did a better job . . . it had been a draw). But his mama had taken right up with another loser dude, and Wilbur had done him some harm, too, and then it became obvious that mama's fun was being ruined by Wilbur, so she kicked him out of the house and he'd been on his own ever since, except for Shelly. And *that* mistake he'd finally rectified.

Wilbur steered the Duck with ease, letting the engine stretch out a bit even though its muffling was spotty at best. But City Boy didn't know that, and anyway, Wilbur wanted like hell to reach their destination. He'd worked up a good case of the hots for the lady doc back there, and he didn't want sloppy seconds after Buck. He turned slightly and checked out of the corner of his eye.

Nope, the doc still showed more leg than she realized, huddled under that blanket. Klug could see Buck leering at her, but he knew the psychotic knife-wielder would yield to his leadership and his size.

Klug couldn't wait for this fringe benefit. The joy of carrying out the assault on the courthouse had already faded. Once done, a feat wasn't nothin' but history. No, he looked forward to the lady doctor's charms and this cop hunt—*wolf, yeah, whatever*—a lot more now. And when City Boy gave them their money, there was a very good chance Klug wasn't gonna feel like sharing.

A very good chance . . .

CHAPTER TWENTY-NINE

SAM WATERS

Huddled in the underbrush not far from the Rivkin place, Sam watched the rust-stained Duck rumble past and drop like a skipped stone into the channel. It was dark, but his eyesight was still good enough to spot not only the three local thugs, but also a stranger—and Doctor Hawkins, who was clearly a prisoner.

Sam raised the shotgun, knowing they were within range, but wild shooting would most likely hurt Jessie Hawkins, too, and he couldn't be responsible for that. He hadn't heard anything about Klug's old Duck being the getaway vehicle. So Klug and his buddies had busted Benton out of jail, but who could have imagined they'd pull off a military-style attack? With *their* wits? And slipping down the channel they'd pass right on by any roadblocks the State Police might have set up by now. Sure, the police had probably considered a boat escape, but this lumbering beast was naturally camouflaged and made little wake. If they hugged the wooded shoreline, they'd probably escape notice from the air.

Sam set the safety on the shotgun again and slung it over his shoulder with the military strap. It was time to make use of his nearly forgotten woodcraft. If he didn't follow the amphibious vehicle, they'd disappear.

He wondered briefly about the wolf. Where was he?

LUPO

His senses alert and the Creature barely muzzled below his skin, Lupo burst through the door of Jessie's cottage. The driveway had given up no clue, nothing to indicate foul play. But the front door stood skewed half-open, with the bookcase's contents strewn across the otherwise neat living room. The phone was unplugged, and the spot rug near the gun rack lay mussed and generally disrupted. Lupo checked the rack carefully. It still held three rifles, but the dust patterns indicated that several other long guns were missing.

Lupo plugged in the phone and played tag until a local operator—from nearby St. Germain—finally connected him with the sheriff's office. He identified himself carefully to the acting sheriff, who explained that all resources were now engaged hunting for the courthouse terrorists. Lupo explained that they were merely criminals, and that a woman—a doctor—had been kidnapped, but the man (who seemed to harbor political ambitions today he might not have had yesterday) spoke with painful bluntness.

"I tell you, Detective, I'm very sympathetic to your problem. But we have no choice but to put your concerns at a lower priority than the capture of these armed men."

"But their capture will also free the doctor," Lupo tried to explain.

"I hear what you're saying," the new acting sheriff said, saccharine-voiced but firm, "and we will find her. But we're busy following up several leads right now, and it's taking up all my manpower. When the feds get here, we'll be able to spread out more. In the meantime, if you would come to my office I'll deputize you—"

Lupo hung up.

He was in this alone.

Reluctantly, he left his weapons and clothing in the car, hid the keys, and took the only option left.

It's a trap.

For me.

Lupo looked up and saw the moon, no longer full, beginning its rise toward the heavens. The chill breeze ruffled his hair and raised goose bumps. He concentrated and allowed the anger, the hatred, and the sadness to swirl together into one mind-set. Could he control the Creature now, when the moon wasn't drawing him on?

He felt his body change, felt his mind begin to split into two entities, and then his head exploded with sensory input.

The woods, the trees, the animals, the night air, the wild, the various scents of humans, several of them familiar. His snout collected it all, and the Creature half-sat, half-crouched on its haunches and howled its warning.

His thoughts were clear, even as he looked through the Creature's eyes.

He sniffed the air and bounded off down the driveway to the road, where he knew immediately they had boarded some kind of vehicle.

God help them when they catch me . . .

MARTIN

He felt like a child. "Are we there yet?"

Klug looked at him as if he were a bug and spat overboard, into the brackish water. He just pointed to the left, behind a very dark promontory.

Martin looked. The tree line was a black felt marker line across his vision between the even blacker water and the indigo of the night sky. But he could see something coming into view—a lighter patch emerging from the black background. A hidden private beach, a narrow crescent-shaped strand of brown sand that resembled snow in the dark.

"That's it?" he asked Klug.

"That's Camp O-Jew-Boy!" The interruption came from Benton, suddenly materializing behind them.

"You betcha, Camp O-Jew-Boy!" Klug laughed, his teeth bright in the moonlight.

"That's where them rich Jew-boys spend their summer vacations, learnin' how to needlepoint and fuckin' each other in the ass!"

"You been there, Buck?" Klug shouted over the sound of the engine.

Buck gave him the finger and a smirk.

They'd made a steady seven knots, Klug had told him earlier. It seemed pretty fast to Martin, who didn't know from fast on a freaking boat. *Whatever,* he thought. *Just let's get this hook baited.*

This was the place Klug had suggested back when Martin had hired them, explaining his needs. A summer boys' camp, it consisted of cabins and a handful of administration buildings and garages, a large boathouse, and a few outbuildings. The boys who were sent here could be seen playing sports in the water, on the beach, and on the camp parade ground from late June to early August, two-week and three-week batches of campers sent away by their well-to-do parents so the adults could "do" Europe or rattle around their palatial big-city mansions without the brats getting underfoot.

It was perfect, Martin thought, even more so now that he saw it.

They headed right for the beach and with little fuss the Duck rolled up the incline, trembled mightily once again as it underwent its bizarre transformation and the wheels gripped the cold sand, then stood for a few seconds, shaking off the river. Klug clutched hard, depressing the pedal almost through the floorboards, then engaged the regular forward gear by wrestling with the gigantic shift lever. Soon, the engine screamed and the vehicle clambered up the sand and toward the cabins. Klug brought the rattling Duck around to face the river in case they needed a fast retreat, then shut down.

Within minutes, Klug made Benton and Kenny carry most of the supplies into one of the cabins. They half-dragged the lady doctor through the jimmied door and dumped her in the corner. Two Coleman lanterns provided all the light they would need.

"You know they're going to catch you here!" she said to them all, in general. "This isn't so far from the city . . . They'll spot you as soon as daylight comes."

Klug nodded at Buck, who immediately gagged her with a greasy rag from one of the crates. She continued to make noises, but then gave up and sat quietly.

"You think he'll track us here?" Klug asked Martin.

"I know he will. He's good at this. And I told you, he has the nose of a wolf."

"Yeah, well, I'll believe that when I see it!" Klug snorted. "Either way, I get a cop. If he's some weirdo magical guy, well, that's cool too."

Martin nodded.

Klug hauled out one of the crates. "Give me a hand, Kenny. Buck, you grab those chains."

They shoved and shimmied, and eventually the three headed out the door into the dark night. "We'll be right back," Klug called out. "Don't go away!"

Martin beamed.

"What's this crap?" Buck asked.

"Wolf traps," Klug explained, as he walked into the

woods. "They're old, but they're just fine, especially after a little improvement, thanks to our friend here. I got a half-dozen of the sons of bitches. Let's see him get past these!"

An hour later, Klug led Kenny and Buck back into the cabin. Their hands and clothes were streaked with flaky rust.

"All done?" Martin asked.

"Yeah, we're set," Klug said. "But right now, I think I have some business to attend to. Kenny, stand guard outside. Take one of the UZIs."

Kenny looked at Klug. Then he looked at Buck, and at Martin. He wasn't that stupid. The lady doctor's eyes bugged out at him as if trying to convey some important fact he'd forgotten. "Wil, I'm not sure I wanna—"

"Fuck that, Kenny. Do what I say, boy. Might be some leftovers for you."

"I don't want any leftovers, Wil." His tone was pathetic.

"Get your ass out there or I'm carvin' my name on it," Buck snarled. "First on you, then on her. Got it?"

Kenny relented. "Yeah, I got it." He shrugged, took the gun, and stepped outside.

Klug stood in front of Jessie while Martin made himself comfortable. Buck leaned against a nearby plank wall, the crossbow slung on one shoulder, sharpening his Buck knife with loving whetstone strokes.

"I think we should spend some quality time with our guest here," Klug said, smiling.

CHAPTER THIRTY

JESSIE

"You come near me, I'll kill you!" she said, but the gag muffled her words into comical cartoon sounds.

When the big guy made his move, she had no time to roll away. He was on her so fast that her attempt to crawl away became in fact detrimental, as it presented him with the view he preferred, with her lying belly-down, her hands still manacled behind her back.

She struggled, but he held one of her legs and let her, until she'd worn herself out.

Then he held her with one hand and roughly tore her shorts down her legs with the other.

She screamed again, but the gag muffled the sound and she realized she could choke on her saliva if she wasn't careful. She whimpered and tears ran like acid streams into her eyes, but by now Klug had torn aside her panties and bared her buttocks. Her struggle was useless, as he seemed to have her like a fish flopping out of the water and onto the bank.

Suddenly, she felt his erection pushing between her thighs, touching her *there*.

She gathered herself for one last effort and scream against her attacker.

Outside, a howl of rage split the night's quiet.

Another howl, then the snarl of a large beast. *Very close.*

Wilbur Klug stopped in midmotion and hastily rolled away from her.

KENNY

Fuck, I can't believe my friends are in there about to rape this chick.

Kenny stamped his feet to keep out the cold. It had always been fun hanging out with those two losers—hell, *he* was a loser, big-time—and he'd happily participated in most of their half-assed, harebrained schemes and petty crimes over the years. Even busting Buck out of prison, that had been exciting! He never thought he'd be shooting UZIs and lobbing grenades, kinda like his favorite movies, *Kelly's Heroes* and *Sands of Iwo Jima* and like them computer games his nephew was always playin'— *Doom* and *Resident Evil* and shit like that. He'd pretended the sheriff and that other dude, the deputy, were zombies or somethin', shooting them before they could get him, and it had been fun, exceptin' all the blood . . .

But now, here, standing sentry while Wilbur and Buck humped that poor lady in there . . . Well, it wasn't right.

He was on the verge of tears.

Shit, my daddy dint teach me to be no rapist!

He cocked the UZI and stood there, hearing the woman crying through her gag. Maybe he should go in there and break it up. Maybe he should . . .

Nah, Kenny wasn't like that. He couldn't make decisions like that. That's why he was standin' guard. The sad thing was, he knew it.

The sudden loud howl scared the bejesus out of him.

He jerked himself around, aiming the submachine gun into the darkness below the trees. Had the howling come from there? He wasn't sure.

Could this be the wolf-man the city boy wanted dead? Was the cop a real werewolf, like in the movies? Kenny screened image after image of movie werewolves in his head. *Sure as hell scary!*

When the second howl came, it was behind him—*right behind him*—and he turned just in time to hear it turn into a snarl.

And in time to see the black blur pounce on him from the shadows right at the corner of the cabin.

He screamed and squeezed the trigger as the claws reached him, raking painfully through his clothes from belly to shoulder, and the jaws closed on his throat and ripped it to shreds while growling with pure, malevolent hatred.

The 9mm slugs tore through the porch roof, some maybe ripping into the wolf itself, but Kenny's backward momentum carried both of them away from the front door, and when the wolf dipped his snout into Kenny's ruined neck once more and tore out muscle and nerve in a shower of warm blood, there was no life left in Kenny at all, his eyes frozen open, staring upward at his attacker as if shocked at his own spectacular end.

LUPO

The wolf shook off the effects of the bullets, stinging hot foreign objects that had traversed harmlessly *through* the magic that surrounded him, and howled again, this time facing the door.

He advanced.

KLUG

From inside the cabin, the rough chatter and sudden silence of Kenny's UZI told the tale.

Klug rolled off the woman, hitched up his pants, and reached for one of the long guns stacked nearby. It was a Ruger Mini-14 from her father's rack. She whimpered in the corner, her eyes still wide, trembling, trying to fumble at her clothes. But Klug didn't care. Martin had unholstered a hog-leg of a handgun, and maybe for the first time Klug believed his strange, stupid story.

There *was* a wolf outside, and it *was* after them.

Werewolf or not, it had gotten Kenny.

It would pay.

He cocked the semiauto 5.56mm Ruger.

BUCK

When they heard Kenny getting mauled, Buck forgot about the woman. He dropped the crossbow and snatched up the other UZI, seeing as how Wilbur was reaching for one of the rifles.

He spread his legs like he'd seen soldiers do in the movies, planting his weight, and squeezed off a burst that ripped through the cabin's front door and wall. He released the trigger only when the bolt stayed open, the magazine emptied. Sizzling brass rained around his feet. A cloud of cordite seemed to hang like haze in the little cabin.

He's not fuckin' gettin' me.

From nearby, a rifle boomed once, twice. Wilbur was firing through the door, too.

"I think it got Kenny!" Buck shouted.

336 W. D. Gagliani

"Fuck Kenny!" Klug kept shooting until the firing pin in his rifle clicked on an empty breech.

Buck shrugged. He found full magazines and loaded up, then kept firing too.

Sonofabitch!

MARTIN

Holding his ground, he watched both the door and the window that overlooked the front of the cabin. The Smith & Wesson felt comforting in his grip, and so did the knowledge that if he did indeed need silver, he had it.

The cabin's simple wooden walls were pockmarked with ragged bullet holes. They'd shot out the window glass, so cold air made its way inside and raised goose bumps along his arms and back. So did the whole wolf hunt idea. He knew now that, journals aside, he had never really believed the story. If he'd given it the weight of his belief, he would have blasted the cop to kingdom come earlier, from afar, with his special bullets. But he wanted the rush of revenge, the great satisfaction of hurting—*torturing*—his enemy for as long as possible, and a quick death would have granted none of the closure he sought. No, the closure he *needed*.

At some point, it occurred to him that he might benefit by staying close to Jessie Hawkins—close enough to lay the gun's barrel onto her skull and back Lupo off. Wolf or human, he wouldn't want his lady friend hurt, would he? On the other hand, if he was a wolf, who was to say he wouldn't maul *her*, too?

Fuck! No use for his consummate acting skills here, not in the woods.

This was the wolf's playground.

And Martin should have remembered that . . .

SAM WATERS

When the gunfire broke out, he was just reaching the out-
skirts of the campgrounds. He'd worked here, one summer many years ago, teaching woodlore, knot-tying, and
canoeing to adolescent boys from big cities. He hadn't
liked it much, feeling like a token Indian on the staff, having to be polite and acting the part of a Tonto—a whited-
up Indian sidekick for each of those acned Lone Rangers.
It wasn't his bag and the pay wasn't all that good, either.
His son had worked there several summers, his age making it more palatable and his athletic good looks working
out well with the girl camp counselors from downriver. It
was just like a movie for Michael, one of those Bill Murray
frat-boy summer-camp golf course sophomoric humor
movies Sam had enjoyed once, but which he could no
longer watch without thinking of his son. So, as much as
he loved movies, he avoided those.

Now the camp was deserted and stuck in the middle of
its typical winter disrepair, but the gunfire clearly indicated where the so-called terrorists had ended up.

He hoped he wasn't too late to help Doc Hawkins, but
at the same time he was all too aware of just how outnumbered and outgunned he was.

But his sharp hearing told him he had one ally.

Perhaps.

If the wolf was indeed also a human.

And if so?

Why was it *his* fight? What brought him here, to fight
this evil?

Was it destiny?

CHAPTER THIRTY-ONE

LUPO

The Creature felt invincible. The humans' bullets had torn through the walls and door, zinging through him without doing any harm he could feel. The human side of the Creature, the part of him that remained Nick Lupo, understood the miracle it represented. That lead and gunpowder could be harmless . . . It was a cop's wet dream. It was like Kevlar from God.

Or the devil.

Lupo and the Creature merged consciousness and became One. He sensed that this had been possible all along, that he could have cultivated this knowledge, this skill, for years—just as Caroline had suspected. But he had been denied, perhaps by the wall he'd erected between the two sides of his personality, unwilling to acknowledge the similarities and the brotherhood. The *duality*. All his life he had continued adding another brick to the wall, just as Pink Floyd said. But now there was more than revenge or hatred or even self-preservation at risk.

Now there was Jessie Hawkins, innocent bystander.

Jessie Hawkins, a pawn in Martin Stewart's sick game, just as Corinne had been.

Jessie Hawkins, his friend.

His lover. How strange that sounded.

Lupo gave the Creature its head and went along for the ride. In a few long-limbed bounds he reached the cabin and burst through the gunfire-weakened door.

He roared his anger to the heavens and entered, his jaws snapping, revenge blocking all other emotions and instincts.

KLUG

When the door seemed to disintegrate, Wilbur Klug had a flash of existential insight. But it was too late to just walk away and go home. He knew instinctively that the wolf, the man, the combination of wolf and man, *whatever the fuck it was*, would not rest until it brought each of them down like weak members of a herd.

Never one for heroism, Klug dove for a side window without even attempting to fire his weapon at the wolf this time. The black beast landed in midstride on his gigantic paws and headed straight for Martin, the only one who stood up in the center of the cabin and faced it. Last thing Klug saw was Martin trying to take aim with his huge handgun. He'd lost track of Buck, but he bet old Buck was also in the regrouping mode.

The hell with this, Klug thought as his big body shattered the window glass and frame and he landed among the wood and glass debris on the hard-packed ground outside the cabin.

He heard the loud report of Martin's handgun inside.

He made for another cabin, his panic streak nearly in control. If he thought he could have made it to the Duck, he would have risked it and got the hell out of Dodge. But the amphibious truck was parked too far away, on the other side of the camp, where they had hidden it in the intense underbrush just off the beach. Whose stupid idea had *that* been?

For once, he had no plan.

Nothing.

Only survival. *That* was the plan.

BUCK

When Wilbur leaped through the goddamned window and the city boy stood his ground, Buck exercised his greater cranial capacity—at that moment—and slid out the door in the wake of the wolf's entrance. He saw the wolf turn and consider him for a split second, and then the city boy was firing that hog-leg of his and the explosions rattled Buck's skull. He thought he saw the wolf flinch in midspring—

and did he yelp like an injured dog?

—and then Buck was out of the cabin and around it, running with Wilbur for another cabin.

Shit! What was the point?

But now his legs were doing all the thinking, and all they wanted was distance and a place to hide.

Huffing like a steam engine, he burst through the locked door at about the same instant as Wilbur, and then they were inside, building a barricade of bunk beds and pine dressers, their lungs heaving and their eyes wild.

Wolf hunt!

What a crock! Who was huntin' who?

MARTIN

He held his fire until the snarling black beast had left the ground and hovered in midair only feet away from his throat, its claws glinting in the lanterns' light and its eyes glowing red and wild with irrational rage.

Martin squeezed the trigger the way Rag had taught him—*rest in peace, Rag-man*—and let his arm and shoulder absorb the recoil. He saw the bullet score and the wolf was knocked out of his trajectory, ending up in a heap near the side wall. Martin was barely aware of Jessie Hawkins still huddled there, staring wide-eyed at the snarling creature and its snapping jaws, which now seemed to be trying to bite its own haunches, growling and yelping.

It took moments to register in Martin's mind. *The silver had done it!* The wolf was hurt. His bullet had hit it, and now it was hurt. He looked down at his hand, which held the Smith & Wesson, and realized that now was his chance to finish the wolf, whatever and whoever he was.

Martin lifted the handgun.

CHAPTER THIRTY-TWO

LUPO

The pain was unbearable.

He had sprung from the door expecting to snap Martin Stewart's neck between his ironlike jaws, but instead the gun had spoken and suddenly Lupo and the Creature both cried out and fell out of the leap, screaming at the searing heat that seemed to skewer their side.

The silver bullets Martin had taken from the gunsmith!

So, he had planned to use them himself, even if he hadn't shared with his buddies.

Lupo and the Creature had never felt so much pain. He looked and saw a furrow where the bullet had grazed his skin and burned off a thin line of his fur and his flesh seemed to be melting there, liquefying into molten burning pain like placing one's hand on a grill, a hot plate, or a griddle. Lupo realized how lucky he was that he'd only been grazed, for this pain would have finished him had the bullet smashed into his body.

He turned his head and saw that Martin was ready to fire again, a cool and collected grim look on his face.

He's got me, was all he had time to think before leaping straight up on all four paws and making for the door, knowing that a full-on assault would only result in his death.

He heard the gun's report behind him, and then Martin swore.

The Creature was out the door and loping toward the trees, still in blinding pain.

Have to regroup, have to think.

Jess was still in there.

Jess!

JESSIE

She rolled into Martin's legs just as he took a bead on the wounded wolf, knocking him aside and throwing off his aim. The bullet went wide, and then Martin swore and brought the gun barrel down on the side of her head. She ducked, but not fast enough, and the front sight raked painfully across the soft skin stretched over her skull.

The wolf escaped, but her triumph proved costly.

She felt her head opening up like a fleshy zipper, blood pouring from the wound all out of proportion to the damage. She knew how bad the blow might have been, but her movement had dulled its effect and now she play-acted a little, screaming in pain (some of it very real) through the greasy gag and letting herself fall heavily back down to the floor.

"Goddamn bitch!" Martin shouted at her, all pretense of civility abandoned. She cringed, expecting a bullet or another pistol-whipping, but he seemed to catch hold of himself.

"You'd like that, wouldn't you?" he said, chuckling.

"Concentrate on you so he goes free! Well, no fucking way . . . You're still useful to me, babe. Very useful!" He giggled insanely.

He didn't even sound like Martin Stewart anymore, as if something inside him had just taken over.

It's all true, everything Sam told me. God help me, if it's Nick.

Martin picked up a lantern and went to the door, searching the darkness outside. Then he came back and dragged her to her feet. He waited until she had awkwardly straightened her clothes. He laid the gun's barrel on her bleeding head, driving it into the jagged cut he'd made and making her whimper with pain, and then he forced her outside as a shield.

By the time they found Klug and Buck, hiding behind their barricade, Jessie was blinded by the ache in her head and weakened by the loss of blood.

The three hunters rearranged their defenses, chastened by the appearance of their quarry, then huddled and plotted in angry whispers.

But Jessie smiled through her pain. She could hear their fear.

SAM WATERS

He'd seen enough of the battle to know what had happened. There were still too many armed men standing, and the wolf seemed disoriented by his wound.

Silver.

It had to have been a silver bullet, but it must have only grazed him. Still, it seemed to have taken the fight out of him, and his senses weren't so sharp, either. The wolf had slipped through the cold forest not ten feet away from him and missed his scent, a fact confirmed Sam's suspicions. The beast would surely have to regroup before attacking again. That made up Sam's mind, too, for he still felt too outnumbered to take on the hunters, and he didn't want to be placed in the position of killing the wolf now, in self-defense. He had a theory about that also.

He decided to wait them out. Destiny would bring them to him. He jimmied the cheap lock on another cabin and slipped inside, spreading over his old, creaky shoulders a small wool blanket he had brought with him and taking refuge from the crisp cold of the northern night.

LUPO

Lupo dreamed he saw this panoramic view.

Jack pines swayed gently outside the cabin, where the woods pretended spring but were still locked in the late northern winter. Too late for heavy snow, but early enough to spread a chilling frost nightly over the landscape. Ice sheets, though thinned by the warmer days, floated on the standing water of lakes and formed crusts on quiet bays of rivers and creeks, wherever the river's bank was protected from running water. Jessie waited for him near a warm fire, inviting him with her smile and comforting him with her body. Her hands reached out for him. Cold hands. Dead hands. The hands of Martin Stewart.

He stirred himself awake like a dog, shaking the cold and dampness from his bones slowly, a limb at a time. He shivered as patches of his skin made contact with the clammy planks of the cabin floor. He felt for slivers, gingerly, and the pads of his fingers brushed across a few nubs of embedded wood, reddened skin. Then the pain-heat hit him, *hard*, and he gasped with surprise. He felt along his side, where the fire-red welt that burned like gasoline in his veins stretched from front to back.

He remembered now. A bullet had grazed him there, gouging out a furrow of living flesh.

A *silver* bullet.

If the bullet had torn through his skin and penetrated, would he be dead now?

The lancing, burning feeling was continuous and somehow sapped his strength. For this reason he had sought shelter, and forced himself to push his Change back to human form. The proximity of the bullet had nearly finished him. Perhaps there were micron-sized chunks of silver shrapnel embedded in his skin even now, radiating pain into his nerves and brain.

Besides the pain, more mundane feelings clamored for his attention.

His parched throat burned and he felt great hunger way down, deep inside. As if to punctuate his realization, his belly roared and grumbled emptily.

He'd killed, yes, but not fed.

One of those three thugs. *Kenny?* The least dangerous . . .

Lupo brought his hand up and brushed his matted hair down against his scalp, then wiped the crud out of his eyes. He cleared his throat and it came out a growl. Sometimes the Change just wouldn't let go.

He sprang up on his haunches in a *lupine* pose and peered out the grimy window again. The other cabins of Camp Ojibway came into view through the lifting ground mist, sheets of which seemed to be torn from the undergrowth at irregular intervals. The cabins formed a square pattern, two on a side, bordering a frosted-grass parade ground in which a single rusty flagpole stood sentry. He was in one of the cabins on the west side of the square and he could see, behind the opposite group, a long flat-roofed building still hugged by the fog. The office and kitchen, maybe, and the dining hall. Or maybe the counselors' quarters and the infirmary. He wasn't sure, because he had never been here, not even during his long winter hunts.

The cabin's shelter had served its purpose, keeping him from the bitter cold, but now the chill had seeped right through his skin and seemed to be trickling down his bones. He knew they were still holed up in that other cabin across the way.

They were just as leery of him as he was of them.

Jessie.

She was their hostage still. He had no doubt she was alive. Without her, this trap wouldn't work. He hoped they hadn't hurt her already, but either way they were in for some punishment of a divine sort.

Lupo weighed his options.

JESSIE

She opened one blood-encrusted eye and surveyed the inside of the cabin. This one was more solid than the first, and when Martin had dragged her here she'd immediately felt warmer, even though she still wore shorts and a light suede shirt. But the night's frost had set in and wrapped her in a blanket of shivering, so that now she suffered from numbness and a blinding headache due to her throbbing head wound.

Early-stage hypothermia, she thought. *And a mild concussion. Loss of blood. Possible infection. At best.*

But it was still better than Klug's attempted rape. It was still better than death. As long as they kept her alive, she had a chance to come out of this. And they needed her. She knew she was the bait that would bring them the wolf. So far, they had been right.

Martin slept sitting up in one corner, his handgun on his lap. He was handsome, if a bit bland, and she might have found him attractive had she met him socially. She had difficulty seeing the blond man as a serial killer of epic proportions, but then Jeffrey Dahmer had seemed all too ordinary as well. She had gone to school barely a mile from Dahmer's apartment, had probably nodded to him out on Wisconsin Avenue. You never knew . . .

Klug and Buck had staked out the bunk frames on opposite corners and now snored lightly through clogged nostrils. They hugged their guns like children, and she wondered what went through their minds. If anything.

Kenny was dead. The wolf had killed him. She'd seen his torn-up remains when Martin had dragged her to this cabin. She couldn't quite mourn Kenny, the simpleton, but she knew he had been the closest thing to an ally she might have had. These guys would rather poke their penises in her than almost anything else, and Martin probably wanted to slice her up, paint her like a whore, and *then* fuck her.

Jesus!

She saw it when a ray of rising sun peeked through the corner of a dirty windowpane.

A small ring holding two tiny handcuff keys. And only a few feet away. It could only have slipped out of someone's pocket, and they hadn't seen it when they dumped her unceremoniously into the corner.

She rolled gently in the direction of the keys, hoping the floorboards wouldn't squeak.

A foot.

Two feet.

A yard.

It was still about a yard away. What if these guys woke up? Then she'd lose her chance.

She started rolling again, a half-roll and half-slither because her hands were still behind her back and, she now realized, nearly useless with paralysis.

Still, she kept getting closer. *Closer.*

She gave a tiny push and rolled a few more inches and felt her hand brush the protruding key ring. Now, could she palm the ring without dropping it and letting it rattle on the wooden floor?

No, she felt it move around.

She held her breath and tried again, willing it toward her. Slowly . . .

Yes!

She'd done it.

The keys were in her fingers. Now, to make the fingers loosen and do their thing . . .

Ten minutes of excruciatingly minuscule motions later, she heard the faint snap of the lock.

The barricaded door was out of the question, but five minutes later she had slithered to the window and five minutes after that she had slid it far enough upward. The idiots still slept.

Jessie prepared herself for the pain. Then she bailed.

MARTIN

He awoke from a wolf-haunted nightmare and turned to see Jessie's legs disappearing through the window.

"No!" he shouted, swiveling rapidly in that direction, trying to bring the gun to bear.

But he was too late. There was no target.

By the time he reached the window, she was gone from view.

CHAPTER THIRTY-THREE

LUPO

If he stepped out as he was, a rifle shot from inside one of the other cabins could finish it. If he forced a Change, he'd at least be a moving target—though he would also provide them with exactly the quarry they sought.

Lupo concentrated, his mind made up. He tried ignoring the cold and his shivers, the pain of his wound, which still throbbed like a searing shish-kabob through his side, trying to bring the alien presence in his mind to the fore, where it could take over. He felt the Creature stir and awaken and his nostrils twitched as the wolf used him to sniff his surroundings. The processing of the information was centered in the wolf's brain, but Lupo realized that he was as a spectator there. He needed to increase his control to that of participant at will. He was almost there. Maybe he needed an emotional spur every single instance.

He sniffed and sneezed unexpectedly.

Now his decision had been made for him. If the hunters

lay in waiting, his exit as a naked human male would draw their fire. If he managed a Change, he would at least have the elements of surprise and speed on his side. Not that those counted for much.

Was a Change even possible in daylight?

Even as he *pushed* and forced the Change, Lupo thought—*too late, too late*—that the hunters might have separated, hoping to draw him into a cross fire.

It *was* too late, because suddenly the Creature stood growling at something it sensed in the cold morning air, snapping its jaws—*his jaws*—and preparing to flee. In one swift move, he bumped the door and watched it snap open, its latch barely an obstacle. Lupo nosed forward on his four paws, catching a familiar scent.

JESSIE

She passed several cabins on her way to the one they'd left. She avoided looking at Kenny, whose ruined body seemed to guard the door. Inside, she found what she wanted and scooped it up.

She ripped off the gag, finally.

Still cold and in pain, but now her father's expertise and his teachings came back strong and true. Bent over, she aimed the crossbow downward and slipped her foot securely into the metal stirrup. Making sure the safety was off, she grasped the bowstring in both hands and centered it, locked her arms, then pulled the string back by using her body, standing upright until it was captured by the latch. The safety now automatically engaged, she plucked a bolt from the quiver and placed it in the flight groove with one fletching facedown, positioning it just slightly ahead of the cocked string.

Locked and loaded.

Because she was an expert, the procedure took a

mere ten to fifteen seconds. She edged out of the cabin and ran.

BUCK

"Get her, Buck!"

When Wilbur had barked, waking him, he'd jumped up and gauged the situation rapidly. The doc gone, the window open, he was It. He'd leaped up and heaved himself through the opening after her, unslinging the UZI only after hitting the ground *hard* and rolling to a crouch.

Where the fuck had she gone so fast?

Had to be another cabin, he reasoned. He wasn't very smart, he knew that, but neither was he an idiot.

Fuck, it's cold!

The breath streamed out of him like steam from a locomotive, as he began checking all the cabins in the nearest row. Their cabin from last night was one of them, he realized—

—and that was when the woman doctor came barrelling out of the door, saw him, and darted for the tree line, cradling in her arms the crossbow he'd taken from her house.

Fuck!

Wilbur would have his balls if he let her get away.

He made sure the UZI was cocked, then gave chase, cursing the day his friends decided he should be busted out of jail. Three hots and a cot sounded a whole helluva lot better than this shit!

JESSIE

She sprinted away from him fast and lost him.

The light of dawn was beginning to spread, touching a

treetop here and there, but mostly creating a morning version of dusk that made sight more difficult below the trees. Now armed with the crossbow, Jessie hesitated.

The rage Jessie felt inside insisted she be an aggressor, but her normal personality preferred a defensive posture. Hurt only to avoid being hurt. Kill only to avoid being killed. Wilbur Klug had tried to rape her, even if he'd been interrupted, and now she had to think clearly. Should she hunt him down, exact payback? He had forced himself on her like an animal—*worse!*—and there would be psychological pain for a long time to come. But did that give her the right to hunt him down? To kill him? He deserved justice, but societal justice, not the lynch-mob variety.

She really believed that, she decided. But . . .

She found a clearing and stood in the center, walking in small circles, partly to think and partly to give herself a chance to warm her frozen skin and numb extremities. It would be hours before the sun rose far enough to reach the forest floor and warm her skin directly. A small shed lay at the edge of the clearing, a depleted woodpile stacked against one wall. An old rusted double-edged woodsman's axe leaned against the pile as if someone had just stopped chopping wood. She flashed for a second on how badly she could have used a warm fire.

Oh, well.

What she needed was breakfast and a shower, but she thought "Fat chance!" of having either one. She wanted desperately to wash Klug from her skin.

Nick! Where could he be? Was he the wolf? Against all her scientific knowledge and beliefs, she had to believe. The magnificent animal had certainly acted as protector, attacking her kidnappers. She wanted to believe she'd seen the kindly eyes of Nick Lupo behind the cold glitter of the wolf's pupils.

What to do?

Before she could dwell further on the question, decisions clicked into place, made for her by the crashing sounds that approached from the woods. Someone—*the psycho, Buck!*—in pursuit, hurtling through the undergrowth like a freight train, apparently uncaring how much noise he made.

Shivering, head throbbing, Jessie raised the crossbow and waited.

BUCK

His tracking skills weren't that good, but the winter grass around the camp was frosted and the woman's steps had messed up the frost enough that even he could follow the spoor. When he reached the area covered by pine needles the going turned tougher, but she'd only just been through here, disturbing enough growth to leave a path if you knew where the hell to look.

Buck careened blindly through the woods, knowing he'd catch her in minutes, maybe seconds. Then he'd have himself a little of what Wilbur tried to take the night before, when the wolf attack had interrupted them. That was freakin' scary, and Kenny was fucked bad, but now it was almost daylight and voodoo bullshit and monsters wasn't enough to scare him off such a prime piece of ass. He'd thought about her so much the time he spent in that cell, he thought his dick was gonna fall off. The city boy didn't seem to care if she got banged up a little, or maybe sliced up, as long as he could use her as bait. Buck figured, *All she's gotta do is still be breathin'*.

He held the UZI close to his chest as he ran, wondering how long before he'd see her sweet ass running away from him, when he crashed into a small clearing and pulled up short, skidding to a halt a few feet in.

There she was. And she had the fuckin' crossbow aimed right at him.

Jesus on a stick! Ain't nothin' easy anymore?

Just 'cause she had it didn't mean she was any good with it, so he grinned a long, yellow-toothed grin and patted the UZI, then he started his approach.

CHAPTER THIRTY-FOUR

LUPO

He had been tracking her scent ever since he'd managed to change, and Lupo now almost enjoyed riding along with the Creature—*it was much warmer inside the fur.*

A confusion of scents throughout the area forced the Creature to hesitate, as he attempted to determine which were most important. When it became obvious that Jessie's spoor had somehow crossed his door but not the others', he directed the Creature's efforts to finding her. Protecting Jessie was his top priority, and he would let the three others go if this outcome posed less danger to her.

Lupo found that he could almost communicate with his Creature side in a strange mixture of thought, image, sound, and a sort of neural messaging. He didn't know how any of it worked, but it seemed as though future experiments would bring communication and further control. He used the connection now to try convincing the Creature the silver wound hurt less, but the pain was too sharp.

When he caught the male scent crossing paths with the female, and then following it, Lupo's Creature growled and snarled with recognition. Lupo knew it was Buck Benton, but the Creature knew him only as Crazy Lead-Spitter from the night before. Lupo edged the Creature into following both, knowing that at any second he might come upon Buck attempting unspeakable acts on Jessie.

He picked up his pace, loping through the forest following the bare path they had taken only moments before.

Suddenly he broke cover and found himself in a small clearing. Buck and Jessie, with blood daubed on her head, faced each other from opposite ends, as if they'd been dancing to some tropical tango and now had separated to cool off.

The Creature snarled and leapt, all four paws leaving the ground and heading for Buck. Before the hunter could bring his submachine gun to bear, the wolf was on him, knocking him over and going for the throat with its bared fangs, drool and spit spraying from his open maw. His eyes seemed to swirl with rage as he clawed at the human and used his jaws to snap the human's forearm.

Buck dropped the UZI and screamed for help, trying desperately to tear the wolf's jaws from his flesh and bones. Lupo felt the Creature lose control and start mauling Buck, ripping into his arms and throat. Trying to hold off the huge animal with his broken arm and open his knife with the other, Buck managed to roll over and take the animal with him, knocking him off balance. Lupo felt his world spin as the Creature rolled away from Buck and regained his legs. Instinctively he crouched, preparing to spring—

—and suddenly he yelped and howled in pain as one of Klug's camouflaged wolf traps snapped shut, its metal teeth biting, ripping, grinding through his left rear ankle.

Excruciating pain shot fiery lances through both Lupo and the Creature.

Metal ground onto bone, puncturing fur and skin.

Again he felt the liquid heat burning through his veins.
Silver? On the trap's teeth?

The Creature sagged back to the ground and opened its jaws, letting out a surprised howl of agony and fear.

Inside its head, Lupo found himself sinking into unconsciousness, the pain obliterating his connection to the beast and short-circuiting his own thoughts.

Then he was suffering through the Change, over and over, back and forth in rapid mind-numbing succession, as if fluttering between the two poles.

He tried to avoid blacking out.

BUCK

Oh Jesus, oh God, it's a fuckin' werewolf and I'm gonna be one, I'm gonna turn into a fuckin' monster, oh God-fuckin'-dammit to hell, the fuckin' thing hurts like hell, fuck-fuck-fuck, I think he broke my fuckin' arm, oh God there's blood all over me, Jesus Christ, I don't wanna die like this, fuckin' bastard werewolf, damn it Wil, where the fuck are ya, you sonofabitch, I was better off in the can, you fucker, oh, man that hurts like hell . . .

Buck knew he'd lost it, and he didn't care.

His words became incomprehensible as he started to bawl.

He lifted the UZI from where it had fallen and raised the barrel, not caring who and what he took with him.

JESSIE

Looking at the wounds Buck had suffered in the attack and at his clear intent with the UZI, and then glancing to see what had happened to the wolf, her protector, drew a snarl out of her and she didn't even hesitate.

She squeezed the crossbow's trigger and in slow motion watched the stretched bowstring straighten and propel the hunting bolt with amazing speed and power to its target.

It took Buck below the chin and exploded upward into his brain, killing him before he knew what hit him. His body dropped to the bloody ground and his limbs jerked once, twice, and then he lay still.

You've just killed a man.

No time to worry about it.

You've just killed a man!

Later, you can feel bad later!

He was a man . . .

. . . who would have killed you and raped your corpse.

She turned and had to believe what she saw.

Nick Lupo and the wolf were indeed the same. But now they were changing, switching, melding weirdly from one to the other, back and forth like a badly lit special effect, like a flickering lantern, alternately screaming in pain and howling.

She rushed to his side, and when he saw her he seemed to exert some sort of tentative control on the wolf side of himself, because he opened his human eyes and recognized her.

"Jessie," he whispered hoarsely. "Jessie, I'm so sorry. This is all my—ahh, goddamn, that hurts!—my fault, it's my fault, they wanted me, not you."

She felt his forehead. Through blood and mud, her hand came away wet. He was burning up. And his ankle was a mess between the steel jaws; blood and gore oozed from the grotesque wound.

She tried to open it, felt his blood on her hands, but it didn't budge a millimeter.

"I—I think there's silver on this trap! I don't have any strength, and I can't seem to change back." He groaned. "This isn't how I wanted to tell you about me."

"No," she said. It was all she could say.

The trap had nearly severed his ankle, having bitten

through the calcaneal and flexor tendons and wedged between the bottom of his tibia and talus.

Not good.

"It's not your fault," she whispered. "Nick, I think I always knew there was something about you . . ."

She took his hand and lifetimes passed between them.

Before they could speak again, they both heard the sound of bodies approaching through the trees.

MARTIN AND KLUG

They crashed through the underbrush as the sun rose higher and they were better able to see. Martin saw a clearing ahead, through the trees, and there were people in it. He held out a hand and stopped Klug, pointing.

"Sshhh."

They locked eyes, hearing the sounds of someone in pain, but not certain who. There was a better-than-average chance that Buck was done for, so they'd still have to finish the job.

"I think he hit one of the traps," Wilbur Klug whispered.

"Then let's go," said Martin with a smile, raising the Smith & Wesson.

SAM

He stepped from behind a large pine and stood in front of them, blocking their path. He had seen enough, and if the lady doctor wasn't afraid of the man who was also a wolf, then he'd at least wait until these bastards were neutered before making a judgment himself.

"Just hold it right there," he said, feeling ridiculous using bad Western dialogue. *Sergio Leone would have done better.*

The two gunmen looked at each other in surprise. Martin because he didn't know who the old man was, and Klug because he hadn't expected to face an old, shotgun-totin' redface.

Klug must have had his finger on the Mini-14's trigger, because there was a loud crack and Sam went down in a heap, his shotgun flying off to the side. "Fuck off," Klug said, as if he hadn't just been threatened by the old man. "We got business . . ."

Sam found himself sitting, his back up against a tree, holding his shoulder and watching his own blood squirt almost comically from the hole the 5.56mm military slug had just made. He felt numb now, but pain began creeping up to his brain, both from the hole he could see and from the one he couldn't, the exit hole, which seemed to have taken a melon-size chunk out of his shoulder blade.

Sam tried to stand up, but instead he blacked out.

LUPO

Lupo was aware of everything that happened around him, but it seemed as if he were watching an IMAX movie. The pain had subsided into a long, continuous burning in each of his wounds, and he felt almost lucid even though he could tell he was running a high fever.

He watched as Jessie tried and failed to spring the trap open. Then he reached down with both hands and also tried to open the jaws, but the burning intensified and scorched his skin. Doggedly he kept at it, trying to gain some leverage against the sprung metal. He gripped the trap tightly and sweated out the pain, attempting to dig deeply into his reserves. Jessie pitched in and they both tried to lever the jaws open.

The sweet-sour smell of his burning flesh wafted up to his nostrils, and when he couldn't stand it anymore he fell back, panting, his eyes closed. Part of him sought blessed relief then.

JESSIE

The gunshot surprised her. Who were they shooting at? They were still far into the trees, but now she heard them approaching again. Whoever it was hadn't stopped them.

Nick appeared to be unconscious. He wasn't blurring back and forth anymore, but that didn't make the whole thing any less weird for her. Still, she was obligated to help him, surely all the more since Nick had sustained two horrific wounds trying to help her.

Jessie turned from the impossible trap and tried to reload the crossbow, but she needed too many pounds of pull to snag the latch and, after everything that had happened to her in the last twenty-four hours, she simply couldn't do it. She strained and almost had it twice, but her fingers refused.

She gave up.

There just wasn't time.

Buck's UZI lay on the ground, but too far away and partially buried under his body. By the time she got it and figured it out, they'd be in the clearing. She looked frantically about for another weapon, and saw the rusted axe near the woodpile. She bounded over and snatched it up by its rough handle, finding its weight almost too much for her, and dragged it over to where Lupo lay, amid the smell of blood, singed fur and skin.

As she watched, Nick opened his eyes.

LUPO

They locked glances for a second, and then when she smiled at him, tentatively at first, his heart leaped. Trite, perhaps, but it lifted his heart and for a moment he forgot their situation, basking instead in the possibility of a better life.

He saw the axe and raised an eyebrow. He could hear the thrashing in the trees. Martin and Klug, coming for the kill.

"I've got one good swing left in me, Nick," she whispered.

Lupo calculated. "They'll be here any time. I think I have the answer, but you're not going to like it."

"What?" Her eyes sprung leaks, tears coursing suddenly straight down her blood-flecked cheeks.

She knew.

He had to talk fast. "I think my, uh, wolf side is more powerful than I even know. I think the magic, whatever fuels it, is strong and I think it can do things I'm just learning. Use the axe! Get me out of the trap, I'll be able to hold them off. *It* will be able to hold them off . . ."

"No, Nick, I can't do it! I won't!"

He looked at the clearing's edge, where the two would appear any second.

"There's no time, Jessie," he hissed. "Do it! Do it now! I'm ready!"

"No! I can't . . ." But she half-lifted the axe, her eyes a mass of confusion and anger.

"Jessie, you're a doctor! You know where—*what to do!* Do it, now! Or we're both dead!"

Martin and Klug called to each other, sounding barely yards away inside the trees.

"Jessie, even if you get one of them, the other one will kill us both. *There's no other way!* Do it now! *Now!*"

JESSIE

All the years of chopping wood came back to her in a rush, and every surgery performed, every autopsy at which she had assisted, every horrible and grotesque scene she'd witnessed as a doctor who routinely stitched up bizarre accident wounds, fight wounds, and self-inflicted wounds. She could visualize his ankle, where the teeth now dug painfully into bone, probably having cracked or fractured the tibia outright, and where the silver had apparently sizzled the skin and flesh as if it were bacon.

She turned once more toward the sounds of approach and saw a flash between the trees.

They were here.

She cried out an oath, and half-raised the axe over her head. She did not want to see, but saw anyway, that Nick had prepared himself, closing his eyes and doing *something* with his mind . . . He seemed to be *pushing* in onto himself, waiting for the blow while summoning up the magic or whatever it was that made him what he was.

She raised the axe the rest of the way. Tears burst from her eyes in a torrent and she ignored them.

She aimed, then took one strong, perfect swing.

LUPO

When the blade bit, finishing what the trap had started, Lupo was in the midst of a Change.

He *pushed* and it passed over him like a shiver, and then the blade hit home true, right on the tibia-talus connection, and both Lupo and the wolf howled in pain as the rusty blade seemed to sever foot and paw simultaneously.

A shower of blood splashed the constricting metal jaws.

But though the wolf was now three-legged, he was still dangerous.

And free!

Fueled by the blade's cruel, screaming distress, the wolf ignored the weeping Jessie, who had sunk to her knees, and leaped instead for the attackers, invaders of his territory.

The wolf snarled its pain and anger and pounced on Klug, going for the throat.

The big man screamed and put up his hands as if to ward off the animal, but the wolf's momentum and his agony catapulted them both onto the ground.

In one great swipe, his foreclaws ruined Klug's hands and tore the gun from them. His jaws clamped on the man's throat, bit down hard, then tore it out in a mass of shredded bloody tissue and nerve.

Before Klug could even shudder and die under him, the wolf had spun and leaped at Martin, his fangs snapping at the man's wavering gun hand and tearing into the exposed forearm. Martin screamed and dropped the silver-loaded weapon. He reached for it desperately with his other hand, but the wolf pressed his attack and the two careened off the spot. They stared at each other for a moment frozen in time, and then Martin grasped his bloody arm and slithered away from the snarling, drooling beast Nick Lupo had become. Before the wolf could pounce again, Martin turned and ran headlong out of the clearing.

The wolf howled its victory and took a few steps to give chase, but he wavered and staggered instead to a stop. He sat down hard and began to lick at his severed paw, whimpering. Inside the Creature, Lupo wept at the intensity of the pain and *pushed,* willing himself back over the line that separated his two sides, though as he regained his human form and the still-gushing stump touched the ground, he wished he hadn't.

And then Jessie was there with her belt for a tourniquet and the calm words of a doctor, as well as the caring words of a friend and lover.

Lupo smiled at her as she administered to him. Then he blacked out.

MARTIN

He ran all the way back to the first cabin, where they had left their gear.

Blubbering, his mind on the verge of a complete data dump, he couldn't stop seeing the man turn into a wolf. He'd waited years to see it so he could end the charmed, magical life of his sister's murderer, but he'd frozen for a second, when the wolf leaped on Klug, he'd frozen and then the wolf was on *him*, and now he was on the run.

This was not how it was supposed to turn out.

Where is it? Where the fuck is it?

He tore through his duffel bag.

Caroline, I wanted revenge for you!

Martin cried. He wanted his Case.

JESSIE

Nick came in and out of consciousness, but at least he had settled into human form and she could administer some first aid.

"We've got to get you out of here," she said. "You need a hospital now. Come on, Nick, wake up! You need a hospital and then you'll be all right. Please, help me help you."

She worked at placing her body partially below his so she could lift him to a kneeling and then slowly standing position, though he threatened to pass out once again as soon as she had him upright.

LUPO

"He's—"

He tried again to speak, but the blood loss had weakened him too much.

"He's back . . ." A hoarse whisper was all he could manage.

The Creature's instinct had broken through to Lupo the man for a split second.

"He's back," he said and, as if to prove him right, bullets splattered all around them.

JESSIE

Ducking, wanting to drop flat on the ground, but also attempting to keep Nick from falling, Jessie managed to turn just in time to see Martin Stewart standing only a few yards away, a tiny submachine gun stuttering in his hands.

Because of his lack of expertise, he'd emptied the magazine of its thirty-two rounds, most of them harmlessly over their heads when the gun's sharp recoil had forced the short barrel upward. Now the breech was empty as the gun fell silent.

Jessie gasped at the sight of Martin.

He had painted his lips a deep violet, making them grotesquely larger, almost clownlike. Tears had slid down his cheeks and he had wiped at them, smearing the dark color bruiselike across his face. He screamed incoherently.

Then she was able to make out some of the words he repeated in a litany from hell.

"Not me! Not me! Not me! Not me! Not—"

Suddenly, his head exploded in a curtain of brains and blood and cranial matter. Without much ado his body slumped to the ground and quivered once, only the echo of the lone blast remaining.

Sam Waters lowered his shotgun and staggered, leaning on a young pine at the edge of the clearing.

Jessie noticed for the first time that a warming sun had begun to burn off the morning chill. She tightened her hold on Nick, whose head hung low as he struggled to keep his eyes open, his naked, battered body clearly wanting to shut down.

"Doc, please tell me this is our Protector, and not somebody else I've gotta shoot," Sam said.

Jessie wasn't sure exactly how, but she managed to smile.

"No," she said softly. "He's our Protector, all right."

She noticed the blood covering Sam's chest, but before she could ask him about it he dropped the shotgun and dug into his pocket.

"Here's my cell phone," he said. "I hope to hell I charged the sonofabitch recently."

Jessie laughed and laughed. For some reason, she thought she'd never heard anything as funny.

EPILOGUE
REQUIEM

JESSIE AND LUPO

Jessie helped him hobble to the gate. He'd become accustomed to the flesh-colored prosthetic device that had replaced his foot, but he still felt unstable on uneven surfaces, and the long concourses at Milwaukee's Mitchell International were on enough of a slant that he'd almost gone sprawling once before she had taken his carry-on bag on her own shoulder and given him her arm. He swung the cane almost jauntily with his other arm.

"Thanks, Jess."

"Least I can do, considering," she said, eyes downward.

"Will you stop beating yourself up about the foot? It's been months. I told you to do it, and neither one of us would be here now if you hadn't, so don't carry this guilt anymore, okay? We've got so much other stuff to fix, both of us, the foot's gonna be okay all by itself."

He was right, of course. It would take her more months, maybe years, to get over everything that had happened.

She could still feel Klug's slime on her and his enormous erection about to batter through her buttocks. Thank God he hadn't been allowed to finish. She still had nightmares.

But she still had the memory of making her daddy proud with that crossbow, too.

She still had the knowledge that Martin Stewart was dead, wiped from the universe he seemed to hate so much.

And she still had Nick Lupo to hold her and make her better, by making sweet and considerate love to her when she wanted it and leaving her alone or holding her silently when she wanted *that,* too.

Everything heals, she thought, *if you let it.*

She watched Nick hobble rather well, barely needing her help. She had seen for herself that in his wolf form (unbelievable for her as *that* still was), the foot—or paw—seemed almost to have grown back. She guessed there was something to the magic of which Sam and she had spoken on that fateful day. She guessed old Sam was right, maybe someday they'd wake up and Nick's *human* foot would be healed, too, through the same magic that should have made him a monster but didn't. Who knew?

She wondered if Sam Waters was kicked back right now, watching a classic Connery James Bond DVD with a frosty Corona in his hands. He'd gotten them hooked on Bond and Corona, too, while Nick had been recovering from his wounds. And David Lynch movies, and Hitchcock and Dario Argento, and even the bizarre Ken Russell. Jessie had never known he was such a strange movie buff, and the revelation somehow made her like him all the more. Sam had taken the silver buckle off his belt, and had shown them the emptied-out shotgun shells. "I melted all the shot down and had a football trophy made for the res high school," he'd said to Nick one day. "They deserve the silver; you don't."

That day Sam had used his silver buckshot to assure no one else would Change, killing their bodies all over again.

When Nick and Sam had shaken hands, Jessie had

sensed that some sort of destiny had come full circle. Sam's son had been a victim, too, of the man who had been responsible for Nick's disease. Now there was a good chance that Nick Lupo could finish what Joseph Badger had begun in hatred, taking his rightful place as Protector of the tribe—but on the law's side this time. If everything went well. There was still a lot to learn about the Change and the fascinating physiological alterations it caused. But there was plenty of time.

Everything heals, if you let it.

Nick had finally allowed some of his scars to heal. The two women he had loved before her, Caroline years ago and Corinne more recently, had died horrific deaths and he'd allowed himself to take the blame. He realized now that he'd been innocent, unable to change things. About Ben Sabatini, though, it would take a long while. Jessie knew he was still thrashing himself and his health over having overlooked the danger for his partner. He had spent much of his free time since he could walk again with Marie and the kids, giving them an Uncle Nick if he couldn't give them back their daddy . . .

They would all heal, too, someday.

If they let themselves.

She wiped a tear from her eye.

Others had died, and they had families too. They'd found Martin's uncle and Stacey Collins frozen together in death. An innocent man, killed for his cell phone. And some woman had come forth, an aging blonde from another escort service, traumatized because she'd *met* Martin Stewart and he had inexplicably let her live. She'd sold her story to Fox for a TV movie.

Jessie wasn't sure how, but Nick had managed to arrange things so the feds attributed the crime spree to homegrown terrorists led by Martin Stewart. With Sam's testimony and hers, it had worked. His prior connection was lost among what CNN dubbed the "bizarre factor" of the terrorist attack, which the networks played for all it was worth.

Finally he cleared the tightened security and she watched him surreptitiously, out of the corner of her eye, as he headed for his gate.

Everything heals, if you let it.

Nick was boarding a plane to see his parents for the first time in years. She knew how much this meant to him, and she wanted him to go. Still, she would miss him. Miss his touch. But she wanted him to take this step almost as much as he himself wanted to.

The time was right.

Everything heals . . .

In the car she had Alan Parsons, "The Turn of a Friendly Card." She smiled and started humming.

From *The Eagle River Post-Press*
(The "Local Lore" Section)
November 26

While engaged in his annual Thanksgiving Day deer hunt, former Milwaukee police lieutenant Donald A. Bowen, came face-to-face with an animal he described as "the largest black wolf I have ever seen." Though North American timber wolves are rarely black in coloring, Mr. Bowen becomes visibly agitated when he describes the encounter, which left him so paralyzed with fear that a rescue team was forced to airlift him from his location in the Nicolet National Forest. Mr. Bowen called for help on his cell phone, claiming to be ill and unable to hike out of the largely uninhabited area north of Eagle River (Vilas County). Asked about his ordeal, Mr. Bowen said only that the wolf made clear his intent to do him harm but backed off when the recently retired police sniper with the Milwaukee PD's Tac-Team laid down his weapon, swearing that he would never hunt again. Mr. Bowen, a decorated Special Forces specialist sniper in Vietnam, has also earned many hon-

ors in various police shooting competitions. Right now, Mr. Bowen claims to have liquidated his trophy collection. "I have no need to be reminded of hunting," he explained, "and all those heads did was stare at me." He is also in the process of selling his extremely valuable rifle collection. "I won't hunt again," he insists, a determined look on his craggy features. "Even if I hadn't promised myself and God, I'd have nightmares about this wolf waiting for me in the woods." Mr. Bowen's spokesman, lawyer and family friend Larry Bolton, refuses to admit that this crisis of conscience may be a reaction to the breakup of his client's longtime marriage to his wife, Helen "His privacy deserves to be guarded," the attorney explains. As to the wolf apparition, it should be noted that local lore does indeed mention a lone wolf regularly romping through the woods in the vicinity of Eagle River during the full moon. But most natives scoff, saying it's a Halloween scary story they've told their children for years. Beyond that, no one is talking. Happy Thanksgiving!